KNIGHTS TEI

CITY OF
GOD

by S.J.A. Turney

1st Edition

For Kerim,

Whose knowledge of the city of

Constantinople is unbounded

and whose efforts helped create this

tale

Published in this format 2018 by Victrix Books

Copyright - S.J.A.Turney

First Edition

Also by S. J. A. Turney:

Tales of the Empire
Interregnum (2009)
Ironroot (2010)
Dark Empress (2011)
Insurgency (2016)
Emperor's Bane (2016)
Invasion (2017)
Jade Empire (2017)

Templar Series
Daughter of War (2018)
The Last Emir (2018)

The Damned Emperors
Caligula (2018)
Commodus (2019)

The Marius' Mules Series
Marius' Mules I: The Invasion of Gaul (2009)
Marius' Mules II: The Belgae (2010)
Marius' Mules III: Gallia Invicta (2011)
Marius' Mules IV: Conspiracy of Eagles (2012)
Marius' Mules V: Hades Gate (2013)
Marius' Mules VI: Caesar's Vow (2014)
Marius' Mules VII: The Great Revolt (2014)
Marius' Mules VIII: Sons of Taranis (2015)
Marius' Mules IX: Pax Gallica (2016)
Marius' Mules X: Fields of Mars (2017)
Marius' Mules XI: Tides of War (2018)
Marius' Mules XII: Sands of Egypt (Summer 2019)

The Ottoman Cycle
The Thief's Tale (2013)
The Priest's Tale (2013)
The Assassin's Tale (2014)
The Pasha's Tale (2015)

The Praetorian Series
Praetorian – The Great Game (2015)
Praetorian – The Price of Treason (2015)
Praetorian – Eagles of Dacia (2017)
Praetorian – Lions of Rome (2018)

The Legion Series (Childrens' books)
Crocodile Legion (2016)
Pirate Legion (2017)

Short story compilations & contributions:
Tales of Ancient Rome vol. 1 - S.J.A. Turney (2011)
Tortured Hearts Vol 2 - Various (2012)
Tortured Hearts Vol 3 - Various (2012)
Temporal Tales - Various (2013)
Historical Tales - Various (2013)
A Year of Ravens (2015)
A Song of War (2016)

For more information visit
http://www.sjaturney.co.uk/
or
http://www.facebook.com/SJATurney
   or follow Simon on Twitter
@SJATurney

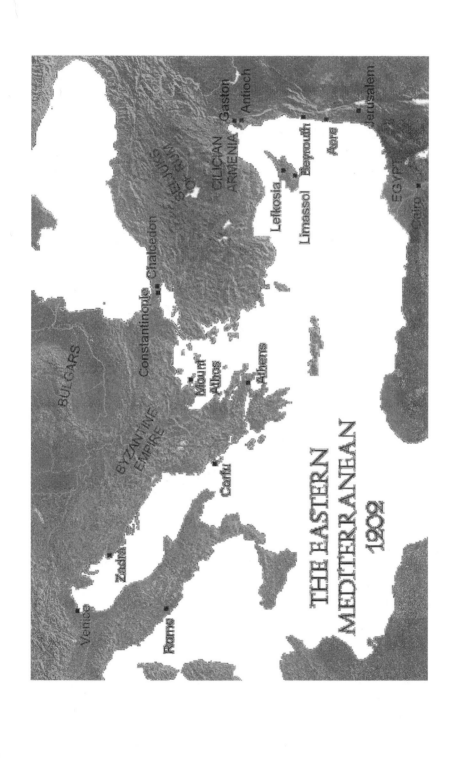

THE EASTERN
MEDITERRANEAN
1202

Venice

Zadar

Rome

Corfu

BULGARS

BYZANTINE
EMPIRE

Constantinople

Chalcedon

Mount
Athos

Athens

SELJUKS
OF RUM

CILICIAN
ARMENIA

Gaston

Antioch

Lefkosia

Limassol

Beyrouth

Acre

Jerusalem

EGYPT

Cairo

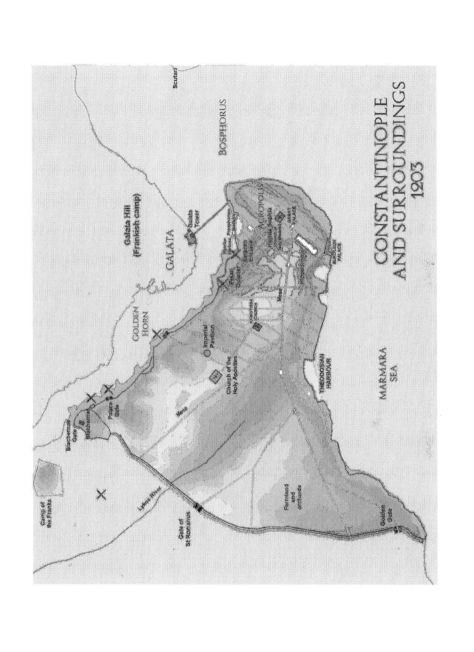

CONSTANTINOPLE AND SURROUNDINGS 1903

BOSPHORUS

Scutari

Galata Hill
(Frankish camp)

Galata Tower

GALATA

ACROPOLIS

Hagia Sophia

GREAT PALACE

GOLDEN HORN

Imperial Pavilion

Church of the Holy Apostles

MARMARA SEA

THEODOSIAN HARBOUR

Camp of the Franks

Blachernae Gate

Blachernae

Palace Gate

Lykos River

Gate of St Romanus

Farmland and orchards

Golden Gate

'...the dirge and the cry of woe and the weeping drowned out

the joyous paschal hymns. While the faithful chanted of the

emptying of the tombs, of the overthrow of Hades and the raising

up of the dead, the cities, one and all, sank beneath the deep of the

earth into the gloomy and frightful abodes of Hades. What mortal

could shed enough tears and adequately mourn the abductions, the

pillaging, the casting of infants into the crossroads, and the

running through of the aged with the sword.'

Niketas Choniates, *O City of Byzantium*

CITY OF GOD

The timbers shook under repeated blows. Arnau de Vallbona cringed as the great wooden portal thudded into his shoulder, dust scattering down from the archway above in a choking cloud. He could hear the shouts outside; no words were audible – just tones of anger and violence.

With a heart-stopping crack, the shining steel curve of an axe blade appeared through the timbers mere inches from Arnau's face. Splinters of wood flew in a dozen directions, one drawing blood from the young Templar's nose as it passed. Even in the midst of this terrible fray, he found the time to say a quick prayer in thanks that only his nose had been blooded. Many a knight had lost an eye or more to the splinters of a lance, after all. A bloody nose was nothing.

The door shook again. He looked up instinctively. The white surcoat, emblazoned with the crimson cross of the order, was visible on the far side of the gatehouse. Ramon, a shining pure-white beacon amid the dun and grey of the local men-at-arms, shook his head with a grim expression. The gate was lost. It was only a matter of time.

An arrow thrummed through one of the many small holes that had already been smashed through the gate, taking a swarthy spearman in the throat and hurling him back to the cobbles to cough and gurgle out his last moments. Arnau paid him no more heed than any of the other poor victims of this terrible fight. He had boundless sympathy for these people, yet even that had been stretched with the chaos, death and disaster all around them.

'The gate is falling,' his fellow knight shouted across the rattle of local tongues, somewhat unnecessarily. Anyone could see now that the gate was done for – certainly the young Templar with the bloody nose.

Before they could do anything more, there was a dreadful crack, and the huge, heavy beam that now constituted the last obstacle gave a little, the iron loops in which it sat coming away from the door with a metallic shriek. The entire gate scraped inwards by a foot, a gap opening in the middle. Arnau could see them outside now – hungry and afire with the desire to kill and maim. *He had seen those looks in another such desperate defence, at Rourell half a decade ago. These men would not be satisfied with anything less than grand slaughter and total victory.*

Arnau lurched back as the gate groaned inwards, and a pike thrust through the gap from without tore through the surcoat at his shoulder, taking wisps of material with it and grating across the chain shirt beneath. This second close call in as many heartbeats drew another prayer of thanks from the young Templar even as he brought his mace down and smashed the head from the pike in the press. Beside him, a man in a gleaming scale shirt suddenly jerked upright, arms thrust into the air and weapons forgotten as a spear slammed into the gap beneath his arms, impaling organs and robbing him of life.

Another thud.

The gate groaned inwards a few more inches. Now grasping arms and jabbing weapons were reaching through the gap, hungry for flesh. Mere moments remained.

Regretting he could do no more, and noting a similar look in his brother's eyes, Arnau de Vallbona withdrew from the defence of the gate, ducking an arrow and backing away.

It was not his fight – had never been his fight – yet leaving it felt like the worst of betrayals.

How in the name of God had it come to this?

Arnau ran.

CHAPTER ONE:
THE GREAT VENTURE

LEVANTINE SEA
LATE NOVEMBER 1202

A rnau heard the call from the deck and nudged Ramon.
'Land, Brother. Must be Cyprus.'
Would that it were Outremer – the Christian kingdom of Jerusalem.

'If they've only just spotted it then I've got a good ten minutes yet,' murmured the older knight as he turned over and buried his head in his blankets. Arnau gave him a fond smile and left him, hurrying over to the ladder to clamber up onto deck. Ramon deserved his sleep. His squire had turned out to be one of the most perpetually seasick men Arnau had ever come across, and the older knight had spent much of every night on board performing both his squire's tasks and his own, as well as playing nurse to the young man. Let him sleep a little longer if he could.

Arnau emerged into the bright afternoon light. His first image of the day was of young Sebastian leaning over the rail, clutching his small wooden icon of the Virgin tight enough to make his hand bleed and retching over the side, sounding like a hungry gull. The poor lad was so thin after weeks of this that he looked like a skeleton in black rags rather than a warrior of God. Since Mateu's death four years ago in the Rourell siege, Ramon had been adamant that he would live without a squire, but his resolve had eventually crumbled under the disapproval of the preceptrix. The rule of the order assigned every knight a squire, after all. Among the pilgrims who had come to Rourell to revere the arm of Saint Stephen that Arnau and Balthesar had recovered during their weird, dangerous and clandestine time on Mallorca two years earlier, Sebastian had arrived with a sick and frail mother who had died before she could even leave the preceptory. The boy had been lost, and like some benevolent grandsire Ramon had taken the boy on. His father had died in some conflict between the Byzantines and the Bulgars a few years earlier and left him the icon to which he clung as though his very life depended upon it. Perhaps the loss of his father and mother had formed some part of the reason he had been so ready to accept the Church of Rome in defiance of his upbringing.

Likely Sebastian was currently regretting it with every heave of his guts. Of course, the ship had bucked and rolled more than Arnau had expected. He'd questioned one of the sailors, who had shrugged and muttered something about winter currents, eddies and coastal circulations. He turned from the sight of the young man just as he heaved his next empty gutload over the rail.

Arnau smiled again. Just this summer, he had taken the vows of a full brother with the blessings of his peers, and had become a true knight of the Temple, discarding his black sergeant's robes for the white surcoat of a knight. Oddly, it had not felt much different. It was made abundantly clear that he was still a junior member of the preceptory. He would always be expected to defer to a more experienced brother, and so with respect to his relationship with Ramon, little had changed other than the colour of his clothes. Moreover, he had not yet been allocated a squire from the recent influx of manpower, though that might not be a bad thing. He had been the first to admit that most of the youths who had come were unlikely to make a good companion for a knight.

He sighed and tried to reflect on the future, though the past insisted on popping up far too easily.

Cyprus lay ahead, and he could see the grey shape of the island now in the centre of the blue swell. Cyprus. His first ever Eastern land. In fact, his first ever non-Iberian land. Oh, he had travelled across the border into French Catalonia once or twice, but his life had been firmly rooted in the dry brown soil of Iberia.

Then the Pope's call had come.

Balthesar had known it was coming. He'd said as much to Arnau, but with settling back into life at Rourell after their return, and with the turning of the seasons, the young Templar had begun to think his friend mistaken, that the Pope was more concerned with keeping his divine rule clear of the interference of secular princes. Then, not long after he had taken the white mantle, it had begun. The Pope had called for all good knights of Christendom to join the holy war and attack Egypt, the heart of all Saracen power.

The call had received a lukewarm reception from the warring kings of Europe, some of whom vied with the papacy in legal and regnal matters, and others who hated one another more than any Saracen to the extent that they would refuse to march to war alongside them.

In the end it had been largely the Franks and Burgundians who heeded the call, with the city state of Venice putting forward their powerful navy as transport, albeit at a high price. Other than them and a few smaller contingents who had thrown in their lot with the Pope's forces, the order had pledged its sword arm to the cause.

Arnau had listened with excitement and trepidation as the news was relayed by the preceptrix. The stronger houses in Iberia were to send men, and since Rourell had begun to grow, they were expected to do their part. Ramon had been the natural choice as senior knight, and despite both desiring and fearing selection, Arnau had almost exploded with pride when he was selected to accompany the older brother. In truth, few men of Iberia became involved in the end. Preceptors argued against sending their men. Who wanted to go and fight for the control of some fabled Eastern city when that same enemy lived but miles to the south, threatening everyday life?

Still, Arnau sailed east with Ramon and his squire at the behest of preceptrix Ermengarda. The two knights and the young squire had called in at several French and Italian ports, passed a couple of days on Sicily, and then spent nights anchored off several insignificant Greek islands. But they had not made true landfall in the East yet. Cyprus would be it.

He crossed to Sebastian as the lad wiped the sick from his mouth and shivered.

'Nearly done,' he smiled. 'And from what I understand we'll be in Cyprus for some time. Something to do with eddies and unfavourable currents.' The young squire turned miserable eyes on him, and Arnau sighed. '*Voítheia krasioú?*' he tried in halted Greek. The squire immediately turned and heaved over the side again.

'All right, no wine, then,' Arnau smiled.

His Greek was coming on in leaps and bounds, which was testament perhaps to the fact that Sebastian would have made a far better tutor than squire. Some arcane path had brought the boy and his mother to the door of Rourell, and their French-accented Aragonese had been so good no one could have guessed their origin. It was only after his mother's death they had learned that he hailed originally from the East, in the lands of the empire with their mysterious Greek Church, and had spoken the Western tongues only for a year or two.

Cyprus. The first step in the great adventure.

They were to rendezvous in Acre with the grand master of the order, there to join the crusading force that would head south for Egypt and the centre of Saladin's power. The moment they had known they were coming east, Arnau had started working with Sebastian on learning the Greek tongue. It was certainly a sight easier than Arabic, and he was managing to master more than just the basics now. He'd never know more than a few phrases of Arabic, but he felt he might one day command Greek well. Only the *spoken* language, of course. The alphabet was still anathema to him.

It irked him more than a little that he had been learning Greek for five months since the call first came, while Ramon had only begun during the voyage, yet the elder knight was already Arnau's equal in the tongue. It might not be of use in the end, of course – their destination was Acre in the Holy Land, and the Crusade as a whole was bound for Egypt. Aramaic and Arabic would be the languages they would encounter. But Greek was the closest geographically, being an Eastern tongue, and it would at least serve them on Cyprus, where the captain had warned them that the winter weather might well keep them for several months.

He strode over to the captain, chest puffed out, still proud of his new white garment with the red cross upon the breast. The man, a Genovese with a bad attitude and a sour face, nodded as he approached.

'Brother.'

'This is Cyprus, then?'

'Aye, sir knight. That's Limassol, largest port of the western shore. Don't say yes to anyone there, or you'll go home a hundred coins poorer but with a sack of fish. They're thieves and vagabonds, the lot of them.'

Arnau nodded as though he agreed. As a Latin captain, the man had the usual disdain for the Greeks with their own alphabet and their schismatic Church. Arnau had argued the first few times, but the man clearly had no interest in reason or logic, so he'd given up.

'My first Greek land,' he smiled.

'Cyprus ain't Greek, sir knight,' the captain said, a sneer creeping in accidentally.

'But it is.'

'No, it was lost to Byzantium decades ago. It's a good God-fearing land now. You should know that. Your order owned it for a year.'

Arnau nodded vaguely. He'd heard as much, but Ramon knew nothing of the island, and Arnau had been able to unpick little more than that simple fact.

'Soon, though, we will head east and join the Crusade.'

He smiled. The idea of being one of God's gauntlets in smashing the Saracen and recovering the Holy City was seductive. The crusading army, called by the Pope, mostly manned by Franks and transported by Venetian ships, aimed to smash the power of the caliph and free the Holy Land. The three Templars would join their brethren at the mother house in Acre and then combine with the western force when it got that far.

Of course, it was almost winter now. No real war against the Saracen would begin until spring, but it was still an enticing prospect for Arnau. He glanced sideways at the captain again. The Genovese seemed to think that sailing in the great central sea was almost done for the year. Ramon intended to be in Acre for the winter, but if the captain was correct, then they would likely wait the bad season out in Cyprus.

Arnau moved to the bow of the heavy merchant ship where salty sailors were busy using their unfathomable nautical language and telling horrendous, off-colour jokes. Cyprus slid towards them.

'This is Limassol?' he checked with one of the nearest sailors, pointing at the approaching shoreline.

'Aye that's the one, masser knight,' the Sicilian sailor replied in heavily accented Aragonese.

'Is it the capital of the island?'

'No, that would be Lefkosia.'

Arnau frowned. 'Why aren't we landing there, then?'

'Because we're a ship and not a fucking eagle, masser knight. Lefkosia's inland.'

Arnau nodded, filled with chagrin, and watched as the island slid ever closer.

Limassol seemed to be a thriving and upcoming port. Having been a coastal dweller throughout his life, Arnau could spot a port on the decline and a port on the rise. Limassol was most definitely among the latter. Ships from half a dozen nations sat wallowing at the jetties and the entire port swarmed with men hard at work, both sailors and islanders. Arnau decided immediately that what time he had on Cyprus was at least going to be interesting.

He saw Sebastian looking up now, taking a pained and grey-faced interest in their destination. The young man apparently hailed from somewhere called Adrianople in the north of that strange Eastern empire of Byzantium, and consequently Cyprus was probably as alien to him as it was to the other visitors. The ship slid slowly into the harbour, swaying gently until it entered the welcoming arms of the sea walls, where the water's surface became glassy calm.

As they made their final approach to the jetty, the sailors rushing hither and thither and shouting in preparation to dock, Ramon finally appeared through the hatch, clambering up onto deck, kit bag over his shoulder.

'Limassol?' he asked, crossing to join Arnau.

'Yes, apparently the capital is inland. Where do we go from here?'

'We'll have to present ourselves at the court in Lefkosia, given that there are no longer any Temple holdings on the island. It's quite a way, from what one of the sailors told me. Probably best to stay in Limassol tonight and then set off early in the morning, since we'll be riding all day. Besides, Sebastian could do with a night to recover before we inflict a horse ride upon the poor lad.'

Arnau nodded. He was still a little unsure as to Cyprus's place in the world, and would defer naturally to Ramon's confident leadership. The island had been part of the Byzantine world until relatively recently. It had been held briefly by the charismatic and bloodthirsty King Richard of England during the time of the last Crusade. It had been given to the Order of the Temple less than a decade ago, but the Order had controlled the island for less than a year before it passed into the hands of the powerful crusading de Lusignan family. A troubled and complex recent history for the island, then.

He was still pondering on the place as the ship touched the boards of the jetty and all aboard lurched for a moment as it came to a halt. Cries went out and ropes were hurled and tied. Sailors began to run out the boarding ramp and bring up onto deck the manifest and other documents for their captain as well as their passengers' belongings. The three Templars' horses were led up onto the brine-coated timbers and then slowly and carefully down the ramp to the jetty.

Arnau smiled as he followed Ramon, both knights now carrying their gear over their shoulders, the rest of which was already strapped to the horses. Sebastian, still weak and grey, was therefore unburdened as yet. As he set foot on the jetty and took his first tentative step in this new world of the East, something made Arnau shiver with discomfort, and he frowned. His gaze turned to meet that of Ramon, and the older knight's expression suggested that he felt it too.

Walking slowly, leading the horses, Arnau peered around him as he went, trying to discern what was making him uncomfortable. It took some time for him to realise what it was, and his boots had alighted onto the stone of the dock proper before it struck him. Few of the folk in the port were looking at them. One thing that Arnau had come to realise over the recent years was that the Order inspired a certain level of awe in most folk. Just as Arnau had gawped in that dreadful skirmish by the Ebro River when the glorious Templar had sung his way into battle, so most people looked up in either fear or respect, or both, when the white and red of the Templar knight passed by. Not so, apparently, in Limassol. Moreover, he was astute enough an observer of human nature to see that it was not that they were raising no interest, but rather that the people were deliberately averting their gaze.

And along with that near shunning came an unexpected undercurrent of anger.

What was going on?

'Note the discrepancy,' Ramon murmured as they walked.

'Discrepancy?'

'The only ones looking at us are the sailors – men from the West mainly, or from the Holy Land, perhaps. The islanders who work the dock will not meet our gaze.'

Arnau nodded with growing unease. That was most certainly the case. What was turning the locals so against them? The new arrivals bore the symbols of the Western Church, of course, but there had always been a grudging acceptance of their schismatic brothers in Greekland, or so he had heard. Why, then, this enmity for the red cross? His gaze slid up from the unfriendly dockside to the white walls and tiled roofs of the city beyond, and to two structures in particular that rose above the surrounding buildings. Just as with most cities: the castle and the church.

'Do we visit the church?' Arnau said. 'Find our bearings a little?'

Ramon shook his head. 'Pious as we must be, it is wise to remember that we live in a temporal world. The fathers in their house of God are wise in the ways of the soul, but if you want to know the workings of the world, visit a tavern.'

Without another word, Ramon angled off towards a low building with a courtyard displaying a sign of three wine barrels above the gate. Arnau followed, as did Sebastian, looking greener than ever, probably at the thought of drink. Sitting at the edge of the port where the streets of the city began, the tavern was a sprawling, single-storey affair, comprised of three wings arranged around a courtyard filled with tables and benches beneath a vine-covered trellis. Wary eyes watched as they approached.

'*Yassas*,' Arnau said amiably in reasonable Greek to an old man with a sour face and a mug of something sitting on a bench by the gate. The man gave him an acidic glare, and Arnau shuffled past, frowning deeper. As they entered the courtyard, Ramon paused and pointed up at the wall. By the entrance, a stone had been mortared into the surface – a flat, white marble stone carved with a stylised lily.

'Franks,' Ramon noted. 'Good. If the locals have some reason to distrust us, at least the Franks do not.'

Leaving Sebastian with the horses outside, Arnau followed Ramon past the tables filled with diners and drinkers, and into the shadowy interior of the bar. The thrum of conversation dropped to a low murmur for a moment as the two Templars entered, but soon rose once more. Good, Arnau thought. At least these Franks seemed comfortable with the Order's presence.

Despite the fleur-de-lys, though, the tavern seemed relatively cosmopolitan. He could hear Greek and French, Italian and English all being spoken in the general hum. Ramon crossed to the bar, where a sweaty man with a shining bald head and a stained apron leaned on the counter and cocked an eyebrow at them.

'Not seen a brother of your order for a while, good sir knight,' the man said in French. Arnau took a moment to adjust his linguistic thinking. French was, of course, the universally accepted court language, and so like any nobleman young Vallbona had a good command of it, but he had been so prepared for Greek that it took a moment to realign his thoughts.

'We are en route to Acre,' Ramon replied casually in good French, 'to join the armies of Christendom as they bring the hammer down upon the Egyptian caliph. Though I fear we will be caught on Cyprus for the winter, if sailors' tongues are true.'

Arnau nodded beside him. Whatever troubles might exist between the islanders and the Order, surely everyone was united against the Saracen, especially this close to their centre of power in Egypt.

'You might be waiting a while, then,' the man said, with a twinkle in his eye and a strange grimace of a smile. 'You've not heard recent news?'

Ramon shook his head. 'We have been aboard ship for some time, with only overnight stops in out-of-the-way places where our captain could avoid expensive port fees. There are important tidings of the army of the Franks?'

'You *have* been out of the way, haven't you?' the man said in surprise. 'It's the talk of every city from here to Paris, and not universally welcomed among my countrymen, I might add.'

Arnau shivered. Was this what was at the root of the anger in the port? He'd assumed it had been something to do with the brief rule of the Order here, but perhaps it was something connected with the new Crusade.

'Tell us, sir,' Ramon said, 'I beseech you. We are starved of news, and this sounds important.'

The innkeeper nodded. 'Very much so. The army of Christendom only reached the Adriatic coast before trouble started. They besieged and sacked Zadra, or so the common tale goes.'

'Zadra?' Arnau asked in confusion.

'A city on the Adriatic coast,' Ramon said knowledgeably. 'Part of Byzantium's empire, nominally, with fealty upon a time to Venice too.'

Arnau shook his head. 'That cannot be. A Christian city?'

Ramon flashed him a look that told him to hold his tongue, then turned back to the barkeep. 'There must be some mistake or misunderstanding. Perhaps the news has been corrupted in transit. If Zadra is an imperial city, then it is true to Christ and part of the Byzantine bulwark that keeps the West safe from the heathen. The Pope would never allow such a thing, I'm sure.'

The man snorted. 'The Pope gave no such order. I hear the doge of Venice was behind the attack. If Count Thibaut had lived to command the Crusaders, he'd never have gone along with it, but the armies of France are led by an Italian now, Boniface of Montferrat. Never trust an Italian statesman, and two of them now lead the Crusade. The Pope has already condemned it all. It's even said that the entire army and its fleet face excommunication for their acts.'

Arnau was still shaking his head. The barman, his grave tidings given, offered them drinks, and Ramon distractedly purchased two cups of wine, then nodded his thanks and urged Arnau along the bar into the western wing of the building and the quietest corner of the room, where he handed one cup to the younger knight.

'This is dreadful news,' Ramon said quietly. 'Absurd. Zadra? What was Dandolo thinking?'

'Dandolo?'

Ramon took a sip of his wine, giving it an appreciative look. 'The old master, doge of Venice. A true political changeling and every bit the untrustworthy Italian statesman the barkeep suggested. You think our friend della Cadeneta was trouble? He was an innocent babe in arms compared with the machinations of the doge of Venice. He is *infamous*.'

'I've never heard of him. But why would he want to sack an imperial city? And why would the Frankish army support him?'

'To the former, I have no answer, other than to point out that Venice once paid homage to the emperor, and not so long ago at that. To the latter, bear in mind that the doge's ships are vital if the Crusade is to hope to ever reach Egypt. It might be stupid and short-sighted, but I can imagine why the Lord Boniface and his council supported Venice in this. That sea city is a rising power – mark my words, Vallbona. Where only generations ago she was a vassal of Byzantium, now she begins to pull strings in the courts of Europe.'

'No wonder the locals are wary of us, if news like this sits in their hearts. What does it all mean for us, though?'

Ramon shrugged. 'I doubt the army will be sailing on now, after Zadra. Winter is too close, and with what has apparently happened, the leaders of the Crusade will want to smooth things over with Rome before they travel further. What use is it engaging in a blessed holy war when the Pope himself turns his back on you? I do know one thing though: if the Pope condemns the Crusaders, then our order will join him and similarly have nothing to do with them. I fear that unless the doge can heal the damage he has apparently caused, we will not be lending our sword arms to the defeat of Egypt after all.'

'Then what do we do?' Arnau said in a worried breath.

'What *can* we do?' Ramon shrugged again. 'We have no master to report to here. We can hardly just sail west once more to Rourell. I was hoping to move on to Acre before the winter tides made it troublesome, but if the Crusade is delayed, perhaps we are better here after all. If we winter on Cyprus, we will receive all the news of the Crusade before even the masters in the Holy Land. And when the weather changes and sailors once more ply the lanes to the Levant, we can journey on to Acre. Depending upon the tidings of the winter, we can either head home or go on to the mother house and present ourselves as ordered.'

Arnau nodded, though he was less than content. Their entire plan had been overturned with that momentous news so casually delivered by a French tavern owner. The sword of

Christendom had been unsheathed, but instead of cleaving the Saracen, it had been wielded against the lands of Byzantium. Against Zadra, a city of God.

Worse, perhaps, was the idea of spending the winter on the island. He had been looking forward to that as they docked, but their reception in the port had changed all that. If the dock workers' attitude was any indication of what they might expect from the island as a whole, the coming months could be less than comfortable.

Arnau took a swig of his wine. It was unlike the brews he was used to in Iberia, much thicker and sweeter and headier, yet somehow it tasted like ash now.

Chapter 2:
The Broken Island

LEFKOSIA, CYPRUS
LATE NOVEMBER 1202

A rnau whistled through his teeth. The number of travellers on the road throughout the day had hinted at the size and importance of Lefkosia, but it was larger still than he expected. The island's capital lay in a wide, flat agricultural basin, bordered to both north and south by mountains that rendered it more or less protected from the coastal region. Its seeming isolation from the vulnerable coastline had not inhibited the city. Indeed, it seemed to be a boon. Lefkosia displayed no sign of walled defences, the city sprawling far and wide, its only nod to security being a small fort poking up from the roofs near the centre.

As they moved closer in the last light of the day, Arnau began to make out things that surprised him. The churches and chapels they passed were nothing like the grand edifices down in Limassol, and far removed from those of Iberia and France. Rather than a belfry and somewhat austere stone walls, these buildings were all apses and windows, and domes with golden crosses surmounting them. They were formed of neat brick that had itself been designed to be aesthetically pleasing as much as stable. They were, in effect, beautiful. And, perhaps more surprising, between and beyond them he could see mosques. They were disused buildings now, or often repurposed as markets or homes, but Arnau had seen enough such examples across Catalunya and Mayūrqa to know what he was seeing.

Lefkosia was the most varied and architecturally fascinating place he had ever laid eyes upon.

As they moved through the town, Ramon continued to annoy Arnau on a selfish, personal level by asking locals, in better Greek than he could manage, the way to the palace. They were guided by a variety of surly locals to a wide square at the heart of the city. Another of the graceful curved churches with their high windows stood on one side of the square, a squat crenelated tower formed of heavy golden-coloured stones facing it – the fortress Arnau had seen over the roofs from a distance. Between the two, standing on the northern edge of the square, sat an odd building. At first glance, Arnau couldn't decide whether it was another form of strange Eastern church or a very decorative fortress. High windows seemed incongruous with what appeared to be thick defensive walls, yet those walls were picked out with marble decoration and strata of red brick that seemed to serve no purpose other than to be pleasing to the eye. A colonnaded balcony overlooked the square, and a huge red banner bearing a rearing golden lion hung above a grand doorway atop a small flight of stairs.

As they were directed towards it, Arnau realised this must be the palace. Its form was old, though, and certainly predated the rule of Western lords. This was almost certainly the old Byzantine palace from when the island was part of their empire. He shivered as he took in the imperial architecture. It was humbling to think that back in Tarragona and Barcelona he had walked amid the shattered ruins of ancient Roman cities, and yet here that same empire continued to exist and rule, for all the odd changes it had experienced in between.

The three men dismounted now and approached the palace. Before they had even reached the base of the steps, the great studded doors opened in response. Two men in mail hauberks displaying the same lion emblem, only in red upon white, stepped aside to flank the open doorway as a third figure emerged.

This man, swarthy and bearded and with a sour expression, wore a long white tunic embroidered with red and gold decoration, and green hose tucked into soft boots, all accessorised with a thick belt of gold and green. His hair was layered and wavy, and shone with a greasy sheen in the late afternoon sun.

Arnau realised that while he was staring and taking it all in, Ramon was bowing, and he swiftly followed suit.

'Templars? Curious,' sniffed the nobleman in perfect French, gesturing absently for them to rise.

'We are en route to Acre, to our mother house, sir,' Ramon replied. 'Seasonal sailing times resulted in us putting ashore on Cyprus, where we may be forced to winter. It seemed appropriate to make our presence known to the king. Might we request an audience?'

The man frowned and pursed his lips, fingers drumming on his hip. 'His Majesty will most certainly make time for the men of the Order, if only to discover why you are *truly* here.'

'As I said—' began Ramon, but the nobleman was already ignoring him, turning away and gesturing for them to follow. Ramon and Arnau shared a look. 'Friendly sort, isn't he?' Arnau sighed. Ramon handed his reins to Sebastian. 'I'm afraid you'll have to wait here until we return, after which we will secure lodgings.'

The squire bowed his head and took Arnau's reins too, and the two knights adjusted their salt-stained white surcoats and set off up the steps in the wake of the supercilious nobleman. The interior of the palace continued the architectural theme as they entered a corridor with doors leading off, high windows and a grand staircase. Its design fell somewhere between religious and military, with a leaning to the sumptuous in an understated way.

Already the nobleman was some way ahead and waiting at a doorway. As the two knights appeared inside the building, he gestured to them and then disappeared through that door. They followed, entering a wide hall in which two more lion-emblazoned guards stood silent and hard-faced. 'Wait here,' the nobleman said, and disappeared through a large ornate door covered with red leather. From seemingly nowhere a servant appeared with a wooden tray laden with fruit, which he proffered to them. Arnau peered at the gleaming delicacies, half of which he could not identify and, being somewhat unadventurous, took an apple. Ramon simply waved the boy away.

They stood in silence for a while, the guards watching them carefully, hands on swords. The only noise was the constant crunching of Arnau's apple. He had finished the fruit, and was wondering what to do with the core, when the door opened once more and the nobleman emerged.

'You will, of course, leave your weapons here. The king will see you for a few moments.'

The two knights bowed again and unbelted their swords, handing them to one of the guards, who regarded the pair with inscrutable eyes. Unarmed, they followed the man through the door and into an even wider room. Once more those great windows that seemed ubiquitous cast the room into a great golden glow from the late sun. A red and white carpet ran the length of the room from the door to a dais at the far end. Four more soldiers in lion tabards stood near the throne, and half a dozen courtiers stood in two groups at the periphery.

The king of Cyprus sat upon an ornate marble seat, padded with red and gold cushions and draped with the emblem of the lion once again. The man who ruled this island wore a red cote, threaded with gold, and a white surcoat with the lion rampant over his left breast. His shoulder-length hair was dark and his beard neat and pointed like a blade. He did not look happy.

Ramon stopped roughly halfway along the rich carpet and bowed deeply, and Arnau followed suit once more.

'I do not like Templars,' said the king suddenly, in an unpleasant drawl.

'Majesty?' prompted Ramon, straightening with a furrowed brow.

'Wherever the Order goes, they leave others to clean up their mess. With their failures at Cresson and Hattin, they effectively handed Jerusalem to the Saracen and lost my brother his throne in Outremer.'

'Majesty,' began Ramon. Lusignan's part in the failure of the dreadful battle of Hattin was well known, but the king held up a hand and the knight fell into a disgruntled silence.

'Whatever might be said about the Order's failures in the Holy Land, their botched command here was yet worse. I inherited a land of foment from the Temple, and I am not pleased to see that red cross on white landing on my island. De Fougères here tells me you are simply passing through. I urge you to do so with all haste, for your very presence on this island endangers a fragile peace. I will brook no troubles caused by you, and if such should arise, I shall take up the matter with your master at Acre in the spring.'

The king lapsed into silence, glaring at the two of them, and Ramon paused for some time. Arnau glanced at his friend and realised that the man was doing what he had to in order to suppress anger and still respond calmly. Finally, the older knight nodded.

'Majesty, we intend no trouble or harm. Indeed, we would rather move on as soon as possible, though we are told by master sailors that the currents east of here in the winter are not favourable.'

'Indeed,' the king said, his face still sour and disapproving. 'Many a fleet has met with disaster in these waters. The king of England conquered Cyprus from the Greeks as a consequence of just such a calamity. Very well, there is a church in the city – the chapel of the Virgin – a monastery church which I grudgingly granted to your order several years ago. It is manned only by a caretaker, but it has accommodation attached and you may remain there during your stay on the island. While in my domain, you shall remove those red-crossed mantles and move around in a more discreet fashion, lest you stir up trouble.'

Again there was a pause while Ramon fought the urge to refuse such an order. In the end, he simply bowed his head.

'Very well, you are dismissed,' the king announced loftily. 'With good fortune I will hear and see nothing more of you until you leave.'

A dismissive wave of his hand bade them leave, and the nobleman who had admitted them now began to shoo them from the hall. Ramon and Arnau turned and strode proudly from the room, chins high and red crosses displayed proudly. Once they were back through the door and retrieving their weapons, Arnau sighed. 'That could have gone better.'

Ramon shook his head. 'I think not. Aimery de Lusignan has a strong reputation. He is astute and no schemer like his brother. If he is as set against the Order as appears to be the case, then he likely has good reason, and he would never have welcomed us more than he did, no matter what we said.'

He turned to the haughty nobleman, who was busy closing the doors behind them. 'Could you direct us to this chapel of which the king spoke?' he asked with forced politeness.

The man raised his face a little, looking down his nose at Ramon as he turned and pointed off to the south, down a street roughly parallel with the one they had taken upon their arrival. 'Follow the Argetis road there. Towards the edge of town, you will pass an old Saracen stable house on the left, with many arches. The next church beyond that belongs to your temple... for now,' he added ominously.

Nodding the barest thanks possible, the two men retraced their steps until they emerged into the square. The sun had now dipped below the horizon and a warm evening glow filled the city. Sebastian stood with the horses, the bored expression on his face a welcome change from the constant grimace of illness he had borne for the past few weeks.

'What now?' Arnau said.

'Now we find this church and settle in for the night. My liturgical hours are all awry since the voyage. I can rarely tell when we are supposed to hold service, and it will be good to do so in a church once more.'

Arnau nodded. It was relief enough simply to be standing on a surface that did not roll with the swell of waves after so long at sea. Actually kneeling in a church would feel like the most sinful luxury now.

Crossing the square once more, they made for the street of the chapel. A small market had been operating in the thoroughfare, and now the stall owners were closing up and boxing away their goods for the night. As Arnau and his friends passed they were unsurprised, but further disheartened, to note how they uniformly turned away from the three passing Templars, an air of distrust and seething resentment filling the street.

Arnau glanced momentarily at Sebastian and noted that with the hand not on his horse's reins he rubbed his thumb reflexively across the icon of the Virgin, a small wooden square covered with the sacred image depicted in ancient, flaking paint. Every few moments he peered myopically at it.

'What is it?' he asked the young squire, gesturing at the icon. 'Why do you examine it so?'

Sebastian looked sheepish and folded the small image away in his hand, shaking his head. 'It is nothing. Superstition, or so people tell me, Brother Valbona.'

'Superstition almost always has roots in reality,' Arnau said, quoting Balthesar easily. 'And when linked to the Holy Mother, it can be of great import.'

The young man looked hesitant for a moment, then opened his palm again and peered down at the icon. 'My ma said that it cried on the morning my papa went to war and never came back. I'd always thought it just a story, but I went to grasp it at ma's deathbed, and it was wet then too. With all the angry looks we're getting and this unknown world, I keep my eye upon it.'

Arnau nodded slowly. He wanted to tell the lad that it was just coincidence and that they were perfectly safe, the icon just a picture. But the Lord worked in mysterious ways, and stranger things that this had been proven true over the years.

'I am enjoying this less and less,' he muttered to no one in particular as they passed the last stall and began to make their way out of the urban centre.

'Caravanserai,' Ramon noted, gesturing off to the left after a lengthy walk. Arnau looked across and noted the building the nobleman at the palace had described. A large two-storey structure which displayed distinctly Arabian-looking architecture, and would have been quite at home in parts of Iberia, stood back from the street, an arcade of horseshoe arches facing them.

'I'm unfamiliar with the word.'

'It's an Eastern one. It's a sort of hostel and stable for travellers, especially merchant caravans.'

'Then that must be our church,' Arnau said, pointing ahead along the road.

They walked their horses on, closing on the small monastic complex. Despite its diminutive size, it was clearly more than just a church. A fairly austere golden stone façade caught the last glow of evening, giving its masonry the hue of rich honey. A plain wooden door sat beneath a window like a half moon over a stone horizon. The church itself seemed to be a heavy, squat rectangular structure with little decoration. Two low grey domes rose from the roof, each surmounted with a golden cross with an extra, slanted crossbar at the lower end. The windows of the church were high and small, set into the stonework below the domes. Beside the church stood two more structures of the same style of construction, connected by a wall taller than a man.

'This would appear to be it,' Ramon agreed. 'A home away from home. Aimery probably thinks such a small church is an insult to us, but then he has not seen humble Rourell. Come, let us enter.'

Crossing to the door, he slid from the saddle and tried the handle. The door remained resolutely shut. As Arnau and Sebastian dismounted, Ramon rapped heavily on the door and waited. There was a long pause before they heard the faint sounds of movement inside. Finally, there was a clank and a rattle, and the door crept slowly open with an ominous creak.

'What do—' began an old, cracked voice in thick Greek, before falling silent as the ageing fellow's eyes widened at the three figures standing outside.

'Good evening, Brothers,' he managed in passable French, though looking extremely confused as he spoke, his face betraying the same distrust as every other islander they had met.

'Good evening. We were directed to lodge here from the palace,' Ramon said politely in Greek. 'I am Ramon de Juelle, a knight of the...' he floundered, not knowing the Greek word for a preceptory. 'The temple,' he settled, 'of Rourell in Aragon, and these are my brothers, Arnau de Vallbona and Sebastian.'

Once more Arnau found himself faintly irritated that the older brother seemed as capable as Balthesar had been of falling into any language with relative ease while Arnau still struggled and had to speak slowly as he formulated sentences.

The old man looked relieved to hear Greek and stepped inside, gesturing for the men to follow. Arnau followed Ramon's lead in handing his reins to Sebastian, who took them without complaint, and then followed the older knight inside.

The church that had looked so featureless and austere from the outside was a different matter entirely inside. Arnau blinked in astonishment. The dying daylight did little to illuminate the church through the small, high windows, but lamps flickered all around the interior in brass holders, giving the whole place a warm, golden glow. It illuminated a marvel the likes of which Arnau had never seen before. Every inch of the church's walls and columns was covered with brightly painted images. Saints and priests and heroes of old wore brightly coloured garments, hands almost touching and raised in benediction on every surface, their swarthy, exotic faces and brown hair highlighted by the golden nimbus surrounding their heads. Every figure stood against a bright-blue or red painted background, each panel edged in gold. Every surface. Every wall. Even the ceilings.

Arnau realised he was staring in slack-jawed amazement when the old man cleared his throat meaningfully.

'Sorry. This is incredible.'

'Needs touching up,' the old man replied dismissively, before gesturing out through the door and telling Sebastian to go around the side.

'These are saints,' Arnau said reverentially as the wizened man closed and locked the door.

'Schismatic Greek representations of the saints,' added Ramon, though there was little real disapproval in his voice. How could there be? This veneration was unlike anything Arnau had ever imagined, and were these not the same saints to whom the men of Rourell prayed, after all? The same Christ? The same Holy Mother and the same God? If Balthesar could see value in the Moor's worship of God despite their heresies, then surely the Greek Church must be little more than a wayward brother to Rome?

'It is incredible,' he said again, and almost walked into a wall as he followed the others through a low doorway.

'Like so many of our old churches, this one now bows to Rome,' the old man said, and Arnau was more than a little surprised to hear a trace of bitterness in the man's voice.

'Are you not a servant of the Order?' Arnau asked quietly as they emerged into an open dusty brown courtyard and strode towards a gate set in the wall between the two other buildings.

The old man snorted. 'I am the caretaker. There have only been knights of your order on the island occasionally since the days of strife. No, I am no servant of your order, nor of your oppressive Roman Church with its vicious need to control the world.'

Arnau felt his face fall into a disapproving frown and was about to leap to the defence of his faith when he caught a warning look from Ramon.

'You are of the Greek Church?' the older knight asked.

'I follow the word of the island's patriarch, yes,' the old man said.

'Is this schismatic issue the reason no one on the island will look us in the eye?'

The old man snorted again as they reached the gate and he slid open the bars to admit Sebastian and the horses. 'The Order of the Temple will never be welcome on this island. Not after what you did here.'

Arnau and Ramon shared a concerned look and waited in uncomfortable silence as the old man and Sebastian rattled off a conversation in native Greek so fast that neither knight could follow it. The squire then took the horses to one of the buildings, opening a large door and slipping inside with them. The old man then gestured at the other building and led them across to it.

'I am afraid we are from a small... temple... far in the West,' Ramon said. 'I do not know the history of this island.'

'It is not history to anyone but the young,' the caretaker said, darkly. 'How the lords of the Temple taxed the high and the low, the rich and the poor, how they forced evictions and reapportioned lands that had been handed down through a hundred generations of a family.'

Again, the two knights looked at one another. The old man's voice was becoming louder and angrier as he spoke.

'How they suppressed our Church and made us worship in ways they approved. How they broke a bar from our crosses to make them look like theirs. How they pushed the people until there was nothing to do but revolt, and then, when the people took to the streets to defy the order's oppression, how they took swords to the old and the young and filled the streets of Lefkosia with the blood of islanders.'

Arnau felt shocked. His skin prickled as though freezing cold.

'So no,' the old man said bitterly, 'it is not because you are not of our faith, but because you are each one of *them*.'

There was an uncomfortable pause, and finally the old man straightened. 'I was putting everything straight here and was then going to douse the lamps and return home. The key to the main door stands inside. I cannot imagine you need me further, so I shall not bother you unless you call upon me. My house stands opposite. Good night.'

Without further ado, the caretaker strode off through the side gate. Arnau and Ramon stood for a long moment, staring at one another. Finally, Arnau hurried over to the gate and closed it, sliding the bar shut.

'Shall I have Sebastian unload our gear?'

Ramon shook his head. 'The boy is busy with the horses and he will still be weak from his days of illness. We will do so in due course, but I fear we are perhaps a little late for vespers, since the lamps are already lit. Let us return to the church and perform our devotions.'

With a nod, Arnau followed the older brother back into the church and into what appeared to be a presbytery in this unfamiliar, Eastern architecture. There, being the senior brother, Ramon led them through vespers, their twin voices rising for each hymn and psalm, Ramon's alone reciting the reading and prayers. When the time came at the closing of the service for the prayer of the Lord, Arnau realised he was putting a great deal more feeling into it than usual, and noted that perhaps the old man's tale of Templar oppression had got to him more than he'd thought.

Our father that art in the heavens,
hallowed be thy name;
Thy kingdom come;
be thy will done
as in heaven and in earth;
give to us this day our bread and all substance;
and forgive us to our debtors,
as we forgive our debtors;
and lead us not into temptation,
but deliver us from evil.
Amen.

When Ramon had given his blessing and the two men rose once more, stretching and moving stiff limbs, Arnau finally voiced what had been eating at him throughout vespers.

'The old man had to be lying, wasn't he?'

Ramon shrugged. 'I cannot say I liked hearing what he said, but he did not strike me as a man creating wicked gossip. He certainly believed what he was saying, and he must have lived through it. It was only ten years ago that the order ruled here. What prompted the grand master to withdraw from Cyprus has never been greatly publicised. Perhaps I am beginning to see why.'

'But surely no knight of the Temple would be so wicked?' Arnau said, shocked.

Ramon shrugged yet again. 'Men are but men, Arnau, and few are saints. If all the members of our order were perfect, then there would be no need for a rule to keep them on the blessed path. Some of the lambs of God stray from the flock from time to time. I have heard tales of less than pious acts on occasion perpetrated by men of our order, though I have to admit this old man's tale is a grand story of wickedness compared with others I have heard. I hope that his bile has driven him to exaggerate. Still, we will clearly not be welcome here and we should look to move on as soon as we can sail.'

Arnau nodded his agreement. He had been looking forward to a sojourn on Cyprus, but now the prospect had been soured beyond all hope.

* * *

Over the following days and weeks Arnau, Ramon and Sebastian fell into a somewhat reclusive routine. They devoted the majority of their time to the traditional tasks of the monastery and to keeping to the liturgy of the hours. On occasion, the sour old caretaker would come over to perform some menial task. His demeanour was always polite, but hovered permanently on the edge of anger. The two knights spent more and more time with Sebastian learning the Greek tongue, attempting to achieve a level of fluency, with ever-increasing success. When they ventured out from the church, which was not often, and ever less so as winter began to make its presence truly felt, they did so in plain tunics and hose, lacking all the symbols of the order, yet retaining their swords against the possibility of violence.

They did manage to make three friends, who together eased their time on the island. The first was Avra, the wife of their bitter caretaker. While old Stathis clearly saw the three travellers as the worst form of evil, it seemed that his wife was a more forgiving sort. She apologised for her husband's manner and explained that the bulk of the islanders saw their present existence as being little more than vassals of a conquering Westerner, blaming that squarely on the lion-hearted English king, and upon the Order to whom King Richard had sold the island. Unlike Stathis, she did not blame these three men for the actions of others, and she brought them cakes and treats whenever she baked, which became a welcome addition to their plain fare.

Their second semi-regular visitor who was sympathetic towards them was a girl of around seventeen called Olympia, who seemed more than a little enamoured with Sebastian. She could be relied upon with each visit to bring news of happenings on the island, though she seemed far more interested in hearing about Sebastian's life than in relaying news.

The third new friend was the most important, and in many ways the most surprising. Father Loukas was the priest of a Greek church a mile out of town, on the road to Argetis. He had popped his head around the door one day on his way into the town, surprised to see the old church occupied. At first, he had been reserved and careful, politely passing the time of day with them but, given their experiences with old Stathis and his wife and what they knew of the island's history, the two knights went out of their way to be friendly, understanding and polite. The result was pleasing. Before long, Father Loukas had become a daily visitor. Often he brought wine and insisted on drinking several cups with them while discussing the difference between his beliefs and theirs which, it turned out, were surprisingly small given the vast history of conflict between the two Churches.

Their debates were often lively affairs, and Father Loukas became their primary source of news, which was how, in the depths of a chilly January, Arnau and Ramon learned of the corruption of the Pope's Crusade. News had finally reached Cyprus of what had happened among the forces of Christendom, and the tidings were far from welcome.

'The army and its Venetian fleet never left Zadra, my friends,' Father Loukas said sadly. 'They are wintering in their ill-gotten land. May their misguided souls torment them for what they have done. Your patriarch in Rome has excommunicated the entire army, including the nobles and the fleet that carry them. They have been denounced as enemies of God, and rightly so, given their actions.'

'Then that is it,' Ramon said with an air of finality. 'The Crusade has failed. It is over.'

'Would that it were so,' the old priest responded darkly. 'For the first time in my long memory, the people of my Church are praising your Pope for denouncing this act. Your own order has joined Rome in condemning the entire expedition, but sadly it appears that greed and the thirst for war are stronger motivations than piety in this wicked world.'

Arnau felt a shiver. What could possibly have happened that was more awful than what they already knew?

'Worse is to come?' Ramon prompted.

'I fear so,' the old priest agreed, lifting his kalimavkion hat enough to scratch amid his wild grey hair. 'It seems the young fool renegade prince of Byzantium has run to the Crusaders for help. There is a rumour that the leaders of the Crusade have agreed to help put the young fool on the throne in return for riches and Rome's control over our Church.'

Arnau leaned back against the wall, eyes wide. Surely this was some kind of twisted joke? The army called to war by the Pope had been destined for Egypt to destroy the heart of the sultan's power and free Jerusalem from his grasp. Was it not evil enough that they had paused in that great and laudable goal to sack and loot a Christian city? Would they now revel in their excommunication? Having sold their souls to the Great Enemy, would they now compound their wickedness by taking the sword of Christendom and using it to usurp the emperor of Byzantium?

Ramon was clearly suffering similar disbelief, with the two men sitting in stunned silence.

'I see the news as unwelcome to you as it is to me,' Father Loukas said, gravely. 'The great empire, which has kept the threat of the Turk and the Saracen at bay for centuries, is to become the target of the papal army. And my Church is a target now also? How far must men fall before Hell opens up beneath their feet and swallows them?'

'It cannot happen,' Ramon said with uncertainty in his voice. 'The Pope will not allow it. An Italian nobleman and a Venetian doge even together do not have the authority to waylay a crusading army.'

But they did. Arnau knew it, and so did Ramon. They shouldn't, but they did. Because the Pope had excommunicated them, and now they had nothing to lose.

Father Loukas left early that day, but he once more affirmed his appreciation of the Order and their stance against the Crusaders, and promised to foster just such an understanding among the islanders. Arnau was silent for some time after the old man left, and it was Ramon who finally broke the silence.

'This is a dark day for Christians everywhere, Arnau.'

The younger knight nodded. 'What do we do? If the Order has condemned the Crusade, we will not be supplying sword arms, even if they change their mind and sail for Egypt when the weather clears. Our mission no longer exists.'

Ramon shook his head. 'We continue on our path, Vallbona. The grand master at Acre is expecting us. Whether the Crusade continues or not, our place is to attend upon the grand master as ordered. If we are required no further, then we will immediately take ship back to Rourell, but we may not return home until we have presented ourselves at Acre as promised. Perhaps the Order will lead some sort of action against the Saracen instead.'

Arnau nodded, though he looked less than excited at the prospect.

The Crusade had not only failed, but had turned upon its allies. Nothing good was going to come of this year. He found himself dreading the coming spring and ships beginning to ply the waters to Acre once more.

Damn the Crusaders.

CHAPTER 3:
THE BITTER TEMPLAR

ACRE
MARCH 1203

It seemed ridiculous, really. Acre, heart of the Templar world and home to the exiled king of Jerusalem, lay less than two hundred miles from where Arnau and the others had wintered on Cyprus, and yet the dangers of eddying currents had forced them to stay on the island until the spring tides allowed for safer sailing.

Though he was loath to admit it, their enforced delay had probably been a boon. Had they rushed straight to Acre they would have been part of the Templar presence in the city when the tidings of the Crusaders came in, and Arnau could only imagine what things had been like in the Order's home fortress then. Digesting the news slowly in the quiet seclusion of the church in Lefkosia would most certainly have been easier, and the late winter had passed much more pleasantly as the islanders gradually opened up to the presence of the three brothers in their midst. It would clearly be a long time before they would trust the Order again, if that ever happened, but at least the undercurrent of malice the visitors had felt upon their arrival had faded.

March came around soon enough, and in a way Arnau had been sad to say farewell to their little monastery. They had slipped back into the Order's daily monastic routine with ease, and it had felt comfortable. Even Sebastian had relaxed and stopped clutching his icon to his heart day in and day out. Now they were heading into unknown territory, and the near future was worrying to say the least. Still, the great adventure of life must go on.

The ship aboard which they had managed to secure passage was a trader from Ascalon, down the coast. Arnau had been rather pleased with their command of the Greek tongue after a winter of concerted study, and had been therefore disappointed when it transpired that the sailors spoke some strange glottal language and his Greek was now clearly redundant. Likely, where they were going he would encounter more Arabic than Greek, the former a tongue which was already becoming vague and distant for him with two years of disuse.

Still, despite their uncertain future, the difficulties of communication and the knowledge that the world was teetering on the brink of something terrible, it was hard not to feel a touch of excitement as the coast came into view as a long strip of hazy brown which slowly resolved into beaches and woodland, villages and parched hills. And then finally, Acre grew out of the haze.

Somehow Arnau had expected a mountainous place with towering walls and turrets, flags of the crusading nations fluttering in the wind and ships prowling the coast, searching for Saracens to destroy. It was a little deflating to realise that Acre was a fairly flat and run-down looking place, filled with low, brown buildings and rabbit-warren streets. There *were* city walls, he could see, but only facing inland. The coast was unfortified, barring occasional towers and one squat, ugly-looking fortress on a headland. The only ships to be seen were the same native traders they had encountered all through their journey. No flags. No mountains. No sign that since the fall of Jerusalem this place was the very heart of the Holy Land, the centre of Christian power in the East and the mother house of the Order.

Still, he rallied. Appearances weren't everything. As the city slid ever closer and they made to round that fortified headland to the harbour on the southern side, Arnau realised that flags *were* flying above Acre, or at least above that heavy, square, golden stone fortress. Black and white flags. The flags of the Templar order. It would appear that the one great military monument in Acre belonged to the Order.

Ramon was peering at the place too, while Sebastian suffered in silence with only the occasional gulp or retch to remind them he was present. As they rounded the heavy stone mole and slid through the waters towards the dock, Arnau could see with surprise ships in port also flying the flag of the Temple. He hadn't realised the Order had its own ships, but then again, this was the very heart of the Templar world. Moments later he was waiting, almost quivering with anticipation, as sailors tied off lines, ran out ramps and brought up horses and gear. The sun was a little past its zenith when they finally set foot upon the dock of Acre.

'To the castle?' he murmured as Ramon tested the straps on his saddle bags.

'To the castle.'

The three men led their horses rather than riding, making their way along the dock and into the streets of Acre. After days at sea, all three of them felt the need to reacquaint themselves with walking on dry land before mounting animals once more. Arnau took in his surroundings like a parched man at a water fountain. Acre was a whole new world, more different from home than even Cyprus. The streets were narrow and paved with ancient stone, the houses centuries old and tightly packed. Awnings of striped canvas covered houses and shop fronts, and stalls seemed to be placed at random, selling all manner of things as if the entire city was one sprawling market. The people here were almost uniformly darker coloured than any visitor, their skin leathery from years of exposure to a harsh sun. Many seemed to be wearing turbans or scarves wrapped around their heads in the manner of Saracens. The entire place smelled of parched horse dung mixed with strong spices, overlaid by the briny salt of sea air. It was a heady combination.

It took just a quarter of an hour to reach the fortress, which stood resolute and powerful, dominating the headland. Constructed in an uneven pentagon to suit the terrain, it sported five towers rising above the battlements. The gate consisted of a single great arch which reached a point at the apex in an almost Arabian style, heavy, studded doors standing open with men in white surcoats bearing the red cross standing to either side, watching any passers-by carefully.

Arnau was concerned to hear the distinctive sounds of combat as they approached, but nearing the gate, he caught sight of figures moving about inside on a cloister lawn of parched brown grass, training in pairs, hammering at shields and parrying the blows of their brothers. The entire place was alive with people. Moreover, now that he looked around, he could see the Order's cross carved above the doors of many of the buildings clustered around the fortress. Clearly Templar control was not limited to the castle. An entire area of the city was under their command. Arnau had never seen so many knights, sergeants and associate brothers in one place. It looked almost like an army preparing for a campaign.

He swallowed his distaste, remembering what he had been told about the Crusade. That was probably exactly what they *had* been doing.

They stopped at the gate.

'Brothers Ramon de Juelle and Arnau de Vallbona of Aragon reporting for the muster. I apologise for any delay. We were caught on Cyprus for the winter.'

'The Iberians,' one of the two men on the door noted to the other, who nodded. 'You are expected.'

'Where do we report in?'

'You've been assigned to Preceptor Bochard,' the first man said. 'Go past the church and to the doorway in the corner. Anyone there can direct you to him.'

The two men nodded and thanked the guards before walking in through the arch and across the courtyard of the fortress, past two dozen men training in a crash of steel and grunts. The sound of voices raised in a pious chant arose from the church as they neared it. Something was nagging at Arnau as they walked. Something about that name…

Finally, he turned to Ramon.

'I know that name from somewhere. Bochard, I mean.'

Ramon nodded, his face sour. 'I'm not surprised. We heard it a few times on Cyprus.'

Arnau blinked with realisation, a cold shiver running through him. That was it. The name had cropped up in the few discussions they'd had with Father Loukas about the Templar troubles on the island. Bochard had been the name of the Templar master on Cyprus who had led the Order through their disastrous year in control of the island. The man who had driven the locals to revolt and who, finding his men trapped in Lefkosia, had led a charge and slaughtered hundreds of islanders.

The chances of the name being entirely coincidental were almost non-existent.

'The same man.'

'Without a doubt. We might tread carefully here, Vallbona. And try not to talk about Cyprus if you can avoid it.'

Arnau nodded vigorously as they passed the church and made for the corner doorway, which led into a huge block that contained halls, chambers and staircases. At the doorway, Ramon once more handed his reins to the grey-green looking Sebastian. 'Find the stables and see to the horses, and then fetch the gear and wait here.'

Sebastian nodded his understanding as Arnau also handed over his reins, then the two knights turned to the building. A sergeant stood just inside the doorway, a hammer in hand, repairing the latch.

'Good day, Brother,' Ramon greeted him in French. 'Can you direct us to Preceptor Bochard?'

The man nodded, three nails held between his teeth. Pausing in his work, he removed the offending articles and licked his lips, wincing at the ferrous taste. 'Up the stairs to the first floor. Head along the corridor with the large window at the end. Behind the last door on the right you will find Master Reynal Bochard.'

Ramon thanked the man and they moved on, climbing the stairs and emerging onto a landing. Half a dozen doors led off this place, and they could hear muted conversation and the occasional low song from them as they passed, before reaching the last one. Taking a deep breath, Ramon shot Arnau a glance that silently asked if he was ready. Arnau nodded once and then the older knight rapped on the door.

'Come,' called a strong, if slightly hoarse, voice from within.

They opened the door and walked into a large room with a low ceiling supported by twin, wide-spanning arches. A window at the far side admitted ample light to give the room a warm glow. The place was clearly no sleeping chamber, for benches sat to each side in pairs and a large table, spread with maps, stood in the centre. A man in a white mantle was leaning over one such chart, peering intently at it. As Ramon closed the door behind them, Arnau took in what he could of Preceptor Bochard. The man was heavily built, barrel-chested and muscular, particularly for a man of his clearly advancing years. His long beard was entirely grey, while his hair was a salt-and-pepper mix, cropped relatively close. As he looked up, his eyebrows were similarly long and grey, throwing the pits of his eyes into shadow. The effect was rather disconcerting. Bochard had almost the same skin tone as the locals, and Arnau surmised the man had probably spent much of his adult life in the Order and in the Holy Land.

'What is it?' barked Bochard, irritably.

'Brothers Ramon de Juelle and Arnau de Vallbona from the preceptory of Rourell in Aragon, Preceptor, reporting as ordered by our preceptrix, Ermengarda. My squire is below stabling the horses.'

Bochard's face underwent a series of odd emotional changes and then settled back into irritation.

'I was beginning to think you would never arrive. You have been assigned to me by the grand master. What do you know about the situation here in the East?'

Arnau remained silent, letting his superior answer for them, though his eyes strayed to the maps on the table. One was of the city, several clearly of this locale and the entire coastal region, heading as far east and north as Jerusalem and Damascus. One seemed to cover the northern lands, up across Anatolia and into the Balkan kingdoms.

'I understand,' Ramon answered, 'that the king of Jerusalem has a number of truces in place with various heathen groups in order to secure the borders while he concentrates on Egypt. As far as I am aware, there are currently no hostilities here. The last I heard the army of the Franks was still in Zadra and may be planning to involve themselves in imperial succession affairs at the expense of their goal in Egypt. As such, I am aware that our involvement in the Crusade is likely to be nullified. The grand master still stands by the papal excommunication, I presume?'

Bochard's brows knitted tightly. 'You are better informed than I expected, given your peripheral position in Iberia and the months spent travelling. But you are far from up to date.'

Ramon bowed his head.

'The Crusade is in danger, certainly,' Bochard said with a hint of anger. 'The army is currently in Corfu, where there seems to be some division between their leaders as to their next move. I understand that a sizeable force has split from the main Crusade, secured their own ships and set sail for Acre, where they intend to put themselves at the service of the King of Jerusalem. Others intend to place this pretender Alexius on the Byzantine throne at all costs, that party being led by the doge of Venice. In fact, the Pope has rescinded his excommunication of the crusading army, hoping that they will all follow the example of those men who have split off and sailed for Outremer. Not of the Venetians, mind, only the crusading Franks. The sea dogs are still outside the arms of Mother Church.'

Again, both brothers bowed their heads. It was heartening to hear that the Crusade might yet recover and adhere to its intended goals. More so that the Franks were no longer suffering excommunication. Perhaps there was hope. And if the Crusaders reached Acre, then maybe the Order would once more join them on campaign.

'The situation here is no less troublesome,' Bochard said, again irritably. 'The king has a truce in place with Egypt, which we will be forced to break if we seek to destroy Saracen power, but which in the meantime has theoretically given us the freedom to consolidate. Yet the Egyptian Sultan has agreed to terms with his neighbouring Saracen princes also, which means that if we launch an attack on Egypt, we risk breaking our truce terms with those same neighbours. We could attack Egypt only to find ourselves with a war on three fronts, fighting on every frontier of Outremer. This is a thorny problem currently plaguing the grand master, though his attention has temporarily been distracted by further difficulties. He has been called north to Antioch, for war has broken out there between Armenian Cilicia and the Antiochene lands. And while they weaken one another, the Sultanate of Rum looks on, anticipating easy pickings among the wreckage.'

'So the Order is preparing for…?' prompted Ramon.

'Anything, to put it simply. Until the troubles around Antioch are resolved – and the king and the Hospitaller master are also there with our own commander attempting to resolve it all – we cannot say for sure where any campaign could be prosecuted, if at all. Everything is in a state of uncertainty at this time. As such, I have been charged with a mission by the grand master, and you shall accompany me.'

'Mission, sir?' prompted Arnau.

'With everything so unstable and troublesome, the court of Jerusalem and our order both have been charged with securing every alliance and border we can. While the masters attend Antioch, brothers of the Temple are on their way as emissaries to the Saracen court in Damascus and even to the emir of Mosul. The support of Aimery of Cyprus is assumed. But even with all those states settled, there is one major worry: the empire.'

Arnau frowned. 'The Byzantines, Preceptor?'

Bochard nodded. 'That heathen empire has ever been hard to predict. Their emperors are as often in league with Saracens and Turks as they are at odds with them. Their relationships with the sultanate of Rum and the Armenian king are complex. We cannot, in the current circumstances, afford the let the empire shirk its duty as a bulwark of Christendom. Despite what happened at Zadra and the presence of the exiled prince among the Crusaders, we cannot allow the emperor to focus on internal problems. We need him supporting our efforts if we are to have any hope of success in the East. Do you understand?'

Both men nodded, though Arnau caught Ramon's eye and knew the older knight was thinking the same as he. How could they hope to persuade the Byzantine emperor to support a Crusade when there was every chance that Crusade would turn on him in favour of his nephew? The very task felt doomed from the outset.

'Good. The grand master was unwilling to commit knights from the local regions to my embassy, for they will surely be needed here in the coming days, and they are familiar with the region and its people and geography. You being uninformed foreigners will be of more use to me than you would be here.'

His gaze hardened.

'And I need you to understand and accept something immediately. Your presence is little more than a matter of show. Like the Romans of old, the Byzantines appreciate spectacle, and the larger and more impressive our embassy, the better. Would that we could send a sizeable force. Still, you will look noble and strong, and yet remain silent and unopinionated. I follow the Rule of our order without question, and I expect those with me to do likewise. That *includes* rule thirty-nine. Do you understand?' he added, his eyes slits.

Arnau felt a twitch creep into his eyelid at the words.

Rule thirty-nine. He knew very well to which aspects of the rule the preceptor was referring.

... all brothers who are professed strictly obey their Master. For nothing is dearer to Jesus Christ than obedience. For as soon as something is commanded by the Master or by him to whom the Master has given the authority, it should be

done without delay as though Christ himself had commanded it.

He caught the eye of Brother Ramon again, and once more noted the same discomfort and worry in his superior's eye. Yet the rules were there, as Ramon himself had said, to keep wayward brothers in place. They had to be obeyed. It was one key thing to which every Templar agreed when they first joined the Order.

They bowed their heads in unison.

'Very well. You have conveniently missed the sext service before your arrival, though I presume you performed your devotions aboard your ship. I expect you to attend none, vespers and compline in the church here in the fortress at my side. We will leave for Constantinople by the end of the week. I live in hope that the grand master will conclude his treaties and return before then, for if that is the case and Antioch is settled, then he might perhaps spare me further support for our embassy. But leave then we shall, whether the commander has returned or no. Until that day, I expect you to take an active part in conventual life as if you were in your home preceptory, treating me as your master, for that I surely am until our task is complete and the Order dispatches you elsewhere. For now, you have two hours until none. I advise you to familiarise yourself with the Order's enclave here in Acre. I also need you to visit the storehouses and arrange everything we need for a month-long journey, since it will certainly take us that long to reach the imperial capital.'

'A month, sir?' Arnau asked.

Ramon shot him a look, but nodded slightly and addressed the preceptor for them both. 'Surely, Master, by ship we can make the journey in a week at most?'

Bochard's lip rose in an odd twitch, reminiscent of a sneer. 'Ships will not be available for our journey. You have a horse. Use it. We shall ride for the principality of Antioch and around the coast of Armenian Cilicia into Byzantine lands. Now leave me. I have much to ponder.'

Bowing, the two men left the room, closing the door with a click behind them. Neither spoke until they were at the top of the stairs, far along the corridor, when Ramon paused and grasped Arnau by the shoulder, pulling him into a corner. 'What do you make of the preceptor?' he asked in hushed tones.

Arnau pursed his lips. 'I'm not sure I trust him, Brother,' he admitted quietly.

'I trust him to do exactly what he thinks is right,' Ramon replied. 'Whether it is sensible or not. I am beginning to see how that disaster on Cyprus might have come about. We shall have a very fine line to walk in the coming days.'

Arnau nodded. 'We cannot disobey him. It is the Rule, and he is more adamant than most.'

'Yet it would be unwise of us to walk into catastrophe alongside him without question. A fine line, as I said. And what of our journey, Vallbona? Why a month-long ride instead of a week-long voyage, do you think?'

Arnau huffed. 'I see no reason. The Order here has its own ships. And even if they are all spoken for, it would not be difficult to secure passage on a private vessel. With the preceptor's squire, we would still only number five men and five steeds. Most ships would be able to find room for us. The Order could afford the cost, and a good God-fearing sailor would charge little for men of the Order anyway. So no, I see no reason. Unless…'

Arnau tried not to dwell on what was rising in his imagination.

'Unless?' Ramon urged him.

'Unless this is all a lie? We only have the preceptor's word that the grand master has set him this mission. If it is but a fable, then that might explain why the preceptor cannot utilise a ship or secure adequate funding?'

Ramon frowned. 'A worrying thought, but I am not entirely sure that Bochard is capable of that sort of lie. I fear he is too rigid. My own notion is that Bochard's sense of self-importance is a driving force and he feels that we are inadequate as an escort on such a task. I think we ride so that we can pass within mere miles of Antioch and the Order's grand master. You heard how he delays so that the grand master might return and grant him more brothers. I fear he means to petition for more men even as we travel.'

Arnau shook his head in wonder. 'Whatever the case, this journey looks troublesome to me.'

'Not as troublesome as the destination. The Byzantine court might not be the best place at the moment, given the threat from the Crusaders. I doubt we sons of the Church of Rome will be wholly popular there.'

Arnau nodded sourly and the two men began to descend the stairs.

'Come,' said Ramon, a smile returning to his face. 'We have two hours to explore. Let us begin with the church.'

The building consisted of a rotunda with a high, pointed roof, from which projected a long and wide nave. A transept jutted off to the north with several side buildings. It was sizeable, though clearly not large enough to accommodate the entire order in Acre.

'There must be other churches outside the fortress,' Ramon noted as they made their way inside the ornate arched western doorway. The church was well-appointed and spacious. Three brothers in white mantles knelt before the altar on some unknown vigil, and Ramon put a finger to his lips, reminding Arnau to keep quiet here. Trying not to disturb the praying knights, the two Iberians moved through the church, taking in all aspects of it. The building was probably only a dozen or so years old, though elements of it had clearly been taken from other sources. A Templar flag hung on the nave wall, its lower edge tattered and shredded, showing the stains of battle and blood, and a similar banner hung opposite. A series of stones built into the nave wall were clearly of such antique origin that their presence had to be meaningful.

They passed into the transept and there discovered two knights standing silent and attentive by a heavy door, which was ribbed with iron reinforcement. A priest nearby was cleaning a crucifix. The two men shared a look and crossed to the old man who, when he straightened at their approach, proved to be immensely tall and birdlike.

'Can I help you, Brothers?' he asked in a soft voice in Eastern-accented French.

'We have just arrived,' Ramon replied in low tones so as not to disturb the praying knights nearby. 'We're familiarising ourselves with Acre. Why guards within the church, might I ask?'

The priest glanced at the two knights standing by the door.

'Our reliquary,' he smiled. 'The contents of which are irreplaceable and of inestimable value.'

Ramon returned the smile and nodded at Arnau. 'My friend here is more than familiar with relics.'

Arnau rolled his eyes. 'I acquired the arm of Saint Stephen for our preceptory.'

The priest nodded indulgently, as though he held the Holy Grail and Arnau had admitted to acquiring a wicker basket. 'Our relics at Acre are the envy of the world. When Jerusalem fell to the Saracen, we were careful to remove every relic we had gathered and transport them here. Not one was lost to the enemy.' A gleam appeared in the priest's eye. Pride might be a sin, but sometimes it was the hardest one to avoid. The man was almost certainly justifiably proud of their collection.

'I would show you, but the room is kept locked, and only three people in Acre have a key. Besides, the bulk of the collection is kept secure in the cellars.'

Arnau frowned. Clearly this reliquary could easily hold more sacred objects than he had seen in his life. How many could they have that they needed a cellar for the overflow?

The priest seemed to read his expression and smiled knowingly. 'We have a number of fragments of the true cross, as well as nails. We have the bones of near a hundred blessed saints, a cross formed from Christ's own lavatorium, thorns from the Saviour's crown, two phials of Christ's untainted and ever-vital blood, a fragment of Pontius Pilate's sacred stair, splinters from the column of the flagellation, dirt preserved from ancient Golgotha, and so much more.'

Arnau felt his pulse quicken at just the mention of some of those incredible sacred relics. They made his own contribution last year seem more than a little paltry. But then, it was said the Order had been gathering relics in Jerusalem for a century now. They had the largest collection since that begun by the mother of Constantine.

'Incredible,' breathed Arnau.

'We also retain a number of stones taken from both the Temple and the church of the Holy Sepulchre in Jerusalem. You will find them built into the walls of our own church.'

Ramon nodded. 'I saw them. And the banners?'

'The flags of our fallen brothers, removed from the field at both Hattin and Cresson.'

Arnau shuddered. Two of the greatest losses in the Order's history. Over a hundred knights of both the Templar and Hospitaller orders and a thousand of their men, including the grand masters themselves, had died at Cresson. Legend had it that only three knights walked away from the dreadful defeat. Hattin had been little better for the Order, and worse for the Christian world at large.

'Perhaps, if the Crusade can be guided back to Egypt, Jerusalem might once again be freed, and the Order can return.'

The priest nodded, though his expression suggested he doubted it.

The two knights took their leave and exited the church. Back in the sunlight, Arnau was still shivering at the thought of what those two tattered banners had seen.

'Come on,' Ramon said with new purpose. 'Whatever we might make of it, within the week we will be riding for Constantinople, and you will truly have a chance to practise your Greek. For now, let us gather everything we need for the journey.'

CHAPTER 4:
THE PERILOUS JOURNEY

NORTH OF ACRE
LATE MARCH 1203

The journey was clearly going to be a tense affair, with the presence of Preceptor Bochard and his squire doing little to improve matters. The two visiting Iberian brothers had pored over maps of the region before they left and had been surprised at how fragmented and disparate the various small Crusader states now were since the fall of Jerusalem and the resurgence of Saracen power. They had been even more surprised at the fact that enemy territory seemed to separate many of the states. Even just north of Acre, Saracen-controlled lands came so close to the coast as to make the connection between two parts of the kingdom little more than a stretch of beach.

Bochard had dismissed their concerns out of hand, proclaiming their safety as a matter of course. The king of Jerusalem in his exile city of Acre had temporary treaties and truces with the local Ayyubid Saracen rulers, and Bochard did not believe that anyone would attack Christian knights and risk breaking the truce. When Ramon, still angling to board a ship, pointed out that there would be bandits to be wary of also, Bochard had sneered and replied that the very reason for the foundation of the Order was to protect pilgrims from bandits, and that it would be a poor lookout for Templars everywhere if they started to panic about banditry.

Stripped of excuses, they had had little option but to fall in line with Bochard's plan for a month-long ride. On the bright side, given their history in Iberia, both men had a little grounding in what to expect. Christian realms with internecine squabbles threatened by a Moorish empire that was more often hostile than pacific described their homeland as easily as it did this region.

So with two horses each and a string of three pack mules, the five men had ridden out from Acre at the end of the week. They had received wishes of good fortune from fellow Templars as they passed through the city, and even odd words of grudging support from members of the rival Hospitaller order and others. They had left Acre in the early morning sunlight after breaking their fast and ridden north along the coast at a steady, mile-eating pace.

The terrain was flat and predominantly brown, with well-farmed land just inshore of golden beaches. Hills rose into what looked like low mountains to the east throughout the day, and they passed a number of small towns and villages that looked as though they had probably changed very little since the disciples of Christ had passed through a millennium ago.

On the morning of the second day they passed the ancient city of Tyre, where a small group of mail-shirted soldiers at a roadside well told them to be watchful and wary further north. Mere miles from Tyre were lands controlled by the Ayyubids of Karak, and they were notoriously lax in keeping to treaties. For the next day and a half, they passed through Saracen lands, though there was no clearly delineated border and no clear indication that the area was any different to the Christian kingdom they had just left. The land and people were exactly the same. Arnau knew from bitter experience in Iberia's border zones how the local populace tended to acquire a jaded fatalism in their approach to authority. Today their ruler was a Saracen. Tomorrow it could be a Crusader king. For them, little else would change.

Mercifully, there was no trouble on that stretch. The only Saracen soldiers they saw were a small troop of horsemen some mile or more distant to the east, and either they held tight to their truce, or they saw little benefit in riding miles out of their way to attack five men who were by their order's very name 'Poor Knights'. Thus, as the sun sank the next day, they approached the outskirts of the city of Beyrouth, safe in the knowledge that they had traversed enemy territory safely and reached lands once more controlled by the king.

Miles north during the next morning, they passed the unmarked border with the Christian county of Tripoli. Thereafter things became a little less tense, though apparently not for Bochard, who seemed to become more and more tightly wound as they approached the city of Antioch, where their grand master was said to currently reside with the other leaders of the East, mediating a dispute. They saw no Ayyubid riders or bandits during those next few days, passing the great city of Tripoli in peace.

Some distance further north they passed through an area which displayed the telltale signs of an increased presence of the Hospitaller order, which further vexed Bochard, who held that rival order in even less esteem, apparently, than most Templars. Still no sign of trouble arose. On the seventh day out of Acre they passed the ancient city of Latakia, and on the eighth drew nearer to Antioch.

Nestled between the great Orontes River and a range of high peaks covered with ancient structures and powerful walls, Antioch remained one of the most venerable and important cities in the East. Its control was currently contested, according to the preceptor, by Bohemond the Fourth, Count of Tripoli and second son of the previous ruler, and Raymond-Roupen, the same man's grandson by his elder boy who was supported by King Leo of Cilicia. A true mess which had brought kings, grand masters, and even a legate of the Pope to the city to mediate.

Entry to the city was easily attained, given their clear Templar credentials, and they were shown to some ancient and palatial building in the city's centre, overlooking the river. There they recovered from the first week of their journey, partook of their first food cooked indoors and with a good range of ingredients in all that time, and waited. Bochard had sent messages to the grand master as soon as they arrived and had become irritable and tense awaiting his summons.

It was some four hours after their arrival that a messenger arrived at their door from the grand master, requesting Bochard's presence. Though Ramon and Arnau had not been included in the invitation and thus remained in silence in their room, both men were secretly glad to be rid of the preceptor for even a short time. His constant tenseness and barely contained anger was wearying to be around, and they had been in its presence now for an entire week without respite. It was only when he had left the room that the other two knights realised just how tense they had become themselves, exhaling slowly and allowing their limbs to unknot.

Bochard's squire Hugues had accompanied his master, and the other three men exchanged knowing looks as the door clicked shut and the booted footsteps beyond echoed into the distance.

'That man is going to be trouble,' Arnau said quietly.

Ramon gave him a warning look. 'No matter your opinion, Vallbona, or even mine for that matter, it is not our place to condemn our superior. No man becomes a preceptor without some strength of character and devotion to the Lord driving it. Bochard may well have hidden depths.'

'So does a latrine,' Arnau replied archly, earning himself another disapproving look.

'He is a martinet and a man, I would say, with a shadow in his past that seems to still be haunting him. You will find more than one brother in the Order whom that description fits. You would find them in Rourell, even. One day, a man might just say that of you. Remember your values as a good Christian and as a soldier of God. It is our place to serve Bochard, and our mission is a peaceful, worthy one.'

'That's another thing,' Arnau said, ignoring the warning signs in Ramon's expression. 'We're going to Constantinople to try and secure promises and contracts that the emperor will maintain his alliances with the Order and the kingdom of Jerusalem and not shirk his duty in the Christian defence of the East. An emperor whose entire reign is coming under threat from a Christian force of whom even the Pope has now accepted validity.'

'Of this I am aware,' answered Ramon quietly.

'Does it not strike you as odd that the grand master would choose the preceptor as the emissary of peace for this duty?'

'Vallbona—'

'Seriously, though, Brother. If you had the pick of every man of the Order to send as an emissary into a fractious and uncertain court, would you really have chosen Preceptor Bochard?'

Ramon sat silent for a long moment, and finally sagged. 'No. In truth I would not. In fact, I might worry that assigning a man known to have been active in suppressing the Greek Church on Cyprus might be too much of a provocation. But the grand master is the leader of our order and a man with the ear and support of the Pope himself. If he has selected Bochard then there is a reason, even if it is not ours to know.'

'And us as his escort, Ramon?'

'Pardon?'

'Newly arrived? Straight from Iberia, setting foot in the Holy Land and immediately being whisked off to play ambassador to the imperial court with Bochard? We know next to nothing of the imperial world and its ways. There will be men in Acre who are familiar with Constantinople and its court. Men who can speak their language and would be better suited. And *more* men indeed. If Bochard is right that pomp and glory is what impresses the empire, then it would be sensible to send an entire *conroi* of knights, rather than two tired and rather out-of-place men.'

'We *do* speak Greek,' Ramon replied somewhat feebly.

'But we didn't until we began our journey, and neither Bochard nor the grand master could know that. Something here does not add up to me. Something is not quite right. And the timely reminder from the preceptor that one of the most critical rules of the Order is unquestioning obedience does nothing to quell my worries.'

Ramon nodded. 'All we can do is our best, Vallbona – obey our orders and trust in the Lord. Unless the preceptor himself flaunts and abuses the Rule, then it is not our place to question or doubt him.'

Arnau sighed. It was true, but that didn't mean he had to like it. He was experiencing something new and entirely unwelcome on this journey. From the day he had put his foot across the threshold of Rourell half a decade ago, he had seen nothing in the Order to shake his faith and his confidence. Despite the unusual presence of a female preceptrix at the house, she instilled nothing but strength and confidence in her people. The sergeants and sisters he had known there had been beyond reproach, pious and wise, and he would have walked off a cliff with a heart full of faith had they but asked. Even the three old knights of the preceptory had managed to secure Arnau's utter loyalty. Lütolf had some dark past in Germany that had driven him to the sandy and dry end of the world, where he gave his life for the Order. Balthesar had been a killer both for and against the Moors in his old life, and despite his worrying obsession with the relic during their recent mission to the emir's island, Arnau had never considered disobeying him. Ramon held his respect in exactly the same way, and he had found no reason to doubt any man of the Order he had met in Acre. Bochard, though, worried him. Whenever he looked at the preceptor, all he could see in their future was trouble.

They sat in silence for some time until the clanging of bells across the city announced the time for none, and Arnau sat up suddenly. 'I think I saw a church back on the road we arrived along.'

Ramon shook his head. 'We shall perform our devotions right here in case the Preceptor returns.'

The two men moved a chair out of the way and dropped to their knees before the plain cross on the room's east wall and Sebastian joined them, hands clasped tight before him. Their devotions lasted a little more than half an hour, after which Ramon turned to whetting and polishing his sword and Sebastian to repacking their gear a little more neatly, while Arnau returned to fretting silently.

All three men stopped what they were doing and straightened at the sound of marching footsteps outside. A moment later the door slammed violently open and Bochard entered with a face like thunder, his squire hot on his heels. Arnau and Ramon remained silent.

'The grand master has seen fit to refuse my request for more companions,' snapped Bochard in answer to an unasked question.

'Then we are to continue on our mission as we were, Master?' asked Ramon quietly.

'Yes. A grand entourage of five men as a deputation to the emperor of a dangerously hedonistic and heretical land, who puts great stock in appearance. And two of those mere *squires*,' he added dismissively.

'With respect, Master,' Ramon said carefully, 'how confident are you that we could influence the decision of the emperor, whether there be five of us or five hundred?'

Bochard shot him a look like a loaded crossbow. 'That depends on many factors, de Juelle. On how persuasive we can be, on what the Venetians and their ships full of Franks decide to do next, on the Byzantine court's current leanings, on events here in Outremer, and even on the mood of the emperor on the day we meet. I can predict nothing as yet. All I know is that with more of us we stood a better chance of making an impression. As we are, we shall be little more than a troublesome horsefly to the emperor.'

The two knights remained silent. Provoking Bochard into further ire would only be counterproductive. In the end, the preceptor drew from his baggage a thick book. Arnau immediately assumed it to be a rare personal Bible. Few men had such a treasure, and brothers of the Order rarely owned personal possessions of any kind, let alone such valuable things. To own a book would require the dispensation of the knight's own superior. Peering myopically across the room, Arnau tried to examine the outside of the book as Bochard lifted it to read.

It came as some surprise to note that there was Greek script on the cover, and he had little or no chance of identifying it. While it came as no shock that Bochard knew Greek – the man had ruled over Greek-speaking Cyprus for a year and had been chosen as an ambassador to the Byzantine court – there was little chance of the book being a Bible. It had to be either some Orthodox religious text or some sort of history from Byzantium – not what Arnau could have anticipated being in the strict preceptor's belongings. Perhaps Bochard was more prepared than he had assumed? Certainly he had voluminous and well-packed bags that were jealously guarded by Hugues when not on the horse in transit.

They attended the other liturgical services together, all five of them, at some grand church in the city's centre, where Arnau had his first glimpse of three of the most important people in the world. The king had not attended, for he was busy with affairs of state and was not bound to the liturgy as were the brothers. However, the grand master of the Templars stood with a number of old knights directly facing a party of Hospitallers, surrounding their own grand master, and the papal legate was also in attendance.

It was with some regret that they rose the next morning and prepared to move on. Antioch was clearly a city of marvels and here, in Arnau's mind at least, the familiar world would end. Once they left Antioch and marched north and west, they would be entering lands controlled by utterly alien cultures.

With their gear neatly repacked by Sebastian, and Hugues loading the preceptor's pack beast with heavy bags, they exited Antioch by the gate through which they'd entered, and rode north. Just a few miles north of Antioch, cutting inland through hilly terrain to bypass a great curve in the coastline, they passed through what Arnau could only describe as an echo of Hell. The land seemed to be intermittently forbidding and mountainous terrain and flat dry land, but there were endless signs of strife around them. Every third village or so they passed had been partially or entirely burned, and perhaps two thirds of them were depopulated and exhibiting clear signs of violence. Graveyards they saw showed signs of greatly increased use, and small fortresses and watchtowers stood crumbling from recent destruction.

Arnau found himself shivering as they rode, taking in the desolation. He noted that Sebastian had lost his sense of ease since their time on Cyprus and had once more taken to vigorous clutching and thumb-rubbing of his icon.

'What is this?' he asked. 'Is it the Seljuks of Rum or the Saracens breaking their truce?'

'Neither,' grunted Bochard, riding slightly ahead. The man had hardly said two words to them since they had left Antioch and had exuded an atmosphere of disappointment and resentment throughout. 'This is the result of the Antiochene war. This was King Leo's advance on the city last year.'

Arnau felt bile rise at the thought. The king of Armenian Cilicia was a Christian. Perhaps every bit as weird and Eastern and heretical as the Greeks, but a Christian nonetheless, and a noted ally of Rome at that. Antioch and its other claimant, Bohemond, were Franks of the Roman Church. This was Christian fighting Christian over a title in the very midst of a world under threat by the Saracen and the Turk. The idiocy and short-sightedness of it made Arnau nervous. In these dark days, all good Christians should be putting aside their differences for the good of Christendom as a whole.

On they rode through miles of ruin and death, through a world that had not recovered from the violence of the war even half a year on. The road they followed passed the eastern edge of a spur of hills some fifteen or twenty miles north of Antioch, and here, as they rode in unhappy silence, they drew up at a gesture from Bochard. Beside the road ahead sat a low stone compound, resembling a toll station or some such, a large banner fluttering above the dry brown walls. As the wind caught the flag and momentarily snapped it flat, Arnau saw a rearing lion in red on a field of white. He frowned, remembering the royal banners he had seen on Cyprus, of which it seemed an almost direct copy.

'Armenians,' Bochard said quietly.

Arnau shivered. This was it. The kingdom of Armenian Cilicia might be Christian and nominally allied, but their Armenian origin made them more distant and exotic and less like the Western Europeans than even Byzantium. These people had come from the eastern steppe, in the lee of the Turks' homeland. And they had been at war in Antioch for years. Everything remotely familiar to Arnau was about to end.

'Do we need to be on our guard?' Ramon asked quietly.

'Always worthwhile,' Bochard replied. 'I have not met them often, but they are not to be trusted. Their king is devious and dangerous and cares not who he aggravates in his quest to acquire all in sight.'

There was something in the preceptor's voice that suggested he felt personally aggrieved by the king and oddly, as he spoke, his gaze was drawn up and left as though caught by a hook and dragged in. The others followed his glance, but all they could see was a craggy and wooded spur of hills. Arnau turned a frown on Ramon, but the older brother's gaze had returned along with Bochard's to the small fortification by the road.

The five men rode slowly towards the walled enclosure, and Arnau's sense of unease rose as they neared and half a dozen men emerged from the building, each with a shield on their arm and a long spear with a gleaming point. They wore glittering coats of wool with small steel plates stitched into a flexible yet protective surface. They did not give off an overwhelmingly welcoming air. Sebastian's attention to his icon became somewhat urgent.

'Be prepared. The Order does not currently face open hostility with the king, but our peace is a fragile thing and liable to break at any moment.'

Arnau nodded. He had no interest in going to war with other Christians simply over who held the title Count of Antioch. Ramon was also nodding and both Iberian knights tried to look imposing, yet with an air of pacific alliance. Bochard, Arnau noted, rested the palm of his hand on his sword hilt.

As they neared, the six Armenians filed into a line, blocking the road. It was a statement, clearly. If the Templars had so desired, they could easily leave the road and pound across the fields, circumventing the footmen and returning to the road perhaps a mile further on. But what the Armenians were doing was defying the knights.

As they closed, and showed no sign of slowing to a stop, the preceptor cleared his voice.

'Make way,' he called in French. 'We are a deputation from the grand master of the Temple to the emperor in Byzantium. Make way, I say.'

The soldiers did not move and from their general attitude it was clear that this was a deliberate decision and not a matter of language. Arnau could feel his muscles beginning to tighten. He was almost certain he knew what was coming. Though Bochard still only rode at a walk, he was showing no signs of stopping as he bore down on the soldiers.

'Make way, or we shall be forced to teach you a lesson in manners, you curs.'

Arnau winced. Clearly the soldiers comprehended French well enough. The Armenians flinched, and changed on their spears, preparing to face potential violence. Though Bochard was hardly defusing the situation, Arnau had to admit that it had been the Armenians who had begun matters by blocking the road in a warlike manner.

The spearmen stood resolute in the face of the advancing horses, and two of them shouted something in what must have been their own language. Arnau had no idea what they said, but the tone was derogatory, even mocking. He did note emphasis placed on the word or name 'Gaston' and by the time he'd turned to look at Bochard, the preceptor had turned a plum colour in anger, his sword slipping an inch free of his scabbard.

'Preceptor...' muttered Ramon in calming tones, but Bochard ignored him, rising high in his saddle and addressing the soldiers in a loud voice.

'Gaston was an insult. There can be no true peace between your heretical king and the Order until Gaston is returned to us.'

'Uh-oh,' murmured Ramon, his own hand now going to his sword. He looked at Arnau, who nodded, reaching for his hilt. The older knight then turned and made emphatic motions at Sebastian. He may be young and but a squire, but for months now he had been practising with a blade under Ramon's tutelage.

'Halt there, Templar,' shouted one of the soldiers in thickly accented French.

'Make way, lest we be forced to ride you down.'

'Preceptor...' tried Ramon once more, readying himself. Arnau wanted to call out too, to try and unwind this dreadful tension. There was still time to ride out and circumvent the line, or even to halt and simply talk this out. Arnau knew little about the Armenians, and they clearly had no qualms about making war on other Christian lands, but still they and the Order were Christians in a world surrounded by enemies, and with no open hostility between them as far as Arnau knew. Yet that word – Gaston – had moved Bochard up from *prepared to defend himself* to *ready to open hostilities*.

'Forgive us to our debtors, as we forgive our debtors,' sang Ramon suddenly and meaningfully, directly from the Lord's Prayer. 'Lead us not into temptation, but deliver us from evil.'

Bochard turned his angry, puce-coloured face on Ramon.

'Debtors they are. And so are we, Brother. We owe them for Gaston.' He turned to his squire, Hugues. 'Guard my bags. You know the ones.'

Arnau shook his head. This was it. The men in the road had regrouped, lifting their spears and holding them forth in the age-old manner to thwart cavalry. One of them shouted something again, and once more the name Gaston was the only word Arnau caught.

Bochard charged.

Taken by surprise despite everything, Arnau immediately put heel to flank to join his preceptor, and Ramon did likewise at the far side.

'Go right and be watchful,' bellowed the older brother to Arnau even as he took the left flank.

The soldiers were prepared, though in truth they had probably expected the Templars to stop in the end. As the horses raced the last forty feet at them, they braced with their spears. Arnau tried to think how best to tackle the problem in the moments he had – those spears spelled death for his horse, he felt sure. At the last moment, as his sword came up overhead and he bellowed the words of a psalm in a confident voice, he yanked on the reins and his horse swerved out to the right. Even as he performed the last-second move, Arnau twisted in the saddle, facing the men he was about to pass. There was an uncomfortable moment as he left the road and almost fell, his horse treading with difficulty in a low drainage ditch, but it was not quite enough to unseat him.

By the time the Armenians had realised he was moving out to flank them and turned to deal with him, he was past the points of their spears, and they could no longer bring those weapons to bear. The man on the end roared some kind of imprecation as he turned, trying to bring his spear round in the impossibly tight space. Arnau's arm fell across his front, between his and his horse's neck, his sword coming down with sufficient force to slam into the man's shoulder and through the padded gambeson and steel rectangles as though they were but cotton. He felt the sword meet the resistance of strong bone and smash through it with ease, and he yanked and twisted, pulling the blade free as he passed.

Arnau knew all too well how much a fight like this relied upon speed and instinct. A general might be able to spend time scanning the field and seeing where weaknesses and danger lay. In small-scale combat, however, pausing long enough to make such judgements might cause death or disaster. Paying no heed to what was happening with the others, Arnau slowed his horse, urging it through crumbling dry mud and another drainage ditch, wheeling it and coming to face the rear of the Armenian line.

His instinct to move without pause had been right. The next man in from the end had kicked his dying friend out of the way and swung his spear in an attempt to deal with Arnau. The spear point came wavering and flailing towards him, and Arnau danced his horse three steps to the right and forward, trying to fall within the spear's reach and make it useless. As he did so, his sword slashing out in a warning arc, the man kept backing up, trying to make room for a deadly thrust with his spear.

Arnau blinked as the man suddenly straightened, his spear flying loose from his fingers and blood rising into the air in a cloud of crimson mizzle. As the spearman collapsed on the road, gurgling, Arnau stared at Sebastian, the young squire's blade dripping blood as he goggled in horror at the carnage he had wrought. It would be his first kill. Such a thing could make or break a man. Still, Arnau couldn't risk spending time consoling him now. His gaze strayed across the scene of combat.

It was all but over. At the far side, an Armenian lay curled up, screaming and clutching his gut. Ramon was busy striking swords and parrying with another. Bochard...

Arnau shook his head in a mix of dismay and awe. The preceptor had been in the centre. He'd had no chance to arc out to the side as the two Iberian knights had done. He'd been facing two men with spears levelled and with no clear way of getting round them... and so he hadn't. He had simply ridden his horse into them, spears and men together. His horse was done for, lying on the ground, shrieking with two broken shafts jutting from its chest, but it lay writhing atop the crushed form of one of its torturers, while the other had been crudely knocked aside in the strike. Bochard had apparently leaped from his horse even as the spears struck, and the man he'd barged aside had lasted only one more heartbeat before the preceptor's sword turned his face to ruined mush. The preceptor's squire had remained uninvolved, staying back and holding the rope to the pack animals, keeping close to those bulging bags Bochard had brought.

The fight was over. Ramon managed to deliver a blow to the man he fought, dropping him to the parched earth with consummate skill. As the knight dismounted to finish his opponent cleanly, Bochard set about the grisly work of dispatching the wounded. Arnau turned away as they were executed cleanly by the preceptor's long narrow misericorde dagger.

There was a sudden intake of breath and the young Templar glanced back sharply. Bochard was crouched over a fallen man whose helmet had come away, revealing the boyish features of a youth little more than fourteen or fifteen summers. Bochard had gone pale, his lips moving in silent prayer as the boy gave a last groan. The preceptor delivered the killing blow swiftly, his face awash with conflicting emotions. He stood there shaking for a moment, and then suddenly seemed to realise the others were watching. With a huff, he pulled himself together and went to retrieve his spare steed.

Arnau and Ramon shared a worried look.

'What was all that about?' Ramon asked flatly as he rose from his kill, wiping the narrow blade on a rag. 'The argument, I mean, not the boy.'

Bochard flinched. 'Gaston,' he replied finally as though that answered all. His eyelid had acquired a rhythmic twitch that worried Arnau.

'But who is Gaston?'

'Not a who. A what. One of the Order's most important fortresses in Outremer. It stands in those hills,' he gestured off to the left of the road. 'Saladin's men took it a decade ago, and Leo of Armenia took it back off them.'

'Is that not a good thing?'

'He refuses to grant it back to us. It is *our* fortress. Our men shed more blood than his in the recovery of these lands. The grand master has demanded the return of the fortress numerous times, even backed with the threat of military action, and still the Armenian king refuses, clinging to our property just as he covets the mastery of Antioch. His greed will be his undoing.'

'I fear our passage through his kingdom just took a turn for the dangerous,' muttered Ramon.

'All will be well. It is less than two hundred miles from here to the far edge of the kingdom of Armenian Cilicia. We shall move at all speed and keep ourselves to ourselves. Once we are away from the contentious area of Gaston, things will be different. In this border zone, soldiers are hot-blooded. In the heart of their lands we will be safe, and once we pass the border into the empire, we shall come to no harm.'

As the five men saddled up once more and began to move out, Arnau found himself pondering that last assertion and not entirely believing it. He glanced sidelong at the pale, wide-eyed face of Sebastian as they began to head north-west again.

'It becomes easier.'

Sebastian turned a troubled look on him. 'That is no comfort, Brother Vallbona.'

'The danger was—'

'There was no danger, Brother,' the young Greek interrupted. 'The Mother *Theotokos* was with me.' He showed the icon he clutched, and Arnau nodded. 'What *worries* me,' Sebastian said quietly, 'is how easy it was.'

His eyes flicked across for just a moment to the preceptor ahead, and Arnau sighed. 'We each follow our own path as the Lord lays out.'

But Sebastian looked no less troubled at the thought as they rode on into the unknown.

CHAPTER 5:
THE BELEAGUERED EMPEROR

THE BOSPHORUS
MAY 1203, FIVE WEEKS OUT OF ANTIOCH

Arnau stood at the rail of the boat, Ramon beside him and Sebastian loitering miserably despite the shortness of the voyage upon which they had embarked. Bochard and his squire stood near the steering oar, subjecting the steersman to an endless series of questions.

The younger knight's eyes slid back to the shore they had just left. The Byzantine town of Chalcedon sprawled across the shore, its solid watchtowers standing proud above the streets and churches. It was one of the largest settlements they had passed through on their three-week journey through imperial lands, but then they had avoided the great cities, keeping to rural roads and settlements. The small vessel's wake churned out across the blue waters, scattering myriad small jellyfish to tumble through the clear deep.

The journey had been an easy one, despite Arnau's fears. A certain view of the empire had formed in the young knight's mind as they travelled, though, and it was both positive and negative. There were signs of a level of control and organisation that Arnau had never seen before. Like the Rome of old, Byzantium seemed to be a land of perfect order, of connecting roads and couriers and way stations. From the minor encounters they had had it was clear that the empire was controlled by a bureaucracy that had been growing and honing itself over a millennium, and had its hooks into every aspect of daily life. Bandits seemed to be non-existent and peace reigned. The churches were clean and plentiful, and powerful fortresses that had stood since the days of yore still protected roads, bridges and passes. Aqueducts still worked, bringing fresh water to cities, unlike Tarragona's, which had long since fallen into disuse. There were bathhouses, which Arnau hankered after, but which Bochard shunned as almost devilishly hedonistic.

And yet there were worrying signs. Byzantium might be likened to a marble palace: magnificent to look at, but on close examination, reveals dirt and cracks one couldn't see from a distance. Prime among these was the military dearth. The empire's fortresses might be the envy of the world, but many stood empty, and as often as not when Arnau did see a small garrison in a roadside bastion, they were clearly hired mercenaries from far outside the empire – hairy, narrow-eyed barbarians from the steppe, with their curved bows and curved swords, or great, golden-haired Titans from Rus-land far to the north. Even, according to the preceptor at least, Turks. It seemed madness to Arnau to protect the border against the Turk with Turkic mercenaries, but the empire seemed to consider it normal. Outside the military sphere, there were other signs too. Towns with low populations, roads in need of repair, churches closed, poverty among the rural folk. Cracks in the marble.

Arnau turned, looking ahead once more, wondering whether the same analogy might be applied to the great capital before them. Constantinople spread across the headland opposite and clearly went back some miles inland. Facing them, on the highest point – an ancient acropolis – stood grand palaces and churches and fortresses, columns and arches and gardens. Some of the churches, in fact, were larger than many castles Arnau had seen in his short life. And below, at the waterline, a set of strong white walls marched around the headland, punctuated every few hundred paces with heavy square towers surmounted by battlements that protected artillery, just visible as complex shapes.

Constantinople was all but impregnable, it was said. The young knight could believe it.

The boat slid across the water and angled upstream. Arnau gestured to a sailor close by, who was coiling a rope. 'Where are we bound?'

'Galata,' the sailor replied in clear Greek. 'All ships from this side of the channel put in at Galata, because of the chain.'

Arnau frowned in incomprehension, but peered with interest at the city. They were clearly not making for the heart of Constantinople, but for the less compact but occupied headland to the north. Galata, he presumed.

As they slid through the water past the headland, he kept watch. A great inlet separated the two settlements, and the sailor's mysterious answer became clear as they passed the waterway's mouth. A great chain stretched from a tower in the city walls to a similar heavy tower that formed part of a small fort on the north side – Galata. The chain was visible even at this distance and Arnau, impressed, estimated that each link in it must be the best part of two feet across. The entire length was kept close to the surface of the water by a series of small skiffs to which it was attached. Arnau could quite imagine the difficulties any ship might get into, entangled in that mess while within range of the artillery from at least half a dozen towers. Even the waterways in this place were fortified.

The boat slid into the dock at Galata, and Arnau was surprised once more by what this suburb held. He hadn't realised how used to imperial architecture and vessels he had become over the past few weeks of travel until he was suddenly confronted by something so different. The sailor saw him frowning and paused in his work.

'Genovese and Pisan enclaves. Traders and the like.'

It was like looking at a small town transplanted from the West and dropped in the heart of the empire. A strange sight. Indeed, the jetties were filled with more foreign traders than local vessels. Something suddenly struck Arnau. During all this time, he had never seen a Byzantine warship. It seemed odd given how much their trade and defence relied upon the water. Even here, at the heart of their domain, he could not see a single warship. Were the Byzantines not famed of old for their navy? He made to ask the sailor, but the man had gone to work elsewhere and a moment later Bochard called for them all to be ready.

The following hour passed by in something of a blur for Arnau. They alighted on the European shore and were met by some functionary of the imperial bureaucracy who offered to escort them to the palace, where someone would deal with them. As the five Templars mounted, the administrator climbed into an antiquated litter, which was lifted by two burly men in tunics and carried ahead of them through the streets. They headed south along the coast, past fishing quays and the European enclaves. Soon they reached the shore of the inlet, and were guided to a series of small ferries, one of which was allocated to take them on the bureaucrat's orders. Throughout, Ramon shared Arnau's clear interest in their surroundings. Bochard focused on his mission, largely ignoring the city through which they passed, and Sebastian had a warm smile that suggested he was feeling the relief of returning to his homeland.

The boat cut across the water towards the main city, which Arnau could now see marched for miles upstream, still surrounded by strong walls, even beyond the chain. As they approached, he could identify two great harbours of similar sizes in the urban mass. The upstream one seemed to be full of small craft and ferries, yet there was still no sign of warships. The downstream one seemed to have largely silted up, and was now home to a shipyard built into the mud.

They slid gracefully into the busy harbour and touched the jetty once more, Sebastian heaving a sigh of relief, not quite having been sick during their two short journeys. From there they were led through a gate in the city wall, checked only briefly by men in steel-plated coats carrying pole arms. Inside the walls the world was different, and Arnau boggled at the great marble buildings, arches and arcades, columns and towers. Churches seemed to stand at every corner, and each was a grand place of domes and golden crosses, high windows and intricate brickwork. They were led past monuments so ancient that they were likely contemporary with the ruins that poked up through the fabric of Tarragona, yet here were still in use. As they crested the heights, across a busy and perfect forum, he could see the arcades of a stadium, stretching down the hill away from him, an edifice of the most incredible size, grace and complexity.

There was no time to marvel at the place though, for they were led through more gates and arches, past more of the ever-present churches and palaces. The official conversed with Bochard and then delivered them into the hands of another functionary in rich silks. Their horses were taken by another servant, to who knew where, Bochard's eyes lingering on his precious saddle bags for a long moment, and then this new man led them through the corridors and gardens and finally into a wide room. 'Wait here,' he said curtly. 'I will send for you.'

As he disappeared through a door, Bochard eyed his companions. 'Good. I had been concerned that our status would not be enough to secure an audience. Whether it be the eminence of our grand master or the emperor's current need, we are clearly to be seen immediately. In the imperial presence, I will do all the talking. The emperor will only speak Greek. I gather, somewhat to my surprise, that you have some command of the language, but this is not the time for your bumpkin accents. Remain silent, stand proud and try to look holy.'

Arnau and Ramon exchanged another look. Neither of them was keen on the idea of speaking to a foreign emperor anyway. Arnau had had enough difficulty with the emir of Mayūrqa.

They sat in an uncomfortable silence for a quarter of an hour until finally the door opened once more and a different functionary appeared.

'Please follow me.'

Along several corridors they went, finally reaching a room where stood three of the most imposing figures Arnau had ever seen. All three wore armour of leather with steel plates stitched to it and leather strops hanging from waist and shoulders, dyed in bright colours. One wore a steel kettle helm and a full face veil of chain mail, his legs wrapped in baggy trousers tucked into steel leg casings. His shield showed a bright sunburst and he held an axe almost as tall as himself. Another wore a helm with a pronounced nose guard and chain coif, mail leggings beneath his coat and a heavy sword at his side. The third wore a skirt of chain to ankle length, with another huge axe over his shoulder. His face was open beneath a conical helmet, and his skin was ruddy and weathered, a great yellow beard covering the bottom half. All three men stood a head taller than any of the visitors. The imperial bodyguard, presumably. Arnau was impressed. Few men would get past these giants to the emperor.

'Please leave your weapons here,' the functionary said, his words relayed somewhat unnecessarily by the preceptor as he unbelted his sword and handed it to one of the titanic guards. The two knights and two squires followed suit and, once disarmed, the functionary led them on. They passed through doors and along another bright corridor painted with images of swans, and into a further antechamber where two more of the giant guards stood glowering at them. The functionary opened the next door and escorted them into the great chamber.

The emperor of Byzantium wore clothes of red and gold silk and a purple robe emblazoned with the imperial crest on one shoulder. An intricate jewelled golden crown nestled within his curly dark hair, and his red boots were clearly of the finest leather. He held a sceptre probably worth more than most noble estates.

Behind the emperor stood four more of the great armoured bodyguards, and a half-dozen courtiers lurked around the periphery, each perfectly coiffured and well groomed.

'Welcome to the ambassadors of the Order of the Temple in Jerusalem,' intoned yet another functionary from a shadowy spot close to the throne. 'You may greet the Basileos Alexios Caesar with gifts now.'

Arnau blinked. This was how foreign embassies were greeted? To his surprise, Bochard bowed his head and fumbled in a leather purse at his belt. Swiftly, he produced a gold chain with a pendant hanging from it. As he turned to display it to the court, Arnau was stunned to see a ruby of incredible size and beauty at the centre.

'My Lord Emperor, my grand master presents you with this, a gift as ancient as it is rich, won at a great price in blood on the fields of Outremer, and which is believed to have been worn in antiquity by the Queen of Parthia.'

There was a brief pause, and the functionary was beckoned to the emperor's side. Alexios Angelos, emperor of Byzantium, leaned close to his servant and murmured to him. The functionary straightened and cleared his throat.

'The emperor accepts your gift with great warmth and grants the freedom of the city of Constantinopolis to you and your companions throughout your visit. He bids you approach the throne.' His voice rose several notches. 'The emperor also commands his court to exit the audience chamber for the duration of this meeting. All except the despot Theodoros Laskaris and the *sebastokrator* Constantinos Laskaris, who should remain.'

As the five Templars, at Bochard's signal, walked slowly across the room towards the throne on its dais, the bulk of the courtiers filed out around the edge. By the time they reached a point where the functionary gestured for them to stop, they were almost alone. The emperor still had his heavily armed guards, but he now even waved away the functionary. As the doors shut, two dark-haired men in rich clothes moved over to the side of the dais, facing the Templars. One of the men had his beard divided into a fork, and his eyes were most disconcerting, one blue and one brown. The other was taller, his beard grown to a point and his hair swept back. They were an impressive pair, clearly brothers and equally clearly of some importance in the Byzantine court.

Arnau was startled as he peered at the emperor to see his analogy for the empire borne out in its ruler just the same. For all his grandness and imposing presence at a distance, this close, Arnau could see the cracks. Alexios Angelos was far from the strong leader he seemed at first. His eyes darted with a nervousness Arnau hadn't expected, and his lip trembled as he looked back and forth between the knights before him.

'It was only a matter of time before deputations came from the south,' Alexios said in a higher voice than Arnau had expected. 'Riders from our Anatolian lands brought news of your approach days ago, but I had somehow expected nobles of Outremer as well as knights of the Temple. I had hoped for support from the king of Jerusalem, given the aid we have shown to him and his over the years.'

'I cannot speak for the king, Basileos,' Bochard replied carefully. 'I am at liberty only to speak for the Order, and even then, only within certain bounds.'

'And such a small deputation,' the emperor mused. 'Did the Temple truly lose so many men at the Horns of Hattin that they can send me but a handful?'

Bochard straightened and Arnau swallowed nervously. He could see from the tremble in the preceptor's hand how he was starting to become irritated already. Still, Bochard controlled himself.

'Basileos, with the war over the Antiochene succession still raging, the Ayyubids constantly probing borders and the potential for an impending campaign, I am sure your nobilissimus self can understand how few men can be spared.'

The emperor slumped back. 'You are aware of the dangers currently facing my throne. Briefly, your master the bishop of Rome condemned the Franks and Venetians over what they did to my city of Zadra, but even he has reconciled with the Franks. Now Doge Dandolo is at sea once more with a crusading army under the command of Montferrat – a man who I suspect lives in Dandolo's purse. They bring my idiot wastrel nephew to Constantinopolis to usurp me. How foolish they can be. My nephew is not suited to rule, and the people will never accept him any more than they would accept his blinded father who now rots in my dungeons. But for all their presumption, I know the danger they pose. I cannot speak of such things before my court, for an emperor must always be seen to be strong. Yet my generals here will be able to confirm all things. The empire is not as strong as it once was. We expend all our military energy keeping the Turk out of Christendom and protecting our border from the Bulgars. To endanger the empire the way the Venetians seem intent upon doing will weaken our ability to hold the borders altogether. As such, you can see my need for foreign support, I am sure.'

Bochard nodded seriously. 'My grand master sent me to seek assurances that you would honour your long-standing alliances and protect the East as always.'

The emperor sighed. 'How can I grant such assurances when Rome sends its dogs on Venetian ships to weaken me? I would love nothing more than to assure your master of my faith, but I cannot in reality do so while I am threatened from the West. Indeed, I have been awaiting your deputation to put a similar question to your grand master. I seek the Order's support.'

'Basileos, as I said, our manpower—'

The emperor waved his hand dismissively. 'I do not seek knights. What use would another handful of men be in protecting my empire? I seek support. If your grand master will affirm the Order's condemnation of the Franks, it might be enough to persuade them, or at least Rome, away from their current course. I do not wish to defend myself with Templar steel, but to divert the danger with Templar voices. The Pope is, I hear, a good and pious man. If the Order speaks out against the Crusaders, the Pope might just listen and do what he can to call back his dogs.'

Bochard shook his head. 'The grand master has already confirmed that the Order does not support the Franks and Venetians. We have withdrawn our offer of men for their cause.'

'That is not *enough*,' snapped the emperor, hammering a fist on his throne. 'I need him to be vocal now. To shout from the rooftops his condemnation of these evil men. If the Order is staunch, other leaders will follow, such is the power of the Temple. Grant me this in the name of your order, and in return I will affirm my vows to support Outremer and the Pope in their fight against the Saracen. Quid pro quo, Templar. I cannot give you my word if you will not give me yours.'

'All I can do, Basileos, is to put your request to the Order. Pending the reply of the grand master, my hands are tied.'

The emperor snarled. 'Then what was the point of your coming here? You test me, sir knight.'

The odd-eyed man with the forked beard raised a hand, and the emperor nodded at him angrily. The man pursed his lips. 'The empire has ships and couriers. Send to your master and put the question to him, but do it fast. If the Franks cannot be diverted, then they are likely already bound for Constantinopolis. Any treaty we can secure will be worthless if it comes too late.'

The emperor nodded. 'Good, yes. Send your messages on fast ships and I will see that they get there. Meanwhile you can wait in the city. If we are to face ruin while we wait for your order, then you can face it with us. You are dismissed.'

Bochard bowed, stony faced, and turned, striding from the room. Arnau, Ramon and the squires followed suit and the five men marched to the door. While they were waiting for it to be opened by the men outside, the two bearded Laskaris brothers approached, emerging into the outer room with them. Arnau noted a strange, uncertain look on Sebastian's face when he glanced at the odd-eyed Byzantine, and made a mental note to ask him about it later.

'That could have gone better,' Odd-eyes said quietly, 'though I concede there was little hope of a treaty here and now.'

'Will the Order consider voicing their support?' his brother asked as a functionary gestured for them and they began their return trek through the palace halls.

Bochard shook his head. 'In the circumstances, I doubt the grand master would defy the Pope, who has lifted his excommunication of the Franks. Only a true offer of support from the emperor might tempt him. And it seems that such is not forthcoming. We appear to be at an impasse.'

Laskaris nodded. 'The emperor will not simply stand down in favour of his nephew,' he said. 'Even if he wanted to, he could not.

Former emperors are routinely executed, often in inventive ways, and the few that survive, like the boy's father, are blinded. And if the emperor will not step down then the vengeful doge of Venice, who has an unreasoning hatred of the empire, and with his excommunication has nothing to lose in the West, might press for a military action.'

'The empire has more men than the Frankish force, surely?' Ramon put in, earning a frown from Bochard.

Laskaris shook his head. 'Spread around far-flung borders, yes. The city has no standing army and few garrison men. Our greatest military asset is the emperor's Waring Guard, who you've seen. Our navy is all but defunct, following a decade of mishandling and corruption by greedy nobles, and it would take longer to pull in sufficient men from the borders than we are likely to have. As a military man, it is my opinion that we may not be able to withstand an assault without aid.'

The preceptor nodded as they reached the gate once more and were passed over to another functionary. Their horses were returned, and Arnau was surprised to see two of the bearded northerners in heavy armour mounted alongside them. The Laskaris brothers were clearly not accompanying them further.

'I pray that you are able to persuade your master,' Odd-eyes said. 'I will call upon you again. In the meantime, these two Warings will escort you to apartments in the Blachernae, where you can compose your messages. The palace staff will be at your service.'

Bochard nodded and thanked the two men stiffly. Moments later they were off once more, riding through the city. Bochard's relief as they were reunited with their horses and gear was palpable and he had Hugues check all the bags before departing.

'This is starting to remind me rather unpleasantly of our time in Mayūrqa,' Arnau muttered to Ramon, who sighed. 'The order will not denounce the Franks if the Pope supports them,' he replied. 'Bochard knows this. Why he is stringing along the emperor with a faint hope, I do not know. This embassy has failed from the start. We cannot give the emperor what he requires, and he will not give us what we want without it. We would be best bowing out and leaving now.'

'The preceptor has agreed to send a message back to Acre,' Arnau pointed out. 'We cannot leave yet.'

Ramon shook his head. 'This is all pointless.'

The two men fell silent as they rode over the hills and valleys of the city, heading west, ever further inland. They listened to the preceptor conversing with one of the Waring Guard, who was describing where they were going and their surroundings as they travelled.

'The Blachernae is only one of five major imperial palaces, of course,' the Waring said conversationally. 'Public business is generally carried out back at the Great Palace. The Bukoleon is often used as a residence for imperial family and high nobles on court duty. The Mangana on acropolis point is used as a summer residence for the emperor. The Botaneiates palace has currently been lent to the Genovese. The Blachernae, though, is the primary imperial residence. That you have been given apartments there is a sign of high honour. The palace lies beside the land walls at the western edge of the city.'

Bochard nodded distractedly, his eyes raking their surroundings as though searching for something. His finger shot towards a large church with many windows, built in a cruciform shape and surmounted by a dome. 'What is that?'

'That is the church of the Kyriotissa,' the Waring replied.

Bochard appeared disappointed. His fingers wandered distractedly down to his belt, where they tapped a large pouch. Arnau frowned, but held his silence. Down another valley they rode, then up onto another hill, the guardsman occasionally pointing out places of interest. As they crested the next rise, they passed one of the largest churches Arnau had ever seen, which would dwarf Tarragona's cathedral, and which the Waring pronounced to be the church of the Holy Apostles. Arnau noted with narrowing eyes how Bochard suddenly sat straighter in his saddle, his fingers drumming on the pouch. They slowed to a stately pace as they passed the grand church and the preceptor examined it in every detail, drinking it all in while Arnau instead watched Bochard carefully. The man was expressing an unexpected interest, but no one else seemed to have noticed. For a brother in an order where lies were forbidden, that man had too many secrets.

Some time later, passing aqueducts and churches and monuments galore, each of which was a marvel in its own right, they finally neared the city walls, which towered over the roofs. Arnau was impressed at the height and strength of the defences. He'd never seen their like, but was afforded little time to examine them in detail, for they swiftly diverted to a gateway in a lesser wall, and were admitted to the sprawling grounds of the Blachernae palace.

As they rode, Arnau took the opportunity to drop back beside Sebastian.

'You know the Laskaris?' he asked quietly. 'The one with the weird eyes, at least?'

The squire looked troubled, but nodded hesitantly after a few moments. 'Not personally. He led the army against the Bulgar king when my papa died.'

'It was his fault?' Arnau probed, remembering the lad's expression.

'No, I don't think so. He's a great general, or so papa used to say. He respected Laskaris, and the man beat the Bulgars, but it was while following him that papa...'

Arnau nodded sympathetically. Sebastian was in the strangest of positions here, both at home and an outsider at once. As the lad lapsed once more into a complicated silence, Arnau let him have his space and moved forward once more.

Twenty minutes later they were in rooms in the palace. Each knight and squire had been given his own chamber, which was a luxury for which none of the men had been prepared, as well as a communal room and chapel of their own. Once their gear was dumped, the two Iberian knights gathered in the common room to share a pitcher of iced water. The squires were busy cleaning and setting out all the gear, and Bochard had disappeared into his room without a word, with an odd, hungry look about him, a new urgency.

Before either man could talk, or even take a sip of their water, there was a rap at the door, and when Ramon rose and opened it, a functionary stood outside. 'The criminal and prisoner Alexios Doukas requests an audience.'

Ramon turned a baffled look to Arnau, who shrugged. 'Shall we get the preceptor?'

'Let's not bother him until we know what this is about. Show him in,' he said to the servant.

The two knights sat down facing the door and a moment later two more men appeared. Once was a clean-shaven man with black curly hair and a smooth, pale face. He was dressed like a rich courtier and walked with a certain swagger. His companion was another Waring guardsman with an axe the size of a small estate over his shoulder and a beard in which animals could hide. The latter man had a strange look on his face, as though he were holding a serious expression in place while a smile threatened to break through.

'Good afternoon, gentlemen,' Doukas said in a strangely hypnotic, lilting tone.

'Criminal and prisoner?' prompted Ramon.

'It is good in Constantinopolis to have a title,' Doukas said with an odd smile. 'Some titles are better than others, but any title is better than none, for only a nobody has done nothing to earn one. I played a minor role in an attempted coup some years ago. My family connections to the imperial house through the Komnenoi saved me from the wall of hooks, fortunately, and I am not important enough to be blinded. And so I remain a prisoner in this palace. A prisoner of wealth and status, but a prisoner all the same. Might I introduce you to my constant companion and very mobile jailor, Redwald of Northumbria?'

The Waring bowed, apparently still finding it hard to hold in his smile.

'An imprisoned usurper?' Arnau smiled. 'Were I to be a criminal I might dream of your prison.'

Doukas laughed – a light, mirthful sound. 'It has been years since I saw the city streets, sir knight. Even a gilded cage is a cage. But come, as soon as I heard men of the Temple were to be housed here, I decided it would be prudent to make your acquaintance. The future of any court animal, free or imprisoned, might rely upon what he knows. I will, however, begin with a warning.'

The two knights straightened as Doukas folded his arms.

'Flee Constantinopolis.'

'Why?'

'This city is heading for disaster. Alexios is weak. His nephew is worse, and the old blind man worse still. The Angelids are weakening the city and the empire by the year with their failures. Why else would I have risked all to put a stronger man on the throne? Even his leading generals, the Laskaris, know he is weak, for all they serve him still. If the Franks come, there will be war, and Alexios Angelos will lose it for us. It would be best for you to be back in Outremer before all this happens. In a perfect world I would come with you. You can do no good here. It is time to go. But before you do, tell me everything you have encountered since your arrival and everything the emperor has asked of you, for I am certain he has begged you for help, first and foremost.'

Arnau looked at Ramon, who gave the very slightest of nods. Nothing they had said was truly a sensitive secret, and the same might be said for the emperor. Certainly a well-informed creature of the court like Doukas likely knew much of it already, and could probably guess what he didn't. Besides, he immediately gave off an air of confidence and competence that seemed to be lacking in the court and their emperor, and it was always worthwhile cultivating alliances with such men.

Ramon took a deep breath.

'All right, criminal and prisoner Alexios Doukas of the imperial house... it starts like this...'

CHAPTER 6:
THE VENETIAN FLEET

CONSTANTINOPLE
JUNE 24TH 1203

A s the three men dismounted in the sizzling mid-afternoon summer sun, Arnau kept himself as inconspicuously at the rear as possible, letting Ramon and the preceptor talk up ahead. More than a month had passed since their audience with the emperor, and the enforced stay in the city was beginning to nag at him, the proximity to the rigid yet secretive Bochard throughout the time doing nothing to make life easier.

He had expected to be gone by now, one way or the other. Bochard had sent his missive to the grand master at Acre more or less immediately following their audience. Even if the message had been sent by rider, it would be expected back by now. Having been sent by ship, it was, by Arnau's estimation, almost a month overdue. The preceptor had brushed aside his concerns, as well as those of the emperor and his courtiers, over the delay. *Yes*, he'd admitted, *there was the possibility that the ship had been destroyed in a storm, or had fallen foul of pirates or some such. Much more likely, though, the grand master had not yet returned from Antioch and the letter has been forwarded to him there. Who knew how long a reply might take to reach the imperial capital in current circumstances?*

The emperor was less than happy with Bochard's calm disregard. Meanwhile reports streamed into Constantinople placing the Venetian fleet and its Crusader cargo ever closer to the heart of Byzantium. Theodoros Laskaris had taken the precaution of recalling all the roving and border military units to the city that could be spared against the possibility of violence, yet his outlook remained bleak.

Arnau had spent the first few days thereafter exploring the city, but had become aware of a strained and faintly angry atmosphere whenever they moved through public places. The Order may have condemned the Crusaders for what they had done, but clearly all the average citizen of Byzantium saw in them was a soldier of that same Roman Church which had sacked an imperial city and threatened the emperor. By the second week, whenever they left the Blachernae's safety, they were escorted by the powerful Waring Guard.

Despite the growing unease over the lack of a reply and the gentle background hum of discontent in the city, Arnau had managed to explore some of the city's more interesting locations, taking an interest in the strange, heretical Greek churches, familiarising himself with the regions of the city and walking almost the entire circuit of the walls, barring those within the Great Palace grounds. As well as the powerful Marmara Sea walls, and the slightly less imposing defences along the Golden Horn inlet, he'd walked back and forth along the four-mile stretch of the impressive land walls, appreciating the large areas of cultivated land within the circuit in the more southerly area. With three levels of wall defences, strengthened with towers and a moat, the entire circuit looked pretty impregnable to Arnau. With Ramon's permission, he had taken Sebastian with him, who was not only able to explain and translate where Arnau could not, but who it seemed had visited the city numerous times in his boyhood and could also help navigate. It seemed to Arnau that the longer the young squire spent in the city, the more he was reverting to his origins and the less tied he seemed to the Order. It was nothing tangible that he could speak of to the others, mind, but rather something he saw in Sebastian's manner. Not that he could blame the lad. These were, after all, his people.

In the main, Bochard seemed content to let the other two wander. He had retreated into a strange cocoon within days of their arrival, only seemingly playing the role of ambassador when he was specifically sent for by the emperor or one of the

Laskaris brothers. The rest of the time he spent going through the imperial libraries, reading voraciously, studying, in prayer, locked in his room or in the company of priests. This latter seemed oddly out of character for a man so avidly set against the Greek Church, yet when queried he claimed to be engaging them in theological debate, stating the superiority of Rome. Whatever he was up to, Bochard spent a lot of time in his room, which Hugues kept locked against any visitors. Those packs the preceptor had brought with him were in there, and Arnau could swear he'd heard the chink and shush of many coins when they were first brought in, which added to the mystery of their master in ways Arnau couldn't fathom. Consequently, Arnau and Ramon were largely at leisure. They had located a small enclave of Pisans in the city, close to the Golden Horn harbours, and had become friendly with a Pisan priest who welcomed them to his services, allowing them to attend to their monastic duty without difficulty and in the company of fellow Christians of the Western Church.

This morning, Bochard had been closeted away in the library once more when a servant arrived, announcing that the preceptor's visit to the church of the Holy Apostles had been approved. Ramon thanked the man and took the news to Bochard, who seemed most satisfied. Arnau had been surprised when Ramon asked the preceptor if they might join him.

Bochard's face had twisted through various expressions at the request. Arnau was convinced that the man had been trying very hard to find a good reason to refuse the request, but in the end had sullenly acceded. As he went to gather his things and the squires hurried off to prepare the horses, Arnau had tapped Ramon on the shoulder.

'Why are you so interested in this church?'

Ramon had given him a sly smile. 'Because the *preceptor* is. He's up to something – we both know that – and I'd like to find out what it is.'

Arnau had nodded, remembering what he was sure were sizeable bags of coin, and wondering what in Heaven's name Bochard could be spending it on in the city.

And so here they were, three men dismounting alongside the servant who had been sent for them, outside the largest church in the city – indeed, the largest Arnau had ever seen. Some twenty paces away, their escort of half a dozen Warings sat astride their mounts and waited. Arnau remembered the preceptor's hungry gaze as they had passed this place on their first day, and the recollection set him to wondering, like Ramon, what lurked in Bochard's mind. That same look had fallen across the preceptor's face again now as they moved towards one of the lesser entrances to the building.

A giant white stone edifice, the church of the Holy Apostles was of a cruciform plan very familiar in Western churches, though its lofty height was most impressive. It seemed to be surmounted by domes with many small windows rising in tiers to one central grand cupola bearing a cross in gold taller than even the tallest of men.

Ramon started to ask Bochard who they were to meet, but the preceptor silenced him with a wave of his hand as he had done several times since they had left the palace. Had he been any ordinary knight of the Order and not a preceptor with great authority, Arnau would have long since pulled Bochard up on his arrogance and lack of manners. Bound by his vow of obedience, though, he simply glowered at the man and nodded his agreement as Ramon glanced over at him.

They left the horses with the servant and crossed to the door, where a man in a belted blue tunic over some sort of white trousers and a long shoulder cloak of russet velvet waited patiently for them.

'Good day,' he said in a serious, yet quiet and lilting tone. 'I am Nikolaos, a *lampadarios* of the Church. The *protopresbyter* has assigned me to show you around. I have to say that you are honoured. Few followers of the Greek rite are permitted to see what you have been granted, let alone heathen Romans. Follow me.'

Arnau and Ramon shared an intrigued look and then followed Bochard, who was thanking the man as he walked, his intent gaze locked always upon the church. They entered the building and began a tour of the interior, which Arnau drank in at every turn, each new sight a mind-boggling one. He was becoming used to the Byzantine habit of covering every inner surface of a church with images in gold lines and figures of bright colour, and had visited several beautiful churches in the city, but the sheer scale of this incredible basilica made it all the more impressive. Oddly, Bochard was focused on their guide more now than on what they were seeing. He listened intently and politely, as did the other two knights, while the lampadarios led them through the church, pointing out everything of interest as they passed.

The church was apparently not the original one on the site, which had been constructed by the great Constantine, but was still ancient, dating to the Emperor Justinian some six and a half centuries ago. Many facts, figures and dates and much of the tour went entirely over Arnau's head as he ogled the magnificence of it all, though his ears pricked up as they moved away from the church itself, unlocking a door and passing into an area that was not open to the public. Here he listened with interest and peered at everything as they were shown the imperial mausolea – the tombs of numerous emperors, including Constantine himself. Ramon was as impressed as he, judging by the expression on his face, yet Bochard still seemed to be waiting, nodding at the information, wanting to move on.

It was when they were shown to the treasury that the preceptor suddenly began to pay a great deal more attention. Arnau found himself frowning at Bochard's sudden enthusiasm as they were shown into some sort of crypt with numerous ornate altars, each bearing some ancient relic or treasure.

'The shroud is not kept here?' he asked their guide, who frowned in surprise at this foreigner's knowledge.

'The shroud of the saviour? No, sir knight. It is kept in the church of Maria Thotokos of Blachernae.'

Bochard nodded thoughtfully. 'And the spear?'

Again, the lampadarios frowned. 'No. At the Mangana monastery. We have here, though, some of the most important relics in the city, not least the body of the blessed Saint Constantine himself in his mausoleum above.'

Bochard nodded again, eyes raking the holy treasures around him. That twitch of the eyelid had returned, Arnau noted with surprise. The young Templar stared in awe at the collection, which near rivalled what he had seen at the Templar fortress in Acre. That memory settled upon him like a blanket of snow, and with it came a deep suspicion. Bochard had known that these great relics resided in this church from the start. That was why he had been so interested in the place upon his arrival. And the shroud and spear? Surely not *the* shroud and spear?

He glanced sharply at Ramon, who had apparently come to the same conclusion and nodded his acknowledgement behind the preceptor's back. The visitors looked and listened as the attendant showed them some of the more important artefacts in the collection, each of which would alone be of such power that anywhere else a grand sanctuary would have been commissioned just to house them.

Bochard began to ask searching questions about the relics, many of which the man answered easily, while Arnau and Ramon continued to share unspoken worries. They were just contemplating leaving when a distant noise suddenly intruded on the conversation. Both men stopped and looked back towards the stairs. Bochard and the lampadarios also turned, their dialogue trailing off.

Shouting...

Alarmed shouting, from the church above.

Consternation falling across the Greek's face, he finished his tour early, ushering the three Templars back towards the stairs. 'Please. We must leave. I should attend the protopresbyter and learn what has happened.'

The three men hurried up the stairs as the man locked heavy reinforced doors behind them at both the bottom and the top of the flight. As they emerged into the church once more, they encountered chaos incarnate. Citizens were kneeling in prayer, beseeching God to preserve them in wailing voices, and more folk were flooding through the door all the time. Despite the buzz of worried voices, there was no clear indication of what had happened.

Nikolaos excused himself and left them standing in a corner as he hurried off to speak to a priest.

'What's happened?' Ramon wondered out loud.

'Whatever it is,' Arnau noted, 'it happened outside, since everyone's coming in to pray.'

Nodding his agreement, Bochard gestured to them and the three men hurried to the door, pushing their way through the crowd and out into the open. The Waring Guard were still there with the servant and the three Templars' horses. Hurrying over to them, Bochard waved at one of the giant bearded bodyguards.

'What has happened?'

The big man leaned forward in his saddle, the blade of the axe on his back catching the bright sunlight for a moment. 'The Venetian fleet is here.'

Ramon turned a worried look on Arnau, while addressing Bochard. 'We should not have tarried so long, Master. It is too late for any message from the grand master to help the emperor now.'

The preceptor glared angrily at him. 'Do not presume to tell me what to do, Brother. I am here on the Order's business at the direct instruction of the grand master. *Everything* I do has purpose in God's plan. You should have more faith, and considerably more humility.'

Ramon bridled and Arnau stepped close to him, lending him unspoken support, yet the Iberian knight held his tongue, eyes dangerous.

'You will obey the Rule of our order, de Juelle,' the preceptor went on, eyelid jumping madly, 'and submit to my command, or you will be sent back to Acre in disgrace to be stripped of your mantle and punished in any way the grand master sees fit. I argued against bringing two provincial unknowns from the barbaric land of the Moor, yet the grand master saddled me with you and I am performing my duties to my master with absolute obedience. I expect nothing less from those beneath me. Do you have anything to say, either of you?'

Arnau could feel Ramon almost bursting with the need to argue, yet to his credit he continued to hold his tongue and lowered his gaze.

'Good. A respectful silence. Maintain that attitude and we shall remain cordial and without recrimination.' Bochard straightened. 'I am satisfied with this visit. I shall return to the palace. Will you join me, or are you bound for your pet Pisan church?'

Arnau simply couldn't hold it in, and burst out with exasperation. 'How can we simply wait in the palace, Master? The Crusaders mean to usurp the emperor with an exile and suppress the Byzantine Church.'

Bochard fixed him with a look of genuine bafflement. 'What care we the name of the man who rules Byzantium, so long as he defies the Turk? And if the place comes under the rule of Rome, all the better for us. See sense, Vallbona.'

Before Arnau could say anything more, Ramon tugged his arm. 'We will away to the Pisan enclave by your leave, Master?'

Bochard nodded dismissively. Still ignoring them, the preceptor mounted and gestured to the Warings, the majority of whom turned and rode off west with him, heading back towards the Blachernae. Two Waring guardsmen remained to escort the remaining knights. As soon as Bochard was out of earshot, the older knight addressed them.

'Where are the Venetians?'

A big man with a braided beard and a white milky eye gestured off down the hill to the south. 'Off the coast, at half a mile, by all accounts.'

'Let's go.'

Ramon began to ride his horse at a brisk trot in that direction and Arnau followed quickly, the two huge guards hurrying along behind.

'What are we doing? I thought we were going to the Pisans?'

'That was for the preceptor's benefit,' Ramon grunted. 'I suspect he might have argued if we went to see what was happening. But we are in a city under threat of violence and that threat just sailed into sight. I for one want to see it.'

Arnau nodded, entirely in agreement and a little thrilled in the privacy of his heart at this defiance of Bochard. As they rode down the wide thoroughfare, Ramon gestured to one of their accompanying Warings. 'Will it be possible for us to mount the walls for a better view?'

Milky-eye shrugged. 'The defences are closed to the public, but the Guard can go anywhere. What is your purpose?'

'If the Crusaders are here, then I want to see what we are dealing with should I end up facing them, which is becoming an ever-increasing likelihood the longer we stay.'

The Waring nodded. 'The Crusaders will remain on the far shore and parlay. They may sack distant outposts of the empire, but even Venice would not be foolish enough to threaten Constantinopolis.'

'I wouldn't be too sure,' argued Ramon. 'Will you get us onto the walls?'

The big northerner nodded. 'But do not get in the way of the garrison. We will accompany you.'

The ride was swift, just a mile down a gentle slope, and before long they could see the powerful sea walls rising up ahead, a strong gate piercing them, leading to a major harbour. As with any grand and unexpected terrible event, while some of the populace had been gripped by panic and ran for the security of a church to pray for their city, others had been overcome by curiosity. Lacking the companionship of Waring guardsmen, and with the walls closed to them, they were flooding out through the gate and trying to find somewhere to view the great Venetian fleet.

As the four men closed on the walls, the Warings guided them off to the left. There a small guard post cordoned off a wide stairway that led up to the wall top, and as they reached the place amid the shouting from a hundred citizens in the nearby gateway, the Warings spoke to an officer in an antiquated cuirass and a skirt of green leather strops. Moments later someone was taking their horses and the two Warings were beckoning as they climbed the stairs.

Arnau was once more impressed at the strength of the walls as he climbed. He had seen the entire city's circuit from below, barring the palace area, but this was the first time he'd had the opportunity to get such a close look. Still, despite everything, he only took in passing details of the ancient and powerful walls, his attention more riveted on what he was going to see at the stair top. The Warings stepped aside as Ramon and Arnau emerged onto the walkway and hurried across to the parapet, peering out at the wide blue Marmara Sea.

For a moment Arnau blinked, wondering what to make of it, for he had expected a fleet of vessels half a mile off, out to sea, perhaps anchored, yet all he could see initially was clear blue sea. Then he realised that the guards were all peering off left, eastwards, along the wall towards the end of the promontory where the Great Palace stood above the mouth of the Bosphorus channel.

Arnau felt his heart rise into his throat along with a considerable quantity of bile.

He stared.

The Venetian fleet was quite simply the largest Arnau had ever seen. In fact, even taking into account the busy port of Barcelona, there were probably three times as many ships out there than he'd ever seen gathered in one place. A number of warships rose high above the fleet, which consisted largely of wide-bellied merchant vessels. Arnau could not imagine how many men and horses a fleet like this could carry. Suddenly the Laskaris brothers' fears about the strength of the Byzantine forces in the city seemed extremely well founded, even with those units that had been drifting into the city over the last few weeks.

'How many ships?' breathed Ramon, more to himself than in any expectation of an answer, though one of the Warings relayed the question to an officer standing at the parapet, who turned, his expression dark.

'Roughly five hundred, we think, including all the ancillary and supply vessels. *Too* many, damn the godless dogs.'

Clearly the presence of two Western Christian Templars was not going to prevent the military men of Byzantium from expressing their hatred of the Roman Church's army that was now at their threshold. Ramon did not seem inclined to take offence, and given everything that had happened, Arnau could quite understand the man's attitude.

'They're getting close to the city,' Arnau said tensely. 'Aren't they worried about the artillery?' His gaze slipped to the looming shape of a massive bolt thrower on the nearest tower.

'They're not officially at war,' reminded Ramon, but the Byzantine officer rounded on them with anger in his eyes.

'The dogs were not at war with Zadra when they sacked it and burned it to the ground,' he snapped.

One of the Warings threw the man a warning look, and then turned to the two Templars. 'Regardless, it seems that they are not stupid, and are staying just out of range. *Only* just, though.'

'May we?' Ramon asked, gesturing along the wall with an open hand. The Waring nodded and the four men began to hurry along the sea walls, all the time keeping the fleet in sight. Soon it became clear that they were catching up. Their speed on foot along the walls was outpacing the fleet, which was continually reorganising as it approached the narrower channel of the Bosphorus.

They followed the progress of the Venetian fleet for a little more than a mile, all the time closing on it. As they neared the end of the great promontory, the nature of the walls changed. They passed an ancient and impressive church and the lower end of the great circus which, from this low angle, presented a massive arc of brick and marble, topped with a colonnade some fifty feet above the city streets. From here, though, the sprawl was left behind and they reached the region of the imperial palaces. Arnau had been this far before but no further, for there was no civilian access to even the inside of the walls once it passed into the territory of the imperial palace.

'Where now?' he asked, gesturing ahead to where the wall came to an abrupt end as it met a grand and decorative seafront palace complex. Instead, the wall marched off inland and uphill, away from the water.

The Waring gestured left. 'I will lead.'

He hurried off ahead and led them away from the water, where they lost sight of the fleet behind the palace. They moved at a faster pace now, hurrying along in the wake of the two Warings, who pounded tirelessly along the wall walk. Here they passed through an area of elegant and perfect gardens and grand imperial structures. After perhaps five minutes of gently curving back to the right, they descended the slope to the water once more, on the far side of that grand waterfront palace. Here they reached the shore again and rushed to the parapet to peer over.

Arnau stared in shock and horror.

The Venetian fleet had deftly reorganised, the bulk of the transports and supply vessels keeping far from the city walls, closer to the town of Chalcedon across the channel, through which the Templars had passed the day they arrived. Meanwhile, most of the warships among the fleet had formed a moving line along the nearest edge and were already opening hostilities in the most despicable manner.

Unable to reach the walls with their light weaponry, archers and artillerists on board the warships were targeting Byzantine merchants and even poor fishermen, peppering their vessels with deadly missiles. Already sails floating forlornly on the water and the skeletons of ships jutted from the water's surface like brown creaking bones as they slowly disappeared beneath, holed by Venetian missiles.

The Waring's earlier comment had clearly been correct, that the wily Venetians were keeping neatly out of the city's artillery range, for missiles being loosed from the tower tops were uniformly plopping into the water fifty feet short of the nearest hull.

'What kind of war is this when a Christian ship feels entitled to sink a fishing boat without compunction?' roared Ramon, gesturing from the wall. The soldiers atop the parapet, who had been eyeing the new arrivals warily, now gave emphatic nods at the outburst, which had been so rancorous and out of character for such a generally good-natured knight that it had quite taken Arnau by surprise.

'This is no war,' a nearby officer barked in reply. 'A war requires a declaration and violence on two sides. This is an *atrocity*!'

It was Arnau's turn to nod now. The Venetian fleet, excommunicated by order of the Pope and carrying an army led by another Italian nobleman more intent on interfering in the Byzantine succession than fighting back the borders of Christendom, had been in sight of the city for less than an hour, and already they had begun to display exactly that unchristian horror which had seen them earn the Pope's ire in the first place.

Arnau was a good Christian, and had been all his life. His belief in the Lord was unshakable, and his trust in Mother Church and her offices total. Now, though, for the first time in his life, he felt doubt. Not in the Lord, for he knew God was eternal and all-powerful, but in the men who ruled the Church in God's name. How in all honesty could the Pope now condone what was happening? Yes, he had maintained his excommunication of the Venetians, yet he had rescinded that of the Crusaders, putting them at liberty to continue in their unholy campaign with the tacit approval of the Church.

Yes, the Greeks followed a heretical doctrine, and one day they would have to see that this was wrong and fall in line with the true Church, but such things were best done with compassion and understanding, not by the sword. This was against everything good and true. Arnau's soul screamed out with defiance at what the Crusaders and their Venetian allies were doing. They may not follow the rule of the Latin Church, but they were still Christians and, from what Arnau had seen in those to whom he had spoken, good men and women of true belief.

He found himself unexpectedly making a silent vow not to let the godless Crusaders destroy this holy city. Moreover, the vehemence with which he made the vow took him even more by surprise.

Realising how ridiculous it would sound to say as much out loud, and also how Ramon might react to such a declaration, he kept silent and watched as the last few endangered Byzantine boats were systematically destroyed by the Venetians, their personnel throwing themselves into the water, where they swam for the shore, many picked off by arrows before they could get far from their sinking ships. When the only remaining Byzantine vessels had managed to come safely close to the city walls, away from the warships, the fleet began to move across the channel towards Chalcedon.

Arnau's heart hardened further against them.

'Where is the Byzantine fleet at a time like this?' Ramon growled.

The Waring beside them snorted. 'What fleet? A century ago or more, this city had a fine navy. Then Stryphnos, the accursed treasurer and admiral, stripped the fleet of anything worthwhile and sold it all off to pad the imperial coffers. What is left of the fleet could hardly stop a barge and sits wallowing in harbours on the Golden Horn.'

Ramon simply grunted again. Such was the short-sightedness of bureaucrats. They watched in silence now. The walls here, in good view of the invasion, gradually filled with more and more soldiers coming to watch the activity in the channel.

Over the following hour, the great and the good of the Byzantine military, accompanied by two Templar knights, watched the Venetians land a huge Crusader force at Chalcedon. Anchoring in the town's sizeable harbour, and all along the neighbouring coastline, the Venetians, their butchery done, simply watched their Frankish passengers ravage, butcher and burn a Byzantine town in full view of the capital.

'Why do the army here not go to help them?' Arnau said, stricken, watching plumes of smoke rise from the town opposite as churches, houses and palaces burned, the population flooding out into the countryside to escape the conquering Westerners.

'You heard Laskaris,' Ramon reminded him. 'He doesn't think they have men enough to save Constantinople, let alone rush to the aid of others. They must sit within the safety of their massive walls. It is a sad rule of war. One cannot sacrifice one's only advantage to save something that cannot be saved.'

Arnau watched as the sun began to sink and the fires across Chalcedon increased. He suddenly turned to Ramon and spoke in Aragonese Spanish for the first time in what seemed an age, a tongue he was confident only the two of them here understood.

'I know what we *should* do, which is to leave and sail for Acre, away from all this and keeping the Order uninvolved. And I know what Bochard would have us do: remain, even in danger of our lives, separate from all this while he does whatever nefarious thing he is here to do with his hunger for relics and his bags of coin...'

Ramon threw a worried glance at him, but offered no argument, so Arnau went on.

'But what I really, truly want to do is put my sword to every neck in that crusading army for what they've done and what they evidently plan yet to do.'

He expected argument from Ramon. He expected recrimination and opposition.

He did not expect a nod.

'But we are bound by our Rule, Vallbona,' the older knight said. 'We must not raise our hand in violence to a Christian brother without the accord of our superior, which we are clearly not going to get here. Bochard would plainly refuse us any involvement.'

'*If* we asked him...'

Again, Ramon nodded. 'But there is an answer, Arnau, my friend. It is Christians we are forbidden to fight. The Venetians conceded all right to that label when they were excommunicated.

They are no longer within the protective embrace of Mother Church. And already the Byzantine nobles will be planning their first reprisal. I believe the time has come, Vallbona, for us to speak to the Laskaris brothers.'

CHAPTER 7:
THE FIRST BLOOD

JUNE 26TH 1203

The two Templars leaned on the balcony and peered out across the water. Behind them a grand ancient column rose into the blue sky, topped by a bronze statue of some long-gone hero. From here, on the acropolis hill, the highest point near the Bosphorus, the view was excellent, affording a much broader range of vision than the city walls below at the water's edge. Here they could watch the progress of the crusading army, and the meagre efforts being put in place to counter them.

They had visited the palace two days earlier, after watching the Franks looting and burning Chalcedon, intending to see the Laskaris brothers, but had been halted in their tracks. It seemed that without the preceptor's authority they would not find easy admittance to the Great Palace, and the two brothers were understandably busy with military affairs.

As such they had returned, impotent and tense, to their apartments in the Blachernae palace. There they had spent the night fretting, relaying to Sebastian all they had seen and not particularly caring that Bochard and his squire were not around.

The next day had brought a visit from Alexios Doukas, the well-informed imperial prisoner. He had been able to tell them a few things of use. Firstly that, to the consternation of everyone with an ounce of sense, the emperor had placed the defence of Constantinople in the hands of Michael Stryphnos, the very man who had effectively destroyed the imperial navy for profit years earlier. According to Doukas, many reasonable voices in the court had called for one of the Laskaris brothers to assume overall command, but the emperor had trusted in his long-time supporter instead.

Doukas had called that decision *the first nail in Byzantium's cross*. He had also been able to tell them that Stryphnos was to lead a unit of the finest veteran cavalry in the empire to meet the Franks and demand their withdrawal. The way he spoke suggested that sending Stryphnos as an embassy was much the same as the notion of dispatching Bochard on the same task. He had also explained that if they wanted to see what was happening on the far side of the Bosphorus, the walls were not the best vantage point. That was to be found below the victory column on the acropolis hill.

And so now here they were, watching events unfold.

The imperial ships were reaching the far bank now. Far from the great warships and transports the empire had once commanded, these were three fat-bellied merchant vessels commandeered in port for the occasion. They had left Galata on this side of the Golden Horn half an hour ago, having loaded their cargo in the dawn's half-light and sailed out towards Scutari on the far shore, loaded with men and horses.

Scutari. Apparently the town's name had something to do with a shield, though it had not provided much protection for the empire. With Chalcedon a burning ruin behind them, the Crusaders and their accompanying Venetian fleet had set off up the coast the next morning, in full view of the watchers in the city. There they had reached the small town of Scutari and repeated their destruction and rapine there. The only saving grace was that many of the town's occupants had fled during that first night, fearing precisely this. Now the Franks were encamped on the edge of Scutari, directly opposite Galata.

And Stryphnos was on his way with his cavalry to parley.

The two knights stood and peered off up the channel, towards the distant roofs of Scutari just visible around a bulging hilly headland on the far shore. Columns of smoke still rose into the morning sky from the second scene of Crusader violence, and the Venetian fleet lay at anchor over a mile or so of coastline up from the burning town. The camp of the Franks was mostly hidden behind the headland, though the nearest edge crowned the hill below which Stryphnos and his cavalry were even now disembarking.

'I cannot see the Franks agreeing to turn around and head home now,' Arnau said with a sigh.

Ramon nodded. 'Things have advanced too far. They might still be bought off and sent on their way – the Venetians are avaricious, after all – but I am not convinced the emperor would be able to meet their price. After all, they have a pet emperor with them. If they can put him on the throne, they can squeeze him for every gold *hyperpyron* in the treasury. How can the current emperor top that?'

Arnau grunted. He couldn't, and they all knew it. What Stryphnos hoped to achieve here he had no idea. Expecting little, they watched the cavalry emerge from the ships and assemble on the far shore, close to the water and at the bottom of the hill. Simultaneously, the camp at the summit burst into life.

An entire *tourma* of Byzantine horse were gathering – the better part of five hundred cavalry. They were visible at this distance only as a silvery mass moving like a murmuration of birds. No individuals could be made out, much less their leader, though Arnau could see what the cavalry were. During the weeks of wandering the Blachernae and the city walls, he had seen enough of the imperial military to be able to identify these men. They were the *kataphraktoi* – the heaviest horse upon which the empire could call. Far more dangerous than the lightly armed and armoured skirmishers and horse archers, and heavier even than the mailed *koursore* heavy cavalry, the kataphraktoi were clad in steel from head to toe, and the same applied to their mounts. Arnau had seen them at practice and had been impressed. He'd certainly not want to meet them on the battlefield.

He fancied he could almost hear the distant honk of horns, and moments later the tourma of steel-clad riders moved off in formation, stomping off up the slope towards the crest and the nearest edge of the Crusader camp.

The two Templars observed tensely, wondering what the Frankish response would be. Arnau found himself gritting his teeth as he watched that silvery mass flowing up the slope like a waterfall in reverse. His gaze was then drawn upwards and he noted with a catch in his breath figures emerging from the edge of the Crusader camp.

If Stryphnos still held hopes of negotiation, then he was clearly about to have them dashed. These figures were mounted, and they were no Frankish noblemen come to parley. They gleamed, and were gathered into a fighting unit. Again, they were much too far away to make out more than the general size. Arnau put it at perhaps a quarter of the size of Stryphnos's tourma.

He watched and waited. What would the Franks do? Less than a hundred horse was not enough to threaten the five hundred strong tourma, but with an entire camp of Crusaders behind them and apparently no intent to negotiate...

Arnau blinked. The Franks were on the move. Incredulously, he watched, heart thumping now, as fewer than a hundred Frankish knights began to charge down the slope towards the vastly superior force below.

'Are they mad?' Arnau breathed.

'Fearless and greedy,' Ramon replied. 'Much the same thing in the end. Stryphnos actually has a chance here.'

'He does?'

'The Crusaders have thus far met no real resistance. They are riding the crest of a wave and because of that they are supporting the insidious designs of the Venetian doge. Stryphnos is at a disadvantage in that he is moving up the slope, but still he outnumbers the Franks by more than four to one. If he can break those Crusaders, it will be the first defeat they have encountered. It will make them think, might make them reconsider. It will certainly make them less sure of themselves. But it has to be decisive. He has to show them that the empire can protect itself.'

Arnau nodded. The weight of numbers certainly *should* compensate for the terrain, though something about it nagged at him. The Frankish knights were thundering down now, a cascade of steel droplets.

The avalanche descended upon that wider Byzantine force climbing the slope, an avalanche smaller in number but so focused, so hard, so hungry. Even watching at this distance, where units of men moulded into vague shapes and colours, Arnau could see it in his mind's eye, superimposed over his own memories of horsemen charging at the Ebro the day he had lost his lord.

It was the moment he knew Stryphnos would lose.

The Byzantines moved up in careful formation like an army of old, like the Roman cavalry from whom they were descended, all signals and manoeuvres and military precision. Conversely, the Franks rumbled down the slope like the berserk northmen from whom they had inherited their horsemanship. No amount of order or military precision was going to withstand that sheer focused brutality for long.

They watched the failure of Byzantium, their spirits sinking. Where the tourma should have braced and pressed to meet the enemy, precisely the opposite occurred. In moments, with the Frankish knights still a quarter of a mile up the hill, the kataphraktoi broke and turned, fleeing back down the slope, every man racing at his own pace back towards the ships. The antiquated army of Byzantium had faced Turks and Rus and Bulgars, but nothing had prepared them for a Frankish charge.

Ramon was shaking his head in dismay.

'No, no, no, no,' he breathed. 'Don't run. You can win this. If you run, you make them stronger than ever. You have to stop them.'

But it was too late; even Arnau could see that. The cavalry plunged back down the slope and raced to the ships. The Crusaders stopped moving only part way down the hill, and that silvery mass remained in place on the slope as the Byzantine horse ploughed back into the ships, which put back out into the channel the moment their cargo was aboard, pulling in the ramps even as they moved in panic.

The young Templar pinched the bridge of his nose. Byzantium had sent its first message to the Crusaders, and it had been an utter failure.

'Perhaps the horses panicked?' Arnau said without great conviction, for he knew precisely what had happened.

'All of them? No. And those were the empire's strongest cavalry. They would not flee from fewer than a hundred men, even up that slope. They were routed by their own command. Stryphnos failed them, not the other way around. They panicked at the sight of the Frankish charge. A good commander would have rallied them and held them tight. Stryphnos instead succumbed to his own men's fear. The fool just squandered the empire's best hope of averting a war.'

They watched sullenly as the three merchant vessels crossed the water once more and docked at Galata, unloading their horse.

* * *

The next morning, Bochard was busily rushing around his room, gathering gear as the other two knights stood in a doorway, watching him for a moment before Ramon spoke.

'Are we leaving?'

The preceptor paused and frowned. 'Of course not. Why?'

Ramon shook his head in wonder and spread his hands as though explaining the obvious to an idiot. 'Because there can no longer be any doubt as to what is going to happen. The Crusaders intend to subdue the empire. And we are trapped here. If we stay, we will be dragged into this, no matter that our order has no place here and no part in this war. We need to get out of Constantinople while flight is still a possibility. I had assumed that was why you were gathering your things.'

Bochard snorted. 'I am engaged in pursuing a matter of great importance to the Order and I shall not leave Constantinople until my task is complete. Neither shall you. I will be out of the city for a few days at a local monastery with a functionary from the palace. In my absence, I cannot prevent you from observing events here, but remember your vows and my orders. You are forbidden under any circumstances to attack another Christian. Do you understand?'

Arnau nodded sullenly, and Ramon joined him. 'We do, Master.'

They watched Bochard's squire saddle his horse out in the courtyard and Arnau peered suspiciously as Hugues brought out one of the bags that he was now convinced contained enough coin to buy a sizeable city and fastened it to the saddle. It looked a little smaller than he remembered. Bochard had been spending in his times alone, apparently. Moments later the preceptor was joined by four Waring guardsmen and a man in a monk's robe on a mule. The small party left the palace, and Arnau sighed.

'We are bound by orders, then. Better perhaps that we stay in our apartments?'

Ramon shook his head. 'You would never make a lawyer, Vallbona. The preceptor ordered us not to attack Christians. He never forbade us from attacking *non*-Christians, nor even from defending ourselves. And he positively *encouraged* us in observing events.'

* * *

So it was that later that morning they found themselves standing on the hill by the column once more with Sebastian and their Waring companions, watching as a small flotilla of ships detached themselves from the Venetian fleet and began to ply their way downstream towards the city once more. The young squire had his well-worn icon in hand once again and was gripping it tight as he watched the threat to his world gradually coalescing. Realising that whatever was about to happen would be close to the sea walls and therefore better viewed from there, the five men hurried down the slope, descending the shining white staircases towards the Bosphorus, passing between elegant gardens and small orchards, odd churches and other unfamiliar structures.

At the bottom of the slope, having now lost sight of the ships, the five of them approached one of the heavy towers in the walls, which connected oddly to one of the city's omnipresent churches.

There, a Waring hammered on the tower door until it was answered and swiftly secured them access.

They emerged from the tower onto the walls in time to see that the Venetian ships were close now. They had, very wisely, stayed just outside artillery range, but were moving very steadily downstream, using their oars to slow the natural pace of the current, as though parading themselves before the city. Ten ships, Arnau counted, and each of them crammed with colourfully attired nobles and bearing hundreds of pennants that snapped in the channel's strong breeze.

The Byzantines had gathered on the wall tops. Every man with the right to be there had climbed from the base of towers or their gate posts and now stood at the parapet watching the ships approach. A single voice was bellowing out from the lead vessel, though they couldn't quite make out his words. However, as the ships came ever closer in their stately parade past the walls, it became clear that the speaker was repeating the same phrases over and over for the benefit of those listening in the city.

'Behold your rightful ruler,' bellowed the impressive voice, in Frankish and then in Greek, repeating the phrase. 'Behold Alexios Angelos, son of Isaac the Second, true heir to the imperial throne.' Another repeat in the second language. 'Rally to your rightful emperor, people of Byzantium, and throw down the pretender who leads you to destruction.'

There were murmurs of anger all along the wall nearby.

'And if you do not rally,' called the voice, now attaining an edge of menace, 'if you do not acknowledge your rightful emperor, you will be reduced to utter ruin.'

Once he had finished his threat, the speaker took a deep breath and then began the refrain once more, making sure that any ear even close to the city walls could hear. The second vessel now slid past, bearing grander flags and banners, and with what could only be the young exiled prince in full view. He stood high in the prow, presumably attempting to look as regal as he could to win over the people of his city.

Even Arnau could see how poorly the display had been planned, for young Alexios was attired as a Frankish nobleman, every bit the great Western king. He looked proud and important, and even regal. What he did *not* look was Byzantine. Arnau shook his head. How could they hope to win over the people of Byzantium by offering them a foreign lord?

Predictably, the display and threats drew from the wall tops not fealty, but derision. Men jeered and laughed. One soldier not far along the wall even turned and bared his backside at the ships as they slid past, earning a sharp reprimand from his commander, even as that same officer grinned his tacit approval.

Someone on the next tower bellowed back that they'd never heard of the prince, their call punctuated by raucous laughter and the thud of a bolt thrower, its missile plopping into the water not more than twenty feet from the figure of the prince.

Arnau shook his head. It was easy to laugh at this, but when the laughter faded and every man here thought hard, they would realise that this was the last moment of peace. This was the moment when they had been given the one opportunity to end this that the Franks were likely to offer. The next thing the Crusaders would bring after this announcement would be steel and blood and fire.

War and death were coming to Constantinople, and Arnau felt a little sick that they were trapped here awaiting it, bound to the city by Bochard's orders. His smile slipped away.

* * *

A week and a day passed without further incident. The threat loomed constantly at Scutari, glowering across the channel. The Byzantine leadership prepared in what ways they could. Arnau and Ramon took to touring the walls daily with whatever Waring guardsmen were assigned to them, watching the enemy, and also the preparations in the city. Bochard remained absent. After four days Ramon and Arnau had begun to be concerned, wondering if somehow the preceptor had fallen foul of roving enemies, but on the fifth day, riders arrived at the Blachernae escorting two chests that they took into Bochard's room and locked up, announcing that the preceptor had extended his stay and would return in due course.

The emperor had been disappointed in Stryphnos's failure with the cavalry, but apparently not enough to remove him from overall command, much to the anger of the Laskaris brothers, as well as to the prisoner Doukas, who became the Templars' source of political news while Bochard was absent. Theodoros and Constantine Laskaris spent much of their time drilling and arranging the disposition of troops, gathering in whatever new units arrived at the city from their border garrisons, and reinforcing the troops at the more vulnerable positions on the walls. Stryphnos seemed to do little more than take credit for the work of the brothers and preen, an impression that Doukas clearly shared.

'Why does the emperor persist in trusting Stryphnos?' Arnau had fumed at Doukas one day upon hearing of the latest debacles involving the empire's senior general.

'You do not understand the ways of the imperial court,' Doukas had smiled enigmatically. 'Stryphnos is a poor general, but he is no threat to the emperor. Since the days the empire was ruled from Rome, all emperors have known how dangerous it is to put too much power in the hands of another. Strong generals make ready usurpers.'

Arnau frowned. 'But isn't Theodoros the emperor's heir designate anyway?'

Doukas laughed aloud. 'Oh but how simple your Western courts must be. Theodoros is indeed heir designate, but the emperor has no intention of giving his heir the opportunity to move his accession forward at the head of an army. No, better for him to put his army in the hands of idiots than men who might dethrone him. Remember, I know that of which I speak, having been party to just such a usurpation in my time.'

Arnau had let the subject drop, more than a little exasperated at the subtle wickedness that seemed endemic in Byzantine life.

On the fourth of July, the Byzantines finally made a move. Pushed into action by the nerve-racking presence of the crusading army on the far shore, the emperor decided to field an army. Doukas reported the details to the Templars that afternoon, and the two knights watched the forces of Byzantium being concentrated near the land walls at the western edge of the city, far from the Bosphorus.

On the morning of the fifth, the emperor, along with Stryphnos and the Laskaris brothers, led the forces of Byzantium forth from the city. A small contingent split off the main force and used what few transports were available to cross the Golden Horn, while the bulk of the army trekked several miles upstream to round the inlet by a large bridge, and then back down the far bank to rendezvous with the ferried men.

Arnau, Ramon and Sebastian stood now on one of the towers near the great chain that sealed off the Horn, watching as the huge army of Byzantium deployed on the slope above Galata, facing the Crusaders across the water, threatening and daring them at once.

Ramon looked nervous as they watched the army moving into position.

'What is it?' Arnau asked.

'This is dangerous. It's like Stryphnos's cavalry all over again but on a larger scale. I can only assume the emperor hopes to frighten the Franks and Venetians into calling it all off and leaving. It's a dangerous gamble. He's got a sizeable force there, and it would make most commanders think twice. But I'm not sure that's going to work against the Doge of Venice and his pet, the count of Montferrat. And if they *don't* flee, they will be forced to act in retaliation. I foresee this turning into a fight by nightfall, and if that happens the emperor had damn well better win. If he loses now, he will have lost too much manpower to maintain the walls against the enemy. It's all or nothing.'

Arnau nodded bleakly. There were now precious few guards left on the walls, the bulk of the military being gathered above Galata.

They watched throughout the morning. Finally, after noon, the deadlock broke. The Byzantine force had stood, sweating, for hours in the hot sunshine above the houses of Galata, while there had been no movement in Scutari, or at least none visible from this distance. Then, suddenly, ships began to detach themselves from the Venetian fleet and steer out into open water. Slowly, as those vessels back-oared to maintain position in the channel, others formed up with them until a row of Venetian ships sat midstream, ready. As the next wave of warships and merchants began to depart the shore, the first group began to move in unison, making for the Galata shoreline.

Arnau found his fingers gripping the stonework of the parapet so tight he was drawing blood in places. He'd been prepared for this, of course, in some fashion anyway, but now that it was actually happening, he stared in disbelief as a crusading army sailed across the strait to meet the Byzantine force awaiting it on the near shore.

War.

Shivering despite the heat, Arnau continued to watch.

The imperial force at this distance was little more than a blob of shimmering silver on the slope, but he could now pick out parts of that huge force detaching and moving down towards the water, readying for the enemy landing.

The Venetian ships held their line like a cavalry charge; wicked, greedy and untrustworthy they might be, but no one could ever doubt their seamanship. They slipped in to the shore in perfect unison and, as they did so, like some delicate dance, they slewed to the right as one, presenting their side to the Byzantine army. Arnau couldn't make out the details, but somehow suddenly the first wave of Venetian vessels were almost at the shore, side on, and in moments a flood of silver emerged from them and raced at the closing Byzantines, a great flow of steel moving uphill at an astonishing pace, even as the ships prepared to make way.

Arnau was stunned. He had seen large groups of soldiers disembark ships before. It was invariably a laborious process, walking steeds down boarding planks and assembling on the shore. What the Venetians and Franks had just achieved should be impossible. In a dozen heartbeats they had gone from ships crossing the water to a force of what had to be heavy cavalry charging the imperial army.

It ought to have been laughable. Even having delivered a force simultaneously from numerous ships, they could not possibly have disgorged an army even a tenth the size of that which awaited them. All the Byzantines had to do was hold firm and then push them back to the water. Arnau could see that, and he was no grand strategist. Even if the Franks were better equipped, heavier-armoured, faster and stronger, sheer weight of numbers made it a foregone conclusion. All they had to do was hold their ground and then push back fast enough to drive the Franks to the water before another wave of ships could land.

He squeezed his eyes shut at what he was seeing.

No.

Even at this distance, at this scale, the unfolding disaster was clear. Just as the general Stryphnos had fled with five hundred cavalry at the sight of a small Frankish charge, the same was happening above Galata. Those smaller groups who had been running down to secure the shore were obliterated, completely disappearing beneath the silvery sheen of the Frankish knights. Barely had the Crusaders dealt with the small advance parties of Byzantine infantry before the main army broke. Arnau watched in dismay as the entire imperial force turned en masse and swarmed back down the slope towards the Golden Horn, leaving the Franks in control of the shore.

'Mother of God preserve us,' muttered Ramon next to him. 'If that's all we can look forward to then Constantinople is doomed. If I hadn't seen the exiled prince for myself, I might be tempted to suggest he could be better for the empire than the emperor is. Doukas was right, though. The Angelids are weak. That force on the hill was large enough to swamp the knights, but either the emperor or Stryphnos, or both, fled the field.'

Arnau nodded. 'Not Laskaris, you think?'

Ramon shook his head. 'Both of them have strength and intelligence. They should have been in command from the start. I'd wager that if Theodoros or Constantine had been with that first cavalry landing, this whole thing would have been different from the outset.'

'They've lost Galata,' Arnau breathed, watching the imperial army flood back through the streets of the foreign enclaves across the Golden Horn. Some were heading for the meagre flotilla of ferries that could carry them back across the water. The bulk of them, though, were angling west, making for the inner reaches of the inlet and that bridge that would lead them back to the city.

'That's it. Without Galata, Constantinople will be under siege.'

'Not yet,' whispered Ramon. 'Look.' His extended finger pointed to a small fortification at the far side of the water.

'What?'

'The Galata fortress. The great tower that guards the sea chain. It's still garrisoned, and I can see that some of the men aren't fleeing the field. Look, they're running into the tower complex. If they can hold that tower, then the future is still unwritten.'

'What difference does one tower make?'

Ramon frowned. 'As long as the chain holds, the Venetians are limited to the Bosphorus, Vallbona. They cannot get into the Golden Horn, and therefore they are of limited use from here on. If they get through that chain, then we really *are* in trouble, but as long as the chain holds, only the Franks present a direct threat. And while if it's these idiots still facing them the Franks alone might be enough, if someone with a little ability is put in charge, the Byzantine forces could win the day. A lot depends upon that tower, though.'

Arnau nodded, watching the fleeing soldiers bolstering the garrison of the Galata tower. Ramon was right, of course. But they needed someone capable commanding who would defy the Crusaders and not break and flee at the sight of confident cavalry.

'We need to get an audience with someone important,' Arnau said. 'The emperor or Stryphnos.'

Ramon shook his head. 'That won't happen without Bochard present, but what we can do is try and meet with the Laskaris brothers and persuade them to take charge regardless.' He turned to the Warings who escorted them. 'Would one of you be willing to deliver a message for me?'

* * *

An hour and a half later they were seated in the common room of their apartment, with Sebastian cleaning their weapons and armour and looking extremely nervous, eyes flicking constantly to the small icon that sat on the table beside him, when the visitor arrived. There came a rap at the door, and when they answered, half a dozen guardsmen stepped back for Theodoros Laskaris to enter. Arnau looked at Sebastian and noted with interest that the lad's earlier unease over Laskaris and his own father's past seemed to have gone, replaced now with a confidence and respect. Another barely perceptible step the squire had taken back into the world of his birth, Arnau suspected.

'Apologies for not having made a personal appearance before now, sir knights,' he said in weary tones. 'Sometimes the simple business of ruining an empire takes up all the court's time.'

'We saw what happened,' Ramon replied, gesturing to a seat and proffering a cup of wine which Theodoros declined with a tired wave. 'I need a clearer head than usual now.' He gestured to the door and the Warings closed it, leaving them alone.

'It was appalling. I think we could have held, regardless, and I think we *should* have held, but in truth I have never seen anything like that.'

'It was incredible,' Arnau agreed. 'They went from aboard ship to charging you in the blink of an eye.'

Laskaris nodded. 'Ungodly, even. Their ships turned side on, and then opened up. I could not have imagined such a thing, but they reached shallow water and dropped the entire side of the ship. The Franks were already mounted in the bowels of the ships. They charged as soon as the sides fell, even through the water. They reached an impressive speed even before they reached dry ground.'

'No wonder your men panicked,' Ramon sighed. 'A Frankish cavalry charge is something no man would wish to face. They have a brutal reputation, and we saw what the mere sight of them did to the kataphractoi at Scutari.'

'We could have held, though,' Laskaris said again with a sigh. 'We'd lost the men near the shore, for certain. Most of them died under pounding hooves, let alone by sword or lance, but we could still have held. I think the emperor himself panicked. The retreat call went up before the Franks had even finished with our vanguard. Now we have a narrow hold on Galata only. There is some discussion as to whether to break down the bridge at the head of the Golden Horn, but it is yet to be decided.'

Ramon leaned forward. 'You have to take control, you know? You or your brother.'

Laskaris nodded. 'Stryphnos is a constant worry. But he is currently at odds with the emperor. He didn't want to field the army at all. He remains in command, but only by a hair's breadth. And if he defies the emperor, then he will fall hard. The empire is not forgiving of failure. We have had a thousand years to become very inventive executioners. I once saw a former admiral who lost a squadron of ships hung on the wall of hooks. His agony was such that his family set fire to him to speed up his death.'

Arnau shivered. 'That is what is in store for Stryphnos?' The man was a fool, but no one deserved such a fate.

'Perhaps if he fails. Most definitely if he refuses.'

'And for you too?'

Laskaris nodded.

'Then you had best not fail. What's your plan?'

The Greek frowned and leaned forward, steepling his fingers. 'My brother took two hundred of our best infantry, including a group of the Warings who are fearsome in battle, back to the Galata tower, which I believe is now crucial.'

Ramon nodded. 'We had come to the same conclusion.'

'I have sent out orders this afternoon, gathering the very best infantry in the city. We shall load them into ferries before dawn and ship them across the Horn. I plan to continue doing so until the place is impregnable, holding off the Franks and thereby preventing the Venetians gaining access to the Golden Horn. And once we have sufficient men in place, we will attempt to fortify what we can of Galata, even if we have to pull down houses and expand, creating a stronger and stronger bridgehead.'

'To withstand a siege?' Arnau mused.

Laskaris nodded. 'We need only hold out until winter. The Franks are used to good farmland and rich pickings. Here they have access only to the relatively dry and unyielding Anatolian hills. With the horses they brought, whatever supplies they carry will not last beyond winter and they will be forced to withdraw. But to be certain of holding out, we need to keep the Venetians out of close waters. Thus, yes, we need to hold the tower and the chain. Is your master intending to leave? I had expected you long gone, since the reply to his letter seems not to be coming.'

Ramon shook his head. 'I have no idea what the preceptor is doing, but I am beginning to think that he sent no letter, or not the one we thought, and I don't particularly care any more.' He straightened. 'Send us a messenger before dawn and we will meet you at the docks.'

Laskaris raised an eyebrow. 'You mean to join us?'

'We have been forbidden to attack Christians, but not to *defend* ourselves from attack. It seems you will need every strong hand the good Lord can offer. Take ours.'

Laskaris smiled. 'In the morning, then. I will show you how an imperial soldier can fight, and you can show me how a Templar knight defends.'

Arnau swallowed quietly. While he'd been itching to deal with the Venetians, the idea of holding a tower against marauding French knights was considerably less inviting.

CHAPTER 8:
THE LAST TOWER

JULY 6TH 1203

Arnau, Ramon and Sebastian stood in the prow of a small skiff that carried nine men including the three Templars. This, the young knight realised, was what had become of the great Byzantine navy in this age of imperial failure: small ships, ferries and commandeered merchants. The fleet that carried the support for the Galata tower was little more than a ragtag flotilla of mismatched boats. It took every hull that could be rustled up in the Neorion harbour to carry the force across in one go, and it was not that large an army to carry.

They had sneaked through the streets onto the dock side in the pre-dawn murk, unobserved by any watchful eye across the water in Galata, slipping into the vessels. The chances of landing without being observed were small, but it was better to get as close as possible without attracting attention.

Arnau's gaze slid past the nervous-looking young squire who was facing the prospect of his first proper fight, thumb working furiously at the faded paint of his precious icon, and to the next boat along. Some twenty feet to their left the largest ship available ploughed through the water, carrying the commanders of the force.

One of the few surviving Byzantine warships, it had seen better days and had recently been patched up and refitted urgently at the coming of the Venetian fleet. A century ago, Arnau suspected, it would have represented one of the smallest and weakest vessels in the fleet. Here it looked like a lord of the sea next to the leaky ferries.

Riding high in the prow in the same manner as the Templars, but some ten feet above them, stood the two commanders of the relief army. Theodoros Laskaris was equipped for war, and though his appearance was probably informed by the fact that Arnau had met the man and knew him to be a warrior of old, he looked like some ancient Caesar, sailing to war against the barbarian. Beside him, the other man looked like some fop in ill-fitting, gaudy armour. Again, Arnau's impression was informed by the stories he'd heard and the failures he'd seen with his own eyes, but already he did not trust Michael Stryphnos, the senior commander of the city's military.

Laskaris had, apparently, confirmed with the emperor his intention to take a force in support of his brother at the Galata tower and there deny the marauding Crusaders any access to the Golden Horn and the city itself. The emperor had been in full agreement, but had saddled Laskaris with the senior commander in the process. Little could be done to oppose it. The empire clearly had as strict a system of obedience to the chain of command as did the Order.

So Stryphnos had been credited with Laskaris's plan. At least it seemed the older man had not seen fit to make any changes.

Fewer than fifteen hundred souls were rushing to the aid of the tower, bringing the total defence to around two thousand. It would be cramped, although the word 'tower' hardly did the place justice, since it was in truth a small walled compound with several structures, turrets and towers all huddled at the water's edge. They would manage. And this was only the initial force, after all. Once they had bolstered the garrison sufficiently to be sure they could hold against the Franks, they could look at expanding their bridgehead and improving the defence force. It was workable.

The skiff slid through the dark water in the early dawn light, the sun's gleam sparkling on the surface like a sea of brilliant diamonds cut through by a fleet of war. The landing places and rickety jetties of Galata's Golden Horn shore were coming close now. As yet there had been no sign of movement atop the hill, where the crusading army had encamped upon the summit overlooking the foreign enclaves. Either the Franks were still unaware of the relief force or, and this was highly likely, they were so confident now that they simply didn't care.

The commanders' ship, being the largest, most powerful and fastest, reached the shore first. By the time the Templars' skiff touched a jetty, the cargo of that vessel was already ashore, forming up and preparing to move off to the tower a few hundred paces away. By pure chance, Arnau's skiff took one of the right-most jetties, close to the tower, and so as they docked, he was able to take in the entire situation at close hand.

The Galata fortress, an outpost of the city walls that stood solely to guard the chain that sealed the water to shipping, was more or less a castle. With a strong curtain wall, it had three smaller towers and one huge square keep into which the sea chain disappeared through a slot. Though he'd not been told how the defence worked, it seemed clear that a windlass inside could tighten or loosen the chain. Unwound, the iron line would sink into the water and the skiffs that kept it near the surface when taut could move to let the chain drop further and allow access for ships. There were only two ways in or out of the fortress: by the main gate facing the hill and Galata proper, and a waterside postern gate in the great tower's base that gave out onto a small private jetty at which sat two small skiffs. It was as defensible a site as any Arnau had seen, and more so than Rourell had been during that awful siege a few years ago.

Moments later he was gathering up his shield, his sword bouncing at his side as they clambered out of the boat and onto land. Arnau felt the uncertainty rise once more. He'd been feeling it a lot during the night. To fight Moors, bandits and Saracens was one thing, and positively lauded in the Order. The men up that hill were Christian knights from France, though, and although the Pope may have initially condemned them, they remained part of Mother Church. Fighting them was at best bending the rules of the Order, if not breaking them outright. It was the just thing to do, of course. The right thing. But at the same time very much the wrong thing. Arnau couldn't quite reconcile how he felt about it. He had early on resolved not to take direct action, but only to defend himself when he had to, and even then he hoped not to have to do so.

The large gate of the Galata tower opened to grant access to the newly arrived force and, as they moved towards it, Arnau could see the face of Constantine Laskaris above the arch, watching his brother's force land.

The three Templars were among the first to arrive, and hurried inside. Ramon turned to the others as they halted in the wide courtyard. 'Fight, defend or withhold as your conscience sees fit, Vallbona. The Lord will judge you, not I. Sebastian, this is not your fight. It is my recommendation that you remain inside and perhaps help supply arrows and water where required. However, I also recognise that these are your people, and this your homeland. If you feel compelled to draw that blade by your side in defence of Byzantium, you will hear no condemnation from me. Just stay safe. I have become attached to my new squire.'

Arnau watched Sebastian's expression as the young squire struggled with the decision. Every day made him more a citizen of Byzantium. He was still Ramon's squire, and Arnau had no doubt that his loyalty remained staunch, but his heritage was taking an ever stronger hold now, and what he would do the day his duty to the order conflicted with his allegiance to the empire remained to be seen. 'Shall we find a place on the walls?' Arnau asked, eyeing the defences above them.

'Let's wait for Theodoros. He might want us somewhere specific. I doubt he wants us in grave danger. The emperor wouldn't like to have to explain to the Order that their brothers had died defending his city from the Franks. It might not go down very well.'

Arnau nodded, once again silently cursing Bochard for not having the common sense to have taken them all back out of the city before the worst occurred.

They stood to one side as files of men entered – small groups of imperial infantry withdrawn from border garrisons and archers from the empire, as well as mercenaries from other, less Christian, nations. Finally, after several hundred men had entered and sought the best position for their skills, the commanders arrived, on foot and surrounded by veteran infantry. No Warings here though – with a remit solely to defend the emperor, they had not left the bounds of the city.

As the commanders entered, Stryphnos turned to a musician beside him and a man carrying the Byzantine flag just beyond. 'Issue the orders. Have the army form up before the walls. All but the archers and a detachment of infantry.'

Theodoros Laskaris stopped in his tracks, his face folding into a frown.

'What? No, they need to line the walls and begin to pull down local housing into barriers.'

Stryphnos turned a nasty look on his second in command. 'The empire has been the power in the East and a God-granted bulwark against the barbaroi for a thousand years. If you think we are going to cower in a turret and let these Western thugs ravage Galata, you are mistaken. I thought you understood, Laskaris. We have crossed the water to do battle.'

'What?' Laskaris was incredulous.

'To drive these Franks back into the water. Without their Venetian masters, they will break. They will soon see their folly. We will push them to the water's edge and there accept their surrender. We will then offer them generous terms to leave the empire.'

Ramon turned a horrified look on Arnau as Constantine Laskaris hurried down from the walls and joined them. 'Did I hear you order an attack, Stryphnos?'

'That's *Strategos* to you,' snapped the older commander. 'I have overall command here, by the divine order of the emperor.'

Constantine pointed a finger, gesturing to the hill beyond the houses. 'There are *twenty thousand* Franks up there. If you take every man in the tower, they will still face ten-to-one odds. You're insane.'

'And you are removed from command,' snapped Stryphnos. 'Stay out of this and I will deal with your insolence on my return.'

He spun back to Theodoros. 'Unless you wish to join your brother waiting in the latrines, you will follow my orders. We will leave three hundred to hold the tower, which is more than adequate. The rest we will use to rout the Franks. They are animals. They understand only brute force and reckless bravery, not culture and sense. Thus we will show them we can fight every bit as hard as they. We will break them against the water.'

Already the force was forming outside, and Theodoros was clearly having difficulty keeping his composure. Carefully choosing his words and speaking through bared teeth, he addressed the general.

'Strategos, it is my duty to advise against this. The odds are so poor we have little chance. There is no horse here, just infantry, while the Franks have heavy cavalry. This will fail and cost us valuable manpower needed for the city's defence.'

Stryphnos nodded. 'Your objections are noted. Fall in with the men.'

Laskaris threw one contemptuous look at his commander and then stomped off through the gate with the men who were forming up between Galata tower and the civilian houses. As Stryphnos turned and marched off with them, Constantine snarled.

'Disaster. This is a disaster. They will all die and our efforts to secure this bank will be weakened.'

'What will you do?' Ramon asked him.

'I certainly will not wait to be upbraided by that lunatic. We will deploy every man we have so that the fortress remains defiant when he fails. Go to the top of the main tower. You will be able to see what happens from there. I will join you presently.'

Arnau and Ramon exchanged glances and nodded, both hurrying to the stairs of the main tower with Sebastian in tow while Constantine began throwing out orders, sending his depleted forces into the best positions around the walls.

Moments later, the Templars emerged onto the main tower's flat roof, where a catapult sat idle, ten baskets of heavy rocks waiting nearby. The only other figures here were the artillerists, for the tower was surrounded by the curtain wall and backed onto the water. It would only come under attack if the main fortress fell.

Arnau watched nervously as the various units under Stryphnos's command moved through the streets of Galata, heading for the open ground on the slope below the Crusaders' hilltop camp. The entire notion was suicidal, clearly. Even spread out as they were on their approach, Arnau could see how small the Byzantine force was compared to the army atop the hill in its sprawling fortifications.

'Do they stand any chance at all?' he murmured.

'No,' Ramon said wearily. 'Barring the intervention of the Lord himself, those men are the walking dead. Joshua himself and all the horns in the Israelite army could not turn this into a victory. Stryphnos is clearly determined to see his city fall.'

The older knight turned to the men behind him. 'If I were you, I would load that catapult. I think its time is nigh.'

Arnau watched, a cold ball of hopelessness and anger settling in the pit of his stomach. In minutes the Byzantine forces were emerging from the far side of the settlement of Galata and forming into a solid block. It would look impressive and strong were it not for the fact that Arnau knew how many men they were arrayed against. Along the wall, Sebastian peered out nervously, sword gripped tight in one hand, icon in the other.

'You will be safe,' Arnau said, hoping to sound reassuring. 'You will not die here, Sebastian.'

'I know,' was all the young squire said, a bead of blood forming where the edge of the icon had bitten into his palm.

The Templars' worst fears were quickly borne out. Even as the infantry force of Byzantium began to march up the hill, horn calls were going out across the Crusader camp. Horses were moving and masses of men forming up. During those first few moments, as the Byzantines covered perhaps a quarter of the distance, sufficient manpower to withstand them was easily gathered.

Half the distance now, the infantry sweating and tiring, marching up the hill. Arnau closed his eyes for a moment as more horns blared and Franks began to issue forth from their camp.

'Lord of might, look down upon us. May the bright angel Michael bring both sword and shield to aid these men and overcome the aggressor. Jesu have mercy.'

'I fear the Lord and his angels all have turned their face from this land,' Ramon said, bleakly.

Arnau opened his eyed and felt his gorge rise at what he saw.

Impressively, the Byzantines continued to stomp resolutely up the slope. Outside the Crusader camp, a force of horsemen had gathered. The gleam from their armour spoke clearly of their individual strength, and in terms of numbers there would near parity. Behind them, infantry were forming up and units of archers were pulling out to the sides and slamming their arrows in a line, point-down into the turf for ease of access.

Stryphnos was insane.

Some call went up from the Byzantine force and the infantry broke into a run. In response horns blared up the slope, and the heavy horse of the Frankish army began to race down the hill to meet them.

Arnau forced himself to continue watching, for all he wanted to turn his face away from this disaster. It came as little surprise when whole Byzantine units faltered and turned, breaking from the force and fleeing. Unlike those cavalry on that first day or the emperor's army on that same hill, these were not ordered soldiers retreating from the field on the command of their general. These were panicked men routing against orders, yet this was the first time Arnau could understand and even support such an act. To stay would be to die.

He watched, sickened, as the officers led their men against that wall of cavalry flowing down the hill. He closed his eyes in another momentary prayer for mercy, and opened them as the two forces met. The instant carnage and destruction was almost total. The Crusader horse hit the Byzantine infantry like a runaway wagon against a rotten fence. They simply rode down many of the men, churning them under pounding hooves with little need for weapons. Here and there lances would pierce men, lifting them from the ground and transfixing them before the shaft broke and they disappeared, dying in agony beneath the press.

The Byzantine army broke. Fully half their number had perished in that initial charge with no appreciable harm coming to the Franks. The imperial troops were running now, making for the illusory safety of the houses and streets, fleeing for the Galata tower and the ferries. Others peeled off, racing for the coast upstream in the hope they might reach the bridge that would carry them back across the upper reaches of the Golden Horn.

The enemy horse dispersed into a melee, some halting and resting after their charge, others pursuing groups of fleeing Byzantines, intent on slaughter. Arnau's eyes slid up from the disaster to the hill, and noted with a sinking heart the infantry and archers already moving. As though the Byzantine march had been some kind of trigger for action, the entire Frankish army was on the move now, heading down the slope towards the tower and the water it protected.

'They're coming for us now,' Arnau breathed.

'Shit flows downhill,' grunted Constantine Laskaris nearby. Arnau turned and could see that a group of soldiers had arrived with the general. A series of creaks announced the priming of the catapult.

'Your brother's banner, I think,' Ramon said, pointing.

Constantine nodded. 'He lives to return, though sadly I see nearby the banner of Stryphnos. The architect of insanity returns to us, having set the entire Crusader force moving.'

They watched in bleak horror as the Frankish knights rode down fleeing parties. Sensibly, they did not stray too far from infantry support, and so hundreds of Byzantine soldiers were making it back into the streets. Some ran for the jetties and the boats, others for the tower.

'Open the gate,' bellowed Laskaris, 'but be prepared to close it swiftly.' Even as the gate creaked wide, fleeing soldiers began to pound through it, pausing to draw painful breaths before their officers directed them to places on walls or towers. Arnau watched the walls slowly filling, bolt throwers on the lesser towers priming, ready to fire.

He turned to Ramon. 'It seems the Lord might yet have a role for us.'

Ramon nodded. 'I will fight if I must, but the tower can hold, even against that host.'

They watched as the Byzantine soldiers fled into the gateway, then something caught Arnau's eye. He peered into a nearby street. Sure enough, he could see Stryphnos's banner along with those of several of his units. Another street showed Theodoros Laskaris's banner and more men, but a third was already filling with lightly armed, speedy Frankish men-at-arms.

'This is going to be close,' he murmured.

Ramon simply nodded. Realising the danger, Theodoros Laskaris bellowed to his men, and they put on an extra, desperate turn of speed, racing for the gate. Men on the walls began to bellow to their fellows, telling them urgently to run. Arnau watched in astonishment. As Laskaris and his men dropped all pretence of a fighting retreat and simply raced for the gate, Stryphnos was sending his men out to the sides, forming an arc to contain the approaching Frankish infantry.

'Strategos,' bellowed Constantine at a volume that almost broke his voice. 'Withdraw! Withdraw now!'

Soldiers were flooding into the gate, yet Stryphnos had slowed his men, attempting to hold back the Franks emerging from the street.

'He can't hold them,' Arnau breathed. Ramon shook his head and pointed right. More Frankish infantry were closing now, appearing along other streets.

'You have to close the door,' Ramon shouted.

'What?'

'Close the gate. The time is up.'

Arnau nodded emphatically. The remaining Byzantines outside were already outnumbered by the men they were trying to contain, and were having to spread out to deal with freshly arrived Crusaders. They would be overrun any moment.

Laskaris uttered a desperate prayer in Greek and shut his eyes for a moment. 'Close the gate.'

As the call went up, Arnau saw panic fill the men still outside. They were doomed anyway, but now the gates were being closed behind them.

'No. *Open* the gates,' bellowed Stryphnos, turning and rushing for the doorway. Their commander leaving the line was all the prompt his men needed, and the entire force outside the walls broke in a panic and raced for the gate. Howling triumphantly, the Franks butchered many turning men, swords punching into unprotected backs.

Arnau watched, heart thumping, as Stryphnos ran for the gate, men flooding about him. As they converged on the Galata tower, his soldiers were already being overrun by Franks, swords rising and falling accompanied by screams and oaths, blood flying into the air to create a mist that filled Galata. Arnau listened in horror to voices in both French and Greek, all crying out to the Lord to save them from the godless.

'No, no, no,' breathed Constantine. He gestured down to the compound below. 'Bar the gate. Bar the damned gate!'

But Arnau could also hear other voices from outside demanding the gate be held. Disaster was coming, and the Templars could see it unfolding, yet were utterly incapable of stopping it. Already the Franks were in among the fleeing Byzantines. The fight outside had become a mess of routing defenders and desperate attackers, all determined to get to the tower gate first, the former to embrace its safety, the latter to capture it and bring destruction.

He knew in a trice what was about to happen. Behind him, Constantine was bellowing urgent, furious orders to close the gate, and some of his men were attempting to do so, but others were holding it open on the orders of Stryphnos, while desperate, shouting men piled through it.

The first clash came sooner than expected, Frankish men-at-arms having mixed in among the Byzantines in the press. In moments, the arch of the gate became a battleground as desperate defenders tried all too late to close the heavy door as Constantine had been demanding, while the Crusaders fought tooth and nail to hold the gate open as more and more of their fellows approached through the streets of Galata.

'Fools. Crazed fools,' breathed Constantine from the tower top. Arnau could see his brother now, leading a small group of defenders in trying to force the Franks back out of the gate, but more of their men were arriving all the time. The place was doomed.

Ramon turned to Constantine.

'Galata has fallen, Laskaris.'

The general nodded angrily, then hurried over to the parapet. The bolt throwers on the other towers were now at work, loosing into the Frankish crowd outside the walls, pressing for the gate, and even the catapult now released, sending a basket full of rocks over the curtain wall and into the mass, pulverising men in droves. Still there were too many. They were in control of the gate now.

Constantine gestured to his brother below. 'Theo, we must abandon Galata.'

The second Laskaris brother looked up, blood covering half his face, and nodded. The fighting below had already moved into the wide courtyard, clearly informing all present that the gate had now fallen to the Franks.

'No,' bellowed Stryphnos, suddenly visible among his men. 'No. Hold the tower.'

'The tower is lost,' cried Constantine from above.

'No!' Stryphnos began issuing desperate orders to bar doors and hold staircases.

'The fool,' Constantine snarled. 'We have to go. He has lost us Galata, but we can still save lives.' He cupped his hands around his mouth. 'All personnel to the boats. Withdraw to the city!'

Ramon nodded his agreement and the two Templars turned. Sebastian had a tear in his eye, which Arnau could readily understand, though this was not the time to grieve over what was happening. They hurried to the city side of the tower and peered down. The postern gate was open now, and men were fleeing along the shoreline, knee deep in the water, for the jetties where the ferries that had brought them across wallowed. Other soldiers had piled into the boats tied up behind the tower and were now pushing off, heading out into the water. One boat remained there. Soldiers were desperately trying to get aboard, but four men with Laskaris's banner were holding it for their master.

'Come. We must go,' Constantine said, and hurried for the doorway.

The three Templars followed him from the early morning sunlight into the gloom of the tower, where they began to pound their way down the staircase towards ground level and their only hope of escape. As they emerged onto the ground floor, a huge, square room filling most of the tower's width, the extent of their peril became clear. The enemy had not only control of the gate, but also the courtyard, and therefore very likely much of the curtain wall. A small group of rabid Franks had pushed their way inside and were now fighting to stop Theodoros Laskaris and his bodyguard getting past them into the tower.

Men hurried to the postern and the means of egress, and Arnau shared a look with Ramon, who nodded. 'Hold the boat,' the older knight said to Sebastian, drawing his sword. With a cry to the Mother of God, he and Arnau threw themselves at the Franks holding Theodoros back. Despite the ignominy of it, they did not wait for the Crusaders to face them, but drove their blades into backs and hacked at limbs, pushing them aside with their shields. The Franks, caught between Laskaris in the doorway and the Templars behind, fought with desperation now, cut off from their fellows. Arnau took a blow on his shield that left a deep groove and numbed his arm, and another blade thumped into his mailed hip, causing him to yelp even as he returned the compliment, breaking the arm of a raging Frenchman. In moments the small party of Crusaders was down, and Theodoros and his men surged gratefully into the tower.

'To the boat,' bellowed Constantine, who had been fighting on the far flank, beyond Ramon. His brother nodded, and the group turned like a wave meeting a sea wall and raced across the room, out to the door and the narrow corridor that emerged on the waterfront.

Arnau was the fifth man aboard the boat, which was likely rated for twenty men and already held thirty-some even as its pilot pushed it out from the jetty. The young Templar looked around. The relief he felt was selfish and brought with it unwanted guilt, but those he cared about most were aboard: Ramon and Sebastian, the former clutching a bleeding arm, and Theodoros and Constantine Laskaris, both similarly bloody.

He watched in bleak horror as they moved out across the water. Boats were departing all along the waterline now, each holding more men than they were meant to. Byzantine soldiers were toppling overboard in the panicked press, disappearing into the water never to reappear, their armour dragging them into the deep. Soldiers were throwing themselves from the walls and towers of the Galata fortress into the water of the Golden Horn. Some hit the shallows and crashed to their death, bones pulverised by the impact. Others made it to deeper water, where their armour dragged them to a grisly death. Few made it to a boat.

Sickened, Arnau watched as in desperation men were trying to climb along the water chain in an attempt to reach one of the ancient skiffs keeping it up. Again, many died in the water there. Few made it more than half a dozen arm-lengths along the chain in the chilly inlet.

It was a disaster. Nothing less.

With a bleak expectation, Arnau watched the chain come loose, unwound at the tower. The Franks had control now, and the one thing that had kept the Venetians out of the Golden

Horn and away from the city sank harmlessly into the depths, the attached skiffs floating free and eddying around in the water. Arnau kept a lookout for the Venetians, heart pounding, urging the boats to reach the safety of the city walls before the enemy surged into the waters here and smashed the fleeing ferries.

Those last defenders of Galata were dying now. The Franks had control of it all, and archers were lining every roof and parapet, loosing arrows into the bodies of the fleeing Byzantines, killing anyone within bowshot. Galata was in the hands of the marauding Crusaders, and the tower along with it. The chain had fallen and the Golden Horn was open to the Venetian fleet.

Constantinople stood alone now, enemies free to range on all sides.

Arnau jumped as Ramon grabbed his shoulder, and followed the older knight's pointing finger. He was distressed over how little sympathy he felt at the sight of Michael Stryphnos being hoisted above the parapet of the tall Galata tower, though he did wince as the figure fell with a shriek, and even more so as the rope snapped tight, cracking the man's neck and almost pulling his head clean off. The jerking, shaking form of the man who had lost them Galata bounced twice against the wall he could have held before finally falling still.

'If you have any faith left in you,' Constantine Laskaris said quietly, 'pray now, and pray harder than you have ever prayed. We are besieged.'

CHAPTER 9:
THE UNHOLY SIEGE

JULY 12TH 1203

Six days. Six days was all it took for the Venetians and Franks to turn a terrible decision by Stryphnos into a full-blown siege of the city. Perhaps it was lucky – perhaps it was not – that Preceptor Bochard happened to return to the city, apparently by chance, in the wake of what had happened at Galata, securing his place in the Blachernae once more just before the enemy set up outside the walls.

Ramon and Arnau had hurried over upon his return to impart all the news to the preceptor, who had brushed it aside as 'unimportant'. No matter how much they pressed, he seemed utterly uninterested in everything they had been through, labelling it 'the problems of heretics' and 'possibly advantageous to Rome'. Arnau and Ramon had finally broken off the argument, sickened, and left Bochard to whatever nefarious dealings had brought a small mule train back with him and required a guarded escort for several chests to his chamber. They could not be coin, after all, for he'd already brought plenty of that from Outremer.

Meanwhile, Constantinople and its enemies both prepared.

The Venetians wasted no time in accessing the Golden Horn. Though they stayed at the far side of the channel, away from the artillery on the walls, they now docked threateningly on the Galata shore facing the city, and any time a Byzantine ship moved from port, it came under attack and was forced to retreat. There the Venetians spent their time building unidentifiable constructions in the privacy of the docks.

Arnau and his friends had received reports regularly as the Franks moved slowly upstream from Galata, consolidating their control as they went, setting up lines of supply and communication from Galata to their proposed new position. As the Crusaders became visible from the city itself, the two knights, standing at the window of their apartment, fumed over how easily the Franks had moved into position, using the bridge over which the Byzantine survivors had fled. In fact, the Laskaris brothers had done what they could to halt the advance, given the lack of time and poor resources. They had demolished the bridge and put small units of archers and skirmishers nearby to harry the Franks. But the Crusaders were strong and confident now, and brushed aside the meagre defenders with little difficulty, repairing the bridge swiftly. All the measures had done in the end was to delay the army by a few days.

The window at which the Templars stood looked west from the city walls that also formed the palace wall to the west, across the lesser defences at this end of the promontory. The gradient of the land denied the possibility of a moat, and centuries of rebuilding about the palace had seen the walls cobbled together over numerous separate periods with various stages of military architecture in place.

The Crusaders were visible from the window now. Just half a mile away an ancient monastery stood upon a low hill, and the Franks had made camp about it, using the monastery itself as their headquarters. The sprawling camp was fortified with palisades and ditches, and what seemed an endless array of off-white tents.

It was as Arnau, Ramon and Sebastian stood at the window, pondering their immediate future and the idiotic obstinacy of Bochard in refusing to leave, that there came a knock at their door and the source of most of their information over the past week made his latest visit.

Alexios Doukas, the political prisoner who wandered the palace with his Waring shadow, and who seemed better informed than most courtiers, greeted them as Sebastian opened the door, and strode across to stand in the window with them.

'I feel more could have been done at the Barmyssa bridge,' Ramon said, frustrated. 'Not enough men to cause them trouble, and they simply rebuilt the bridge. Had you left it in place, you could have fielded a major force and kept the Franks funnelled through the narrow bridge, trapped and at the emperor's mercy.'

Doukas shook his head. 'You are thinking like a Frank, de Juelle. Not like a citizen of the empire. Gone are the days, sadly, of Roman generals fielding armies that win great lands and destroy whole empires. Our manpower is low, spread out, and often reliant upon foreign mercenaries. Witness the failures of every force the city has fielded since the fleet arrived.'

'That was poor planning and generalship.'

Doukas shrugged. 'To some extent, yes, but there is more to it than that. We have not been a conquering empire for centuries. We fight mostly to stop rebels seceding from the empire.'

Arnau glanced momentarily at Sebastian's troubled face. That was precisely how his father had died, after all.

'Much of our foreign policy for centuries has been one of negotiation and pacification,' Doukas went on. 'And now, with a strong and violent enemy at our gates, we simply have not the skill to meet them in the field. But we do have walls that have kept this city safe for a thousand years. Yes, the hinterland has been sacked once or twice, but still the walls hold strong and the city has never fallen. The people remember that and rely upon it. Better not to waste men at a bridge we cannot hold, but put thcm on the walls and make sure the Franks begin to starve in the winter and finally desert their cause.'

'But the chain is gone now,' Ramon reminded him. 'The Horn is filled with Venetians.'

Doukas shrugged again. 'Others have done the same. Vile Rus and imperial rebels have both got past the chain in their time, only to founder against the walls. No, with good leadership, relying upon our fortifications is still the way. As long as our weak-livered emperor relies upon good men like the Laskaris brothers, then we can hold and eventually drive them away. The loss of Stryphnos is a boon, but mind that the emperor himself is every bit as foolish and impulsive. We have a chance, but we are not out of danger yet.'

Ramon nodded, and Arnau kept watch on the camp full of Franks. They looked a little too close and too powerful for comfort, regardless of the massive walls behind which the Templars stood and upon which Doukas seemed content to rest his hope.

* * *

The next five days were tense and unpleasant, yet fascinating and often eye-opening. As with all sieges, events began slowly and moved with ponderous progression. The Crusaders spent much of the first week gathering supplies, cutting wood, fortifying their continued settling in for the duration. The secretive Venetians continued to build and prepare on the far side of the water, performing some kind of arcane works on their ships that no one could identify from the walls. Daily, a deputation was sent from the enemy camp to just outside bowshot from the walls, displaying the young pretender and warning the city that denying his claim would be their undoing.

Within the city, the people still seemed surprisingly calm and confident. The walls thronged with men, all of whom continued to spit at the prince when he appeared and who were prepared to hold out as long as they could. The walls were strengthened wherever Constantine Laskaris identified a weak spot. Gates were shored up and some blocked. Tower-top artillery was kept primed and with plentiful ammunition in place. All was made as ready as possible.

One thing that surprised and impressed the watching Templars was the piety with which every heart seemed filled. Every day, a great icon of the Holy Mother was brought forth from the church in the Blachernae palace and paraded around the city before the defenders, escorted by a dozen priests, several nobles and officers and a score of Warings with hands on axe handles. Wherever the icon passed, there were cheers and prayers, and the spirit of the defenders lifted noticeably. Their closeness to the Virgin Mother, when placed against the incessant violence and pressure of the Crusaders, made it ever easier for Arnau to see these so-called 'heretics' as the innocent and godly victims of temporal aggression. Like Zadra before it, Constantinople was besieged by men who should know better. Like Zadra, Constantinople was truly a city of God.

The Byzantines did not limit themselves to bolstering their defences, though. By the third day, when the Crusader siege engines began to loose and test the city, it became clear that their weapons were outsized monsters developed solely for the destruction of castles and with an impressive range, while the city's artillery was more incisive and accurate anti-personnel equipment, but with a much shorter range. The Franks set up siege weapons halfway between their camp and the walls, each with their own small defensive circuit and garrison. There, with skilled artillerists, they were just within range of the city, as the first shot they loosed proved. The closest missile launched from Constantinople, however, fell eighty paces short of its Frankish target.

Consequently, the new, dreadful counterweight trebuchets of the Franks began to pound the city walls with impunity while the city weapons fell silent, conserving their ammunition. Having sought the emperor's permission, Theodoros began leading a series of cavalry sorties at night. Carrying pots of what they called 'Greek fire' and torches and jars of pitch, they managed to reach several of the larger siege engines the first night and set fire to them. Arnau had been impressed to watch thcm burn throughout the hours of darkness, leaving only charred bones in the morning. He pressed Doukas on the matter.

'Why do they not just wet the timbers and use water to extinguish the flames? The fires burn unassuaged.'

Doukas had smiled an unpleasant smile. 'The secret of the ancient fire handed down through the generations. The fire sticks to surfaces and defies water. It even burns on the sea.

Nothing can extinguish it. Once the engines are alight, they are doomed.'

Arnau had been horrified at the notion of a fire that could not be extinguished but was still, in a way, grateful at least that it was being used *by* the city and not *against* it. Over the next three nights, repeated forays met ever-increasing resistance from the angry Franks, but Theodoros was clever and his sallies were rarely unsuccessful. By the sixteenth of the month, every engine the Crusaders had fielded had become ash, leaving only a few small dents and cracks in the city walls to show they had ever been used.

Every day half a dozen funerals were held for men who had died in the forays, yet they were not seen as sombre signs of loss and failure, but as the joyous celebration of deceased heroes who had helped their empire defy the invading army. And their success was notable. For the first time since the fleet had arrived, Byzantium had bloodied the enemy nose and achieved an unqualified success. The enemy's siege weapons had been destroyed, and the sorties had taken enough Crusader lives that they began to pull back their pickets and foragers, keeping their men within the safety of their camp whenever possible.

And while this dreadful war progressed, every day saw a procession of junior priests, administrators and nefarious characters visiting Bochard and leaving, Arnau suspected, with fat purses.

The city hailed Laskaris as a hero, and even the somewhat dour and fatalistic Doukas lauded the actions of Theodoros. That last day, the sixteenth, all activity among the enemy ceased, as their plans for assault were rethought. Clearly siege engines were not going to win Constantinople for the Franks. A new tactic had to be found.

The morning of the seventeenth of July saw that tactic come into play. Doukas arrived at the Templars' room with his Waring escort, the taciturn and menacing Redwald, just after first light.

'I fear the true siege is about to start,' the prisoner said with a mix of trepidation and anticipation in his voice.

'There is movement?' Ramon crossed to the window. 'I can make out a little activity in the camp, though this view is not the best.'

Doukas gestured upwards. 'Lookouts atop the towers have warned that several divisions have formed up within the camp as though for battle. Moreover, the Venetian ships have been made ready and are being loaded with equipment and men.'

Arnau breathed slowly, deliberately. 'This is it, then.'

'It would seem so.' Doukas narrowed his eyes. 'The Order of the Temple, of course, has no place in this war on *either* side.'

Ramon nodded. 'Of that I am painfully aware. But having been, in a former life, an advocate for the Church of Rome in the courts of Iberia, I am more than a little familiar with legal minutiae, loopholes and how to exploit them. There are at least half a dozen rules in our order that prevent us taking any action against your enemies, though in court I would utterly destroy all arguments based upon them. The only unbreakable rule holding us back is obedience to our master. Bochard will have the final say, and there is little I can do about that.'

'But you will find a way,' Sebastian said suddenly.

Ramon turned in surprise and the squire, his face a picture of fury, gestured at him, icon gripped tight. 'You will find a way. Because when I came to the Order, it was made clear to me that you were men of God. That you had vowed to protect the innocent and God-fearing from the wicked and the vicious. I turned from the Church of my birth and embraced Rome's teachings because you took us in, and you were noble and just and right. And if that is true, and you are all those things, you will find a way to help. And if you are not, then I am done with the Temple.'

Arnau blinked in surprise. Sebastian had ever been quiet and accepting. He had never shown a hint of pride or defiance, yet here he stood, tall as a giant, making demands of his superiors. But Arnau had watched as the months rolled by and the young squire slipped ever further into the arms of his people. And he was right. Arnau walked over and stood beside him. 'Find a way,' he added, simply.

Ramon looked at them for a short while, his brow furrowed. Then he nodded. 'Sebastian, have our war gear made ready. Arnau, come with me.'

Moments later, Ramon was hammering on the preceptor's door. It opened quickly, Bochard's wary, dark eye appearing at the crack.

'What is it, de Juelle?'

'The Crusaders are making ready for a great assault, and we must stand with the soldiers of Byzantium.'

'No, de Juelle. This is not our fight.'

Ramon snarled. 'It never was, and we should not even *be* here. We should have left for Acre months ago, but you insist on our remaining so that you can... what? Gather icons and relics? Is that why we are here? But you've left it too long. We're part of it all now, because you kept us here. We either throw in our lot with the Crusaders or with the empire and, heresy or not, I cannot in conscience take arms with our Roman brothers against these men. Remain locked in your room if you wish, Master, but you must give us permission to do our part.'

Bochard shook his head, drawing the door open a crack wider. Arnau could just see past him where his squire was packing things carefully into a chest.

'Out of the question,' the preceptor snapped. 'I forbid it.'

'You forbid what?' growled Ramon angrily.

'You will not fight the Crusaders. You will not draw your sword against any son of the Church. Do you understand me?'

Ramon growled again. 'Perfectly.'

With a sharp nod, Bochard slammed his door closed and Ramon marched away, Arnau at his heel.

'What now?'

'Now?' Ramon hissed as they returned to their own apartment. 'Now we obey Bochard's commands. To the letter.'

'What?'

Doukas and Sebastian looked up as they entered.

'We obey Bochard,' Ramon repeated. 'We will not fight Crusaders, and we shall not draw a sword against a son of the Church.'

'I don't understand.'

Ramon reached for his arming jacket and began to pull it on over his tunic. 'The enemy will come on two fronts, Vallbona. The Franks will hit the walls near this palace where they are weakest and there is no moat. The Venetians can only assault by water, but they will do so close to the Blachernae, so that both attacks hit the same sector of the city at once from two angles. We are forbidden to fight the Franks on two counts: they are Crusaders and sons of the Church. The Venetians, however, are fair game, not being men of the Crusade, but simply their transport, and no sons of the Church since their excommunication remains in place. Bochard's rules apply only to the Franks.'

Arnau broke into a savage grin and hurried over to where Sebastian had laid out his gear, grasping his arming jacket. The squire was also collecting up his own meagre equipment, bearing an expression of grim determination.

'Fight if you will,' Ramon told him. 'These are your people, after all. But keep yourself safe. Be careful and stay close to us.'

Sebastian nodded and held up his icon proudly. 'The Theotokos watches over me this day, fear not.'

Ramon laughed darkly. 'Would that we all had such a treasure, Sebastian.'

Doukas smiled a weird smile. 'War makes for strange bedfellows, does it not, Brother de Juelle?'

Ramon nodded. 'Tell us where the weakest point on the Horn walls is,' he said. 'The Venetians are cunning enough to strike there.'

* * *

Half an hour later, with a three-man Waring escort, the Templars ascended a staircase at the bottom of the steep slope of the so-called 'Sixth Hill', where the walls towered above the

Golden Horn and a narrow verge of marshy land that lay in between.

Already a few of the tower-top artillery pieces were thudding, throwing out missiles, and as they emerged onto the wall top close to a gate and hurried to the battlements, Arnau could see why. The Venetian fleet was mid-channel, sailing for the city en masse. Truly the invaders intended to take the city today. This section of wall had been identified by Doukas as the most likely trouble spot, and it seemed the city's commanders agreed, for he could see along the wall, close to the next tower, the figure of Constantine Laskaris, his banner flying atop that tower beside the imperial flag and several others.

'They come,' Laskaris bellowed as he saw the Templars arriving. Ramon nodded. 'Your noble brother?'

'With the emperor, dealing with the Franks at the land walls,' Constantine replied.

Arnau took in the other defenders with a sweeping gaze. They seemed strong and confident. Many were armed with long spears or similar pole arms, ready to use them to fight off men down below. Interspersed were archers, and each tower held a piece of artillery. Braziers burned along the defences, supplying fire to the archers should they need it. Here and there he could see pots of pitch too. Briefly, he caught sight of Sebastian among a unit of Byzantine spearmen some distance down the wall, saw the young man kiss his icon of the Holy Mother, and then lost sight of him as men moved about once more.

'How will they attack?' Arnau breathed, watching the ships getting ever closer.

Ramon shrugged. 'They will have to land and raise siege ladders, I think, unless they mean to pound us with missiles from the water.'

'Then surely there is no real danger?'

The older knight frowned. 'These are Venetians. There is always danger. Be ready.'

The two knights waited tensely, Sebastian close by, as numerous warships closed on the walls, keeping pace side by side.

The artillery atop the towers began to fire in earnest now, stones and bolts hurtling from the defences to slam, thud and crash into the ships. There were screams and the sounds of shredding timber, but the ships kept coming.

'Their masts,' bellowed someone along the wall. 'Look to the masts.'

Arnau did so. He couldn't quite make out what he was looking at, though. The masts, with their many ropes and canvas sails, seemed somehow bulkier than usual, but he couldn't make it out. He was still frowning at them in confusion when the ships began to turn. Riding with the momentum of their erstwhile speed, they continued to drift towards the walls, side on.

Arnau stared, realising what had been done to the masts only as they broke into action. Spars and ropes and acres of sailcloth had been reworked to form strong ladders with thick sides attached to the mast. As the ships closed on the walls and towers, ropes were untied and released, those new, ingenious walkways pivoting and lowering, forming boarding ramps high up amid the masts.

As the ships drifted the last thirty paces or so towards the walls, men began to swarm up the ropes, their shields on their backs and weapons at their sides, racing for the mobile boarding ladders. Arnau watched in fascinated horror as a ship closed on his stretch of walls. The ladder swung and wavered, and he realised in shock that, given the height of the mast, the boarding ladder was above the level of the wall.

Byzantine archers began to do their duty, peppering the ships with arrows, some burning, trying to pick off the men swarming up the rope ladders to the walkways at the top. As they did so, archers suddenly rose from those same ladders, hidden there by the voluminous sailcloth. They stood, bows drawn and arrows nocked, and in an instant missiles were flying downwards at the men on the walls. Their aim was careful, and the bulk of the missiles that struck home did so in the flesh of an archer. Thus in moments the Venetian bowmen had more or less neutralised their opposite numbers on the walls.

The bowmen continued to loose arrows as the walkways swung over to the rampart. Arnau watched the walkway closing on him and swallowed his nerves. There was a dreadful thump and the whole thing lurched as the ship below touched land, and two archers fell from the walkway with screams, their bodies dashed to pieces far below.

'Take ye lore of chastising,' Arnau said, glaring at the walkway swinging towards him and quoting the second Psalm, 'lest the Lord be wroth sometime and ye perish from the just way. While his wrath shall burn out in short time, blessed be all they that trust in him.'

Ramon, drawing his sword and taking a deep breath, replied in deep tones. 'For the great day of their wrath cometh, and who shall be able to stand?'

Revelations… Arnau shivered. He wasn't quite prepared for the end of days yet, though perhaps the Venetians were. Ropes down below were let go and the mobile walkway shook for a moment, and then descended.

With a thud, the shaking ladder with its canvas walls slammed onto the wall top. The first men to appear were the archers who had been hidden inside, though now they had drawn blades and ran forth, desperate to gain a hold of the wall.

Arnau brandished his sword, turning so that his shield faced the charging men. He braced himself, running through several other appropriate psalms as the first Venetian ran at him. The archer, his bow held low in his left hand while his right held a short blade, raised that latter weapon, bellowing something in a thick Italian accent. He never reached Arnau, for the artillerist on the nearest tower had turned his bolt thrower and aimed carefully. The archer was plucked from the ladder, impaled with a two-foot missile that had punched deep into his torso, and thrown him from the bridge, hurtling down to the water or earth below, gurgling his last invective.

The man behind him was not fazed. In a heartbeat he reached the wall top and leaped from the bridge, sword swinging. Arnau caught the blow contemptuously on his shield and punched outwards, foot braced against the stone. The archer, turned aside by shield and push, fell to the left, barking out his surprise, where a nearby Byzantine infantrymen in a shirt of bronze scales swung a heavy mace and stoved in the man's head. Arnau tried not to feel jealous. What he would give right now to be wielding his favourite mace and not a sword.

No time to brood, though. The men were coming from the ship thick and fast now.

Ramon was beside him as a third man piled off the ramp, swiftly followed by a fourth. They leaped at the Templars fearlessly, hammering down with blades and knocking the knights back with the ferocity of their attack. Arnau pushed the man back, hacking down with his sword and scything a deep cut into the man's unprotected thigh. The Venetian screamed and fell away, but there was instantly another man in his place. Arnau realised what the men were doing, though there was precious little he could do about it. These men, lightly armoured and armed, were selling their lives cheaply that their fellows might gain the advantage. Leaping into a fray they knew would kill them with the single goal of pushing back the defenders on the wall top sufficiently to allow more and more men to emerge from the bridge. It was working too.

Arnau fought back hard, his sword rising and falling almost mechanically, butchering men, but those initial few leaps had driven them back and the men swarming up from the ships' decks were coming in force, pouring along the ramp. Arnau felt a weapon strike his sword arm elbow, the mail preventing serious injury, but the blow hard enough to temporarily numb the arm. He resorted to using his shield as a battering ram, hammering out at the ever-increasing sea of Venetians flowing onto the wall. Ramon was under pressure, fighting like a madman, and they had now lost sight entirely of Constantine in the press.

The bodies of the Venetians underfoot were becoming troublesome now as they fought to maintain what looked like an increasingly tenuous hold on the walls. Arnau felt the pain now in his fighting arm, and tested his swing. It hurt like hell, but he retained full use of it at least. Gritting his teeth against the pain, he went back to work with his blade, hacking and slashing at the Venetian mob. The defenders were in trouble. He could see that. The men coming along that bridge were better now. The light-armed archers and men-at-arms who had formed the initial assault and gained a foothold were almost gone, and the Venetians coming now wore chain shirts and had shields and helmets.

The foothold had been gained and now here came the real warriors to take advantage of it and capture the walls. Arnau roared a prayer and threw himself forward into the fray. His sword swung and stabbed, chopped and thrust, biting into chain, wool, flesh. He felt the hammer blows of enemy weapons battering his shield and helmet. Something stamped hard on his foot, causing him agony, yet still he fought madly.

At one crazed moment in the fray he found himself face to face with another of the Byzantine footmen, and both of them had to pull in a blow meant for one another before turning and finding the next target. Momentarily he wondered where Sebastian was, and prayed that the young squire's faith in the protection of his icon was well founded.

Arnau fought on, marvelling at how this had all happened so easily for the enemy given how ready the defenders had been and how impregnable the walls had seemed. The answer was clear, though. The city had rarely faced a threat here. The Golden Horn had been protected by the chain and enemies hardly ever managed to penetrate it. Consequently, the walls here were not quite as tall or powerful as those exposed permanently. Add to that the unlikelihood of a man on a ship's deck posing a threat to the walls, and no one could have predicted this peril. The Venetians had used extraordinary cunning and ingenuity, turning their very ships into siege weapons, gaining sufficient height to look down on the walls.

The Byzantines had simply not been prepared for it. How could they have been?

Something bumped into him, and a blade skittered off the chain on his shoulder, tearing a hole in his surcoat. Arnau was forced to step back and to his left. A flurry of blows from two opponents almost pushed him from the wall, and he fought hard to keep his place, sword and shield smashing out.

Something suddenly hooked over his shield and pulled. He felt his left arm yanked painfully, almost jerked from its socket, and he was forced to relinquish his grip on the shield before the pulling either dislocated his arm or dragged him to the floor. The shield fell away, a Venetian gripping it triumphantly for only a moment before a Byzantine defender punched his blade through the man. Arnau caught a momentary glimpse of his shield before it was knocked away by staggering feet and fell from the wall. It was already so battered and scarred that he could hardly make out the design on it any more.

He raised his sword and caught a descending blow with it, the blades scraping horribly along one another. Contemptuously, he kicked his opponent hard between the legs, and was rewarded with a crunch audible even over the fight. The man fell away, screaming, as Arnau lowered his foot, the heavy leather boot reinforced with chain mail coverings. The bastard Venetian might get away, but his line would now die out with him.

Arnau was suddenly pushed back by another opponent. The wall was too crowded to make out too much of what was happening now, but he caught occasional sightings of Ramon, struggling in the press. One thing was clear: they were losing.

The young Templar could not even estimate how long he fought on that wall against a seemingly endless tide of fearless Venetians, but the sun was riding high in the sky when the fight hit both its lowest and highest points at once.

Somewhere ahead, east along the wall, someone was blowing a horn. Arnau didn't know the Byzantine signals, of course, but the urgency and direness of the sound made it fairly clearly a call to retreat. Someone had decided the walls were no longer defensible, that it was hopeless, and the Venetians had control. Momentarily, he caught sight of Constantine Laskaris fighting like a madman, and knew that at least the call had not come from the commander.

But perhaps the signaller was correct. Arnau could see four Venetians now for every Byzantine. It did look hopeless. Even as he watched, the invaders along the ramparts were taking the opportunity to tip the burning braziers from the wall, where they plummeted into houses and shops of dry wood and tile, which burst into flame in moments. Even as Arnau dispatched another screaming Venetian, the conflagration took hold and began to spread.

They were lost. They were at that lowest point. Arnau knew they had to withdraw, lest they die among the Byzantines at the mercy of the vicious invaders.

Then came the reprieve.

A new call.

A new melody blaring out over the fight. Arnau could not identify this one either, but it came from behind him, from back towards the palace, and it sounded angry, yet positive and fierce. It sounded somehow like a mother bear realising her cub was in danger. Whatever it was seemed to give new heart to the Byzantines, and they began to fight once more like lions, shouting prayers and curses as one, stabbing Venetians and desperately trying to regain control of their walls.

Arnau was struggling, fighting off two Venetians at once, when the reason for the new call became apparent. The Venetian to Arnau's left made to take advantage of his lack of shield, lunging for his armpit. The blow never landed. Instead, the snarling Venetian disappeared in a cloud of flying gore and fragments of bone.

Arnau stared, and struggled to regain his wits and hold off the man he still faced as a Waring guardsman, a clear foot taller than him and wider in the shoulder than most horses, stepped forward and yanked his great axe from the bifurcated remains of his victim.

The tide turned in that moment as giant warriors from the north, bearded and fearless, appeared in droves, fighting back the Venetian plague.

'Never mind, little knight,' grinned the Waring, pointing at the man he had obliterated. 'I'll save some for you.'

With a grin, Arnau nimbly dispatched the remaining man he'd been facing and went back to work alongside the emperor's guards, pushing back the Venetian tide in an effort to regain control of the wall. He laughed as he fought and chanted out his favourite psalms, carving his hatred and defiance into the Venetians.

Behind him, Constantinople burned.

CHAPTER 10:
THE IMPERIAL ARMY

JULY 17TH 1203

'They're on the run,' someone shouted.

Arnau, jammed between two hulking Warings with bloody weapons and sharp tongues, wiped the spray of blood from his face, yanked his blade from a shuddering body and stepped back. Enough had changed in the last half-hour that now at least he had room to do so.

It was true. The Venetians seemed to be thinning out, and he could see figures pounding back along the attack ladders, heading for their ships. He looked back and forth along the wall, trying to spot a familiar face. Finally, in the press of flailing blades and bobbing heads he spotted Ramon, who was looking in his direction but waving and pointing with his left hand even as he fought on with the right.

Arnau turned and looked at where Ramon had been pointing. The next tower west, marking the edge of the Blachernae palace grounds, rose above the crowd, and he could now see Constantine Laskaris atop it, beneath his own banner, throwing out commands and pointing hither and thither. The young Templar turned back to his friend, who had been joined by a blood-soaked figure Arnau believed to be Sebastian. Ramon was indicating that he should go to the tower even as the pair also pushed their way in that direction.

In a matter of minutes, Arnau was emerging onto the relatively clear tower top. Waiting patiently nearby, by the time Laskaris had finished with his latest set of orders and spotted the Templar, Ramon and Sebastian had joined him. The squire seemed hale enough, though his left arm hung by his side, covered in blood. His expression was certainly fierce, rather than pained.

'Have we won back the walls?' Ramon shouted, crossing to the imperial general.

'We have,' Constantine confirmed, pointing out to the water. Perhaps half the boarding ladders had survived the attack, the defenders concentrating on destroying them wherever possible, and the remaining ones were even now swinging back onto the ships, their crews moving to depart. Ships were pushing away from the bank and the walls, out into the water.

'They run,' nodded Arnau.

'Look again,' Laskaris said

Arnau did so and frowned in realisation. The Venetian ships were not fleeing back across the Golden Horn as Arnau had expected. In fact, they were moving up the channel, inland.

'Supporting the Franks?' Ramon murmured.

'It would appear so. But to abandon a fight they might yet have won? We were making headway. But the struggle could still have gone their way.'

Arnau turned and looked back inside the city wall where whole blocks of housing were now a roaring conflagration, desperate citizens running back and forth from fountains, cisterns and bathhouses, trying to douse the flames, though with little success.

'Perhaps they're leaving the city to burn,' he said with a shudder.

'What?'

'I've been in burning buildings twice now. It's not something you seek, believe me. Perhaps the Venetians think they're done here. They've fired the city and moved on.'

Constantine nodded grimly. 'Certainly ours has been a costly victory.'

'It may yet not *be* a victory,' Ramon reminded him. 'If the Venetians are heading upstream, we should find out why.'

The general shook his head. 'You go. My duty is here, securing the sea wall and overseeing the fighting of the fire.'

Nodding, Ramon gestured to the others and disappeared inside the tower door. Arnau and Sebastian hurried to catch up, pounding wearily down the stairs to emerge onto the wall top. The euphoria of battle had begun to fade now, and with it his energy was waning. The aches and pains of combat began to make themselves known and Arnau winced. His sword arm shrieked with pain every time he moved it, and he thought that he probably had at least one broken toe.

'I'm almost spent, Brother,' he said.

Ramon turned his head as he walked purposefully. 'Aye, myself also. And Sebastian here needs to have that arm looked at. But we are not running to a fight. I might be content to push back the Venetian advance, but Bochard strictly forbade us from attacking the Franks, and that is where we are heading, so I sheathe my blade.'

Wiping it on the rag from his belt until it shone grey once more, he did just that. Arnau glanced at the hard face of young Sebastian. He was not convinced that the squire shared their determination to obey even in the face of Frankish aggression.

All along the wall, Byzantine soldiers were cheering and jeering, having won back control of their fortifications and bested the Venetians despite their ingenious plan. Arnau knew, even as they moved back west and south around the Blachernae perimeter, that the success could only be pinned upon the timely arrival of the Warings. He had adjusted his thinking now. Before today, he had more or less written off the imperial bodyguard. Oh, they were big and impressive, but their remit was the protection of the emperor and they would only be committed to a fight on his order. Thus Arnau had thought of them purely as bodyguards. Now, though, he had seen them in action. The Warings were every bit the dangerous foe they had been centuries before when drawn from the ranks of the Norse berserkers.

He couldn't help but feel that despite the ancient organisation and discipline of the Byzantine army, the survival of the city would hinge upon the Warings. Indeed, as they moved along the walls, trying to identify what had spurred the withdrawal of the

Venetians, keeping pace with their ships as they hurtled west, they found the next area of engagement also being held together by the great armoured northmen, fighting alongside the Byzantine infantry.

Here, where a gate from the palace complex gave out through the main walls, a sizeable Frankish force was doing its level best to swarm across the defences and gain a foothold in the city. The land walls, though, were far, far stronger than the sea ones, even here where they lacked something of the impressive design of the main stretch. Between the strength of the defences, the lack of attacking siege engines, and the sheer violence of the imperial force, the Crusaders were making precious little headway. Arnau could see no great likelihood of this area falling today. Was this where the Venetians were coming to help?

Some Byzantine senior officer, marked out by his archaic uniform with knotted ribbons and red leather strops hanging from shoulders and skirt, was busy giving out commands, and Ramon paused nearby until the man turned his attention to the blood-soaked Templar.

'Yes?'

'The sea walls are secured and the Venetians are sailing west. What happens up ahead?'

The officer frowned, clearly unaware that Templars even existed in his city and likely wondering what part they played and whether he could trust them. In the end, noting the signs of battle upon them and their claim to be fighting for the city, he gestured south, along the main land walls.

'The emperor has led out the army.'

Ramon and Arnau exchanged a look, then thanked the man and ran on along the walls with Sebastian immediately behind, picking up their pace. At the southern edge of the Blachernae palace grounds the land rose to one of the city's great hills and, wheezing and sweating, the three Templars pounded on up the sloping wall, passing towers and artillery. Here the defenders were thinner on the ground, the bulk of the forces in the area having moved towards the gate to help defend it from the main Frankish assault.

As they neared the top of the slope, Arnau noted a familiar figure ahead atop the tower. Bochard's white surcoat with the brilliant red cross and his steel helm marked him out among the uniforms of the Byzantine infantry. The preceptor stood at the parapet of the highest point on the walls, looking out across the land away from the city. It was only then that it struck Arnau that this was the first time the preceptor had emerged from his private business and paid attention to the war. Had he finally realised the danger?

In a matter of moments, the other three entered the tower and pounded up the stairs.

Emerging onto the tower's flat top near a loaded catapult and a small force of imperial soldiers, they crossed to the preceptor, who turned at the sound of approaching boots. His face shifted quickly through a number of expressions, none of which were remotely welcoming, settling upon puce with anger.

'What have you done?' he roared, gesturing at the three blood-soaked figures.

'No more than we had to,' Ramon replied quietly. 'What is happening out there?'

'I ordered you not to fight them.'

'We engaged no Crusaders,' snapped Ramon. 'We found ourselves under attack by Venetian dogs and we fought them off.'

Arnau nodded emphatically. It was the truth, strictly speaking.

Bochard's arm was shaking angrily, and his mouth opened and closed a few times, trying to find fault with them. Unable to do so, he shut it angrily for a moment, then wagged a finger at Ramon, his gaze dark and threatening. 'You may have *initiated* nothing, de Juelle, but you invite chaos by placing yourself among the enemy. I know your game, Brother. Do not think to fool me. I shall be more explicit with my commands in future.' He relented, still angry, but calmer. 'How stand the sea walls?'

'They are secure.'

'Mmm,' the preceptor murmured. Arnau frowned. The inflection of the noncommittal noise suggested that Bochard was in some way disappointed. What was he waiting for, standing here and watching the Franks carefully, seemingly disappointed in their ability to hold out?

'The emperor and his general may turn the war their way today,' the preceptor said, and Arnau again caught a note of regret in the words. Surely Bochard couldn't support the Crusader cause in this? But thoughts hit him thick and fast now. The preceptor had suppressed the Greek Church on Cyprus. He'd driven the island to revolt and had no qualms about butchering countless citizens. Why would he care about those same imperial citizens just because they were in the capital? Bochard favoured the Franks. Of *course* he did. And realistically, many others in the Order would likely do the same. Bochard would not be able to understand why Ramon and Arnau favoured heretics over soldiers of the Church of Rome. A thorny problem. Not one to confront now, though.

Instead, he turned his attention to what was happening outside the city. If the preceptor was right, and the emperor could fight off the invasion today, this could be it. The saving of the city and the withdrawal of the Crusaders. Certainly Bochard's disappointment suggested it was more than a possibility.

Arnau's breath caught for a moment at what he saw.

The forces of Byzantium had issued forth. What seemed countless regiments of infantry and cavalry had emerged from the city to wage war. The Crusaders had committed a large force to the walls of the Blachernae, where they fought for control of the gate. Behind them, some distance from the defences, the bulk of the Frankish cavalry sat. During the assault they had been largely impotent, since noble knights preferred to stay in the saddle and not get their hands dirty, yet even the strongest cavalry were no use against a city wall. Thus, they had waited in support, perhaps halfway between the fight at the walls and their own camp.

The Byzantine army had split into two distinct units. One, bearing all the banners and colours of the emperor himself, was lined up facing the Frankish horse at perhaps a third of a mile distance. Arnau could see the second force further away, threatening the Crusaders' largely empty camp. There, the Byzantines were clearly enjoying great success ravaging behind the enemy's lines. He could see no banners, but it seemed certain that Theodoros Laskaris would be commanding there.

Arnau could imagine the havoc. Men would be scrambling to defend their tent city with whatever stores they could find – even frying pans. And the Crusaders could not rush to their aid. The men-at-arms were busy being committed at the Blachernae walls, and the cavalry were facing off against the emperor's force. If they raced off to save the camp, the emperor could fall upon the rear of the wall assault and annihilate the infantry. Thus all was in a dreadful stalemate close to the city, while Theodoros and his highly mobile force ruined their camp.

This was it. They could win. This was why the Venetians had withdrawn from their own assault: to come to the aid of the Franks, who were in dire straits, yet they would not arrive in time to do anything. All it would take was a little courage and not falling apart under pressure, and the emperor and his general could break the back of the Crusader siege.

Arnau found himself shivering, almost breathless, leaning on the parapet and willing the Byzantines to break the Franks. Almost as if the stalemate had gone on too long for all concerned, calls went up almost simultaneously from both the emperor's force and the Frankish cavalry.

Slowly, inexorably, the two forces began to move forward. Arnau tensed. The bulk of the Byzantine cavalry were with Laskaris at the Crusader camp, and if the Franks managed a full cavalry charge, it would all be down to how the Byzantine infantry dealt with it. They could hold and stand it, and if they did, the day should be theirs, but twice now the imperial forces had broken when confronted with the charge of the Frankish knights.

Arnau's gaze slid to that silvery tide of steel-clad Crusaders. They *were* fearsome. As fearsome even as the Warings in their way. They were Titans. They were…

'A strong man in the midst, that goeth before the host and is ready to fight against one of the enemies in singular battle, went out of the Philistines' tents, Goliath of Gath by name, of six cubits high and a span, and a brazen basinet on his head; and he was clothed with a mailed habergeon, and the weight of his habergeon was five thousand shekels of brass. And he had on his thighs brazen boots, and a brazen shield covered his shoulders. Forsooth the shaft of his spear was as the beam of webs and the iron of his spear weighed six hundred shekels of iron.'

Ramon turned to him.

'A Frankish Goliath? Then the emperor is your David?'

Arnau trembled a little. 'I hope so. I hope Doukas is wrong about him.'

They watched the two armies converging, knowing that this confrontation could end the siege entirely. Ramon suddenly let out an explosive breath and pointed furiously into the distance. 'There. See? Laskaris comes to his aid.'

The second force, speedy and strong and formed largely of cavalry, had broken off from ravaging the enemy camp and was now racing back towards the two armies closing on one another. Arnau glanced to his right, down the slope to the Blachernae. The fighting there had slowed, the bulk of both forces paying more attention to what was happening on the field outside the city, knowing full well how important that clash was.

'Come on, Laskaris,' urged Ramon, hammering his fist on the battlements. Arnau saw that Bochard was watching them both with hawk-like eyes. The preceptor did not want the emperor to succeed, clearly, though he could hardly shout as much here, amid the Byzantine defenders on the tower top.

They continued to watch. Laskaris and his men came ever closer. The two armies were almost within bowshot of one another now and still the Crusaders had not yet broken into a charge. Arnau shook his head in wonder. The Franks *should* have charged by now. They would be too late. He felt a small ripple of elation flow through him. The two forces were too close now for the Frankish cavalry to charge properly. They couldn't do it. And the Byzantines were about to have their numbers bolstered.

They were going to win.

Arnau watched the Frankish horse moving with uncertainty. Several different divisions, flying the flags of various lords, were only moving forward because their fellows were doing so. They were doing it all wrong, playing into the emperor's hands.

Then, to make matters worse for the Crusaders, one of their lords suddenly broke from the force and turned his division, hurrying back to guard their flanks from the coming cavalry of Laskaris. The Frankish advance faltered. They still came on but slower. Less certain.

'They have them,' Ramon said quietly. 'Laskaris will break their flank, and they cannot charge now. Their commanders are at odds and the argument has ruined the day for them.'

Arnau nodded, watching with barely contained delight as Laskaris urged his second force to new speed, racing for the Crusaders' flank and the single division of horse settling in to face them.

Calls went up.

The Crusader force came to a shuddering halt.

Arnau found himself hammering the battlements with his fist. It was coming. The Crusaders had stopped. They were afraid. Unsure. Ready to break.

Then the imperial force halted too, amid new calls.

Arnau stared in astonishment.

'What is he doing?' he breathed.

Bochard gestured down to the Golden Horn beyond them. The Venetian fleet were visible now, offloading their personnel, who were forming up to come to the Franks' aid.

'The emperor is afraid of facing them with Venetian strength in support,' the preceptor declared.

Ramon shook his head. 'No. He thinks his job is done. He rode out to threaten the enemy and pull the Venetians away from the walls, and it's worked. He's saved the sea walls. But he can win this. If he fights, he can break the Franks before the Venetians reach them.'

Arnau was shaking his head. 'No, no, no, no. He can't stop now.'

But the emperor had done just that. New calls went up and the imperial force began to withdraw, still facing the Frankish horse. Arnau watched in utter dismay as the emperor pulled his army further and further back towards the gates close to where the Templars stood.

With his withdrawal, the atmosphere across the peninsula changed in a heartbeat. The Crusaders, close to panic only moments earlier, suddenly let out a victorious roar, jeering at the retreating Byzantines. Arnau's gaze flicked up to Laskaris's secondary force. Unprepared for the emperor's withdrawal, he had engaged the Frankish horse. Even now, the Byzantine cavalry were butchering Crusaders, but while the fight was hard pressed, Theodoros's signaller was already blaring the call to retreat.

The cavalry broke off their attack at the last possible moment and raced away, those few light skirmishing troops with them running to keep up. Even as they fled, Franks were chasing them down, killing the slowest. The tables had turned and Laskaris, about to utterly rout the Franks, had instead been forced to flee lest he find his smaller force facing immeasurable odds without the emperor's army.

Arnau watched, lost and downhearted as both Byzantine forces raced for the walls and the safety of the city. The Venetians were cheering now, loud enough to hear even from such a distance, and the Frankish assault on the Blachernae Gate had redoubled in its ferocity.

An opportunity missed.

'The Lord, it seems, is with the Franks,' Bochard said in French with some satisfaction. 'Now perhaps you will cast aside your ridiculous notions and remember that you are brothers of the Temple and servants of the Church of Rome, just like those Franks on the hill. Clean yourselves up and go pray for your salvation, you fools.'

With a heavy heart, the other three Templars turned their backs on the retreating Byzantines and made their way back along the wall to the Blachernae. With a sense of defying the preceptor in the smallest of ways, both knights and the squire made extensive use of the bathhouse close to their accommodation, enjoying the hedonistic luxury of the Byzantine institution that Bochard considered heretical and decadent.

It was over an hour before the three returned to their apartments, their newly scrubbed clothing dripping wet and displaying the stains of battle despite their best efforts. They entered the common room, dressed in simple white habits, to find Doukas and the Waring called Redwald waiting for them. Swiftly hanging their drenched clothes over a balcony, they crossed to greet the 'prisoner'.

'You'll know what happened, of course,' Ramon said quietly, taking a seat.

Doukas nodded. 'It is inevitable with the Angelid dynasty in command. I warned you that they would be the downfall of the empire. The fight goes on at the gate, though there is little chance of the Franks taking control there. The city remains safe for now, but for how long?'

'I'm not sure *safe* is the correct word,' Arnau argued. 'Much of it seems to be burning.'

Doukas nodded. 'It is a dangerous fire, but this city has survived many fires. It will be stopped eventually. The real trouble is that Alexios has lost his one chance of victory. Now the city once more languishes under the threat of violence, waiting for the next push from the Franks and their Venetian allies.'

'What will the emperor do next?'

Doukas laughed mirthlessly. 'If he has any sense at all, he will put a blade through his chest like a failed general of old. His future is bleak.'

Arnau frowned. 'He is still the emperor.'

'Not for long,' Doukas said quietly. 'Already every noble tongue in the court wags against him. He had a chance to prove himself to them and instead he failed utterly. The imperial court is unforgiving. I believe I have mentioned this before. Men have met their ends in the most dreadful ways for failures such as this. Even emperors. Strangled with a bowstring, blinded and castrated, hands and arms hacked off, beheading, burning, stoning and dismembering, even beaten to death with a bucket. My own distant cousin the emperor Andronikos Komnenos met a particularly repulsive fate when I was fifteen summers old.'

Arnau shuddered as Doukas elaborated with grisly glee.

'Had his teeth, eyes and hair pulled out. He was submerged in boiling water, hung by the feet and then torn apart. I remember watching it all in the hippodrome. No, my friends, it doesn't do for an emperor to fail. Already men will be plotting his end.'

Ramon's lip curled in distaste, and Arnau felt faintly queasy at the notion. He'd seen plenty of death and wounding in his time, and the punishment of criminals and sinners in brutal manners. He'd even seen a man burned once. But nothing like the inventiveness of the Byzantines.

Doukas left shortly after delivering his gruesome history lesson, throughout which Redwald the Angle had sat stony-faced. Then Ramon and Arnau drank more than their expected single cup of wine, and their prayers during the liturgical services throughout that day, even when news came that the attack on the gate had ended and the Franks withdrawn, were more fervent than usual. Notably, Sebastian no longer joined them, having sought the company of his fellow Byzantines in the Blachernae's church. Another step away from the Order, Arnau suspected.

The following morning, as they returned from prime, the light of the morning sun beginning to illuminate the higher roofs and towers of the city, Doukas made his next visit, filled with urgent news.

'The emperor is gone.'

'What?' Ramon frowned as he picked a grape from a plate and popped it hungrily in his mouth.

'The coward Alexios fled during the night, knowing, I imagine, what was coming. He took his wife and his mistress, his favourite daughter and half a dozen pretty concubines, along with enough gold to bury an elephant, and boarded a ship in secret. He has been gone from the city for hours. All is chaos.'

'What next, then?' Arnau said quietly, trying to imagine what must have gone through the desperate emperor's head.

'A council of nobles met first thing to decide what to do.'

'And?'

'And the fools turned to his predecessor,' spat Redwald, breaking his usual silence with unrestrained anger. 'Alexios had a readymade heir in Theodoros Laskaris. The man is married to the emperor's daughter, after all. But no, they turn to the old blind fool.'

Doukas gave his guard a sympathetic smile. 'Redwald here, being bound in service to the emperor, likes his commander to be worthy.' He sighed. 'Laskaris would have been a good choice, I will admit. He might well be able to turn this around yet and drive off the Franks. But Isaac...'

He made uncertain motions with his hand.

'Isaac is another Angelos,' growled Redwald. 'So inept that he was blinded specifically to *prevent* him ever regaining his throne. How can I serve a blind madman?'

Ramon sighed. 'I can only apologise for this, Doukas, but I fear our time here must end. We must find the preceptor and arrange to leave.'

The political prisoner gave a short bark of a laugh. 'I can hardly condemn you, sir knight. Indeed, I am inclined to ask that you take me with you.' He smiled sadly. 'But no. This is my city, and no matter what happens, I will stay with her to the end.'

Redwald gave his prisoner a nod of approval and stood beside him. It had not struck Arnau until then how the Waring seemed always more of a bodyguard to his charge than a jailor. But then Doukas seemed to be considerably brighter than many of the courtiers, so perhaps that was not too much of a surprise.

When Doukas had left the apartment, Ramon folded his arms. 'We must persuade Bochard to leave. If what we hear about this Isaac is true, his hold on power here will be even more tenuous than Alexios's. I foresee the Franks getting their way. Their young pretender is the closest thing to a legitimate emperor here now.'

Arnau nodded unhappily, remembering the preening youth dressed as a Western prince aboard that Venetian ship. Somehow Arnau could picture him on the throne in a way that ended well.

CHAPTER 11:
THE BLIND FOOL

AUGUST 1ST 1203

'How desperate does a city need to be to make a blind madman their emperor?' Arnau sighed.

Ramon snorted. 'You saw the alternative. That pomped-up child the Franks keep parading around. Can you imagine *him* ruling the city?'

'No more than a shell of a blind man who's been made insane by years of incarceration. The choice should have been Laskaris. We all know it. Everyone knows it. Heavens, but he was even the coward Alexios's chosen heir!'

'And that is why he is unacceptable to the nobles, Vallbona, even if they know he's best for the city. They cannot bring themselves to support Alexios's choice, and so they turn to the man who had opposed him: his brother Isaac.'

'Every step this city takes is one determined pace further into the maw of hell,' Arnau grunted bitterly.

Ramon could not argue, and nodded sadly.

Whatever the older knight had planned to say next, he fell silent at a knock on the door. Inviting their visitor inside, the two men relaxed at the sight of Doukas, wearing his robe of office. If there was one positive Arnau could make out about the flight of the emperor and the reinstatement of blind Isaac, it was that Doukas had been released from his custody. Having never stood against Isaac Angelos, he had been given his freedom and, because of his obvious intellect, had even been promoted to the position of finance minister. It made Arnau smile a little to note that the burly Waring guardsman, Redwald, remained at Doukas's shoulder at all times, though now as a guard rather than a jailor.

'Minister, it is good to see you. I thought you would have little time for social visits in your new role.'

Doukas smiled. 'Life has become more than a little busy, for certain, my friends. The city is not wealthy these days. Generations of mismanagement under certain grasping rulers and greedy councillors has left the treasury depleted. The true financial blood of Constantinopolis has always been mercantilism, and if we are to regain control, we must foster and nurture that trade. But with the city surrounded by enemies as it is, trade is in a rapid decline where we need it to grow. It is a troublesome situation and I bend every effort to solving the problem, but my fiscal worries were not what brought me here this morning. I came to deliver the latest tidings. I know that unless I do so, no one else in this benighted place will talk to you. In truth I was surprised to learn that you were still here at all. I would have assumed that your preceptor would wish to depart with haste.'

'The preceptor is up to something,' grunted Arnau, earning a sharp warning look from Ramon, who cut in.

'Preceptor Bochard does not believe he has fully accomplished his task here yet.'

'His task? I thought he was here to elicit promises from the emperor?' Doukas's face, and an odd twinkle in his eye, plainly suggested that he knew a lot more than that was going on.

'Yes,' Ramon said blandly, 'and that failed, but now there is a different emperor on the throne. Bochard cannot leave without at least attempting to achieve his goals for the grand master.'

Doukas sighed. 'His plan is futile, I'm afraid, if indeed securing alliances *is* his plan. The new emperor is in no better a position to grant that which you desire, and in his current mood, he is much less likely to be inclined to negotiate.'

'He is mad?' Arnau said.

This time, Doukas shot him the look of warning. 'Saying such things about the emperor is both illegal and foolish. You would do well to watch your words, no matter how incisive they may be.'

A confirmation, then. Arnau turned his gaze on Ramon, who gave an almost imperceptible shake of the head.

'The news, then?'

Doukas nodded. 'The emperor is keenly aware of how precarious his position remains, though he cannot afford to show any weakness. This is a problem, as you can imagine. To consolidate his reign, the fugitive Alexios Angelos the Third has been made an outcast and an enemy of the empire. He will find no succour throughout our lands. His wife has been arrested, though her fate is as yet undecided.'

Ramon nodded slowly. 'Unfortunate and unpleasant, though also predictable.'

'The problem facing us now remains the Franks and Venetians. The emperor, upon his accession, sent a message to their leaders, Dandolo and Montferrat. He sought terms for their lifting of the siege, given that the emperor who defied them so openly has now gone.'

'I cannot imagine their terms are any more acceptable now,' Ramon murmured.

'Quite so. Dandolo has hated the empire since the day he was blinded in this very palace for transgressions against the state.'

Arnau and Ramon shared a startled look. No wonder the Venetians were so rabid.

'Their reply was flat,' Doukas went on. 'Their original terms remain, with one alteration. They have demanded all the payments that they have been promised by their pet exile, which, I might add, currently amount to around six times the entire financial wealth of the city. They have called for the patriarch to step down and the Church to submit to the rule of the Roman Pope. They have demanded that young Alexios out there be crowned as emperor, though they have offered to have him share the throne in joint rule with Isaac, for after all, they *are* father and son.'

'A blind fool and a puppet of the Franks sharing the throne,' Arnau spat, this time receiving that warning look from all the room's occupants. He shook his head and went on. 'That will be unacceptable, surely? It would be the death knell for the city. And while I cannot in conscience complain about the overlordship of the Pope, for I feel that unity of our faiths could only strengthen Christendom, I cannot see it being popular in the city. Worse still, bankrupting Byzantium to pay off the Venetians.' He glanced at Sebastian who wore a sour look at the very idea. His connections to the Church of Rome through the Order were weakening daily these days, yet somehow, despite that, he still felt closer to Arnau than their master.

Ramon took a deep breath. 'His mouth runneth over, but with wise words. Doukas, the city cannot accept this. It will put Montferrat and Dandolo effectively in control of the empire.'

Doukas sighed. 'The response is currently being considered by the council of nobles, and despite the unacceptability of the deal, I am uncertain as to the outcome. Many nobles of the empire think far more of their personal comfort and wealth than of public service or the health of the Church. Such men could prosper under a new regime, for their private fortunes would likely remain untouched if they support the Franks and their position would become more secure. Honourable voices like those of the Laskaris could well be drowned out by an avalanche of avarice.'

'When will the answer be given?'

Doukas shrugged. 'That depends entirely upon how long the nobles argue. I have stated my case for a refusal and left them to it. I will be warned of their decision once it is made, though, and will pass on the news as soon as I have it.'

Ramon nodded. 'Thank you for letting us know all this. It is good to see that there are still men like yourself in power. Let us hope you can sway the fools.'

Doukas nodded and turned, leaving the room. Redwald fixed Arnau with an inscrutable look for a long moment, and then followed his master. As the door clicked shut behind them, Ramon frowned at Arnau. 'No matter how correct you might be, think ahead on what might be prudent before you flap your lips, Vallbona.'

'Doukas agrees with us.'

'And even *he* warned you. Bear in mind that the Angle Redwald is one of the emperor's own guards, no matter how close he might appear to Doukas. Just be careful.'

Arnau sighed and flopped back. 'What was that you were telling him about the preceptor? He's said nothing of the sort to me.'

Ramon sucked air in through his teeth and rolled his shoulders. 'Thinking on my feet. I think we both know what Bochard is up to, but I could hardly tell Doukas that we weren't leaving until the preceptor has raped the city of any relic of value. I cannot imagine that going down well.'

'You lied?' Falsehoods were very strongly frowned upon by the Order.

'I made assumptions. What I said makes perfect sense, and if negotiation is our prime purpose for being in the city as the preceptor maintains, then what I said is almost certainly true. If it is not true, that is because Bochard is lying himself. I am only false if Bochard also lies.'

Arnau sighed again. 'What will happen if they accept the terms?'

Ramon shrugged. 'Latin control. The suppression of the Eastern Church and its gradual integration into the Church of Rome. Poverty and distress, for to meet the financial arrangements they will have to tear coins from the hands of every citizen. But they will have peace and the city will survive. The question that must be asked is whether that is worth the price they will pay.'

Sebastian was shaking his head, a sentiment with which Arnau agreed entirely.

'Peace at such a cost?' Arnau shook his head. 'And already an area of the city lies in ashes since that last attack. Surely that will gird them to further defiance?'

'To the common man it might have entirely the opposite effect,' Ramon noted.

'And if they refuse and hold out?'

The older knight shrugged. 'Then it depends upon whether men like Laskaris can continue to lead a strong defence and hold until the winter drives the Franks away, or whether weak men will continue to fritter away what chances they have. The result is far from certain. Whatever the case the city will, I am sure, become more and more troubled in the coming days. I have half a mind to have it out with Bochard once more and attempt to turn him to departure.'

'He won't go.'

'No.' Ramon shook his head. 'I don't think so either.'

'How long is it until sext?' Arnau asked wearily.

Ramon glanced out of the window, looking up into the deep blue filled with the whirling shapes of birds, trying not to dwell on the distant looming shape of the Crusader camp below.

'Less than an hour. I will prepare shortly. We should by rights be using our time wisely to practise or clean our weapons.'

'Sebastian has our weapons and armour in perfect condition, and I think we're getting plenty of weapons practice,' he added wryly. 'Fancy a walk out? Think I'd like to take a look at what's happening across the water before we head to the Pisan church.'

Ramon shook his head. 'I think I'm going to wait here in the hope of news from the council. If I hear nothing, I will meet you at the church in time for sext.'

Arnau nodded and strapped his sword to his side. For a moment he contemplated gathering up his shield and helmet, but decided against them. Saying farewell to Ramon and pulling his white cloak around him he left the room, allowing the door to clunk shut behind him. He glanced momentarily to the right at Bochard's apartment. There was no sign of movement and no sound. Presumably the preceptor was once more out and about his seemingly nefarious business. Arnau gritted his teeth. Years of service to the Order had changed him. Learning, serving and fighting alongside men like Balthesar and Ramon had opened his eyes to the base levels of goodness and wickedness in the world and the fact that the two did not always correlate with whether or not a man bent his knee to the Pope. But what it had done most was convince him of the rightness and goodness of the Order. Men like the preceptor, he felt, did nothing to promote the image of the Poor Knights of Christ.

A secretive, untruthful and possibly even larcenous brother?

Lip fluttering in anger, he turned his back on Bochard's door and marched out of their small area of the palace complex. He frowned as he emerged into the courtyard. In months of residence here, he had found Waring guardsmen either waiting in a small chamber near their rooms or at least out here. Now there were none in sight. Actually, that was not strictly true. He could see the big northerners here and there, moving up stairs or through doorways or strolling along parapets alongside more mundane city soldiers. But no small group stood waiting for him.

As a burly mailed man with golden braids hanging from his steel coif strolled past, axe hooked over his shoulder, Arnau gestured to him. The big man frowned as he paused.

'Yes?' he said in thickly barbarous Greek.

'We usually have a Waring escort.'

The man shrugged. 'New emperor. New rules. All assignments outside the imperial person and palace and court protection have been withdrawn. Sorry, little man.'

Arnau was too busy being surprised at their loss of Waring support to bother being offended at being addressed thus, and watched the blond northerner stride off to his duties. He still had access to parts of the palace and city even without the imperial guards, for each of the visiting Templars carried a small document bearing the imperial seal and granting them certain privileges. It would have to do.

How long before those were withdrawn by the new emperor too, he wondered?

He strolled through the palace grounds and corridors, relishing the sizzling play of hot summer sunshine on his face every bit as much as the respite of cool, shady interiors. The hum of city life joined that of bees and of birds, and it was difficult at times to remember just how troubled imperial life was right now. Emerging at one of the lower gates in the boundary wall of the Blachernae palace complex, Arnau nodded amiably at a man in a coat of shining plates with a tall pike. The man nodded back, uncertainly. A quick proffering of the document, a scan through it and a nod, and the gate was opened to allow Arnau out into the city.

Here the palace walls were particularly tall and impressive at the lower slopes of the Sixth Hill. The retaining wall at their base was hugely thick and formed at an angle against the hill, with the more decorative work with its arches and windows, and finally the battlements, rising some thirty feet above him, towering over the lower city and the Golden Horn.

The street that ran around these walls had been left deliberately wide, some twenty paces between the palace walls and the buildings facing them. In the West such a decision would have been made for military and security reasons. Here, Arnau suspected, it had more to do with propriety and aesthetics.

He strolled out across the wide street and at the far side began to descend the hill towards the walls stretching along the waterfront. It was only as he was closing on the defences that he remembered he was lacking the usual Waring Guard escort. He reached a doorway and knocked. When a Byzantine soldier with a suspicious face opened up with a mace in hand, Arnau held out his papers and asked politely whether he might be permitted to climb the walls and view the water. It came as no real surprise, but a little disappointment, when the soldier flatly refused his request and closed the door on him. It seemed that without the support of the Warings, he was of little import to the soldiery of Byzantium.

With a sigh he turned away from the walls and strode on through the city, making for the Pisan enclave and the church where they habitually attended all the services in the Litany of the Hours. For a short stretch of his journey he moved back inland from the walls, strolling along a narrow backstreet. He paused to buy an apple from a stall, and crunched upon it as he strode under the clear, warm azure sky. For a moment, things seemed less terrible…

His heart lurched as he rounded a corner and was treated to a bleak vision of hell.

The street turned where it had once marched back downhill a short way and emerged close to the walls, but as Arnau rounded the corner, he saw no such vista. Instead, what his eyes fell upon was the aftermath of the Venetian assault.

Two houses down from the corner the buildings ended in a pile of blackened rubble. From there, he could see clearly across a vast swathe of the city, almost to the Pisan enclave for which he was bound. He realised now why Ramon had led them to every service since the attack along the hilltops and past the great church. He had been skirting the huge blackened field of destruction.

For the better part of a mile, nothing had been spared by the inferno. Here and there the brittle bones of churches and a few other rare stone or brick buildings rose like imploring arms above the blackness, pleading to heaven to be put out of their misery. Most of the area, however, had been almost entirely rendered down to ash and charred beams, the majority of housing and shops being of timber construction. It was impossible even to identify where streets had been. So utter was the destruction that even the wildlife was avoiding the place – there were no scavengers amid the ash and no carrion birds resting on the jutting remains. The charnel field was quieter than the grave, stretching out into the distance across the city, and reaching almost from the sea walls up to the crest of the hill.

Arnau tottered to a halt, staring in horror at the ruination of a huge portion of the city.

'Lord, forgive us all,' he whispered.

This had been the outcome of the fight at the walls. As the Venetians had fled up the water to support their Frankish allies, Arnau had cheered. He had felt elated, as though they had won such a profound victory, keeping the crafty doge and his men out of the city. Now he was being forced to acknowledge the cost of their victory. How many men, women and children had perished in this immense conflagration? How many had lost their houses and their livelihoods? How many ordinary, God-fearing folk who had no say in what their empire did had perished?

Faced with this spectacle, he found himself reassessing what he had said back in the palace.

Peace at such a cost? Surely that will gird them to further defiance?

Was it unreasonable to believe that the people who had gone through this nightmare might be willing to pay almost any price to prevent a recurrence?

Lowering his gaze, he closed his eyes and lifted his hand, folding his fourth and fifth fingers back and tracing the sign of the cross with the remaining three representing the Trinity. In low, reverent tones, he began to pray for the welfare of all those whose lives had been touched by this dreadful tragedy.

Arnau's prayer tailed off, the words scattering into the barely noticeable breeze as he lurched in surprise when something bounced off his shoulder. Deep, thumping pain began immediately to course through the joint. Something had struck him hard enough to bruise badly. Had he not had the benefit of a chain shirt beneath the cloak, the blow might well have broken his shoulder.

He saw a brick rattling to a stop amid the ashes in front of him and turned sharply, trying to identify his assailant, for it had to have been a deliberate act. The angle at which it rolled to rest indicated it had come from behind him, not above.

He felt his pulse quicken. Three men stood in the street behind him. One had another chunk of rock in his hand. Another brandished a short blade, while the third held a hefty length of ash. His alert gaze took in the rest of his surroundings. There was nowhere to go other than past them along the street, or back across that huge and treacherous swathe of ash and rubble where any number of obstacles could be hidden beneath the veil of grey.

Damn it.

One of the men said something to his companions and Arnau missed much of it, though he caught the word 'Frank'.

Damn it, damn it, damn it. Here he was in a city of Byzantines dressed as a Crusader, more or less. How could he not have anticipated this sort of trouble? For the first time since joining the Order, he truly regretted the red cross emblazoned on his chest and shoulder. For him they represented his place as one of the Poor Knights of Christ and his devotion to the Lord and his Church.

To the locals, they represented the horde of savage invaders who had assaulted their walls, killed their fellow citizens and burned down a huge swathe of their city.

Damn it.

'I am not what you think,' he began, holding up his hands in a gesture of peace.

'Fuck off,' snapped one of the three men, an oath punctuated with violence as his friend let fly with his half-brick.

Arnau ducked urgently to the left as the missile whooshed through the air beside him and clattered to a halt amid the destruction behind. Still he kept his hand away from his sword hilt. 'Listen, I'm not a Frank. Templar. See? Templar. I fought with—'

His speech was clearly having no effect, for the three men snarled and shouted and advanced on him, weapons brandished. Arnau noted with some disappointment how the few people in the street behind the men were nodding their agreement and showed little indication of any intention to intervene. He was on his own.

He sized the three up as they stomped slowly towards him, spreading out a little as they came. He could probably manage to overcome them. He had a long sword with a good reach, while they were poorly armed, and they were likely street thugs at best, entirely untrained civilians more realistically. But there was a nagging doubt floating around at the back of his mind. He and his brethren were here under the sufferance of the emperor and his court. If one of the Templars were known to have killed or injured three citizens, how would the court react? He remembered vividly the tales of torturous methods of execution Doukas had listed. And it would be self-defence, for sure, but with the only witnesses clearly sharing the attitude of the three attackers, of what value was Arnau's word?

'I have no wish to hurt anyone,' he tried at last. Still they came on.

Arnau, unsure how best to proceed, stepped a few paces back among the ash and charred timbers. What non-lethal weapon could he employ? His searching eyes played around the ruins, but came up hopeless. There were few items in the wreckage a man could wield, and those he could would be so charred and weak they would break on impact without causing any real harm.

With a deep breath, he unfastened his sword belt and lifted it, still stepping gingerly back to buy time from the advancing citizens. Unthreading the belt, he let it fall away into the ash and lifted the sword, its leather and iron scabbard still covering the blade. It would still cause wounds, but at least not such brutal ones. It was the best he could do.

'See? I do not want to kill.'

His words fell upon deaf ears. The bricks cast, the three men now had one short blade and two wooden cudgels. He had to deal with the blade first. The three had spread out, and the outer two were pacing slightly faster now, moving to surround him. A quick flick of the eyes backwards and he spotted one of the rare survivals of a brick wall, little more than five feet high, close by. Praying he wouldn't stumble over something underfoot, he steadily backed away towards the wall fragment.

It was an immense relief when he felt his back touch the blackened bricks. The three men were advancing slower now, watching their footing.

He found himself recalling all those times he had found himself on his backside in the dust with Brother Lütolf's blade at his throat. Don't do anything impulsively. Leave no tells for them. Concentrate and move decisively. This was not battle.

This was a duel, just with more than one opponent. He cleared his mind, breathing slowly.

'Dread I not them, for the Lord our God shall fight with me,' he said quietly. 'Deuteronomy.'

He kept his gaze on the central man, but allowed his eyes to defocus just slightly, increasing his peripheral alertness. The man with the sword was to his left. The blade was wavering. He was coming in for a blow at the earliest opportunity. The one in the middle looked a little nervous. He knew he was directly facing Arnau, and by now they must have seen the chain shirt he wore amid the white and red. Good. Nerves would make him slow and hesitant.

He gripped his sword hilt tight, sheathed blade horizontal across his midriff, still staring at the man in the middle. They closed. His anticipation paid off immediately and in the last moment he thanked his departed German brother for all his lessons. The nervous one in front was hanging back a little. The other two were coming in for a strike.

Arnau attacked.

His sword suddenly lashed out towards the man on his right with a short club. The swing was enough to make the man lurch back, which was all Arnau had hoped for, as his sheathed sword continued through the swing, towards his left. There, the man with the blade was taken completely by surprise. The leather scabbard, weighted with the steel blade within, struck the man's arm with an audible crack and the attacker shrieked, that shining blade falling from his grasp.

A broken arm. Bad enough.

The man backed away, crying in pain, clutching his arm.

Arnau's attention flitted back to the other two. The man he'd feinted towards was in trouble. He had lurched back from the expected blow and had fallen over something in the wreckage. As Arnau turned towards him, he was floundering in a cloud of ash, shouting angrily and trying to stand.

The nervous man in the centre had swallowed his fear, though, perhaps in the realisation that he was now in a win-or-lose situation. Arnau tried to bring his sword back to bear, but the man got there first, his length of ash smashing forward.

Arnau felt the tip of the club coming for his chest and tried to duck back with the blow and rob it of much of its strength, but he was too close to the wall. His back hit the brick just as the cudgel struck his torso. The mail shirt did much of the job of defence, but he felt a rib crack with a fiery pain that spread across his chest. Roaring angrily, he swiped out with his sheathed sword and caught his assailant on the side of the head. The man spun away in a mizzle of red, jaw probably broken. As he collapsed into the dust, the third man was up again.

Arnau was struggling now to control his temper, wincing at the pain in his chest. Damn these fools. He was one of the few men actually trying to *save* them! Before he realised he was doing it, he had ripped his sword from its sheath and was holding the gleaming blade towards the grey-coated figure.

'Do you really want to do this?' he gasped angrily, free hand against the pain in his ribs.

The man answered him in a heartbeat, dropping his club and fleeing across the wreckage, careless of obstacles underfoot. The man with the broken arm was gone too, almost back at the street.

Arnau sighed and bent. He yelped in pain as the movement made his rib hurt as though it had broken all over again. Gritting his teeth, he gathered up his shcath and grumbled at the state of it. Coated in black crud. Gripping both it and his sword in his left hand, he braced himself against the pain and reached down, grasping the arm of the man still down there and sobbing.

With a great deal of effort and no small amount of pain, he helped the man to his feet. The attacker reached up and tested his jaw. It had not broken after all, but by God it must hurt. The man made some muffled, pained attempt at speech, then shook himself free of Arnau's grip and backed away as fast as he could.

The young Templar watched in pained silence for some time as his assailants melted away into the city and the witnesses disappeared indoors, leaving him alone with charred ruins and an empty street. At least he hadn't been *in* this fire. That made a change, at least.

With a sigh, he scoured the ash for his discarded sword belt, considering how he would apologise to Sebastian for undoing all his attention to the equipment. Then, with a deep breath, he began the journey to safety.

Back at the Blachernae, after a tense and nerve-racking trek through the streets, he related his encounter to Ramon, who had been about to set out for the sext service. Instead, Ramon helped him to the palace's resident doctor, who labelled Arnau's wound 'non-threatening', cleaned him up and bound him with lengths of linen. He was given some powdered herb or other to mix into wine for the pain and otherwise left alone. In the continuing absence of Bochard, Arnau spent the next few hours lying in his room, occasionally yelping and wincing, and eventually drifted off to sleep. When he stirred it was dark, and his waking had been caused by Ramon opening the door, remaining silhouetted there in the square of light.

'Brother?'

'Good,' Ramon replied. 'You're awake.'

'How long...'

'Long enough. The nobles have voted to accept the Franks' terms. The Crusaders have won. Their deputations are in the city now, and there will be two emperors, the young pretender crowned alongside his father. The Greek Church will be no more and Dandolo will have his money by hook or by crook.'

Arnau sagged. 'We fought for nothing.'

'We fought for what was right and for our conscience, Vallbona. That is never a mistake. And while we are seemingly bound to remain for a time, Doukas has pledged to have Warings assigned to us once more to prevent a repeat of your little misadventure.'

As Ramon left him in peace, Arnau sighed and tried not to move in case it hurt.

That was it, then. Byzantium was now under the control of the Crusaders.

CHAPTER 12:
THE BLOOD MONEY

AUGUST 11TH 1203

It was over... and yet it also so very clearly was not.
Over.
From this vantage point on the walls close to the so-called 'Golden Gate', Arnau could only see the south-western area of the city which was mostly given over to cultivation and dotted with monasteries and small private estates, and the wide grasslands stretching west outside the walls towards Thrace and Greece.

Here was the great decorative three-arch triumphal gate with the shining golden doors through which victorious emperors returned to the city. Here was one of the focal points of imperial power and grandeur. That gate said as much as anything in the city that the emperor of Byzantium was untouchable and powerful and ruled with God-given right.

Which was why it was so heart-sickening to see the new young co-emperor astride his Frankish warhorse and accompanied by steel-clad Westerners in bright colourful surcoats leaving the city on a tour of his provinces. Perhaps half a dozen sycophantic and hopeful noblemen were with him, and Doukas, in his capacity as finance minister, all accompanied by only four Waring guardsmen, for it seemed that the newly crowned Alexios the Fourth trusted little in his imperial guard and far more in his Frankish friends.

The tour was ostensibly to bring troubled cities and regions back under imperial control, and the force of Byzantine cavalry outside the walls awaiting them backed up that notion, though the fiscal situation in the city and the presence of Doukas in the party made it clear what it truly was: a tax-gathering army. Having squeezed the city until it bled silver to pay the Venetian debt, the new emperor was now taking soldiers into the hinterland to bleed them too.

Over.

And the heavy taxation of town and country was not the only reason for the presence of Franks in the city. Arnau couldn't see them from here, in this more cultivated, less built-up area, but back to the northern side of the city and towards the promontory, where the urban mass lay thickly packed, no street seemed to be devoid of armoured Westerners stomping around and making their superiority known. Having been unable to take Constantinople by force, they had finally gained the city with just demands and threats, and now they were avenging their losses during the earlier struggle by making the citizens' lives a misery, taking property without payment, ignoring age-old laws and causing violence and misery wherever they went.

Over.

The priests among the Crusader army had been around the city's churches, knocking the heretical second and third cross piece from every crucifix, confiscating their holy books as unacceptable and replacing them with Bibles written in Latin, which was completely incomprehensible to the local priests. Vows had been forced from people and Frankish and Italian priests had led compulsory masses in open spaces to introduce the city to how it was now expected to worship. Sebastian had been understandably torn in his support, born as he was to the Byzantine world, but a willing convert to Rome in recent years. Perhaps, in some ways, this was a balm to the young man's soul. An end to the conflict that had been tearing him in two since they arrived. A Venetian priest had even been installed in the city as the patriarch, the old one being kicked out to learn his new faith in a monastery. In some ways, Arnau felt sick over that. Had it been a Frank, he might have been able to accept it more readily, but the Venetians en masse had been excommunicated. Even if this priest had not been, his loyalty and motives had to be considered highly suspect at least. The more Arnau learned about the sea dogs, the more he came to the conclusion that greed alone drove them, and that at the peak of that greed sat Dandolo, using it to steer his people on a track of personal revenge.

Over.

Men like Constantine and Theodoros Laskaris had retreated from their true places in open council, biding their time, unwilling to deal with the enemy leaders as they rewrote the entire culture of Byzantium. Those who made the laws now and administered the empire were those living in the purses of Frankish nobles.

Over.

While the new young emperor drained every coin he found from the city to pay the Venetian doge his blood money, his father, the blind Isaac, simmered in his chambers. He had put in few public appearances. It was said among courtiers that he was ashamed to show his blinded, ruined eyes in public, given the reason for his blinding in the first place. It was said more widely that the ruined man was a quivering wreck, wholly insane and bitter from his years of incarceration. Likely in truth it was both. Whatever the reason, the only man who might have the authority and strength to champion his city's survival was less than useless, and his son actively promoted its ruination.

Over.

And yet it so very clearly was not. Arnau had realised that within days of the silent conquest. The nobles might fawn over their new lords, and the emperor cower in his rooms. The army might submit as expected, and the Warings live up to their vow and obey their new mad emperor. But the people of Byzantium were not done. They suffered the humiliation and violence of their Frankish visitors, but Arnau could see the defiance in every eye. He never left the palace now without at least two Warings at his side – he had argued for the protection – for the atmosphere had changed in Constantinople. As if the day that the three men had attacked him for being a Westerner had been some sort of trigger, a malaise and aura of xenophobia had spread across the city entire. Silent, seething resentment clung to every door and wall, ran through the gutters and aqueducts, blossomed on the trees and settled in the morning air. It buzzed through the wildlife and rumbled along with the carts. It lapped at the shore and hummed as an undercurrent through the new popish songs warbling across the city.

The city waited, but it was not done.

Arnau saw it as a pot of bitter stew. The fire was burning beneath the iron, and the stew was bubbling. Every gobbet of phlegm spat from a Frankish mouth at a Byzantine citizen enhanced the flame. Every incident, every insult, every new restriction fanned those flames and brought the stew to the boil that little bit faster. Arnau could see it, and so could Ramon, as well as men like the Laskaris. What seemed unfathomable was that the Franks appeared to be entirely blind to the danger boiling up around them.

Not so the wily Venetians, mind. While the Franks strolled the city streets causing trouble, the Venetians remained with their fleet on the far side of the Golden Horn, encamped in their own safe little enclave. There they simply took the money being delivered to them in chests and waited. They might be damned by Rome for wicked thieves, but they were not stupid.

No, it was not over. It was just a matter of time.

The pot boiled.

Ramon stood beside him, watching the imperial force depart to squeeze money from the provinces, with Sebastian beyond them leaning on the parapet with a face like thunder. The young man had said little since that day he had fought the Venetians, but his face expressed enough. He felt much the same as any number of his countrymen. He would give every drop of blood in his body to bring down a curse from on high against these men who were oppressing and ruining his city.

Arnau was not surprised to realise that he shared that anger.

So did Ramon, though he was always more circumspect in what he showed publicly.

'The only question,' Arnau muttered over the rumble of carts and clop of horses leaving the city, 'is whether Byzantium will rebel in his absence or wait for his return. The prince might come back to find the gates shut against him.'

Ramon nodded. They continued to refer to the new co-emperor as 'the prince', an insult they had picked up from the Laskaris, who had refused privately to acknowledge his lordship over them, as had many good men who now waited quietly in the shadows for the next move.

'It cannot last more than a few months, maybe even weeks,' Ramon agreed. 'I can feel the city crouching, bunching its muscles, ready to rise once more. And this time, when it does, there will be no negotiation or quiet tolerance. It will be cataclysmic. The end of days for one force or the other.'

'Bochard is insane. You know that?'

The older brother turned to him, lacking his usual recrimination over such a remark.

'No, Arnau. Not insane. Dangerous, for certain, but not insane. He believes he is doing the right thing, and he is utterly focused on it. I cannot say precisely what, but he is clearly gathering relics, and that is hardly new for the Order. Moreover, he seems to be doing it on the grand master's orders. And whether we trust him or not, in fairness he has survived half a year of this city so far with nothing to show but success. The trouble we have met we have invited.'

'You don't think he's doing this for the Order, do you?' Arnau scoffed, turning away from the parapet and gesturing back north. 'Nor is he doing this for the grand master. He's doing this for himself. I worked it out a while back. He failed utterly on Cyprus. He was given a whole island to make part of the Order's territory, and he left a boiling, rebellious land of warring citizens, tearing down our red cross. He failed. And he's been living on the margins of the order ever since – a preceptor without a house to rule. A failure. And he's been given a task. It was probably even given to him as an afterthought to keep him busy and out of the way, but he sees it as a way to redeem himself. He thinks that if he brings great treasures back to the Order, it will erase his failures and make him a valued brother once more. You might not say he's insane, but I think I can happily apply that term.'

Ramon said nothing, which to Arnau felt like tacit agreement.

'Back to the palace?' he asked. The older brother nodded. Behind them four hulking Waring guardsmen in colourful leather and gleaming plates turned and shadowed them. Through poor rulers, insidious invasions, local grievances and siege warfare, the Warings were the only thing in the city upon which Arnau felt he could truly rely. No matter who ruled, they seemed utterly loyal and fearless. He respected their stance.

'We need to leave, Ramon,' he said quietly. 'More than ever we need to leave.'

Still nothing.

'Brother, when this pot boils over, what happened last month will look like a play-fight at a local fair. The next time conflict comes it will only end with Hell rising to the living world.'

'Do not say such things,' snapped Ramon.

'But that is what it will be like. We both know that. What Bochard went through on Cyprus will be nothing compared to this. If we stay in the city and the Franks win, we will just be five more bodies to ruin in the conquered city. Do you think they'll care that we wear the red cross? And if the Byzantines somehow win, against all odds, then we'll be in no less danger. Their leaders owe us nothing and will see us as the same as those men out there. We are sons of the Church of Rome. At best we can expect a knife in the dark. Ramon, we need to leave this city before the next rising.'

Again, that silence with its tacit agreement.

They strolled along the walls, heading the three miles back to the Blachernae. After a while, Sebastian broke the bitter silence.

'I will not be coming with you.'

'Brother,' Arnau began, but he had been half expecting this, in truth, and the young squire shook his head.

'I cannot leave. This is my city, my empire and my people. As long as the Franks remain a threat, I will hold my sword and defy them. If you stay, I shall stay as I vowed, by your sides, but if you leave, consider my involvement with the Temple done. I shall offer my sword to the Lords Laskaris. I will not leave Constantinopolis undefended.'

Ramon eyed him sidelong. 'You must do what you believe to be right, of course.'

They strode on in silence, the hot summer sun gradually making their chain shirts less and less comfortable, such that Arnau began to long for a simple white habit once more. They had packed away those habits now, though, certain that armour would be the order of the day for some time. They walked along the walls, watching Frankish horsemen practising on the grass beyond the city's wide moat, passing the last areas of farmed land inside the walls, past the monastery of the Holy Martyrs and the great Gate of Saint Romanus through which the previous emperor had led his failed attack. Finally, they crossed the shallow valley of the Lykos and climbed the Sixth Hill to the Blachernae.

As they approached, Sebastian silent and determined behind them, Arnau fixed Ramon with a look. His eyes bored into the older knight until they reached and entered the palace gate. Finally, clearly irritated by the glare, Ramon's head snapped round.

'All right. We will make one more appeal to the preceptor.'

Satisfied, Arnau turned his gaze back to the squire.

'Head to our apartments and wait there. We shall not be long.'

A short time later they were standing before Bochard's door. They had approached along the corridor, shushing and clanking with their armour and belted swords, and yet had clearly not been heard by the chamber's occupants, who were engaged in an argument. It seemed rare these days to find the preceptor in his room at all, let alone arguing with someone. They paused for some time, listening.

It was impossible to make out the details through the thick door, and Arnau surmised that the voices were probably in a far room of the apartment, but there were clearly demands being made and refused. When the argument finally ended, Ramon lifted his hand to rap on the door, but it swung open before he could do so and a man in a priest's robe left, his face thunderous. Arnau noted that though the man wore the red garment he had seen on so many Byzantine priests, a Western crucifix hung around his neck like a millstone. The young Templar frowned. He vaguely recognised the man, but couldn't recall where from.

As Ramon stood there with his knuckles ready to rap on the open door and the priest passed, throwing him a black look, Bochard appeared in the chamber beyond, his face puce once again, eyelid dancing.

'What do you want?' he snapped.

Ramon looked over his shoulder at Arnau. 'Bad time.'

'Do it anyway.'

They strode into the room, where the preceptor poured himself a cup of cold water and stood drinking it. Arnau couldn't help noticing how the cup shook in the man's hand and hoped it was down to the anger clearly coursing through him.

'Well?' Bochard demanded curtly.

'The war here is over, Preceptor. The Church of Rome is triumphant. The Franks will finish up here and sail on for Egypt as originally intended and the Venetians will leave, mollified by enough gold to sink their fleet. Whatever happens now is beyond our control. And with the Pope leading their Church and a man in the pocket of the Franks on their throne, the vows we sought to protect Christendom are rendered pointless. We have no ostensible reason to be here now. We should return to Acre and prepare to join the true expedition against the Saracen.'

'No.'

Ramon's fists bunched. 'All right. I was playing the fool's game there, Preceptor. Look around you. We are in the eye of a great storm. We've weathered the first blast, but the second will be worse. This isn't over and the city is going to rise against the Franks. When it does, this time we may not be so lucky. And the Order has no official involvement here. We *cannot* be here. We must leave before the real trouble begins.'

'No.'

'Then you owe us an explanation.'

'I owe you no such thing. 'Tis *you* who owes *me* obedience, as per the Rule of our order.'

'There have to be limits to such obedience. Would you obey the grand master if he told you to murder the Pope? Of course not. The Rule is there to instil order, not to force men of God into blind servitude. Believe me that I have no wish to disobey you, but we cannot risk remaining here and falling in with the chaos that is coming simply to facilitate your theft of icons.'

Bochard's face went from puce to white, as though all the blood had drained down through his neck. His eyes bulged.

'*How dare you*, de Juelle! I am a brother of the Temple and a man of God. What I am about is far from theft. Very well. You seek clarity, you may have it. This place is a warren of heresy. I have secured some of the most holy relics of Christendom for the true Church, and I will continue to do so until I have saved all that can be saved. There remain some of the greatest treasures of the faith in this city, jealously guarded by men who refuse to acknowledge Rome's supremacy. If I cannot retrieve such items, they will as like as not be destroyed along with their keepers in the angry flame of crusading zeal. They must be preserved. And I am *not* stealing them. Despite the fact that as their betters they should *willingly* give items to us, I have secured many relics with the consent of their former keepers, and others I have purchased with good coin. The city needs gold to pay their Venetian debt, and they are willing to part with the most wondrous things for that coin.'

He wagged a finger at them. 'It is every bit as important to retrieve our sacred items from the heathen Greek as it is from the Saracen. I am doing God's work, and what is more, I am doing it on the orders of our grand master. I shall not fail again!'

Arnau's brow creased. That tic had crept back into Bochard's eye stronger than ever, and that accidental slip at the end had confirmed everything Arnau had suspected. The preceptor sought redemption for what had happened in Cyprus. Some men believed you could buy your way into heaven, despite the scriptures, and Bochard's coffers were not yet full enough for him to be sure.

'The city boils over,' Ramon reminded him.

'And if there is war again? If there is a siege that succeeds and the city is sacked? What do you think will happen then, de Juelle? Fire, theft, rapine and massacres. What then of these important relics? They will burn with their churches, or be taken to private estates in the West in Frankish purses. What I am doing will *save* these items from destruction. I care not whether we are caught up in war. What we are about is more important than that.'

Arnau stepped forward now. 'I know a man,' he said quietly. Somehow he knew that confrontation would achieve little now. Gentle encouragement might succeed where anger had failed. Bochard was on the verge of mad anger, and he could see it. 'I was with this man on a Moorish island,' he added, 'hunting just such a relic. He learned the hardest way that sometimes faith in the unseen is more important than a mouldering bone, no matter to whom it belonged. Avid acquisition brings with it its own madness, Preceptor. Do not fall into the trap of avarice.'

Bochard's eyes darkened. 'Do not presume to tell me my business, boy. I will save all that can be saved. You have no idea the work I have accomplished. Already treasures beyond your ken are bound for Rome and Venice and Acre aboard ships secured by our brothers outside the walls. *They* know the value of the work I do.'

Arnau blinked. They'd not seen much of Bochard recently, but it had not occurred to him that the preceptor had been dealing with the Franks and Venetians. Now that he knew, though, it came as no surprise. How else would Bochard have expected to shift such a weight of sacred reliquaries from the city? They had to go by ship and, until the young prince had been crowned weeks ago, the Venetians had been sinking Byzantine ships attempting to leave the city. Now they were ferrying Bochard's ill-gotten gains away. Almost certainly that was why Bochard had been atop the walls that day, watching the siege. Had he seen his ship-owning contacts among the enemy?

His gaze raked the room, and it did indeed look less like a storeroom than the last time he had seen it. Something caught his eyes, though, in the tense silence that had now settled in the room. On the desk opposite sat a silver reliquary, edged in decorative gold, but Arnau could have sworn he glimpsed a spatter of dried blood on the silver before the preceptor caught his gaze and stepped very deliberately in the way, blocking the view of the casket.

'I have business in the palace. I no longer have time to debate your desire to disobey me. Return to your rooms and simply thank God that the heathens have submitted and the Pope can instil the true faith in this place.'

Arnau glanced at Ramon, who flicked his eyes back towards their rooms. With stiff, formal bows, they departed. In the corridor, they almost bumped into three insufferably smug looking men in long dark-green tunics. The young Templar was momentarily taken aback to realise that they were Westerners, visiting the palace. They bowed their heads respectfully and stepped aside, waiting as the Templars passed before continuing on to Bochard's door.

'*Scusa*,' the lead one said in a thick Italian accent, his expression containing little more than distant disdain for all this politeness.

Arnau nodded in return, not trusting himself to speak, and slipped past them, half-inclined to remain and eavesdrop on his master. In moments, back in their room, the squire looked up hopefully. Ramon nodded with a sigh. 'Be assured, Sebastian, it appears we are to remain in the city.'

'We are not to disobey him, then?' Arnau said.

'His points are all valid, no matter how much we might dislike them,' Ramon responded. 'Any number of masters of our order would support him and condemn us for leaving. No, we must remain for now.'

'Did you see the reliquary he hid? It bore blood marks. Not all his icons and treasures were bought or accepted from willing hands, I'd wager.'

'You think he would kill for a relic? Kill an innocent, I mean?'

Arnau squared up. 'You think he wouldn't?'

Ramon looked troubled then, and Arnau frowned. 'He had business in the palace, he said.'

'Yes.'

'Not in the city, but in the *palace*. With whom? The important Franks are all away with the new emperor or in their camp.' He shook his head in sudden realisation. 'And not those three oily curs in the corridor. I think they were Venetians, but that priest in red? He's a priest in the palace. You know that important church down near the water in the palace grounds?'

'Saint Maria's?'

'That's the one. The one where they keep that icon they parade round in times of war as a protection for the city. He's the priest from that church. I've seen him around the palace. He didn't look happy.'

Ramon frowned. 'You think the preceptor is trying to take the city's protective icon?'

'It seems likely, does it not? And will the city stand for its most sacred protection being taken away?'

'No.'

'We need to stop him. He's going too far.'

Ramon nodded. 'I doubt he can be persuaded, but we should try. Sebastian, you stay here. We'll go alone.'

'What about the Warings?'

'We don't need them. We won't be leaving the palace grounds, and I'm not sure it would be a good idea if they learned what Bochard was planning anyway.'

They nodded and left their apartment once more. A quick visit to Bochard's room confirmed that the preceptor had already left. Hugues answered the door, opening it only a crack through which Arnau could see the dark green of those Venetian visitors, and told them. Leaving once more, they hurried down the stairs and out into the open. There was no sign of Bochard, of course, but that mattered not, since they were sure where he was bound. They moved through the gardens and vestibules, past baths and towers, along tree-lined arcades down the slope of the hill towards the Golden Horn. The church lay at the lower end of the huge complex, a fairly grand building, if not by the standards of the great basilicas of Holy Apostles and Holy Wisdom. Still, it was accounted one of the more ancient and important churches in the city, housing the most significant of relics. Indeed, as well as the church itself and an attached baptistery, there was a purpose-built relic house, the Haghia Soros.

The two Templars closed on the end of the church complex, rounding the corner and taking deep breaths, preparing for a troublesome encounter. Arnau's heart leaped into his throat as they rounded the brick edge and the door came into view. Two heavily armoured men in great helms and long mail hauberks with full sleeves stood beside the door, shields on arms and hands gripping sword hilts. Though neither of the two men were known to Arnau, both were clearly Franks, their shields and surcoats displaying their allegiance – one red and white checks with black lys flowers, the other the same colour but with a strange design of shields within shields.

Ramon grabbed his shoulder and pulled him back around the corner.

'What?' Arnau whispered.

'They didn't see us. Great helms, no peripheral vision.'

'We need to go in.'

'I fear things are beyond that. It seems Bochard is now not only visited by Venetians, but guarded by Franks. I doubt we will be given a warm reception.'

Arnau nodded, shivering. Something about those coats of arms was oddly familiar, though he couldn't say why. Ramon gestured back the way they had come and Arnau nodded, following him.

They passed back through the gardens and palace buildings. At one point, a servant hurried past them, carrying a lipped tray of pomegranates. He ducked round the two men, not slowing his pace, and several fruits fell. With deft speed, Ramon reached down and grabbed one as it dropped, lifting it and looking at the hard red shell.

'Good fruit. Better than the rotten fruit of our situation, eh, Vallbona?'

They reached the courtyard outside their apartments, which was quieter than usual. The nearest guards and Warings were up on the wall tops, and the place was quiet without dashing servants. Crossing to the doorway and the stairs, Ramon frowned.

'What?'

'Where are the Warings? Since Doukas's new order, they're always out here waiting for us. Hadn't occurred to me.'

Arnau joined the frowning and ducked instinctively at a dull twang and thud. He was immensely lucky that Ramon was apparently more alert then he, for the missile had been aimed at his back, and ducking would do little to save him. Fortunately, Ramon pulled him sideways at the same time, and the crossbow bolt clunked against the stone wall a foot from the younger knight.

They spun in time to see a figure disappearing into a dark doorway. Arnau, hand going to sword, started to run and Ramon, in a fluid move, hefted the pomegranate and hurled it at the figure. His aim was true and there was a muted yelp from the shadowy doorway, but the figure was gone and the broken fruit rolled back out into the sunshine.

Arnau reached the door and ducked inside, but stopped there. He could hear distant footsteps padding up stairs. Their assailant would be long gone in the palace complex before he caught up. The figure had been in colours seen only briefly and in shadow, but indicative of any ordinary palace servant. All he had to do was drop his weapon and disappear among the other staff and they would never identify him.

Disgruntled, he crossed the square once more and joined Ramon in the doorway.

'What was that about, do you think?'

'Take your pick,' Ramon answered. 'Angry Byzantine trying to remove a Western knight from the equation, angry Frank recognising one of the Templars who fought on the walls? Maybe even just someone who hates the Order. We're not universally loved.' A thought seemed to strike him. 'You don't suppose the Baron de Castellvell or his cronies are on the Crusade?'

Arnau shook his head. 'Castellvell has his work cut out with the Almohads. But you don't think that Bochard...?'

Ramon turned a sharp look on him. 'No matter how much we might disagree, this is not the work of the preceptor. Never suggest such a thing, Vallbona. A suspicion like that is beneath you.'

With that he turned and stomped on up the stairs.

But it didn't *feel* beneath him. As they strode on back to their rooms, watching every shadow for another would-be assassin, Arnau found himself wondering about Bochard. The man had massacred the citizens of Cyprus. Had he killed to get that silver casket with the bloodstains? How far might a man like that be willing to go to accomplish his mission?

He shivered despite the heat.

CHAPTER 13:
THE VICTORIOUS FRANKS

AUGUST 18TH 1203

Was it a good thing or a bad one that the Franks had withdrawn from their encampment outside the walls and returned to Galata and their original place of repose? Arnau couldn't decide. Ostensibly it represented a good thing for the people. Not having siege machines aimed at their walls and the countryside outside ravaged and foraged by an occupying force was clearly beneficial. But that force remained a strong threat sitting just across the Golden Horn alongside their Venetian allies. There was speculation in the city that when the emperor returned from his tour with the Frankish leaders, the Venetians would be paid and the army and fleet would move on, returning to their Crusade.

Neither Arnau nor Ramon were remotely convinced.

The more hopeful and naïve of the people believed that their life would more or less return to normal when that happened. That they would be able to pay lip service to the Pope and privately go on with their heretical Eastern devotions. That they would return to being an empire with their own government, without Western interference.

Not at all convinced.

Ramon and Arnau descended the stairs from the sea walls close to their favoured Pisan church in good time for the service, wearing their full regalia with the red cross, earning reserved and careful looks from the Byzantine soldiers around them. Never had Arnau been more grateful for the bulky Waring guardsmen that accompanied them. They wore their white mantles at all times now, displaying the proud red cross of the Order which labelled them 'Crusaders' among the majority of the imperial citizenry. Ramon had approached Bochard carefully and requested permission to spend their days in the city in simple drab tunics, or at least plain white, the red cross being so negatively associated with the Franks in the city's eyes. Bochard had flatly refused. In his view it was unnecessary, and the Order's symbols, he said, would prevent them becoming a target for any angered Crusader. Thus they had left the palace via the city walls, using them to cross half the city to the Pisan enclave without ever descending into the disgruntled city itself.

Father Bartolomeo would have everything ready for the service, and the two knights prepared themselves as they passed through the few short streets from the walls to the church, shrouding themselves in fresh cloaks of serenity. It did not do to bring the troubles of the mundane into the house of God, after all. Arnau walked quietly, wondering how much longer they would remain in this boiling pot of anger.

Such was his internal focus that he failed entirely to note the noise until Ramon suddenly halted, hand going to Arnau's shoulder to stop him.

'Listen.'

The younger man did so. It took him a moment. There was the ever-present symphony of the seashore – lapping waves, creaking timbers, splashes and the endless coarse cries of gulls. And closer there were the sounds of soldiers atop the walls. There was the hum and susurration of city life all around them. But no, there *wasn't*. That latter was gone, replaced by something entirely different. The sound of violence.

Arnau blinked and turned his head, cocking his ear. It came from directly ahead, from the direction of the Pisan church. 'Trouble.'

Ramon nodded and both men drew their blades. Along with the stricture to wear their cross in public, they had made the decision to be armed at any time they left the apartment. Shields hefted into place, swords brandished, the two men hurried around the corner and along the next street. Arnau was acutely aware that even with the Warings, there were only six of them. He was glad that

Sebastian had remained in the palace, making himself unpopular with Bochard by shying away from Latin services being held in Constantinople's churches, though in a tiny, selfish way, he missed the extra sword.

Two more corners and narrow streets, and each one brought with it more audible clarity of what was happening. The sounds were not that of a clash of arms between soldiers, but of large-scale angry violence that was wholly one-sided. In the city? Franks marauding once again?

They rounded the final corner to see the small church at the junction of streets, and the sight that greeted them was appalling. At first glance it seemed to be a sizeable portion of the city's native population attacking the Pisan settlers. From three streets citizens poured, wielding makeshift clubs and kitchen knives and whatever weapon came easily to hand. Clearly numerous Pisans had already fallen to the onslaught, judging by the distribution of crumpled shapes on the ground amid the chaos, and others were fleeing through the street towards the church, yet more disappearing into their houses and barring shutters and doors.

It was a riot, plain and simple, and it did not escape Arnau's notice that the whole thing was more or less a grand-scale copy of what had happened to him that day among the burned ruins of the city. He had been waiting for the city to explode, but he had expected it to be focused against the Franks and Venetians across the water, not against others within the walls. Yes, the Pisans were loyal to the Roman Church, but they had been residents of the city for decades. Their menfolk had rushed to the walls to lend their aid when the enemy had arrived, regardless of their faith. In fact, Arnau understood that entire units of Pisan, Genovese and Amalfitan soldiers numbered among the city's defence force now. Had their shared faith with the invaders been enough to turn the city against them?

Arnau fumed. The city was in enough danger without them tearing each other to pieces within view of the Franks.

'Look,' Ramon said. 'The cause, I would wager.'

Arnau followed his gesture. Half a dozen Franks in bright surcoats and with shields bearing varied designs were among the beleaguered Pisans, pushing their way back, trying to get away from the Byzantine mob.

'You think they finally broke the peace? Enough to turn the city on any non-Greek?'

Ramon shrugged. 'It's possible. Who knows? But it seems likely to me.'

'What do we do?' Arnau said, uncertainly, watching the violence moving through the street ahead of them.

'Nothing.'

'What?'

Ramon gave him an exasperated sigh and sheathed his sword. 'We do nothing. There is no part in this for us.'

'You jest, Brother.'

Ramon turned on him angrily. 'What would you have us do, Vallbona? Should we attack the innocent Pisans and support the Byzantines? But they are not only innocent, they are God-fearing Christians and both our Rule and the direct order of the preceptor prohibit that course.'

'No, but—'

'Or should we attack the Byzantines? Those men and women we have been fighting alongside for months, seeing them as the righteous in all of this. Men and women who are now officially within the arms of the Church of Rome? Again, an act forbidden by both Bochard and the Order.'

'No, there's—'

'The Franks? Men of God. I say it again, forbidden by all. And to get to them you would have to wade through Pisans and Byzantines. Vallbona, this is one fight we cannot afford to become part of.'

Arnau gestured helplessly, muttering 'But...' over and over. Ramon was right. He had no wish to fight Pisans or Byzantines, and he had been expressly forbidden from attacking the Franks. 'But this is appalling. If it doesn't stop...'

Ramon nodded. 'It might be the trigger we've been anticipating. Come on, we have to get out of here.'

As they turned and fled back towards the walls, Arnau couldn't escape the feeling that the Warings were every bit as glad to get out of the area as they. No one wanted to take sides between two groups of citizens. They reached the walls and climbed the steps, turning at the top to look back. The entire Pisan quarter was in an uproar now. The noise had risen to a din, the rioting spreading. Likely something similar was happening now in the Amalfitan and Genovese quarters, judging by where the noise was coming from. Arnau pinched the bridge of his nose, shaking his head. Stupid. These foreign enclaves had fought alongside the Byzantines for the good of their city for months and now they were being attacked while the Franks and Venetians sat watching, smug, across the water.

Arnau turned and looked over the parapet at the water. The Neorion harbour sat only a few hundred paces away, busier now than at any time since the Templars had arrived, with everything from full galleys to small ferries and fishing boats moored there, taking Franks back and forth across the Horn. He switched his glance back to the city again. The violence was spreading and the citizens were either fleeing this way or being driven hence. At least there seemed to be no sign of smoke, but then the Byzantines, no matter how angry and aggrieved they might be, were far from stupid enough to set fire to their own city.

It was minutes only before the Italian peoples began to arrive at the gate in the sea walls, which remained resolutely shut these days unless opened by the soldiery. Arnau peered down at the first half-dozen citizens to arrive at the gate. The lead man, who held a long staff which gleamed wetly at one end, shouted something in his native language at the gate. Ignored, he tried again in Greek.

'Open the gate. We are being massacred.'

There was some discussion among the Byzantine soldiers, and while more and more refugees appeared at the gate Arnau noted something wrong with that spokesman. His head was bloodied and messy. It was only as the man turned in Arnau's direction in desperation that the young Templar realised in horror what it was. Someone had carved a Byzantine crucifix with its three cross pieces into the man's forehead with a blade.

This was *insane*.

A decision was reached, and the gates thrown open.

Arnau watched with sinking spirits as the various Italian residents of the city fled through the gate in a constant flow, pouring onto any ship or boat they could find in the harbour and putting out into the water, fleeing for the dubious safety of the Franks and Venetians across the Golden Horn.

'What have they done?' Arnau said in hollow disbelief.

'They have turned on their own. Those men will throw their support behind the Franks now.'

The two knights stood in bitter impotence on the wall top, joining in three murmured psalms, a muted hymn and the appropriate recitations and prayers for the service they were clearly going to miss as they watched the foreigners pouring out of the city, driven to the water by the brutal row and violence behind them.

'Nevertheless, my soul be subject to God and my hope of deliverance in him, for he is my God, and my Saviour; mine helper, I shall not be shaken.' Arnau wondered whether Ramon's odd choice of the sixty-second Psalm had been as a plea for their own deliverance from this entire mess as much as for the fleeing Italians passing them by.

For two hours the pair stood and watched in quiet gloom as men fled the city until the rioters back in the streets, robbed of anyone to take out their anger upon, set to work looting and destroying. With a sigh of regret the knights watched the gates being closed once more and, in the company of their Waring escort, began the trek back around the walls to the palace.

When they returned to the apartments, it was with a sense of foreboding and unhappiness. Conflicting reports reached the palace throughout the rest of the day, and without Doukas being present, they had to actively press whoever they could find for information. The Laskaris brothers were nowhere to be found, and so the main source of news were the palace staff and those few Warings who deigned to speak to them beyond matters of direct duty.

Depending upon who Arnau listened to, there had been a number of causes of the riot. A few voices suggested that the people of Constantinople had simply had enough and had passed their breaking point, lashing out at the nearest perceived oppressor, those being the Italian enclaves in the city. Others suggested some grand conspiracy between the Pisans and the Venetians, and that their duplicity had led the citizens to finally rid themselves of a snake at their bosom. Yet more folk claimed that Franks had raped a nobleman's wife and when confronted about it had gone on a rampage of mindless violence until the citizens rose against them. That they had taken refuge with the other non-Byzantines in the city in desperation and that the mob had been so incensed by then that they had failed to distinguish between guilty Franks and other Westerners. It sounded horribly possible to Arnau, as did the simple possibility that the natives had just had enough and erupted wildly.

Whatever the cause, while reports varied wildly in their numbers, the gist was the same. The foreign enclaves on the northern edge of the city near the water had emptied in a matter of hours. Every last Pisan, Genovese or Amalfitan had fled across the water to seek safety with the Crusaders. Those who had received sufficient warning managed to take their wealth and possessions with them. Many had not, fleeing with only the clothes on their back and losing everything in the process. In the aftermath, the rampaging Byzantines had left bodies strewn in the streets, had daubed their heretical cross over any Western markings, had torn down signs in Western tongues and destroyed them, painting proud ancient slogans in Greek in their place.

And then it had subsided.

It had not quite been the trigger Arnau had fretted over. He had seen it as the first phase of a general rising and a complete closure of the city against the Westerners. It seemed that something had failed to ignite that spark though. With the flight of the Italians, the mob dispersed unchallenged, melting back into the streets. All went quiet. Life went on.

To Arnau and Ramon, listening to the reports coming in at the palace, it represented another step closer to the Hell on earth of which the young Templar had spoken. The general mood of simmering discontent that had pervaded the city for so long now had taken a subtle but noticeable shift into violent anger – xenophobia, even.

They contemplated speaking to Bochard again that evening, but eventually decided against it. Little good would come, they thought, from provoking him further. Nothing would change for them. Nevertheless, Arnau hovered outside their common room for some time late that night with an unaccustomed second cup of wine, and he noted with sinking spirits the preceptor's door creak open, emitting the sound of hushed conversation.

A man emerged, wearing a knight's surcoat and with a very expensive sword buckled at his side. Three men-at-arms accompanied him, and as he emerged into the lighter area of the corridor, Arnau felt a lurch of recognition. The surcoat the man wore had the same red and white squares with the black fleur-de-lys that he had seen on the shield of one of the men guarding Bochard at the church days earlier. That Bochard was fully in league with at least one of the Frankish nobles was now impossible to deny. Arnau ground his teeth as the man walked past, and tried not to look too belligerent as the knight bowed his head in acknowledgement of the Templar in the corridor.

Behind him, the preceptor's door shut tight once more, and Arnau stood seething for a moment. Then he hurried over to the nearest window and looked down in time to see the knight emerge from the doorway below with his soldiers. Another dozen men stood outside with the man's horse – some men-at-arms and some archers. Clearly, given what had happened, this nobleman was not going to venture into the city without adequate protection.

Something else struck Arnau, and he peered down at the Franks for a moment before pulling away from the window and hurrying back into their apartment, shutting the door and crossing to Ramon.

'Bochard had a Frankish visitor,' he said in a quiet voice.

'Hardly a surprise. And realistically, since there is now no state of war in place, there is no reason not to.'

'Same coat of arms that was outside that church door the other day. And he had crossbowmen with him. I tried to see if any of them had pomegranate stains on their tunic, but it's getting dark and they were too far away. But I would bet my teeth that one of them did.'

Ramon frowned. 'I've been thinking about those coats of arms. I'm sure I saw one of them back in Acre before we set off.'

Arnau blinked and slapped his head in irritation. 'That's it. I've been trying to place it ever since the church. I knew that I recognised it from somewhere.'

'And if that blazon was in the mother house in Acre, then the man has a Templar connection. No wonder he and Bochard are in collusion. One wonders how he came to be in Acre and then also here, but he is a direct link between the preceptor and the Franks. The perfect man to negotiate between them. Good money says that this knight is the man who secured transport for Bochard's relics.'

'And there were Venetian soldiers at his door earlier too. Men with access to ships. Why would his man shoot at us though?'

'*If* he did. You cannot say for sure. But yes, it is a worrying question.'

They lapsed into silence, and the rest of the night passed, tense but uneventful.

The following morning the two knights joined Bochard at the church of Saint Mary of the Blachernae for the services, as they were denied their usual haunt of the Pisan church now. Arnau couldn't help but feel throughout the entire proceedings that above and beyond the general feeling of discontent from the various forced converts sitting through the to-them incomprehensible Latin service, there was a special and specific resentment being aimed by the formerly Greek Church priest against Bochard. There was a tension between the two men almost bowstring taut. It was actually a relief to leave the church and venture out into the hot sunshine of the dangerous city once again.

The preceptor, without a word to them, returned to the palace proper. Arnau and Ramon made their way instead around the sea walls of the city, taking everything in. The scars of the past months lay like stinking lesions upon the place, and the buboes of the coming days looked fit to burst into open rot too.

From the Blachernae, they first passed the site of the furious fight for the walls, with the damage that remained to remind all that it had happened. Almost seamlessly, they moved from the site of this violence to the burned-out region of the city, acres of black and grey civic bones rising from the hillside all the way to the crest at the heart of the city. And almost immediately beyond the edge of that ash-scape, they walked alongside the empty and sepulchral enclaves of the Italians who had left the city in haste. By the time they had reached an untouched area of the city bearing no war wounds, they were almost at the ancient acropolis, most of the way along the Golden Horn, next to the old silted-up harbour now used largely for shipbuilding. Here remained the only surviving foreign enclave in the city, such as it was. A small trading post nestled at the base of the great headland, centred around – of all things – a mosque. There were few residents there, but Arnau found its presence fascinating. Despite the constant troubles in the East and the Crusades called to free the Holy City over the past century, pragmatism, combined with the fact that long periods of peace and stability interrupted the wars, had led to the emperors allowing a small mosque within the city for the Arabian and Saracen traders that still brought distant and exotic goods to the empire. It was almost a relief to see the simplicity of the Saracens here, for they represented no dogmatic headache for a brother of the Order.

'Heaven help us,' Ramon said suddenly. 'Looks like trouble again.'

Arnau turned from the small Saracen enclave and peered out across the water to where Ramon was looking. It took him moments to spot the small flotilla. Perhaps ten boats had set off from the wharves of Galata, angling directly across the Horn towards the city proper.

'Franks. Nothing new.'

Ramon pursed his lips. 'I disagree.'

Arnau looked left and right. Little seemed to be troubling the soldiers along the wall. He frowned. 'Why?'

'Because they usually come two at a time, or three at most. Ten is more like a fleet than a ferry. Ten boats betrays a grander purpose'

'Maybe a deputation?'

'Maybe, but that usually means nobles on horses with an entourage. They would come around the land side to where the Blachernae palace lies. No, I don't like this.'

Arnau watched. The boats were making directly for them, for the less popular and often treacherous docks in the silty Prosphorion harbour. That was also unusual. 'Come with me,' Ramon said quietly.

They descended the stairs and reached the bottom, where the Warings hesitated. Their leader, a blond, barrel-chested beast called Octa, cleared his throat. 'Where are you bound?'

'Trouble comes across the water on boats,' Ramon replied. 'We go to see what *sort* of trouble.'

Octa frowned. 'I advise staying on the walls. We are forbidden by imperial command from becoming engaged in trouble with the Franks.'

Arnau rolled his eyes. The weakness of blind Isaac showed through the cracks in the empire every day. 'Stay here, then,' Ramon advised them in return.

The two men stepped down into the street and crossed to an archway in the walls, hidden in shadows, where they waited. Octa and his Warings remained on the steps, torn between protecting their charges and steering clear of Frankish warriors by imperial order. Shouted voices outside the walls opened the gates with no argument and the two Templars watched as mail-clad men, armed and with shields strapped to their sides, stomped in through the gate as though they owned the city. Ramon hissed and pointed and Arnau followed his gaze until his heart leaped into his throat. Some of the men carried unlit torches, pitch-coated and so, so dangerous in the tinder-dry summer city.

'Holy Mother of God,' Arnau breathed. 'They can't be?'

'It looks like it.' Ramon turned to the stairs nearby as dozens of men thumped past carrying all the tools of destruction and death. Once the last man had passed and they were not in danger of being spotted, Ramon emerged once more and waved to Octa. 'How dear is the city against your oath of non-interference, Waring? They carry *torches*.'

To their credit, Octa and his men looked extremely worried and uncomfortable.

'The Lord watch over all his children,' Ramon said and gestured to Arnau, walking purposefully in the wake of the Franks. There was a brief pause only and then, with curses in some northern Angle tongue, the Warings hurried after them.

The six men trotted through the streets as lightly as knights and Nordic giants in armour could, following the path of the Crusaders. Arnau's initial fear, born from the direction of the boats' travel, was being borne out. There were several major thoroughfares that led into the heart of the Byzantine city up the slope or to the headland acropolis, and yet the Crusaders had instead forged ahead into a warren of narrower streets.

Straight for the Saracens.

'A fine time for the Franks to remember they are on a Crusade,' Arnau grunted.

Ramon nodded. 'The mosque. Perhaps they see it as a holy duty. More likely, I fear, they think it will turn the remaining city in on itself.'

They rounded a corner and entered a wide square, surrounded with buildings of old-fashioned Byzantine construction and yet adorned with very Moorish-looking arcades. The mosque sat at the centre of the square, a squat minaret rising from it.

They were too late. The Crusaders were already entering the mosque, swords drawn and roaring passages from the Good Book as though the Lord might condone their actions. Someone had clearly brought and used a flint and steel, for those pitch-soaked torches were now dancing with golden light. Cries and shouts arose from within the mosque. Ramon threw out an arm as Arnau made to race forward, stopping him.

'What?'

Ramon gestured to the scene before them. Saracen traders and their local contacts who lived in the enclave were gathering up whatever they might be able to wield in anger and were racing for the mosque.

'This is not our fight, Vallbona.'

'What? You were the one who dragged us after them.'

'To observe, not intervene. They are sons of the Church. We are forbidden by Rule and command. Need I walk you through it all again?'

Arnau felt the frustration building. Yes, the Saracen occupants were theoretically more heretical even than the Byzantines. But they were merchants and women and children, living in peace. The Franks might be nominally Christians, but the values they were currently displaying were more Satan's work.

'This cannot be allowed.'

'We are *forbidden*, Vallbona.'

'The Rule should guide us to acts of forgiveness and mercy,' Arnau spat.

'And Bochard—'

'*Fuck* Bochard.'

Arnau was truly angry. In fact, it was fair to say he was about as angry as he could remember ever being. He was angry at the preceptor for supporting mindless hatred and what appeared to be theft without a hint of compassion. He was angry at the Franks for their stupidity in ravaging this place all because of the Doge of Venice and his hatred. He was angry at the Venetians for engineering this whole thing. He was angry at Ramon for his refusal to intervene. Most of all, he was angry that the men who supposedly championed the word of the Lord for the West seemed to be either committing acts of depraved wickedness, supporting those acts, or refusing to do anything about them, while those men who seemed to embody the true peace of the Lord in their hearts were heretics and Mussulmen.

It was all so wrong.

With a roar, he pushed past Ramon's hand, sword torn from his sheath. Fuck Bochard and fuck Ramon if he disagreed, but Arnau couldn't watch this happen and not do something. Ahead, the Saracen imam had been hauled from his mosque's doorway by two burly armoured men. His long white robe was already drenched in crimson. Smoke had begun to pour from the mosque's various apertures, and other Crusaders emerged, coughing.

The local residents met them in the most appallingly mismatched fight, shopkeepers with sticks against Frankish knights with great steel blades. Before he could justify himself further, had he felt the need to, Arnau pushed a feeble-looking old Saracen out of the way, wincing at the sudden pain as he moved sharply and his rib shifted, his sword rising and then falling to bite some unwary Frank in the shoulder. The man wore a chain shirt, which prevented the heavy blow from cleaving deep into flesh, instead spreading the impact. It did not save the man, though. The blow landed with enough force to utterly shatter the shoulder, arm and several ribs. The knight screamed and dropped his sword, falling back.

Arnau didn't care. Even the pain of his broken rib was nothing, a note lost in a song of war. He was not working to a strategy. This was no duel. This was one man standing against a massacre, and if he died, he would approach Heaven's gate with a clear conscience. Right now, Arnau could not have planned his attack if he'd tried. He had surrendered himself to something deep within that he'd not been aware was there – a primal anger riveted to a cross of justice.

His sword lashed out again, this time taking a man in the unprotected face, turning it into a mush of red and white. The scream died away in a moment, lost in the ruined mouth, but Arnau was implacable, unstoppable. He felt something thud against his leg; two blows on his shield. He felt the ache of what would be bad bruises later.

He yelped more from the shifting of his damaged rib than from the blows that were seemingly raining down on him constantly and yet with little more effect that light taps. God was with him. The Lord was shielding the righteous, he was sure, just as Sebastian had claimed the Holy Mother protected him. He swept low, breaking the thigh of a man who disappeared into the press with a cry, then rose and smashed his shield into the raised sword arm of another Frank, who cried out at his breaking knuckles and dropped his weapon.

Slash and hack, hammer and barge, he pushed his way ever onwards, amid a sea of colourful Frankish surcoats and drab local Saracen garments. His voice rose in a melodic roar.

'Thou hurtlest down to me the instruments of battle, and I shall bring down nations with thee, and I shall destroy realms in thee.'

Then suddenly he was moving backwards. His arm seemed unable to move. He cut down with his sword, but his arm would not fall. His boots skittered off stone and his shield wouldn't move. He shook his head. He was at the far side of the square now, away from the fight. Suddenly he saw the oddly mismatched figures of Octa and Ramon holding off angry Franks making to follow him.

He blinked.

His eyes spun as his head twisted this way and that. He was being dragged by two huge Warings, who had his arms pinned. He struggled, but already he could feel his righteous fury ebbing, giving way to some sort of exhausted sadness.

The mosque was properly aflame. Black, roiling smoke rising into the clear blue. Those few Saracens who had remained were being butchered. Most had fled. The headless body of the Saracen imam lay on the stones of the square, pooling in blood. Already two more buildings around the square were alight, sparks carried by the channel's strong winds from the burning mosque. Even with attention, the chances of arresting the fire swiftly were small, but the population had fled, and only blood-hungry Franks remained, men with little intention of preventing a fire. Indeed, some were already looting the stores.

'You fool,' Ramon snapped, suddenly arriving once more at his side. 'And what is it with you and fires? You seem to carry a conflagration with you wherever you go.'

'They deserved to die,' Arnau spat. 'They still do.'

'That was never in doubt, but it is the Lord's place to punish them, not ours.'

Arnau turned angrily on Ramon. 'What are we if not an instrument of the Lord?'

'Save your philosophy until we are safe in the palace.'

Arnau shrugged out of the grip of the Warings, who continued to watch him carefully until he wiped and cleaned his blade and then followed along with the others.

'My conscience is clear,' Arnau said with an accusatory look at Ramon. 'How yours is, I cannot imagine.'

'I'm glad your conscience is clear. Now we will have to see whether Bochard decides to punish you or even cast you from the Order.'

'I'm no longer sure I recognise Bochard's authority,' snarled Arnau.

Ramon stared at him for a long time, and Arnau deliberately held his fierce expression. Finally, the older brother nodded. 'Perhaps it is better that he doesn't hear about this at all.'

'This city's descent into Hell proceeds apace,' Arnau grunted as they reached the walls and began to climb.

CHAPTER 14:
THE ANGRY CITY

SEPTEMBER 1ST 1203

'**D**o you think he has any intention at all of doing as he promised?'

Ramon turned to Arnau. 'The preceptor is learning from my examples. I used his vagueness to find loopholes that allowed us to face the Venetians, and Bochard has picked up on that. His strict adherence to the Order's Rule will not permit him to outright lie, even to heretics, but I have heard him come close at times now. He suggests, intimates and agrees, but not once have I heard him confirm that he will *definitely* do something. I may have created a monster in that regard.'

Arnau sighed. Sebastian had begun talking to Bochard's squire more in the last few days, and information had leeched through him back to the two knights. The preceptor was now dealing directly with the new Venetian patriarch of the city who had, in theory, overall control of all churches in the city and their priests. Through that channel Bochard was now acquiring relics at an increased rate. But he had been more and more cunning in the past weeks. As well as using the new regime to achieve his ends, he was playing the sympathetic ear to the disenfranchised Greek priests and offering to save their treasures from the Franks by shipping them to the great monastery at Mount Athos, where the Greek rite was said to hold strong. The chances of any of those relics loaded onto Venetian ships reaching Mount Athos was next to nil, to Arnau's mind.

Ramon had waited until Bochard had been in a particularly buoyant mood following an important acquisition, and had once more carefully posited the notion of leaving. He had been shouted down in an instant. Far from this increased success glutting the preceptor and leaving him ready to depart, it had made him hungry for ever more. Arnau was of the opinion that Bochard would not leave Constantinople now until every church roof had lost its lead.

Ramon had been so silently disapproving of Arnau's violent outburst at the Saracen enclave that the younger knight had forced his anger and all memory of the event deep down inside where it would not come between them, where it simmered, hidden but not forgotten. He both liked and respected Ramon, and had no wish to be at odds with him. Moreover, it was enough to be at loggerheads with one fellow Templar without doing the same to the other, and in Bochard's case Arnau was just a few short steps from outright rebellion, whatever Ramon might say. He had always thought Ramon one of the more easy-going of Rourell's knights, but it seemed that he had reached his limit in this dreadful place. Arnau couldn't help but wonder what Balthesar's responses would have been had he been here instead. He suspected the old knight would have been up to his eyebrows in Frankish blood by now, denying Bochard at every turn.

'Do we have to go? It's a job for servants,' he grunted, fastening his sword belt.

'Simple choice, Vallbona: defy the preceptor or obey him. I might not agree with what he is doing as such, but I am still not ready to break my vows because of him. The day he steps outside the Order's Rule himself, I will act. Until then, my vows mean more to me than my disapproval of a superior. You are still young in our order, Arnau. I know your idealism is getting the better of you. I know you want to wear your heart on your breast alongside the cross, and to defend the weak whatever the cost, and I laud you for it, but there must be structure. There must be obedience, lest our order simply comprise a gang of disparate brothers who act each according to his own will. Can you imagine the chaos and the danger in that? There are strictures in place. When Bochard steps out of line, there are avenues for us to follow to put things right. But think what you like, the preceptor has yet to actually do anything wrong. And as long as he acts within the interest and bounds of the Order, we will obey him. So the answer is yes, we have to go.'

Arnau didn't trust himself to answer, instead jamming on his helmet and gathering up his shield. As he bent, he felt the ache in that rib once more. It was definitely on the mend now, but sudden movements still pained him. The medicine he had been given to mix into wine certainly helped, though Ramon had warned him against taking too much.

'Come on,' Ramon sighed and strode from the room.

Down the corridor and the stairs they went, emerging from the doorway below. Four Warings stood there with six horses, all harnessed and saddled and ready to go. Something made the skin on the back of Arnau's neck prickle – a preternatural feeling, and as they moved to the horses, his gaze strayed up and across their surroundings. Three men stood by a marble bench beneath a shaped tree, each in a long dark-green tunic and chaperon. Perfectly innocuous. Three men who had, in the current situation, every reason to be in the palace, standing in the garden at the edge of the courtyard and talking among themselves. And yet Arnau was almost certain that they had been watching him and then looked away as his face came up. He had not that good a memory for faces, but he would be willing to place a hefty wager that they were the three Venetians he had bumped into outside Bochard's door. He glanced back up at their room.

'I'd still have liked to take Sebastian.'

Ramon shook his head. 'He's more use wheedling information out of the preceptor's squire,' he said quietly before greeting the big northerners in a loud, friendly voice. Octa nodded at him, and the two knights mounted and headed for the nearest palace gate with two Warings riding before them and two behind. Arnau glanced back as they left, to see the three green-clad Italians heading for the stairs to their apartments. Bochard. He almost turned to follow. Had Bochard sent them away just so he could have his clandestine meetings with the architects of this whole mess? Ramon gave him a meaningful glance and he tore his gaze from the doorway once more and turned his attention to their task. He had to acknowledge that Doukas had been thorough with his protection of the visiting Templars, and the absence of the minister had not seen that protection falter.

They left the palace and headed south, along the crest of the Sixth Hill towards where the Mese – the great central thoroughfare that ran the length of the city – emerged through the walls. They passed one of the most impressive and sprawling monasteries in the city before emerging out into that region of greenery and fields, meeting the Mese and the next built-up area. They turned onto the great street and passed east along it on their errand for the preceptor, passing a great open-air cistern full of clear blue water.

Arnau could not help but feel utterly hated and unwanted. Every citizen they passed threw at them a look of malevolent disgust. Several times small gangs of locals stood deliberately in their way, glaring at them and muttering imprecations in Greek until the Warings threatened them and demanded they move. Each time they did so, slowly and raking the two knights with looks of utter hatred as they went, but each time Arnau was not quite certain that they would actually move. If one group happened to decide that it was worth taking on four of the emperor's guards in order to kill two Westerners, it might spell real trouble. The six of them were professional killers and could hold their own in combat, but numbers played a strong part in any fight. A single show of defiance by the city folk might draw support from the rest of the population. The small party of warriors might defend themselves against a dozen shopkeepers and youths only to find themselves suddenly facing a hundred angry Byzantines. Arnau could now quite easily picture how those few Frankish knights had ended up retreating into the Pisan enclave, chased thence by a huge mob.

He shivered. They were one small act of defiance away from a repeat of that disaster, but with Templars as the prey this time. He only hoped that the presence of the Warings would be enough to put them off.

It was the most nerve-racking hour of Arnau's life, even given everything he had been through in his time with the Order. They walked their horses at a slow, steady pace the three and a half miles to the acropolis headland, partly to project an air of calm and peace and not spook the locals into any foolish act, and partly, Arnau suspected, to preserve the beasts' strength in case they needed to flee. That thought was not encouraging.

They followed the Mese across the whole city, through ancient fora with grand Roman columns and arches, colonnaded buildings that had once been pagan temples and numerous churches. Arnau was grateful that the clutter of buildings on their left hid the northern slopes of the city with their burned-out regions and empty enclaves. No one would travel through there now. The second fire, started by the Franks at the mosque, had burned for three days and destroyed much of what remained on those northern edges of the city. Fully a quarter of Constantinople had now been rendered to ash, according to reports.

No wonder it was now almost unheard of to see a Frank in the city. They were keeping away, across the Golden Horn, fearful of triggering another riot. No wonder the locals were glaring with such hate at the symbols of the Western Church, despite the fact that the Templars had only ever tried to help the city. No wonder Arnau felt so damned nervous.

Still, finally, they passed the end of the great hippodrome, came close to the Great Palace and reined in before the great church of Holy Wisdom, a marvel unrivalled in Arnau's experience. As they passed through the doorway into the immense domed structure, Arnau allowed himself to shrink into the background. He had little wish to be involved in Bochard's thefts, and was happy to leave the details to Ramon while he stood behind with the Warings and took in the grandeur of the building around them, trying his best to ignore the seething resentment on every face. It seemed the Warings were the only citizens who didn't hate them, but then the Warings had been with them through it all, knew what part they had played and valued them accordingly.

Right now, beyond his own companions, the Laskaris brothers and Doukas, they were the only people in Constantinople that Arnau really trusted.

He stood looking up at the dome and around at the painted images of the saints and the Christ and sacred Mother that adorned the massive nave of the church while Ramon met some sour-faced Greek priest wearing a Western cross as though it might burn him. They spoke briefly and the priest handed over a silver box almost a foot long. The priest hesitated for a moment, unwilling to relinquish his prize, but soothing words from Ramon did the trick. As the priest let go, Arnau could see the wrench of loss in his eyes. The man hated them no less than any commoner in the street. It was making Arnau's soul itch to be so universally despised.

As the priest stumped disconsolately off and the Warings escorted them back to the door, Ramon carefully undid the catches and turned the tiny key in the lock, lifting the lid with reverence. Despite everything, Arnau felt a tiny thrill, even as his face soured.

The true cross. Little more than ancient, rotted splinters, really. Four tiny slivers of rotten wood on a bed of purple silk. But those splinters had once been a beam that had held the Saviour aloft on his last day as a mortal husk before rising to stand with the Father.

He shivered at the proximity of such an incredible treasure.

A bitter part of him reminded him that Bochard had been so unconcerned about them that he had sent his knights to collect it rather than go himself. Was it that he was gathering such unearthly treasures in his rooms and on his ships that even slivers of the true cross were relatively unimportant? Was it perhaps that Bochard feared crossing the city? He damn well should, after all. Perhaps he felt that sending others was sensible. Was it, as he'd suspected, just a matter of getting them out of the way while he spoke to the oily Venetians? Or perhaps, the darkest part of him suggested, Bochard hoped that they would fall foul of a riot and be out of his hair for good.

That was a nagging thought that wouldn't go away. Arnau and Ramon were becoming an inconvenience. Had Bochard even been behind that crossbow bolt? As they left the church and mounted once more, Arnau found himself pondering his theory. Every new idea and connection fitted well, and every one was more worrying than the last. It was all about convenience, or rather, *in*convenience.

Bochard had been troublesome. The grand master had concocted some distant task to send him on that took him far away and kept him busy. And because Bochard had nagged about needing companions, the grand master had looked at the resources available. He clearly would not send important brothers who knew the Holy Land and were already acclimatised, but two brothers from far-off Aragon who would be peripherally useful at best. Of course. And neither was expected to speak any useful tongue, either. They would be little more than pointless muscle to send with Bochard. Thus had the grand master disposed of his inconvenient preceptor with two of the less important brothers for his campaigns.

But Bochard had taken his mission far more seriously than anyone expected. He felt he had much to prove. And once he had realised that his companions were not only relatively bright, but actually spoke Greek, he had tried to keep his true purpose hidden. Then, when that had no longer been possible, he had tried to keep them contained and quiet, using the rule of obedience to keep them in line. But no matter what the preceptor tried, Ramon and Arnau kept getting themselves into trouble.

Kept threatening Bochard and his mission.

God above, but Arnau was more than half convinced. The preceptor *was* mad, despite Ramon's protests. Perhaps he was not behind the crossbow, though. That was maybe going too far, but the man's Frankish friends were a different matter entirely. And sending the pair off on a simple collection task through the dreadfully dangerous boiling pot of a city? Did he truly hope that they would fall victim to a riot and stop causing him difficulties?

Was the man willing to sacrifice such a relic just to get rid of them?

He couldn't broach the subject with Ramon of course. The older knight would not countenance such a notion. And it did sound far-fetched, but the more Arnau pictured Bochard's puce face as he ranted, and his avaricious glee as he beheld his hoard, the more he became convinced.

For half an hour of the ride back he tried to talk himself out of the idea, though he failed repeatedly. He jumped as one of the Warings suddenly held up a warning hand and yanked his steed to a halt. The others did the same sharply in response. Arnau peered ahead. At first, he could see nothing, but he could *hear* it. A similar sound to what he had heard near the Saracen mosque. His heart beat fast at the realisation.

Moments later, half a dozen Franks emerged from a side street, brandishing swords. Behind them came a huge crowd of Byzantines with makeshift weapons, shouting angrily. Arnau's hand went to his sword hilt, but Octa shook his head. 'Do not fuel their fire.' Arnau let go and grasped his reins tight, noting wryly that Octa's warning did not seem to apply to their escort, as the Warings all unslung and brandished weapons.

The Franks were cornered against some building, swinging wildly, trying to hold the mob back. The citizens were hesitating, each reluctant to be the first to enter the arc of swinging steel. The stand-off would not last long, though.

Arnau felt sick as one of the Franks spotted the men on horseback with their red crosses, accompanied by imperial guards theoretically loyal to the regime who had allowed the Crusaders in. Imploring arms jerked forth and, in a moment, as most of them continued to swing and hold off the mob, several started to shout at the Templars desperately, beseeching them to help.

Ramon's face was stony and bleak. Arnau could see how conflicted he was. At one and the same time, the older Templar wanted to save fellow Christians, but he also wanted to let the Byzantines have their vengeance for what had been done to them. He took a deep breath. 'Continue to stand down, Vallbona.' Arnau nodded. He had no desire to help the ravaging, savage Franks anyway. Besides, he couldn't imagine the Warings letting them interfere.

'Can you order them to disperse?' Ramon quietly asked Octa.

The Waring snorted. 'I can order the wind not to blow, but it will not listen.'

Thus it was that with the bitter taste of powerlessness in his mouth Arnau sat astride his horse and watched as the first citizen moved, cut down easily by Frankish steel. He was replaced instantly with another, then another. The Byzantines were butchered mercilessly but suddenly there were too many of them and they were within the sword arc, lunging and swiping. Octa shook his head, gestured to the right and led them into a side street. Arnau watched as they left the Mese, seeing the first Frank fall beneath a flurry of blows. He never saw them die, but the sound of their demise as the small party skirted around through side streets would come back on more than one occasion to ruin a night's sleep for Arnau.

For the sake of safety, they moved down the northern slope until they emerged from a ruinous street to the burned wreckage of the city's Perama region. Here and there, the more concerned citizens had begun to clear off and renovate the surviving walls of various churches, reconstructing the houses of God that had been a central facet of Byzantine life for a millennium, but still the majority of the region lay as black and grey bones.

The rest of the journey was unpleasant but uneventful, and on their return, Arnau made good use of the palace bathhouse to clean off the dust and ash of their journey before the next service. During that mass he performed every action expected of him, but his eyes never once left Bochard. The man seemed so innocent and pious here in church that Arnau at last began to doubt his earlier suspicions. Bochard was a Templar. He would never have reached the rank he had if he'd had such a diabolical, murderous streak. No, Arnau's notion had been fanciful. Bochard had simply delegated work, and the crossbow bolt had come from some dubious Frankish lord… or Venetian? Memories of those three silent, attentive, green-clad foreigners drifted back.

The preceptor joined them for the various services in the liturgy over the following days, in between which times he negotiated with politicians, nobles and religious figures of the city. Since his purpose was now open and he had nothing to keep secret, the local priests being subservient to Rome and the Crusaders controlling the land, Bochard no longer had to leave the Blachernae to go about his business, with other folk coming to him instead. At least those three Venetians seemed notable now by their absence.

Summer's roll into autumn did nothing to improve matters. As September gave way to October, the division between the seething and rebellious Byzantines and the Franks and their allies continued to widen. The Byzantines were repressed in their own city and in the name of their own blind, insane emperor and his Frank-loving pup of a son. The Crusaders continued to consider themselves the de facto masters of the city and its empire, though they would rarely dare cross the water and pass into the city. Far too many Franks had died at the hands of angry mobs now. There had been purges in the name of the emperor and the Doge of Venice after such incidents, but it was pointless, for they strung up a few random citizens, never knowing who was truly responsible, and the Templars watched every punishment drive the citizens further into rebellious hatred. The green-clad Venetians began to visit Bochard again, though now they came to the palace through the gate in the walls, avoiding the city's streets entirely, and in greater strength, rarely numbering fewer than eight and all heavily armed. Arnau habitually avoided them. His spine itched when he found them watching him.

Late in October Arnau and Ramon spent a nervous few hours abroad in the city once more, helping Franks who sneered at them load Bochard's latest haul on board a Venetian ship called *La Figa* to take it to 'safety'. The presence of green-clad Venetians all around them felt more oppressive and threatening than anything they had felt in the battle on the walls. Arnau vowed silently to himself that it was the last time he would assist in such sickening and blatant theft, no matter what the preceptor called it. November came around with a turn in the weather, bringing a chill to the air and rain in vast swathes that suppressed the ash clouds at last, but which turned the northern shores of the city into a vast swamp of grey sludge, the rain carrying the remnants of a burned city down the slopes to pool in streets close to the walls. The more Arnau saw, the more he felt that his prediction of Hell on earth was coming true.

On the morning of the eleventh of November, news arrived that the emperor's force had been spotted north of the city. Unwilling to risk the city's violent streets, Arnau and Ramon strode the three miles along the land walls to the Golden Gate, which seemed certain to be the place the emperor would enter the city, since it had long been the gateway to the heart of Byzantium for victorious emperors.

Sure enough, that afternoon Alexios the Fourth passed between the great golden gates under the decorative triumphal arch to a fanfare like some Roman hero of old, flags waving and gleaming knights in a hundred colours in his wake. Behind them, protected by the comparatively dour imperial army, came carts laden with loot, ripped from the desperate clinging hands of Byzantine peasants and provincials. Having impoverished the city to pay the Doge of Venice, the young emperor had now repeated the process with the hinterland. Arnau found himself wondering whether even now they had managed to cover the massive sum promised. He doubted whether, even if they had, the doge would relinquish control so readily.

Inside the walls, the leaders of the army turned from the long main street and began to pass through wide connecting roads and then out into the open farmland enclosed by the walls, heading for the imperial residence in the Blachernae.

Arnau and Ramon kept pace on the wall top, watching the imperial party returning. The emperor was garbed like some antiquated general. Doukas followed among several other courtiers, perhaps a dozen of the Frankish nobles alongside, all escorted by brightly coloured knights, dour men-at-arms and Byzantine soldiers. The citizens watched them all with simmering hate. No Frank was safe in the city these days, but no mob was going to attack such a large army, and probably the emperor was unaware of the danger in his own streets anyway.

They closed on the Blachernae's gate, the imperial party proceeding along a wide thoroughfare and the Templars keeping a parallel course on the wall. Passing from the city ramparts into the palace's enclosing curtain, Arnau and Ramon soon reached the gate top and watched the emperor and his cronies return to the palace. They would see Doukas as soon as they could, learn what he had to tell and inform him of all that had happened in his absence before the court could provide a sanitised version of events, shifting any blame.

Arnau glared at the party until Ramon nudged him and pointed across the wide courtyard. Arnau peered and saw Bochard emerge from the stairway to their apartments. At the preceptor's shoulder was the Frank in the white and red surcoat and black fleur-de-lys design. Both had squires with them and several men-at-arms followed.

Quickly, at Ramon's heel, Arnau descended the tower and emerged beside the gate. In the courtyard, the preceptor and his Frankish friend had met with two of the returning knights. Arnau felt something click in his mind as he saw that one of them bore the same white and red shield-in-shield design that he had seen outside the church all those weeks ago when someone had attempted to shoot them. The other was dressed impeccably in the latest Western fashions, forgoing armour, but his cote of dark green drew Arnau's attention almost as much as the red-and-white coat of arms displayed on his horse's caparison.

Two Western knights, a Venetian dog and Bochard.

Arnau looked round in surprise at a call of greeting to see Doukas walking in their direction, peeling gloves from his hands. His boots splashed in the shallow puddles left by the morning's rain, and he came to a halt with a shiver. Redwald stood at his shoulder as always, treating the two Templars to a simple nod of recognition.

'I am sure we all have much news,' Doukas said in weary tones.

Arnau nodded vigorously, but Ramon waved it away with a hand. 'Do you know who those men are?' he asked, pointing at the knights who had been in the minister's company on the journey but had now joined the preceptor. The young Templar looked back. The two knights in red and white moved with that haughty pride typical of the Frankish lords, but the man in dark green and with rich gold adornments was something else. Moving along behind them like a sour shadow, he felt wrong, suspicious. Arnau was moved, with a shudder, to even say *evil*. He did not so much walk as stalk, not so much stand as lurk. Arnau took an instant dislike to him. That man was trouble.

Doukas nodded, brow furrowing. 'The white and red fellow with the big nose is called de Charney. He is a dangerous one, I think. He likes to hurt people and see them killed. The emperor pleased him greatly on our journey by hurting a great many people before fleecing them of coins.'

Ramon nodded, and turned to Arnau. 'De Charney. Big Templar family. One of them, possibly his father or uncle, was a preceptor back in France. I met him once. De Charney and a man from Acre. Bochard has contacts within the Crusade.'

Doukas frowned at them. 'The other is a Venetian by the name of Balbi. Almerico Balbi. I would not trust him as far as I could spit a wolf, though much the same could be said of all Venetians.'

Arnau nodded. A succinct appraisal that very much supported Arnau's own. Balbi – the man who supplied Bochard's ships, no doubt. And given the other two, probably with some connection to the Order. The preceptor was shrewd, clearly, using those with a vested interest in the Temple to acquire, gather and ship his haul. How far could he trust his Crusader allies and their Italian ship masters though, Arnau wondered.

'The hinterland is officially secure,' Doukas said wearily. 'That is the *official* line. In truth rebellion lurks a few fathoms below the surface, and our little financial forays did more to drive disaffection into every heart than draw them back in. I would not be at all surprised if whole regions did not defect to the Bulgars in coming months. Not that the emperor will care now that he has his coin.'

'You gathered enough to pay off the doge?'

Doukas gave a hollow laugh. 'There is not enough gold in the empire to pay off the doge. All we have done is compound our problem and doom ourselves.'

'Why?' Arnau breathed.

'The emperor has managed to gather sufficient coin to pay the Venetians for their services thus far. Nothing is now owed. But if the Franks wish to sail on to Egypt, then they will owe more. The Venetians will take them no further without coin, and the Franks do not have the funds. But between them they more or less control Constantinople and they cannot believe we are not hoarding more wealth away from them. This is far from over, my friends. All we have done is guarantee that the Franks and Venetians will stay for the winter.'

Arnau closed his eyes in dismay. 'Can the Crusaders not simply cross the land from here on their way to Egypt?'

'They would have to pass through areas with poor forage and dangerously close to the Sultanate of Rum with whom tenuous treaties exist. That way disaster lies. No, they need to go by ship. Which means the Venetians, which means raping the city of every last coin.'

Ramon sagged. 'That will force a war. You've missed much, Doukas, but I tell you now that a single kick or slung insult these days could drive the entire city into open rebellion.'

Doukas sighed, looking up as it started to rain again.

'Tell me everything.'

CHAPTER 15:
THE LINE DRAWN

DECEMBER 11TH 1203

'Trouble,' Ramon said, looking back through the apartment door from the corridor where he had been standing at the window like some lovelorn prisoner mooning over the world outside. But then in a very real sense, prisoners was exactly what they were.

Prisoners confined to the city by Bochard's ongoing obsession with acquiring and shipping artefacts. Without the preceptor's permission, they could not leave Constantinople unless they deliberately broke one of the most important rules of the Order: obedience. Ramon would not countenance such a thing without Bochard breaking the Rule first and giving them justification.

Prisoners within the Blachernae palace, too. The city had come to the boil, using Arnau's now frequently voiced analogy. There were no longer punishments for citizens attacking Frankish visitors, not because of a change in the regime, but because there *were* no Frankish visitors. Since one unfortunate and foolish Burgundian man-at-arms had chanced the city in mid-November and had been sent back across the water in a small fishing boat, moaning, with his eyes put out and his hands and feet removed and sealed with hot pitch, no one else had felt inclined.

Now no Frank crossed the water, the entire crusading force sitting glowering at the city from Galata's slopes, the Venetians on the waterside opposite the city's strong white walls. Arnau could imagine how much the situation rankled among the Crusaders and their naval allies. In theory, the younger of the two emperors currently ruling the city was their creature, and therefore they more or less controlled Constantinople. Yet they dare not enter the city as free men, for to do so invited a gruesome demise. Moreover, they had no legitimate reason to complain. The emperors had punished men for what had repeatedly happened, for all the good it did, and the city had paid over the money demanded of it... thus far.

It irked Arnau – Ramon and Sebastian too, he was sure – that they had fought and shed blood against the Venetians for the sake of the city, yet because of the cross that Bochard insisted they continue to wear, they themselves could not enter the city without facing exactly the same peril as the Crusaders with whom they would be connected in the public eye. Even an escort of four burly Warings no longer seemed adequate protection from the furious city, so they had now spent weeks trapped in the palace.

The only visitors these days – which consisted almost entirely of either priests insisting on Papish practices being followed by the city's churches or the occasional visits by those few nobles dealing with the preceptor – came to the city heavily armoured with an entire conroi of knights and associated men-at-arms. They came around the Golden Horn by the higher bridges and approached the city by land, entering through the Blachernae Gate, straight into the palace without braving the perilous streets of the city itself.

The situation was deteriorating daily and Ramon was convinced that open warfare was just days away once more. Their window of opportunity for leaving the city had almost closed, yet still Bochard refused.

The only visitor Ramon and Arnau regularly saw was Doukas. Even the Laskaris brothers had begun to keep themselves to themselvcs, staying out of the court's circles, safely anonymous. Doukas was permanently busy, trying to stretch the tiny funds of the city to pay all that needed paying, but when the strain became too much, he would visit the Templars, acquaint them with the latest news and sag in a chair with a cup of wine, retreating from his fiscal nightmares for a short while.

Arnau joined Ramon at the window in the corridor and peered down, his spirits sinking at the sight of red-and-white clad men below, side by side with dark-green Venetians.

'Wonderful.'

The two men stepped back into their doorway. Blocking the corridor to the preceptor's room would be unlikely to improve anything. Footsteps echoed up the stairs, and after a few moments, figures emerged from the darkened stairwell. The Lord de Charney stepped out onto the flagstones, flinging the two Templars a look filled with a haughty superiority not often displayed before the Order's knights. The two men returned his look with stony glares of their own. Then Almerico Balbi appeared. Once more, Arnau's neck hairs rose, and he shivered. The Venetian's face was the precise opposite of de Charney's. He radiated good-natured interest. At first glance, it would be tempting to step over and shake his hand. But Arnau knew the man better than that now.

Some men put forth an aura that seduced the eye and the heart, distracting them from the truth of things. Balbi was such a man. The very moment Arnau forced himself not to see that warm exterior, he noticed the cold flat look in those eyes. Balbi assessed the value of everything. In the man's eyes, Arnau could see his own worthlessness reflected. Balbi considered him nothing, yet that warm smile kept people unaware of his reasoning.

Balbi bowed his head respectfully, and without even intending to, Arnau found himself responding in like manner. Lord, but the man was charismatic. They stood in silence as de Charney rapped on the preceptor's door, which was opened to reveal Bochard already prepared for the outdoors. Leaving his room in Hugues's care, Bochard stepped out, following the two foreigners back down the stairs. The master treated them to a look no warmer than de Charney's, and was gone. The two knights watched from the window as the small party moved off across the Blachernae complex and out of sight.

'De Charney displays all the warmth of a snake,' Ramon said with a curl of the lip.

'De Charney is nothing compared to his friend.'

Ramon nodded. 'Did you get a good look at him?'

'Better than he'd like, I think. The man has the Devil in him.'

'He seemed perfectly angelic on the surface,' the older knight said quietly.

'So did Lucifer. That one is a dark heart hidden behind a golden smile. If Dandolo is half what Balbi is then it is no wonder the Franks betray everything they believe in at his mere whim.'

The two men returned to the room, peering at the half-polished armour sitting on the table. Had things been normal and they in their full monastic routine, Ramon would have reprimanded Sebastian for leaving a job half done. As it was, the young squire was off somewhere on his own business, as was increasingly the case these days, and both knights felt inclined to give him space. He was struggling so much more than either of them, after all. Thus it was that the two knights were alone when the impeccably dressed eunuch reached the top of the stairs, his Waring escort and three attendants at his heels.

'Good morning,' the man said politely, inclining his head, standing in the light of the window at which Ramon had recently stood.

'Good day,' the knights replied, bowing curtly.

'I bear a message for your master.'

Ramon and Arnau exchanged glances before the latter straightened. 'I am afraid Preceptor Bochard is absent. I am not sure when we are to expect him. Can we be of assistance?'

The man's face dropped into a crease of uncertainty. 'It is a matter of some urgency. Where might I find the commander?'

'I truly have no idea, I am afraid,' Ramon replied.

Again the man seemed worried and doubtful. 'The emperor has summoned the representatives of the Order in confidence. The summons is, as I say, a matter of some urgency.'

'Then we will join you. Vallbona here and myself are full brothers of the Temple and quite capable of representing the Order's interests.'

Still the man hesitated, peering intently past them at the far door as though Bochard might suddenly materialise if he concentrated hard enough. Finally, he nodded slightly. 'Very well, if you would follow me.'

Ramon again looked across at his younger companion. An imperial summons sounded important, and the words 'in confidence' were intriguing. Arnau shivered in anticipation. They had spent time in the company of several courtiers, some of them repeatedly, but they had personally experienced an imperial audience only with the former emperor who had fled in the night. Their entire involvement with the current emperors had been limited to watching the younger Alexios being paraded by his Frankish masters. They had yet to even set eyes upon the ageing Isaac, whose blindness and frailty had made him something of a recluse, hiding away in the palace, according to rumour.

Which emperor, Arnau wondered? Who had issued a confidential summons to the Templars?

The functionary led them from their accommodation across the courtyard outside, through a garden with high hedges and into another part of the huge palace complex – a part into which they had not yet ventured. Their meetings with the emperor and his court had always been in the Great Palace on the far side of the city or in their own rooms. This place would be the palace proper where the emperors now held court, for it was only at the Blachernae where the Crusaders could visit without passing through the city itself.

Arnau marvelled anew at the ancient marble grandeur of the place. Statues from antiquity of emperors long dead lined a vestibule with a floor of multichrome marble. They clumped, clicked and rattled their way along it, Warings behind them, functionary in front. Entering a wide room, they were delivered into the hands of a different eunuch in even more sumptuous silks, who bowed.

'Good morning, sirs. If you would follow me.'

The man turned sharply and strode off through another door, alone. Ramon and Arnau shared unspoken thoughts, shrugged and followed. It was only as they entered the new corridor that Arnau realised they were now alone with the man, the attendants and guards left behind. Their intrigue grew as they were led up a staircase, through a door that required unlocking and along a narrow corridor into a small room. The room was little more than ten paces long and six wide, with seats but no table. The only light was provided by a single oil lamp standing on a narrow shelf. There appeared to be three arched windows in a columned arcade, each covered by a thick red curtain.

The knights turned frowns upon the man, who smiled oddly. 'If you would kindly wait here until you are sent for?'

With that, he withdrew and closed the door. Arnau felt a tiny thrill of alarm at the sound of the door being locked. For whose security, he wondered.

'Well, what do we make of this?' Ramon muttered quietly.

'All very clandestine,' Arnau agreed. 'A strangely obscure antechamber or waiting room, wouldn't you say?'

A nod. 'Where are we, I wonder?' Ramon murmured and crossed to the window, edging aside one of the curtains and peeking through. Arnau heard him take a sharp breath, and he let the curtain drop, turning with wide eyes.

'What?'

Ramon gestured to the windows, and Arnau repeated the procedure, lifting one edge slightly and peering through.

He stared in surprise.

What he had assumed to be draped windows did not look out onto wide gardens or courtyards, but down into a wide and well-appointed chamber. A throne room, it appeared, or perhaps an audience chamber. The large room was decorated with purple drapery, and on a raised dais at one end were two great thrones. Arnau peered at the figures of the two emperors in fascination. He had seen Alexios before, and was surprised to see the young man finally dressed as a Byzantine ruler and not some Frankish princeling. The man's court dress was incredibly rich and complex, decorated on every inch of fabric, scattered with priceless jewels and plates of gold, from his crown decorated with pendulous chains and rubies to his red leather boots with gold adornments. The ageing Isaac the Second was garbed just as richly, his face cadaverous, empty white eyes staring out above a greying beard that had been trimmed down to a spade-like point. Arnau wondered how much of the Venetians' debt could have been covered by the imperial costumes alone.

Behind the emperors' dais stood a small crowd of servants and eunuchs, and richly dressed courtiers lined the two sides of the room, standing silently, the only two seats in the room those in which the emperors sat. The gathering was completed by numerous heavily armed and armoured Warings, bristling with pointed steel for the emperor's protection. Arnau spotted Doukas among the courtiers, as well as the rarely seen Constantine Laskaris. Redwald and Octa were both present, standing like deadly sentinels.

'What is this?' he whispered.

'We are in a musicians' gallery, I suspect,' Ramon replied quietly. 'It would appear that we are to eavesdrop by imperial order. How curious.'

Carefully, being as silent as possible, the two men brought across wooden chairs and placed them by the curtains. As subtly as they could, they edged the red drapes back just a touch, leaving a crack through which they could see down into the room without being plainly visible from below.

The old emperor Isaac turned his head momentarily, lifting sightless eyes to the windows at which the two men sat before returning his blind gaze to the room before him. Ramon looked across at Arnau and nodded, then turned back at the sound of movement below. The doors at the far end of the room swung open to a distant fanfare. A richly dressed official appeared in the doorway and stepped to the side.

'The chevaliers Conon de Béthune, Geoffroi de Villehardouin and Otho de la Roche.'

Three brightly attired knights from the Frankish force strode into the room, one slightly ahead of the men at his shoulders as though forming an arrow head to punch into an enemy body. Arnau chewed at his lip pensively at the sight of one of them. The man at the far side was the one wearing the red and white with the black fleur-de-lys whom he had seen occasionally with Bochard.

As the three men filed in to stand on one side, facing the thrones, heads held high and proud and making no sign of deference to the emperors, more footsteps approached, and the functionary took a deep breath.

'The Venetian patricians Andrea Dandolo, Filippo Falier and Cristoforo Minotto.'

Three impeccably dressed noblemen entered side by side and strode down the hallway to stand beside the three Frankish knights. A dozen followers, all armed and armoured, entered without being announced and formed a small force behind the six men who clearly represented the interests of both the Crusaders and their naval allies. Once the entire deputation was in place, the doors were closed behind them and another functionary stepped forward at the foot of the imperial dais.

'The *basilis pistoi Romaion*, Isaac the Second and Alexios the Fourth, pious and noble kings of the Romans, give greetings to the emissaries of Venice and Frankland and would hear their entreaty.'

Initial formalities complete, the leader of the Frankish trio, the central figure, stepped a pace forward.

'Greetings to the emperors of Byzantium. We represent the interests of the holy and most sacred army of God and his earthly representatives the Bishop of Rome, Pope Innocent the Third and the Count of Montferrat, as well as His Serenity Enrico Dandolo, Doge of Venice.'

The emperors both nodded their acceptance, and so de Béthune bowed his head and cleared his throat.

'With regard to the promises made by your imperial majesty, calculations have been made again and again in order to be certain of the facts, and it is my unfortunate duty to inform the court that the figure agreed upon has yet to be fully paid. Despite the efforts of the emperor and his court, there is still a sizeable shortfall in the coins delivered to the Venetian fleet.'

There was a rumble of discontent throughout the court and Arnau and Ramon glanced at one another. To their understanding, the debt thus far had been fully paid. Still, the Frankish spokesman did not look nervous. If this was a lie, then he was an exceptional liar. Arnau wondered silently whether perhaps the Venetians had deliberately miscounted and the Franks remained unaware. Certainly from the looks on the faces of the emperors, they were unaware of any such shortfall. Yes, Arnau decided, the Venetians without a doubt.

'I am charged with delivering this unpleasant reminder and also words of caution and encouragement for the benefit of all concerned. If you will only fulfil your obligations, then everything will be well. But I must warn you that reneging on them will lead the commanders of this most holy Crusade to withdraw all further communication with a view to severing our current ties of friendship.'

Arnau had to stifle a bitter laugh at the notion that any of this had been conceived in friendship. There was a dreadful silence, which was filled with a second voice sporting a thick French accent as another of the ambassadors stepped forward.

'The forces arrayed across the water are noble soldiers of God. As such we will never open hostilities without due warning, for it is not our custom to act in a treacherous manner.'

Again, Arnau felt his lip curl at the blatant untruth issuing from the lips of men whose arrival in Byzantium had been heralded by the sinking of fishing boats, and who had sacked a Christian city with neither warning nor declaration of war the previous year. He changed his angle to get a good look at the emperors.

Isaac's face was a mask of hatred and disdain. He might be labelled mad and feeble by some, but at least there was a touch of defiance still in his white, sightless eyes. It occurred to Arnau that the two forces meeting here in conflict were both ultimately commanded by bitter and blind old men. What did that say about the world, he wondered. Young Alexios, who had come east with the Franks, and who had been put on this throne by the very men now threatening him, looked utterly astonished. Had he not expected such treatment from men he had considered allies? Was he actually foolish enough to think himself a valuable asset in whose prosperity the Franks had a vested interest, and not simply a tool for their own advantage?

An Italian voice now cut through the knife-edge silence that had followed the threat.

'We give you until the new year to make good on your promises and then, if debts are not paid in full, the period of peaceful negotiation will come to an end and a state of open hostility will once more be declared. You have been warned.'

With that, the Venetian trio turned and marched away without a further acknowledgement of the imperial presence. Arnau winced. He had seen enough now of Byzantine court life to know that everything was highly regimented. Everything was achieved through a dozen layers of subtlety and formality, and nothing was ever delivered with such brashness. The court were staring open-mouthed at the departing Venetians. To give him his due, de Béthune also looked around at their retreating forms with distaste. He might have delivered his blunt warnings and reminders, but even he would not go so far as to turn his back on the emperors and leave without due deference.

The three Franks bowed smartly.

'Thank you for your time, Your Majesties,' de Villehardouin said formally. 'I trust when we meet next, it will be under more positive circumstances.'

Even this was clearly outrageous form given the looks on every Byzantine face, and the Franks turned and left, taking their small party with them.

Arnau let his curtain drop back and stood. Ramon did the same and they crossed to the far side of the room, near the door.

'That was dreadful,' the young knight breathed quietly. 'Did you see their faces?'

Ramon nodded. 'That was never going to end well. The money was fully gathered and delivered, according to Doukas, and he is not the sort of man to lie about such things or to make mistakes, either way. Which means that the demand is a deliberate act by either the Franks or the Venetians, or possibly both in concert. I fear that Dandolo was probably highly disappointed when the money was actually paid and he lost his pretext for attempting to control the city.'

Arnau nodded. 'Whatever the case, it would appear that January will bring another war. I presume there is no hope that we can persuade Bochard to leave now, while we still can?'

'Doubtful. Now let us find out why the emperor treated us to this little exchange.'

There was not long to wait. Just ten minutes later the same functionary reappeared, unlocking the door and bowing his head. 'If you would follow me again, my Lords.'

They set off at the man's heel, back along the corridors and down the stairs, though not to the grand throne room. Instead, they were led through the labyrinthine palace to a door protected by two heavy Waring guardsmen. A swift rap on the timbers and an order to enter, and the doors swung open. Inside, Arnau saw the older emperor, Isaac, sitting on an ornate seat up a pair of steps. Of his son and co-emperor there was no sign, nor indeed of any of the nobles they knew or might expect to see. There were just the two minor functionaries who had opened the doors, a dozen more Warings looking alert and dangerous, and a man in the robes of a Greek priest, which came as a surprise.

'Knights of the Temple,' the old emperor wheezed, turning his sightless eyes eerily on the two men. 'I was under the impression there were three of you.'

As Arnau wondered how the blind emperor had known how many men stood before him, Ramon bowed deeply. 'Your Imperial Majesty, greetings. We are honoured to find ourselves in your august presence. In answer to your question, our leader, Preceptor

Bochard, was absent about his business when your summons arrived and, given the timing, your eunuch decided it would be better to bring two men he could find than miss the meeting entirely looking for the third.'

The emperor nodded his understanding. 'And you are empowered to speak for him?'

Ramon took a deep breath. 'If there are matters for which only the preceptor can speak, I will convey your words to him and seek a repeat audience, Majesty. But in many matters, I can assume authority. How might we help?'

'You heard the embassy of the Franks.'

'Yes, Your Majesty.'

'Constantine Laskaris warned me in advance what to expect, and he was close to the mark. Given what he had anticipated, I felt it might ease matters between us if you were fully aware of the situation. I would ask your opinion of what you witnessed.'

Ramon sighed. 'An appalling ultimatum, Majesty. I would say that the entire deputation was intended as little more than an insult, from its manner to its content and even its brevity. I fear the Venetians have deliberately miscounted their money in order to deliver such a demand. I believe that your august son, the Basileos Alexios, is no longer of use to them, and now they turn their threats upon the empire and its rulers.'

'Astute,' Isaac snarled. 'Yes, they insult us in every possible way. Your own bearing and manner might be crude and even lacking by imperial standards, yet you who owe us nothing show vastly more respect and deference than the so-called *nobles* of the West. I am content that your opinion of them and their demands is not far removed from my own. Even my feckless son, whose avarice and arrogance brought this entire situation about, is now horrified by what the Venetians and their pet Franks are demanding.'

'I presume, Majesty, that you have no intention of paying any supposed shortfall?'

Isaac snorted. 'Had I the money in these very hands I would swallow it before I gave it to the *anti-Christos* Dandolo. But the simple truth, which I am loath to admit, is that the city simply could not afford to do so if we wished it. To cover our supposed debt, we would have to sell everything of any value in the city. Our churches would have to be stripped, our army unpaid, our nobles driven to poverty. And you know as well as I that if I sent the money to the Crusaders, there would just be a further demand made that we could not meet unless we can turn the Franks against the Venetians somehow. You are correct in your assessment of the enemy. I know Dandolo of old, from the days before he was doge. I remember him when both of us had eyes with which to judge our hatred. Dandolo intends nothing more than the destruction of the empire entire.'

Arnau shivered, but Ramon simply nodded. 'What is your question, Majesty? That for which you summoned us and allowed us to witness your jeopardy?'

The emperor sat back in his chair. 'Thus far I have not treatied with your order. I am aware that you spoke with my brother before his ignominious flight, but given the situation since then, there seemed little point in dealing with you thereafter.'

'And what has changed, Majesty, might I ask?'

Isaac's brow furrowed, a strange effect with those white, sightless eyes. 'Doukas informs me that the receipt of a small amount of money had alleviated some of the worst privations of our beleaguered churches, through the somewhat strangling mercantilism of your preceptor.'

Arnau winced. Bochard's acquisitions coming to the attention of the emperor himself seemed sure to be a bad thing.

'While I deplore the priests of my city selling off the great treasures of Byzantium to your order, especially for the paltry sums your commander seems willing to pay, I can neither condemn nor argue with their decisions. Money is desperately needed. It occurs to me, however, and Doukas supports my notion, that the small-scale alleviation these sales have brought could be carried out on a much grander scale.'

Arnau closed his eyes. Was this it? Was the emperor of Byzantium about to turn to the Order in desperation for a loan? It seemed impossible that the empire could be so desperate.

'I have a mind to put a proposal to you,' the old emperor said. 'I need money and security for my throne, my city and my empire. The Temple can grant all of that. It is said that your order is exceedingly wealthy. Indeed, it is the subject of jokes I hear that the "Poor Knights of Christos" are wealthier than some kings. Your order could cover any payment we need to make. Moreover, you could grant us security with mere words. An oath of support from the Order would be seen as Rome's endorsement of our power. I despise the fact that I must go to the children of the Pope with my crown in my hands like a pauper, seeking their endorsement, yet this is what must happen. If the Order will speak out in favour of the empire and against the Franks and their sea-rat friends, then the knights of God could be turned from further violence. If we can then cover the figure spoken of, the Venetians will also have no valid reason to stay. We might turn this tide.'

Ramon sucked on his teeth. 'Your predecessor had similar notions of support from the order, Majesty. The preceptor, however, seemed disinclined to entertain them, writing to the grand master in a letter that has yet to be answered after all this time.'

'I am aware of this,' Isaac nodded. 'But I am also aware that my brother offered only a nebulous set of promises to aid the security of the East in return. I offer more. I offer the Order property and authority within Constantinople and other cities of the empire. A chapter house in this city and others. Lands and other interests. No such thing has ever been considered or offered to any organisation of the Latin Church. I presume the value of what I propose is not lost upon you.'

Arnau's eyes widened with every word. It represented *huge* value. To be the first group under the Roman Church to be granted a place in the empire. To link the Order's future to that of the Byzantines. For centuries the Genovese, the Pisans, the

Amalfitani and even the Venetians had worked to gain just a small stake in the lucrative world of Byzantium, where the exotic trade routes of the East met the merchants of the West to the profit of all. Arnau was in no doubt whatsoever that any number of senior members of the Order, including probably the grand master himself, would leap at such an opportunity. A sickened part of him, though, remembered Bochard's face whenever he was confronted with Byzantine culture or the Greek Church. That he consorted happily with the Franks and was unconcerned about the fate of the city beyond his raping it of value. Almost certainly Bochard had never actually written that letter to the grand master. Would Bochard throw his support behind the emperor even for such a fantastic reward? Somehow, Arnau doubted it. Bochard would see it as demeaning his order.

A glance at Ramon told him that his companion shared his opinion.

Damn it.

'Majesty, your offer is beyond generous, and most worthy of consideration. It is, however, of such great import that these matters could only truly be settled by the grand master and the mother house in Acre. I fear your surest course of action is to bypass us entirely and seek the agreement of Acre.'

'Impossible.'

'I would be willing to act as the intermediary, Majesty. To write such a missive or even travel and deliver the offer myself.'

Arnau felt his heart leap. Ramon was on the cusp of securing a departure from the city for them both. While he might not disobey Bochard willingly, delivering such tidings to the grand master would have to take precedence.

'That is not a possibility,' the emperor repeated, irritably. 'You heard the Franks and Venetians. It is less than three weeks until January, which to the Venetians is their new year. In little more than three weeks' time we will be at war. If we are to get what we need in time to avert disaster, it must be agreed now. Even by a fast ship, it would take most of the time we have just to reach Acre and return.'

Ramon shook his head, as though the blind old man might see it.

'Then all I can do, Majesty, is to put your proposal to the preceptor and ask him to meet with you. I strongly suspect, however, that such a course will either fail or, if it succeeds, will do so with such torpidity that it will be of little value to you.'

The emperor straightened once more. 'Then I can only pray to God that you are wrong. Put my proposal to your commander. He may secure an audience at any reasonable time through any channel in the palace.'

Ramon bowed, and the opening of the doors behind them clearly signalled the end of the meeting. Thanking the emperor with due deference and as many honorifics as he could remember, Ramon led them back out of the chamber, remaining silent until their eunuch escort delivered them out of the building and into the cold open air once more.

'That offer was generous,' Arnau said.

'*Beyond* generous,' Ramon agreed. 'It would have hurt for a man like that to make such an offer, which is an indication of the level of distress the court is now in. There will be no appeasement by coin, and no further negotiation. Bochard will never agree to this, even generous as it is. I have half a notion to send a message by fast ship to Acre myself, going over his head, though I doubt anything could be arranged in time anyway. I note that the wily Venetians left it long enough before their embassy and gave a short enough deadline that there is little chance of the emperor achieving *anything* in that time.'

'It's inevitable, then?' Arnau sighed.

'I fear so. We have not witnessed the end of this city's siege, but merely of the first wave. And what is coming will be cataclysmic, as you so cleverly predicted. Byzantium teeters on the very edge of Hell.'

CHAPTER 16:
THE KINDLED FLAME

DECEMBER 30TH 1203

U ndoubtedly the Crusaders and their Venetian friends saw no change in the city languishing across the water over the following days. As the Franks in their camp settled in for three weeks of celebrations, beginning with the Yuletide Christ Mass and leading up to the end of their year, they likely thought the same would happen in Constantinople. Arnau had assumed so too. But the Franks and Venetians remained across the water, looking only at the unchanging walls and not the troubled city behind them.

Christ Mass was a muted affair in the city. Arnau attended the services, of course, and the city *did* celebrate, though it seemed that the holy day was of lesser importance to the Byzantines than Epiphany, which was the real time for celebration. Moreover, the Byzantines began their new year in September, rather than in January like the Franks.

So while the Franks and Venetians revelled in their festivities in Galata, living a lavish life with rich goods bought with Byzantine gold from the many smaller towns in the region, the population of the city celebrated quietly and swiftly and prepared for the worst.

Needless to say, when Bochard had returned from his day's work, he had flatly refused to be involved in integrating the Order within the Byzantine world, when in his opinion it was just a matter of weeks before the forces of Rome controlled the city once more and the Order would have the opportunity to gain lands without sacrificing their sanctity by 'dealing with heretics'. He had visited the emperor and, though Arnau and Ramon had not been there, clearly the audience had gone particularly sourly from the look on Bochard's face when he returned. Still, Ramon had taken it upon himself to write a letter with the emperor's offer and privately see it onto a fast *dromon* – one of the few remaining from the ruined Byzantine fleet – bound for Acre. He had little hope of a reply coming in time to do anything, but still he had to try.

Arnau and Ramon, ignoring their preceptor as he rushed to acquire all he could before war made it impossible, watched the city change in small, subtle ways. The first was the closing of gates. One thing that had been manifest since the change in emperors and the nervous peace with the Crusaders was that the gates remained accessible. Even when the troubles had started, at least the Blachernae Gate had opened freely at the command of any Frank or Venetian. Now the city had been sealed. Since no Frank came, they could not know, but already many of the gates had been bolstered and blocked.

Secondly, every Western cross, Frankish flag and symbol of the Crusaders had been removed from Constantinople. Arnau was fairly sure that the Templars were now the only Westerners in the entire city. The emperors had drawn their line. No matter that young Alexios had arrived as a puppet of the Franks and his father was blind and considered half mad, both stood by their empire now, refusing to capitulate and bleed their city any further for the benefit of avaricious foreigners. Of course, they were also well aware of the danger they faced, and in the absence of any deal with the Temple, overtures had been sent to the Seljuk Turks and the Tsar of Bulgaria. And while they prepared the city for disaster, there was no sign of any attempt to take the war to the Franks.

In the city, the Western Church had been denied once more. The churches of Constantinople rang out in Greek voices singing hymns of heresy, and cross pieces had been added to the Western crucifixes, returning them to their former pattern. The city had reverted, casting aside all that had been imposed on them in the unacceptable deal.

So Constantinople prepared and waited, watching the enemy revelling. The court sat tense, waiting for word from Acre or Bulgaria or the Turks. Any one of them might be enough to make the Franks think twice. But time would be tight. No word came.

Arnau stood at the window of his apartment, peering out at the distant hilltop where months ago the Franks had camped, lobbing stones at this very wall. Ramon lay on his bed murmuring almost-silent prayers, and Sebastian sat in the corner, polishing armour.

A knock at the door turned all three heads, and Ramon bade the caller enter. As the door swung open, Arnau was surprised to see the figure of Theodoros Laskaris. Neither he nor his brother had been visible much in court circles since the day of capitulation five months ago, yet suddenly there was a gleam in the eye of the former general. Behind him stood two men in the uniforms of Byzantine officers and one man in the rich garb of a court official.

'Brothers of the Temple, greetings.'

'Laskaris,' Ramon nodded. 'It has been a while.'

'It has, and my apologies for our absence. As you are undoubtedly aware, we opposed any deal being struck with the Franks, and time has borne out our view, I believe. Here we are near half a year later facing the same situation, but with little in terms of money or support, having seen it all leeched out by the enemy. And our emperors flounder. Neither is willing to do what must be done to defy the enemy. They do not believe we can win any engagement, so they send out desperate pleas to our neighbours for support. But stout hearts remain, and this city's walls have held for a millennium. We will see off the Franks if only we can commit fully to facing them.'

Arnau nodded. 'But the emperors will not sanction such a thing.'

Laskaris folded his arms. 'We intend to give them no choice. The Franks and Venetians will besiege us once again in less than two weeks, when their new year is upon them. If we do nothing before then, they will have all the initiative and advantage. We must take our chance now.'

Ramon sat up on the edge of his bed. 'Why come to us?'

'Courtesy,' Laskaris said simply. 'We have fought side by side and you proved yourselves honourable men. I have no wish to see you caught up in what is coming. When we move tomorrow, and we *will* move tomorrow, then war will be upon us once more, and this time it will only end in destruction for someone. I advise you to leave Constantinople before nightfall tomorrow, else leaving may no longer be an option.'

Arnau glanced sharply at Ramon, who shook his head. 'Our preceptor will not allow us to leave.'

'Then you will become part of this great tragedy,' Laskaris warned.

'What is it you are planning?' Arnau asked.

Laskaris paused, perhaps weighing up the danger of revealing plans to the outsiders.

'A two-pronged attack,' Theodoros said, glancing over his shoulder. The men behind him nodded. 'Already Constantine gathers his forces and my men gather the equipment. It is clear that any move, if is to be decisive, must target both the Franks and the Venetians simultaneously.'

'How will you attack the Venetians?' Ramon frowned. 'Their navy is strong, and yours is all but non-existent.'

Laskaris smiled unpleasantly. 'With fire. We have the bulk of the military commanders on our side. They will follow Constantine. He will lead the army around the upper Horn and against the Franks. Already our forces gather outside the city, unknown to the enemy and even the court. It must come as a surprise. They will begin marching early in the morning on the first, with a view to reaching the enemy camp at dawn.'

Arnau nodded. A good plan.

'In the meanwhile, I have given orders to seize every boat and ship in the city and port them, if necessary, to the Neorion harbour. There they will be filled with kindling and pig fat which we have already begun procuring. Jars of pitch and Greek fire will make them floating explosives. You may have noticed over the last two days a shift in the winds. It is not uncommon at this time of year. A southerly wind that rips along the valleys in the city into the Golden Horn and across to Galata. It is not something that happens throughout the year but on such odd occasions makes sailing north unusually easy. The fleet will be sent out at midnight.'

'Fire ships,' Ramon breathed.

'Quite so.'

'It is the most appalling method of waging war.'

Laskaris shrugged. 'There I fear our worlds differ. Fire has long been the chosen weapon of the empire. No imperial mind would shy from such a thing, whereas the lack of diplomatic respect that seems to be second nature to the Franks is unthinkable in our court.'

'Your timing is out,' Arnau noted. 'The fleet will engage in the small hours and that will all be over before your army reaches the Crusaders.'

'I am counting on that,' Laskaris said with a malicious grin. 'The Venetian fleet will burn throughout the hours of darkness. The disaster will wake the entire enemy force. With luck the Franks will rush to help their Venetian allies. If not, they will at least be kept awake. Our army will have slept well and rested for a day before the attack and will have marched only four miles to engage, while their entire army should be exhausted, soot-stained and demoralised. If all goes well, by sundown on the first, the Venetian fleet will be destroyed and the Franks resoundingly beaten.'

'You are defying the emperors,' Ramon noted. 'Doukas has told us some of the consequences of that.'

'Unless we win. If we save Constantinopolis in the name of the emperors, they will look favourably upon us. Success breeds success.'

Arnau looked across at Ramon. 'It has the makings of a workable plan.'

Ramon nodded. 'It is ambitious.'

'At this stage nothing humble will suffice,' Laskaris said quietly.

'True.'

Laskaris straightened. 'I would ask you to keep this to yourselves until the time comes, but I still urge you to leave, whether you go with your master or not. If this succeeds, then your preceptor's easy acquisitions will end and he will have no business here. If it fails, you will not want to be in the city.'

'Thank you for the warning,' Ramon said. 'It will all unfold as God wills it.'

'For certain.'

With a polite nod of the head, Laskaris turned and left, taking his small cadre of officers with him. The door clicked shut, and Ramon turned to Arnau and Sebastian. 'It is a very good plan, and if it succeeds, it will almost certainly put the city in the ascendant and make the Crusaders beg for terms. But there are many things that can go wrong, and he is correct that if that happens this city will be the most dangerous place to be in the world. As such, I think we have decisions to make.'

'We do?'

'I will not break the Rule of the Order. I cannot leave as long as Bochard intends to remain. I will state here and now, though, that the very moment he breaks the Rule himself, I shall consider myself freed of his authority and shall act accordingly to save whoever I can. Vallbona, you are a brother of the Order. As such I would humbly submit that the same strictures apply to you, though your soul and your conscience are your own, and I will not stop you if you wish to leave.' He turned to Sebastian. 'You are my squire and a friend, and an associate of the Order. I have come to rely upon you, and wish to see you preserved. I hereby release you from any vow or command. You are free to choose your destiny. If you wish to leave before your city teeters on the edge of destruction, I will help you. If you wish to stay, that is your choice.'

He fell silent and folded his arms.

Arnau felt torn. The Order had become everything to him in his five years of service: a home, a family and a future. And any early misgivings he might have had were long since cast to the wind as he took the vows of full brotherhood. He swallowed a resigned swallow and shook his head. Being a brother of the Poor Knights meant following *all* the rules. Obedience was no less important than any other, and more so than many. If Ramon would not go until the preceptor either commanded it or broke the Rule and proved himself unworthy, then neither could Arnau.

'I am with you.'

They turned to Sebastian, who had paused, polishing rag held close to the steel. 'No,' the young man said, 'I will not leave. I will hold my sword and stand fast and push two feet of iron into the gut of any Frank who thinks to end my people.'

Ramon took a deep breath. 'We are agreed, then. I will not see Bochard, nor tell him what has transpired. He is far too fond of his Frankish friends, and I fear he would consider it his duty to warn them. Moreover, if we visit Bochard he will command us to remain uninvolved, and I have a mind to watch Venetian ships burn.'

Arnau nodded vigorously. That was a sight he would relish for sure.

The evening passed at a crawl. As they had since the city's churches had returned to their Greek traditions, the two knights went through the liturgical services appropriately in the privacy of their apartments. Sebastian, instead, continued to visit the Blachernae church for the Greek services and Ramon did nothing to stop him.

Their visitor that night came as the most unpleasant surprise. Ramon answered the door to a quiet knock, presuming it to be one of the many palace functionaries or perhaps Laskaris with an update on his plan, or even Doukas with new information to impart. Instead, the older knight backed away from the door, hands coming up in a pose of surrender. Arnau rose sharply from his bed, hand going to sword hilt until Ramon barked at him to desist. The two men stood, frozen, as four green-clad men-at-arms entered, fanning out around the room, small, light crossbows already loaded, aimed at the two Templars. One itchy finger would mean a painful, lingering death. The two knights retreated against the wall.

It came as no further surprise when Almerico Balbi appeared in the door, wearing his Morningstar smile.

'Please, gentlemen, do take a seat. I will not take up much of your time.'

As Arnau and Ramon sank slowly to the beds, Balbi plonked himself down in a chair opposite them as a fifth man-at-arms closed the door to grant them privacy.

'You will forgive the manner of my arrival, I am sure. The streets of Constantinople are unsafe for a God-fearing Roman these days, and the palace no less so.'

'You may lower your bows, Balbi. I give you my word our swords will remain sheathed.'

'My, my. A Templar's word. A valuable thing, I'm sure. Let me come to the business at hand. I had initially considered you peripheral at best to my work here. Bochard is useful and lucrative in many, many ways, while you were merely his muscle. Upon further investigation it appears that you yourselves took an active part in the defence of the city walls against my countrymen. Some Venetians might take offence at that. I am more... flexible, let's say. Then it seems, from what de Charney tells me, that you have been prying into Bochard's affairs more than one might expect from hired muscle. Then, most recently and most interestingly of all, I am informed that you receive visits from the finance minister and even the city's most rebellious generals. What am I to make of all of this?'

Ramon's expression remained unreadable. 'We simply bide our time and survive as best we can in this dreadful world where an army of the Pope·attacks a city of God.'

Balbi gave a deep laugh. 'I have always found the monochrome thinking of monks to be exasperating. The world is built upon many layers, my friend, not just a black and a white.'

'What do you want, Balbi?'

'I am a lover of expediency, Templar. The deals I strike with Bochard and his crusading friends aid them and will make the house of Balbi wealthy enough to become pre-eminent among the families of Venezia. I do not like unknown quantities, and you represent just that. I fear that you are averse to your master's work here, but are too bound to him to leave. My offer is simple. I will secure for you from the preceptor permission to depart, and I will grant you free passage to a port of your choice on one of my own vessels. Your only part in this is to agree to leave without further incident.'

Arnau frowned. 'We present such a danger to you that you will whisk us away for free?'

Balbi's smile slipped for just a moment.

'I am a businessman, Templar. Sometimes one can make the greatest profit with an initial outlay. In the end it can be more lucrative. But rest assured that I am equally capable of threats. I would rather we resolved this swiftly and simply without the need for unpleasantness. I will have a place kept on my next departure until New Year. You may take it at any time. Beyond New Year, I cannot speak for your safety. You know what is coming.'

With that, he slowly rose from the seat. 'Again, apologies for the interruption. I pray you have a good night.'

Arnau sat, teeth grinding, as the Venetian left, still with that Luciferian smile, his men retreating after him, weapons still trained on the pair until the door closed.

'I have half a mind to follow them and make them regret that,' he grunted.

'Personally, I rather favour burning their ships to ash,' snarled Ramon.

'The bastard. Who does he think he is?'

Ramon turned. 'I thought you were still desperate for us to leave? Here Balbi is offering you that very chance.'

'I find suddenly that on having the door opened by Balbi, I am looking for the tripwire. No.'

'And Balbi will not back down,' Ramon sighed. 'His sort are driven by greed. You heard him. Lucrative deals with Bochard.'

Arnau nodded. 'Balbi's ships carry Bochard's treasures away. I would be willing to wager that a number of priceless items are diverted on the journey to a treasury in Venice. Balbi is becoming rich on Bochard's mania.'

'I wonder how many of Balbi's ships we can burn on the morrow?' Ramon smiled nastily.

* * *

The following day Arnau and Ramon, with their usual Waring escort, toured what they could of the city, without descending from the safety of the walls. Trying not to spend too long lingering on the sight of the scarred, burned-out parts of the city, they watched the Byzantines' quiet, subtle preparations throughout the day. In addition to keeping their plans secret from the enemy, the two brothers had done what they could to hide them from the emperors who might decide to halt them in their tracks.

Ships were being readied in the Neorion but at such a slow pace that it would not attract undue attention, the loads not being revealed for what they were until they were aboard, when they were distributed to be ready. Seventeen large vessels and sundry small boats were being prepared. If aimed correctly, they should be enough to ignite the entire Venetian fleet. Moreover, as the two knights had stepped out in the morning, they had witnessed Laskaris's predictions coming true. The southerly wind blew so strongly with wintry chill that ash and brick dust was being gusted through the burned-out parts of the city and settling on the waters even now, months after the fires. All seemed in order.

At the other side of the palace, on the land walls, they watched with fascination as small military units continually departed the city in groups of no more than a dozen, drawing no undue attention from the authorities. No one could see the gathering army, but it would be less than two miles away, beyond the hills and close to the upper waters of the Golden Horn.

The Laskaris were preparing well and had planned everything to within a hair's breadth.

Having spent much of the day watching the subtle preparations, the two knights returned to their rooms in time to perform the service for vespers. Outside the sun sank behind the slope of the Sixth Hill and the city burst into the light of a thousand twinkling lamps. The temperature dropped, but the wind kept up its pace and the clouds remained high – light scudding fleeces with no threat of the rain that Ramon had worried might just be the thing to ruin the entire plan.

Two hours passed in tense silence as Sebastian joined them once more for an evening meal of which none of them managed more than a few bites. Arnau was surprised at how tense he was. He had prepared for battle numerous times and was capable of adopting a stoic calm in the face of a coming storm, and this was not even his fight. Indeed, he *could* not draw his blade for it, as their vows prevented violence against the Franks, and the Venetians were to be targeted only with burning ships. All he would do was watch impotently as Laskaris's plans unfolded, yet he felt more nervous than he usually did before a fight.

The last service of the night, compline, was a muted affair. The knights went through the form appropriately, but the focus for both men was on silent and very avid prayer.

An hour later, they threw on their cloaks against the chill wind and left the palace before Bochard could find them and interfere. Passing from the palace walls smoothly onto the Golden Horn defences, they made their way along those ramparts, heading for the harbours.

As they neared the Neorion, the signs of what was to come were there for those who knew. The abandoned foreign enclaves, where they remained standing and untouched by fire at least, were occupied now by men. They gathered in numbers behind the walls, ready. The figures on the parapet remained few, for fear of alerting the watching Venetians. The ships in the harbour were ready.

Arnau, Ramon and Sebastian stood on the top of the Neorion Gate as the night's inky blackness deepened. They could see the lights of the Frankish camp spread out over the slope, unaware of what would face them in the morning. The Venetian fleet sat at its jetties across the water not much more than a quarter of a mile away. Arnau's attention was drawn to the brazier close by. Sparks leaped from it in the strong wind and hurtled from the wall, drifting down like falling stars to vanish above the black waters of the Golden Horn. Arnau shivered at such a portent of what was to come.

They stood for almost two hours on the wall top, watching, the tension increasing by the minute, especially in the last half-hour as the houses behind the walls emptied of their population, who poured down through the narrowly opened gate and into the Neorion harbour. In a matter of minutes, as the day drew to an end on the stroke of midnight, the sails of two dozen vessels were suddenly unfurled, men directing and even rowing the incendiary nightmares to the harbour entrance, where the entire small fleet caught the wind in bellying sails and burst forth with impressive speed.

Arnau watched, heart racing, as brave men ignited the ships and threw themselves over the sides, swimming for the small six-man rowing boats that waited to ferry them back to shore. In the space of mere minutes silent, skeletal vessels by the dockside had become floating infernos, carried across the water by a strong prevailing wind.

It was going to succeed. Arnau could see it. The ships were perfectly on target. One or two at the periphery would drift of course, but it would only take a few barging into the midst of the Venetian ships to set the whole fleet alight.

Arnau stood tense, watching the golden bonfires spitting sparks and belching black smoke as they raced across the water. The Venetians would not have time to move their ships, that was certain.

Galata was bursting into life now. The Venetians were racing for their ships, and beyond them there was increased activity in the Frankish camp. All seemed to be proceeding according to plan. The Venetians could never move their ships in time, and the Franks were awakening with urgency.

Ramon straightened and crossed himself.

'And I saw a glassy sea mingled with fire,' he intoned breathlessly, 'and them that overcame the beast and his image and the number of his name, standing above the glassy sea, having the harps of God; and singing the song of Moses, servant of God, and the song of the lamb, and said Great and wonderful be thy works, Lord God Almighty; thy ways be just and true, Lord, King of Worlds. Who shall not dread thee, and magnify thy name, for thou alone art merciful?'

Arnau shivered. The revelation of Saint John the Divine.

'The end of days,' he said, his voice wavering.

'Quite.'

But if the lord was merciful, then it apparently was not going to be that for the Byzantines. Arnau watched, bitterness rising into his throat. The Venetians were not even attempting to move their ships, but they were creatures of the sea, and nothing the Greeks could do might faze them on the water. Even faced with the horror of fire ships, the Venetians worked feverishly. Men flowed across the ships at the extremity, where the true danger lay, taking up spars and poles. There they reached out over the sides of their vessels.

The wind was strong, and for a moment Arnau thought the plan might still work, for the flaming vessels could not be stopped, but the men with poles in every case managed to deflect the approaching bows, turning the ships so that they drifted into the Venetian vessels at a quarter angle, robbed of sufficient impact to sink their target. There the gangs of men worked hard, those with spars heaving the burning vessels back away from their own hulls, while others threw buckets of water over any spot where the fire began to take hold.

Still, there was incredible danger. Perhaps two thirds of the Byzantine fleet had sailed true. Those that had not now floundered on the shore, burning out. Those that made it, though, were still a threat. One enemy merchant vessel was already alight. The wind kept pushing the Greek vessels at their targets and the Venetians had to work constantly with their poles to keep the burning hulks away and to extinguish any fires caused by flying sparks.

But the danger began to pass. The ships' sails burned away fast enough that the pressure of the wind diminished rapidly until there was nothing left driving the vessels against the Venetian fleet.

Then Arnau realised what the enemy were about. Dozens and dozens of small Venetian skiffs flooded around the edge of the near disaster. As they neared the great burning ships, long ropes and grapples were thrown out. Though it spelled doom for the assault, Arnau could not help but be impressed as, calm as anything, the Venetians anchored the burning hulks with a dozen grapples each, put muscle to oars and began to tow the danger away from their fleet, assisted by the pushing of men with spars. In less than a quarter of an hour the Byzantine fire ships were already burning out and were far from endangering any other vessel, towed out into the fast waters of the Bosphorus where they were released to be carried by the strong waters down past the city to be rendered to ash in the deep of the sea beyond.

Still, despite everything having so unexpectedly and so resoundingly failed, the Templars continued to watch as the single Venetian ship that had caught fully alight – a fat-bellied merchant – was towed out into the waters and allowed to burn away out of sight of the rest of the fleet.

'I am astounded,' Arnau breathed. 'These Venetians must be part fish and half fireproof.'

'The days of Byzantine naval eminence are gone,' Ramon said quietly. 'Witness the rise of the Venetian monster, more at home in the water than on land. What you are watching, Vallbona, is the future.'

'Heavens, but I hope not.'

'Seven angels having seven plagues went out of the temple, and were clothed with a stole clean and white and were girded with golden girdles about the breasts. And one of the four beasts gave to the seven angels seven golden vials full of the wrath of God, that liveth into worlds of worlds. And the temple was filled with smoke of the majesty of God, and of the virtue of him and no man might enter into the temple till the seven plagues of the seven angels were ended.'

'I wish you would stop quoting Saint John,' Arnau grunted. 'I prefer to hope that the end of days is some way off yet.'

'I fear we may be living through it,' Ramon replied.

'There is still a chance. Yes, the Venetians are untouched, but they alone represent only so much danger. The Franks are in disarray, see. Their camp seethes and lights abound. No matter that the fire ships failed, when the army arrives the Franks will be tired. Constantine Laskaris can still win a land battle and sue for peace on his terms.'

'Perhaps,' Ramon replied. 'But unless we are willing to share the Franks' exhaustion, we had best away to our beds for a few hours. We shall perform matins before sleep and return to the walls before dawn to watch what happens before lauds prayer.'

Dispirited, Arnau waved Sebastian along with them, but the young Greek shook his head and remained where he was, peering over the water at the disaster they had witnessed.

'Leave him. Let him mourn,' said Ramon quietly, and they turned, taking two of the Warings with them and leaving the others with Sebastian. Arnau started as he spun. He'd not heard or seen the people approaching, so intent had he been on the activity across the water. The attack had come to the attention of the people of Constantinople, and hundreds, perhaps even thousands of figures had emerged from their slumber and hurried down to the waterside where they had flooded through the gates to stand on the shoreline and watch the very embodiment of the rebellious spirit that had been building in their hearts for months now.

The two knights with their bearded northern escort trudged disconsolately between crowds of bitter, horrified citizens, along the wall and back to the palace. Entering the building where their rooms were, the two men prepared themselves for their devotions, though their swiftly sought serenity fled once more as they opened the door of their apartment to find Preceptor Bochard seated at their table with his arms folded.

'Did you know about this?'

Ramon nodded. 'If you refer to the Byzantine attempt to dislodge the heathen Venetians, then yes, Master.'

Bochard's eyes flashed dangerously. 'That they are still under excommunication is neither here nor there. I have warned you not to become involved.'

'We were in no way involved in the planning or execution of Laskaris's assault, Preceptor. We simply observed events from the wall top.'

Bochard looked unimpressed, but nodded irritably, robbed of what he'd felt certain to be a legitimate target for his anger. 'When you are aware of such matters it is our duty to apprise the emperors of them.'

Ramon shook his head. 'Surely when you order us not to become involved, that includes the spreading of rumours around the court, Master? Besides, with the Laskaris and probably Doukas all being aware, we had no reason to know the emperors were unaware.'

We *did* know, Arnau thought, but we had no *reason* to know. Lord, but Ramon had a lawyer's mind.

'Hmmm. Well the time for such foolishness is over. Laskaris will find there are consequences for doing such things, and his brother is already under arrest for attempting to leave the city and lead an illegal army. The officers supporting him have all been arrested and that force returned to its rightful place in the city.'

Arnau sighed. It was over, then. One brief flare of defiance, snuffed by Venetian ingenuity and imperial cowardice.

'No man might enter into the temple till the seven plagues of the seven angels were ended,' Ramon repeated.

'What was that?'

'An excerpt from the scriptures, Master. An apt one, I thought.'

Those questing eyes remained on Ramon, then slipped to Arnau. 'Stay uninvolved. Keep quiet. Our work here is almost done. Soon we will watch the rule of Rome take root in this place, and we will leave in triumph for Acre. Do not do anything to jeopardise that.'

Rising, Bochard glared at them both for a long moment before striding from the room.

'You know what will happen when news of those arrests and of the army's failure to march gets out in the city, don't you,' Ramon said quietly as he shut their apartment door once more.

'What?'

'Remember Alexios the Third? He led out an army to the cheers of his people and then led them back in again without engaging. Within a day he was fleeing through a city gate with all he could carry. The court and the Byzantine people all turned against him. Constantine is popular. And the people need hope and something to cheer. When they find out that the one chance the Laskaris gave them was snuffed out by the emperors? A Frank-supported boy and a blind, bitter old man? Ask yourself out of which gate those two will flee. And who will be next.'

Arnau nodded slowly. 'A coup, you think? A change in the emperor again.'

'I think it has been inevitable since the day the previous emperor ran. This joint rule of puppets and madmen was never going to last. It is the job of a council of nobles to select the next emperor if that happens. It is my great hope that they choose one of the Laskaris. Both have connections with the Angelids. Both are viable, and either might still stand the chance of saving this place.'

Arnau nodded. Being a Waring guardsman in Constantinople must be difficult, vowing utter loyalty to a throne that changed occupants like a waterwheel. It was clear to him why they were not required to wear the blazon of the emperor's family. The seamstress's bill would be enormous.

CHAPTER 17:
THE BYZANTINE REACTION

JANUARY 25TH 1204

In the event, the young Latinised emperor Alexios and his blind, frail father seemed to cling on to power with their fingernails over the following days. Despite being challenged by the nobles of the council, they remained in place, becoming ever more reclusive. The two emperors retreated into the safety of the Blachernae's main palace block where none but the imperial family, their guards and any invited guest – of whom there were now none – would go. There, the Waring Guard gathered in force, watching every window and every door, for Alexios and Isaac both were well aware of how precarious was the position of an emperor deemed by his people to have failed.

Indeed Doukas, still the Templars' main source of news, had informed them that in the wake of Laskaris's action, Alexios had sent a desperate message to the Franks. He had not only apologised unreservedly for what he called a 'cowardly attack', but begged the Franks to send a force of knights to the palace to help protect him. Perhaps it was a sign of the panicked state of mind of the young emperor that he felt he could not even rely upon the staunch Waring Guard. He had even offered the heads of the two Laskaris brothers to the Franks in mollification. The Franks had not replied. Instead they had begun to prepare for war once again, as had the Venetians.

Power seemed to be slipping away from the two men, though, despite their tenacity. They might wear the robes of emperors and sit upon thrones, but their influence spread only as far as the walls of the Blachernae, and sometimes not even that far. The city itself was now being administered by the council of the nobles, lacking the three figures that Arnau felt were most competent to do so. Constantine and Theodoros Laskaris languished in an extended tower, at the wall edge of the palace complex, known ominously as the 'dungeon of Anemas', and Doukas, though he made his position known in council meetings, seemed to remain apart from them to a larger extent.

Challenged upon his non-participation a few days ago on one of his semi-regular visits, Doukas had turned a resigned and unimpressed expression upon them.

'The council of nobles is failing every bit as much as their emperors. I cannot sit in on their verbose meanderings, for it makes my flesh itch to listen to them debate the most unimportant of matters or argue over whose lineage is the most acceptable while the city faces the peril it does.'

Arnau and Ramon had nodded sagely. Somehow those tidings surprised neither of them.

'Did you know that it is universally believed among the nobles that the time has come for a change in leadership?'

Again, the pair nodded. They had not heard as much, but had increasingly assumed that to be the case now for weeks, ever since the failed assault on the ships. Every day had seen the emperors withdraw in paranoia that little bit more, while the city's nobles took up the reins of state. Such a situation clearly could not be maintained for long. Moreover, since the only action either emperor had taken in all that time on behalf of the city was a grovelling apology to the Franks, the imperial line looked doomed to change. Isaac and the young Alexios, however, seemed determined to hold out to the last, not to run in the night like their predecessor.

'Three days now,' Doukas had said. 'Three days the council has debated over a successor. Even if they can settle on a name, they cannot be sure how the Warings will take it, of course. Remember that the guard are by oath loyal to their emperor beyond all else.'

Arnau's eyes had slid then in curiosity to Redwald, the hulking Angle of the Waring Guard who had hovered at Doukas's shoulder, whether prisoner or minister, throughout all the months they had been in the city. Redwald, clearly, was one of very few Warings not currently cramming the emperors' palace home. Moreover, he did little more than narrow his eyes a little at the words of the minister.

'They chose an emperor on the first day,' Doukas said with a sigh. 'Nikolas Kanobus. A likeable soul with a good heart. About as politically and militarily effective as a slap in the face with a wet cloth. Such a reign would be disastrous. Fortunately Kanobus, when presented with their decision, laughed until he coughed and refused the honour outright. He was the first of several to do so on that day, in fact. No one wants to grasp and drink from this particular poisoned chalice, of course. Now they still debate back and forth. The most sensible choice, of course, would be either of the Laskaris brothers, but there are enough fools in the council to block that decision. The failure of both brothers to break the enemy have made them just unpopular enough to be unacceptable to the council.'

Arnau shook his head. 'Both of them failed only because of their emperors.'

'*I* know that, and *you* know that, and Lord but the *brothers* both know that. But you are *thinking*, and such an activity largely escapes the mindless drones of the council.'

Doukas had then left to go about his work.

Days passed in that strange, taut expectancy. The Crusaders and their naval allies made their last preparations for war, readying themselves to begin the final assault on Constantinople. The ineffectual and cloistered emperors remained in their palace, unseen by anyone and surrounded by a sea of Waring guardsmen. The nobles argued and debated in the great nave of the Haghia Sophia church which they had adopted for their meetings. Emperors were proclaimed and discarded in the same breath in those meetings, with no real change. The city seethed in a combination of anger and fright, fearing what was clearly coming almost as much as they desired it, to remove once and for all the threat of the invader.

Throughout it all, Preceptor Bochard went about his business apparently entirely unconcerned, still stockpiling his relics. No longer were Franks or Venetians visiting the rooms, for their access to the city was more and more difficult and far from advisable. On the rare occasions Arnau caught a glimpse of the inside of Bochard's room, he knew that the treasures gathered there were now so numerous they must soon be moved, lest they become too many for the space. He had a mental image of Balbi's ship lying at anchor somewhere awaiting this haul, some of which would never reach Acre, instead filling a vault in Venice.

And the rest of the Templars? Sebastian had long since ceased his cleaning and maintenance, and even Ramon had not spoken to him about it. The young man stalked the walls of the Blachernae, cursing and gripping his sword hilt, waiting for the opportunity to gut the enemies of Byzantium.

Arnau and Ramon also walked the walls on occasion, and they prayed. They kept their steel sharp and their minds alert. They listened carefully to every nugget of news that came in, as any tiny piece of information might make the greatest of differences now.

Thus it was on the cold and crisp afternoon of the twenty-fifth of January that they were standing at the window in the corridor, watching almost a thousand Warings at weapons drill in the gardens outside the emperors' palace, when they saw Doukas and immediately knew that something was wrong.

The finance minister burst through the gate that led into the Blachernae complex from the city proper, on the far side of the wide courtyard from their window. The Waring Redwald was at his shoulder as usual, though for the first time since Arnau had seen the big man, he had his axe unslung and gripped in his huge ham fist. Doukas's face was tense and dark, and Redwald's set in a deep frown of violence. The two men strode purposefully across the frosty white stone of the courtyard, but not towards the building that housed the Templars, angling instead east, down the slope towards the palace itself.

Arnau and Ramon nodded their tacit agreement before they turned from the window and hurried off down the stairs. By the time they emerged into the courtyard, where crows circled in the bitterly cold air, Doukas was already striding away through the gardens close to the palace.

Ahead, the Warings were busy shouting and grunting, clanging and banging, training with axes and swords and spears. Ramon glanced at Arnau and then started to run. Something was most definitely happening.

'What is it?' the older knight called ahead to Doukas as they closed on the pair, but the minister was preoccupied, his attention elsewhere. As Doukas and Redwald approached, the purposeful manner of their arrival rippled ahead through the Warings, drawing their training to a close. In moments, the ripples had reached the far side of the gardens and every axe and sword had lowered, silence echoing across the palace with every bit as much presence as the noise it supplanted.

'To arms,' bellowed Doukas. 'To the walls, men of the Waring Guard. To the Blachernae gates. The blood of the people is up. A mob comes for the emperors' blood!'

Without further explanation, Doukas marched on through the crowd, Redwald still at his shoulder. Arnau was impressed how the sheer power and strength in the minister's manner made the enormous guardsmen melt out of his way like the sea before the staff of Moses, parting and flowing back across the lawns.

'To the walls,' bellowed Redwald with a voice like the crashing of falling mountains. While Doukas's announcement had stalled the Warings, to hear it repeated by one of their own with war on his face and his axe unslung seemed to galvanise them all.

The Warings broke into a run, hurtling past Arnau and Ramon, who had to remain very still, like branches poking out of fast flood waters, until the tide of northerners had passed, heading for the gate into the city and the walls flanking it. By the time the two Templars were alone once more and able to move freely, Doukas and Redwald had reached the imperial palace and entered the main doors.

'A mob?' Ramon said in a tight voice.

Arnau nodded and they broke into a run once more. It was hardly surprising, really. In fact, it was more surprising that this had not happened sooner. Two emperors who had failed their people holed up in a palace behind thousands of Warings, a council of nobles unable to agree even upon a potential usurper, and a vast array of enemies across the water waiting to destroy the city. After all, mobs had risen several times in the past few months. It was easily done. From Doukas's manner, the angry crowds must be close, approaching the Blachernae. What was the minister doing? Planning to get the emperors out by the external gate? Surely he would not lend his aid in helping the emperors flee to the camp of the Franks?

As they neared the imperial palace, more Warings began to flood from the main doors, and the two Templars kept to the left-hand side, managing to close on the doors as Warings erupted from the building like ants from a kicked nest, unsheathing swords and unslinging axes as they ran, shouting instructions to each other. Arnau hadn't realised just how many of the Warings there were in the palace until he had to struggle past them. Someone had once told him there were six thousand in total, though rarely more than five thousand in the city, and it was unusual to find more than perhaps five hundred of them on duty in one palace. Yet they had seen probably two thousand already in the past few minutes.

As they managed to push their way into the building and through the vestibule, they laid eyes once more on Doukas. He and Redwald were standing in a wide hallway at the base of an enormous staircase as the finance minister continued to issue commands like a general on a battlefield. Arnau was impressed, partially at the sheer presence and control Doukas was exhibiting, but more at how the Warings were obeying without question. He'd known Doukas to be clever and strong since the day they'd met, but this was the first time he'd seen the man truly take charge.

'Should the Warings be following his orders?' he said quietly. 'I mean, he's a *finance* minister.'

Ramon shrugged. 'He's authority. The other ministers are probably all busy arguing over the succession.'

They watched as Doukas hurried on now, up the stairs. Redwald here departed from his charge and instead beckoned to two of the Warings and disappeared through a doorway. Ramon, his face betraying worry and fascination in equal parts, looked back and forth between the two. 'Up or down?'

Or both, Arnau thought silently, but discarded the idea. Something was definitely up, and they needed to stay together. 'Up,' he said, finally. Ramon nodded and they hurriedly climbed the stairs in the wake of Doukas, who had already reached the top and moved on.

The two men were halfway up the stairs when another half-dozen Warings passed them on their way down, barely sparing a glance for the two Templars in the heart of the palace.

By the time they reached the top, there was no sign of Doukas. The two knights stood on the wide landing above the staircase. Corridors led off, some into gloom where the walls were windowless, others bathed in the bright winter sunlight pouring through the glass. All doors were closed and there were no people to be seen. Arnau paused, concentrating. He felt, given Doukas's urgency, that he ought to be able to hear the man, yet he could not do so over the ambient din of thousands of Waring soldiers making their way to guard positions around the Blachernae. His eyes searched the ground for footprints, for it had been frosty outside and there should be marks of the passage of feet. Futile. There had been so many Warings in the palace this morning that the marble floors were a mosaic of footprints anyway. Arnau had the suspicion that the emperors were living in squalor, unable even to trust their servants and staff enough to allow them into the palace. If the floors were not being kept clean, then how few servants were working?

A muffled voice drew both men's attention suddenly, and instinctively holding their sword hilts to stop the blades swinging and clonking, the two knights hurried off towards the noise, down one of the shadowed corridors.

A sense of foreboding began to settle upon Arnau as they entered the dim passageway. Something was wrong. *Very* wrong. More murmured voices, and they both identified the door that was the source of the sound at the same time. As they closed on the rich, decorative door, they paused, looking at one another. Arnau shrugged and Ramon shook his head, backing away. Something had spooked the older knight suddenly, and he retreated behind a wide porphyry pillar a little further down the corridor. Arnau hurried after him and dropped back into the shadows, frowning a question at his friend.

Ramon shook his head and pressed a finger to his lips.

Arnau bit off his unspoken words and fell silent, lurking in the shadows. It made him feel extremely uncomfortable doing so, as such subterfuge had with Balthesar on Mayūrqa. It seemed unnatural for soldiers of God, knights and noblemen, rather than thieves and assassins and low types. Still, something had alerted Ramon, and the older knight certainly had good instincts. Arnau watched, his breath coming in faint, tiny gasps

He had become so tense that he actually jumped a little when the door swung open once more. Ramon leaned back, swallowed by the shadows behind the wide, purple stone pillar. Arnau watched from the gloom as Doukas emerged, leading something. Arnau's eyes focused, brow furrowed, as he peered at the shape. A person, hunched over, bent beneath the folds of a voluminous cloak.

It had to be the emperor – one of them, at least. Where was Doukas going to take him? Where, other than with the Franks, could he possibly hope to be safe against a mob of his own people demanding his head?

As the minister and his covered companion approached the top of the stairs Arnau leaned out of the shadows, his gaze following the activity. Doukas approached the staircase, making encouraging, supportive noises that echoed back along the corridor as little more than a murmur.

Arnau stared in shock as the pair reached the top of the stairs and the minister suddenly jerked aside and shoved his companion roughly. The cloaked figure gave a terrified squawk, the cloak falling away as he slipped from the top step and fell.

Arnau was moving before he'd decided it was a good idea. Ramon was at his heel, though the look on his face suggested he hadn't planned to and had only reacted because Arnau had emerged.

As he passed the door from which the men had emerged, he turned his head and glanced inside. He could see one other figure in there, sprawled out on the floor. In that brief moment he noted no sign of blood or fracas, just the figure of Isaac Angelos lying on the floor, one hand reaching out, imploring in death, his face a mask of pain and shock.

Then Arnau was past the room, slowing as he approached the stairs, Ramon with him.

Doukas turned to them, a strangely authoritative, challenging expression on his face. Arnau looked at him in disbelief, then down the stairs, where his shock increased.

Alexios the Fourth had fallen the full length of the staircase, bouncing all the way down, acquiring bruises, fractures and broken bones from the marble. He had hit the bottom and lay there, bloodied and moaning. A circle of Warings stood around the man. Whatever oath they had taken, these few burly men showed no sign of leaping to the aid of the fallen emperor. Arnau felt slightly sick, even as Ramon stepped in front of him.

'There is no mob, is there, Doukas?'

Doukas nodded once down the stairs. At the bottom the Warings, led by Redwald, hauled Alexios Angelos off the marble floor roughly, stripping him of his rich garments. As the fallen emperor panicked and tried to fight them off with one arm, the other broken and hanging limp, the Warings exhibited no care, smacking and kicking him into submission.

'Take him to the dungeons and make sure he is secured,' Doukas commanded. 'And while you are there, see to the release of the Laskaris brothers.'

'No mob. No danger. Not from the city, anyway,' Ramon said again, a note of accusation in his voice.

Finally, Doukas turned a languid and calm face to the two knights.

'Of course not. But the Warings needed diverting. You disapprove?'

'This is usurpation. Whether for your own gain or to crown Theodoros Laskaris, it is still usurpation.'

Doukas shrugged. 'You Westerners and your odd definitions of honour. You cannot abide the idea of a coup, but have no qualms about insulting an emperor in his own palace during a diplomatic audience. Have you any idea how many emperors have ascended the throne over the body of a failed predecessor? More than had been born to it by far. It is a time-honoured and quite acceptable method of ascent, believe me.'

'It isn't right,' muttered Ramon. 'He was appointed by God, according to what I hear.'

'And removed by the hand of man. De Juelle, use your head, not your heart. Isaac and his son were weak and dull-witted. At a time when Constantinopolis needed a giant, we bred rodents. Had this happened months ago, we might now be at peace, with the Franks gone.'

Arnau frowned. It was true, of course. The method of succession might not be pleasant, but the motive could hardly be argued with. 'He's right, Ramon.'

'Right?' snapped the other knight, pointing down the stairs to where the naked former emperor was being dragged away, sobbing and leaving bloody smears on the floor.

'One thing Balthesar tried to teach me on Mayūrqa was not to always judge other peoples by my own cultural rules. It doesn't always work. Remember your Book of Kings, Ramon: "In the eight and thirtieth year of Azariah, the King of Judah, Zachariah son of Jeroboam, reigned upon Israel in Samaria six months. And that which he did was evil before the Lord, as his fathers had; he departed not from the sins of Jeroboam, the son of Nebat, that made Israel to do sin. Forsooth Shallum, the son of Jabesh, conspired against him in Samaria; and Shallum smote him before the people, and killed him, and reigned for him."'

Ramon grunted. 'You liken Alexios to Zachariah the evildoer, and his father, the reprehensible Jeroboam, to blind Isaac? Then you make Doukas here your Shallum? And shall he now reign in Israel?'

Doukas remained placid, his face emotionless. 'A true Roman emperor is not made, knights of the Temple. He makes *himself*. Neither of those men had the mind or the strength to rule. The Angelids have been slowly ruining the empire for generations. And perhaps you forget that I have something of a history in this area. Four years ago, I saw the danger and the rot of the Angelids and I supported Komnenos the usurper. Had we succeeded then, we might not now be facing extinction. No, I am unrepentant over the fate of that snake down there. I would have him strangled now were I sure I might not yet need him for something.'

'But the council of *nobles* has the duty of selecting an emperor, yes?'

Doukas sneered. 'I gave them three days. Three days to pick one name. I even tried to steer them to the Laskaris brothers, but with three whole days of debate they are further from a decision than when they began. And while they do nothing, the Franks and the Venetians prepare to annihilate us. Someone has to take the rudder of state and steer us from disaster, and the more I watch fools and cowards fail around me, the more I am convinced that the man to do it is me.'

Arnau was nodding. He'd not meant to show his blatant support, at least not without talking through with Ramon, but Doukas was right. Apart from the Laskaris brothers, he could think of no one he had seen in his months in the city who had a better chance of success than Doukas.

'You will free the Laskaris?' he said.

'I have given the order. The city will need their skills and minds and their leadership in the coming days.'

Arnau turned to Ramon. 'You have to admit that with this man on the throne and the Laskaris leading the army, at least Byzantium stands a chance.'

Ramon remained still for a long time before finally giving a small nod.

'The time for serious war is almost upon us, knights of the Temple,' Doukas said darkly. 'I do not wish to sound crude, but in this situation, the Warings have an expression: defecate, or leave the latrine.'

Arnau gave a bitter smile. 'Fight or flee, you mean?'

'If you do not leave before the Franks come again, you may no longer have the option to do so. If you would like I can have your preceptor forcibly expelled from the city.'

Arnau almost laughed at the notion, but Ramon shook his head, his face plastered with disapproval. 'Bochard sees himself as saving the treasures of God from heathens. If you eject him, it will simply feed his hatred of Byzantium and make him all the more determined. If he is pushed from the city, he will join the Franks and you will find one more man on that hill willing to see the city fall. No, better to leave him. I will make one more entreaty.'

'You will be caught up in the war.'

'It will all be as God wills it.' Silence fell for a moment, and in the stillness, Arnau could just hear chanting outside.

'Alexios the Fifth?'

Doukas shrugged. 'Perhaps not the best of precedents, I suppose, but we can do little about the names our parents choose. Should you decide to leave, seek me out and I will make sure you are escorted to safety. Should you choose to stay, I fear you cannot avoid involvement. There is always a place in the defence of the city for men like you.'

Ramon gave his tiny nod once more, accepting, if unhappy.

With a last smile, Doukas turned from the two men and began to make his way down the steps. At the bottom he paused for a long moment, looking down at the bloodied smears on the floor,

CITY OF GOD

shook his head sadly, then skirted the pile of rich clothing, including the red boots that marked an emperor, and left the building. Outside a thousand Waring voices chanted his name.

'I have never witnessed the succession of a crown before,' Arnau said quietly.

'With luck you will never do so again.' Ramon, his face still radiating his displeasure at events, turned and strode back to the imperial apartment. Arnau followed. The room was quite simply the most sumptuous he had ever seen. Any two square feet of the chamber contained enough gold, ivory, silver, silk and gemstones to pay for an entire palace. He mused ruefully that the contents of this room might have been able to pay the city's debt to the Crusaders without taxing the citizens.

Ramon strode across to the body and crouched.

'No sign of violence,' he confirmed with audible relief. 'In truth I would say the shock took him. Perhaps that is a blessing.'

'Certainly after what Doukas told us they usually do to failed emperors. Young Alexios has little to look forward to, I suspect.'

Ramon nodded bitterly. 'I knew a change was coming. I had thought it would be more of a public decision than this.' He sighed and straightened. 'But no matter how little I like it, I fear this is all part of God's plan. Perhaps Doukas is the man to stop the Franks. Perhaps he always was.'

'Too little, too late,' said a booming voice from the doorway. They turned to see Redwald standing there, axe once more hung over his shoulder.

'What?'

'Doukas would have been the man. But I think it is too late now. I urged him to move the day the exile was crowned, but he remained loyal for too long. Until it was too late, I think.'

'You *knew*,' Ramon said, accusingly. 'You took an oath to protect the emperor, yet you violated it. You and men around you. Oaths are important. They are the very heart of our order. Are they nothing to you?'

~ 266 ~

Redwald snarled. 'Do not think to lecture me on loyalty, you who aid the Greeks against your own Mother Church.' Arnau recoiled, at both the force of the man's anger and at the unpleasantly accurate accusation. The Waring sighed. 'I was not alone. We take an oath to serve the legitimate emperor, and we all did so with the Third Alexios. But Isaac was no emperor. He had been blinded and usurped, and a blind emperor cannot rule. It is Byzantine law, centuries old. My oath cannot be given to an illegitimate emperor, and Alexios the Fourth was not crowned by the city. He did not stand on the omphalion for his coronation. He was imposed on the city by enemies, and was a puppet of the Pope and his Frankish mob. So no, I have never considered myself bound by oath to the dog. Neither of them were emperors in the eyes of many.'

'That is just semantics,' Ramon accused, though with considerably less vehemence now.

'You are the legal expert,' Arnau said quietly. 'You know the value of details.'

'What will happen now?'

Redwald straightened. 'There will be a coronation. A proper one, in the Haghia Sophia on the omphalion, overseen by a true patriarch of the Church and not some Venetian wolf. The Laskaris brothers will marshal the army, and we will prepare to fight the Franks and the Venetians one last time. That,' he pointed at Isaac, 'will be entombed with his forebears. His son? Well, I think Doukas is bright enough not to let the dog live. He will be strangled and dumped before the fighting begins.'

Arnau nodded. 'May God walk with you in the coming days, Redwald.'

'And with you,' the Waring replied, bending and throwing the body of the frail, blind old emperor over his shoulder and then leaving once more.

'You know Bochard will refuse to leave, yes?' Arnau said

Ramon turned to Arnau. 'Of course. I will try persuasion one more time, but I fear we must be prepared to fight for our lives, no matter who it be against.'

'I fear it is time they began to circulate with the icon of the Holy Mother again,' Arnau said quietly. 'She will bring hope and strength. Remember Chronicles two: "He called together all men in the street of the gate of the city, and spake to the heart of them, and said, Be ye manly, and be ye comforted; do not ye dread, neither be ye afeared of the king of Assyrians, nor of all the multitude that is with him; for many more be with us than with him. A fleshly arm is with him; but the Lord our God is with *us*, which is our helper, and shall fight for us. And the people were comforted with such words."'

Ramon nodded. 'The people might just take heart from such a sight. Assuming the icon is not in a chest in Bochard's room.'

Arnau couldn't help but let out a hollow laugh at that.

CHAPTER 18:
THE EMPEROR'S VALOUR

FEBRUARY 25TH 1204

Arnau and Ramon stood at the top of the staircase that led to the top of the gatehouse and the Blachernae's walls, watching the force being assembled below. Here, in the security of the Blachernae, no word of what was to come could leak out, since the time had come for action.

As had seemed to be the case throughout their time in Constantinople, the ongoing war with the Franks and Venetians proved to be a staggered, stop-start affair. The attempted burning of the enemy fleet and the Franks' preparations for war, the coup that placed Doukas on the throne had all been a staccato and rapid succession of events. Then, as Arnau had felt certain they would fall directly into brutal combat, in fact they had hit another lull.

On the part of the Crusaders it was not so much a lull, in truth, as a shift in focus. Leaving sufficient forces to keep the city closed in, with the Venetians prowling the waters, bulky Frankish forces had marched and ridden around the Byzantine hinterland for weeks, sacking and raiding other towns and cities, giving them the supplies they needed for another season of war. All up the coast almost to the lands of the Bulgars they had destroyed and looted.

As for the Byzantines, they took the opportunity to prepare.

The Laskaris brothers had been reinstated and made the senior generals of the Byzantine armies. Doukas, though, had refused to leave *all* military matters in their hands. While he would defer to them strategically, he was determined to be a leader for his people. Just as the sacred icon from the Church of Saint Mary in Blachernae and other great relics were paraded for the morale of the people, so also Doukas made himself visible at all times, bedecked for war and not for court, leading the soldiers and marching the walls of the city. The emperor seemed to be everywhere. Arnau approved.

Preparations were made. The army was thoroughly reorganised, and the Warings told that they were expected to form a solid part of the city's military throughout the crisis, regardless of what their emperor did. The gates of the city were sealed, strengthened and bolstered. Using the rubble from the burned-out districts, walls were strengthened. Those ramparts damaged by the Venetians the previous year were rebuilt, as were parts of the Blachernae walls. Most importantly, to prevent a repeat of the Venetians' cunning mast tactics, the towers and walls of the Golden Horn defences were raised by twice the height of a man, using some stone and a great deal of timber. No Venetian ship could now spill its men onto them.

Doukas's preparations were not all military, though. In order to fund the rest of the campaign, Doukas levied a new tax across the city. While this was not the most popular move, the public were largely mollified with the knowledge that their money was going to sharpen swords and man artillery to save them from the Franks, rather than being loaded into chests and given to the Venetians. Moreover, Doukas was known to have donated great wealth from the palace to match the funds raised by the tax.

He was becoming tremendously popular. The emperor who stood against the Latins and defended his people – a far cry from any of his recent predecessors. After an initial demand sent to the Crusaders thàt they depart forthwith had been derisively rebuffed, Doukas had decided that his predecessor would serve no further purpose, and his continued existence could only serve as a motive for Frankish violence. Consequently, the young Alexios was quietly strangled in his dungeon and interred without fuss alongside his father in a monastery within the city. The calm and accepting, matter-of-fact feeling around the court at this officially sanctioned murder set Arnau's teeth on edge, and he was forced to remind himself not to judge everyone by his own standards.

All seemed to be progressing with more consideration than Arnau had noted throughout the past year. If Byzantium could be saved, then it seemed that Doukas was the man to do it.

Then, one day, the roving Franks returned to the city, a sizeable force setting up camp in their old position on the monastery hill facing the city walls, while the rest returned to their place at Galata. It seemed that the siege was about to recommence in earnest. Equipped with almost adequate supplies now, the Franks began to forage the area to supplement their stores and prepare for the long term.

Arnau had wondered what the Byzantine leadership planned. With Doukas now almost wholly occupied with the business of empire and the Laskaris brothers assisting him, no one seemed to have the time to visit the Templars any more and keep them informed. Bochard, of course, redoubled his efforts, gathering what he could, fearing that if he did not, they might be destroyed during the siege.

The answer came early that morning. Arnau had heard the quiet but unmistakable sounds of soldiers gathering. The gardens and courtyards of the Blachernae were filling with men: archers and swordsmen, as well as cavalry both heavy and light. Doukas and both Laskaris brothers were there, marshalling their men.

It was inevitable in a siege that word of anything big would leak out. Surprise attacks were incredibly hard to organise and took much secrecy and preparation, as had Laskaris's fire-ship attack, yet even that had come to the attention of the emperors who had halted the companion land attack. Hoping to avoid word of this one reaching the Franks in advance, the new emperor had gathered his troops over hours within the walls of the Blachernae. Even now, though there was a sizeable force in the palace complex, it could easily be mistaken for training, for each unit was gathered in a separate garden or courtyard. It did not look like an army until you took it all in together, which would be near impossible to do from outside the palace walls. Doukas and the Laskaris were taking no chances.

'Hello, that's unexpected,' Ramon said, his voice tight. Arnau followed his gesture. Bochard had emerged from the doorway of the tower that led up to the Templars' apartments. He strode out across the frost-rimed paving of the near courtyard with purpose, breath frosting in the air.

Arnau peered suspiciously. The preceptor was armed for war. Of course, Arnau and Ramon had been armed for war for months now, but then they had fought and struggled and learned the hard way that they needed to be armed and protected at all times. Bochard, conversely, had spent most of his time in negotiation with priests and noblemen, either in his rooms, in churches or in the court. Not once, to Arnau's knowledge, had he gathered up his helmet.

Here he was, though, shield strapped to arm and helmet held tight in mailed grip. Arnau looked ahead, and sure enough the preceptor's squire was busily leading out Bochard's horse.

'Surely he doesn't intend to fight? Not after all the lectures he's given us?'

Ramon snorted. 'The day the preceptor lifts his bared blade in Byzantium, the good money says it will be among the Franks and aimed at a Greek. I don't know, but I'm intrigued. Where is Sebastian?'

'I have no idea. These days he belongs more to Laskaris's army than to the Order, I fear.'

'I cannot truly blame him. But in his absence, I think we might want to gather our own steeds.'

Arnau frowned. 'Why?'

'Wherever he's going, it's by horse. Personally, I want to see where, since I doubt he's thrown in his lot with Doukas.'

Nodding, Arnau followed Ramon to the stables. The place was in chaos, though of the more organised kind. Though the cavalry, traditionally quartered at a place called the Hebdomon a mile or so outside the city walls, were now garrisoned in a temporary camp within the farmed land inside the defensive circuit, and therefore their stables stood there, the horses of nobles and commanders were still often kept here at the Blachernae, hence the frenzied activity.

Skittering slightly on the frosty stone, they hurried to tack and saddle their steeds. At least, since they did not expect to be in the saddle for any great length of time, they did not have to fit the saddle bags and load up with supplies. Thus in a matter of minutes they led their horses out.

Arnau stood shivering, peering around them at a large unit of Byzantine infantry, their kite-shaped shields painted brightly in red, shirts of chain gleaming, axes or swords in hand. He couldn't see Bochard for some time, then finally spotted the mounted figure of the preceptor over in one of the other gardens. Ramon put a hand to his arm, holding him back.

'Don't follow too close. Whatever he's doing, I suspect he will not want us with him, else he would have commanded it before now. Let us follow him at a distance. He is bound for the Blachernae Gate in the city walls, I'd wager. Let us move circuitously to the same place.'

They led their horses rather than mounting, being less conspicuous among the infantry that way, and passed through two gardens and across a courtyard behind the main imperial palace building. As they moved, they passed heavy *cataphracti* cavalry, armoured from head to toe, horse included, a unit of stocky, narrow-eyed men in fur hats with composite bows, and infantry with long lances. Doukas meant business.

At the lower end of the slope a small internal gate led out of the palace complex proper and met the Blachernae Gate. Arnau and Ramon approached and, spotting Bochard sitting astride his charger close to the gate, dipped into a side alley where they positioned themselves so that they could just see around the corner enough to observe Bochard. There they waited.

'This feels wrong,' Arnau murmured quietly after a while.

'Why?'

'It feels as though we are spying on the preceptor.'

'That is because we *are* spying on the preceptor. I am no great lover of such subterfuge either, Vallbona, but we cannot afford to be left in the dark now. Bochard has lurked, cajoled, negotiated and visited numerous monasteries and the like, but I have never seen him without the company of a priest or a noble or one of his Frankish contacts. I have never seen him armed for war, and with what is about to happen, such changes make me nervous. The man has done nothing yet outside the bounds of the Rule, and I simply cannot challenge him until he does, but if we do not keep our eyes open, how will we know whether he does or not?'

Arnau nodded. He still didn't like it, but he couldn't argue with the logic either.

They continued to wait, and after perhaps half an hour a short chorus of horns blew in the palace, followed by the distinctive sound of several thousand men and horses moving. Arnau steeled himself, and at Ramon's silent signal he mounted. The two men sat ahorse for a few minutes more until the imperial army approached the gate. Arnau watched with interest. Doukas led his troops in the military finery of an emperor, looking like a Roman of old, several hundred Warings and his senior officers accompanying him, barring the Laskaris brothers for they came next, with Constantine leading the infantry and Theodoros the cavalry.

Further noises drew the Templars' attention then, and they turned to see a small mounted party of officers accompanying three priests on horseback, the central one of whom bore the sacred icon of the Blachernae, the Holy Mother with the infant Jesu on her arm, gesturing to him in the old Eastern way, with three fingers extended.

This was the icon that protected the city, which brought hope and morale to the people. It seemed it was now to accompany the army. Several things clicked into place in Arnau's head and left him feeling distinctly nervous.

'Ramon…'

'I know.'

'The icon.'

'I know.'

Clicking into place. Bochard had been gathering relics, and his hungry eyes had repeatedly fallen upon the most precious items in the city: the shroud of the Saviour, the nails of the cross… the icon of the Holy Mother. *Click.* Bochard had made many, many visits to the Blachernae church where the icon was kept. *Click.* Arnau remembered the face of the Blachernae's priest when he'd left Bochard's rooms in anger. *Click.* The preceptor had been there again with an escort of Frankish knights, on the day when Arnau and Ramon's curiosity had earned them a crossbow bolt. *Click.* It came as no surprise that Bochard coveted the icon. That was plain. That he had tried to obtain it by purchase, by argument and possibly even by force that day with the Franks. Had he even tried theft? But the icon was the city's most precious relic, and no one within Constantinople would willingly let it go. The fact that the icon was accompanying the army and Bochard was here ahorse and armed for war was no coincidence.

Click.

'Would he really?'

Ramon shrugged. 'For his soul's sake I hope not, but it rather looks that way.'

Arnau leaned forward once more to peer around the corner. Bochard was sitting by the gate, but his eyes were lifted to the tower's top, and he gave a small nod. Arnau's gaze slid upwards, just in time to see a figure backing away from the parapet, no more.

'He's up to something, Ramon. Something I don't like the look of.'

Moments later the lead elements of the army were past and the gate groaned open ponderously. The icon with its holy and military escorts fell in behind Doukas and his party, in front of the bulk of the army. Arnau's professional eye roved across the force as it thundered from the city through the gate in the walls. Doukas and the Laskaris brothers had been wise in the army's composition. There may be cavalry, infantry and archers here, but there was not a slow man among them. The heaviest infantry were mail clad and bearing shields. They could move at speed for a short distance. The entire column would be highly mobile for a short time.

Arnau waited, tense. Ramon sat, quiet and apparently calm. Finally, at the back of a column perhaps two thousand strong, the rearguard of a hundred Warings passed by. Peering around the corner once more, they saw Bochard step his horse forward. The preceptor fell in at the absolute rear of the column, following along perhaps twenty paces behind them all. Arnau started to move, but Ramon held his hand out again, and began counting quietly. When he reached fifty, he nodded and gestured to Arnau. They rode softly out from their side street and towards the gate.

The army having now fully departed and being out in the grasslands beyond, the soldiers were busy closing the great timber doors, and the pair had to pick up the pace and call for them to hold the gates. The soldiers did so, and Arnau and Ramon emerged into the open land outside the city for the first time in many months.

Being out of the city felt at once liberating and very odd. They had been closeted within the city since the day they arrived, and had become more used to the urban life than they had expected, yet for months they had been lobbying to flee Constantinople, and right now they were outside. They were free. All they had to do was angle their horses west and ride for Achaea.

Instead, they fixed their gaze on the army.

They were making for a foraging force of Franks in the hope of overwhelming them and winning the first real victory for the city. If rumour held true, they would outnumber the Franks perhaps two to one, and success should be assured. There were other Franks in a position to come to their aid, but only with adequate warning. They would not have that warning. While no one could miss the thunder of hooves and feet, nor the cloud of dust and steam rising into the winter air – the foraging army would see them coming – they would have far too little time to do much about it other than brace themselves.

The Byzantine army suddenly broke into a run, yelling, horns blowing. Bochard turned his mount aside. Arnau frowned as the preceptor rode to a small hillock and sat there, watching. On one level, the young Templar was relieved that Bochard was up to nothing more underhand than watching the battle, but on another he was a little disappointed to discover this was the case. He'd felt certain Bochard was up to something.

Realising that they would shortly catch up with the man, he turned at Ramon's signal and made for a similar rise, a little further back. The view would not be as good, but they would be behind Bochard and not likely to attract the attention he kept riveted upon the battle.

They found their rise and crested it, then turned and reined in.

The battle was about to be joined.

Arnau's heart suddenly thundered. Whatever Doukas had been expecting, this could not be it. The force they faced was larger than their own, not smaller. As the Byzantines raced at the Frankish knights, the enemy horses shifted fractionally and crossbowmen stepped out in front, each with the bolt already in place, string taut and weapon lifted.

Arnau swore under his breath as the crossbowmen released their dreadful barrage and then disappeared back between the heavy knights. Arnau saw a dozen horsemen or more in the front of the charge go down, hurled from their steeds or simply disappearing beneath a charge in which those behind were forced to jump their horses over their fallen comrades.

He had to give it to the new leaders of Byzantium. In every engagement the previous year, the moment the enemy so much as bared their teeth, the Byzantine forces had fled or withdrawn. Instead, here, faced with superior odds and a force that was unexpectedly prepared for them, the Laskaris brothers instead drove their men on to greater speed and savagery.

Arnau could see little in detail, but managed to take in a general sense of events. The battle could go either way as far as he could tell. The Crusaders had the numbers and seemed more prepared than they should have been, but the ferocity of the Byzantine attack would make a difference, spurred on as they were by their respect for their commanders and the knowledge that drawn by her icon, the 'Theotokos' Mary was watching over them all.

For several moments Arnau thought the Byzantines were about to rout the enemy. They had hit the Franks so hard and so confidently that they were truly carving pieces off the Frankish force and spreading panic among them. He watched as the Crusaders, unable to charge or use their long lances in the press, discarded their primary weapons and drew short blade sand daggers, stabbing around them at the savage Greeks who fought with the ferocity of polecats.

But the Franks had one more surprise waiting.

As the Byzantines committed their entire force, suddenly the rear of the Frankish army moved out to the sides, flanking the imperial force, almost enveloping them. Hidden behind the knights had been a force of highly mobile light infantry, who now enfolded the Byzantines in a square of sharpened steel, hacking and maiming. Arnau turned his face away.

'Disaster,' muttered Ramon. 'They have to withdraw or they'll lose everything. How could the Franks be so prepared? How could they have known?'

Arnau exhaled miserably. 'They had prior warning, I fear. As we left, I saw Bochard nod to someone atop the gate. I can't say what they did, but it is conceivable that someone on the gate house could signal the Franks, if they knew what to look for – as if they were expecting it.'

Ramon's lip curled. 'I hate to think that Bochard would be that devious.'

'I tell you, Ramon, he's a bad seed. We need to overrule him and leave.'

Ramon shook his head. 'He's done nothing wrong. I mean, the emperor would tear the flesh from his back if he found out about this, but nothing he's done would even get him a dressing-down in Acre. We might not like it, but we can't defy him unless he breaks the Order's Rule.'

'The seething, avaricious bastard just sold out the emperor and his army. And for what?'

'For that,' Ramon said, his arm suddenly reaching out, finger pointing away to the north.

Arnau followed the gesture. The Byzantines had clearly come to the same conclusion as Ramon. Signals to withdraw had gone out and the imperial army was already breaking into a retreat. Arnau bit deep into his lip as he watched whole regiments of imperial soldiers fall, swamped by howling Franks. The cavalry were the first out, but it was neither the massacre of the army, nor the flight of the cavalry to which Ramon had drawn his attention.

Out ahead of the retreat one unit raced back for the city at full pelt. Just a dozen men on horseback, they consisted of a senior officer, two cataphractii, three priests and a handful of Waring guardsmen. The icon of the Virgin flapped and rippled in the wind as they rode.

Arnau's suspicious gaze slipped to the figure of Bochard on the next summit. The man had not moved. His hands remained on his reins. Yet somehow, Arnau knew there was more to come.

He did not have to wait long to discover what.

The small party accompanying the most sacred relic of Byzantium, the icon that defended the city in the eyes of its people, crested a low rise and slammed straight into a small party of Frankish knights coming the other way. Now Arnau knew the whole thing had been engineered. There was nowhere for those Franks to have come from by accident. They couldn't have been there as the army passed on the way out. They had to have circled around the periphery as the fight began and come far behind the Byzantine lines solely for an opportunity like this. Possibly they meant to capture any fleeing officers, of course. That made plenty of sense. Yet deep down, Arnau knew it was not the case. He knew the force had been dispatched with the sole purpose of capturing that small group. And he knew that somehow Bochard was behind it.

He cursed under his breath again. Ramon might consider his vows too important to consider challenging the preceptor without adequate cause, but Arnau was close to breaking point. He gripped his reins until his hands hurt, observing, forcing himself to obey and not race to intervene.

He watched in disgust as the Franks dealt with the icon's escort. They knew precisely what they were doing. Two groups broke left and right and engaged the Warings, drawing them away so that the remaining third could ride directly into the centre and butcher the officer and the priests.

The Warings were good, and they put up an impressive fight, but they were outnumbered and facing fresh men. The only advantage the Byzantines could claim was the two cataphractii who were hard to take down, so heavily armoured were they. For a heart-stopping moment, it looked like they were going to make it. The Warings were keeping the bulk of the ambush busy, and the two cataphractii forged their way through to the priest with the icon and escorted him forward amid swinging maces. Then, finally, the Franks got the better of one of the armoured Byzantine horsemen. It took three knights and all their strength and fury to batter the cataphract rider from his horse and keep him down.

The priest fell a moment later, and Arnau felt his gorge rise. How could these Crusaders call themselves soldiers of God, butchering a priest carrying an icon of the Blessed Virgin? He silently prayed that the Lord would open the gates of Hell this very day beneath the hooves of the Franks. His prayers went unanswered.

There was a cry of dismay as the icon fell to the dirt. The other cataphract rider tried desperately to sweep down and gather it up, but the move opened him up to attack and, as his fingers touched the staff holding the blessed relic, he was smashed across the back with an axe. The mail prevented the drawing of blood, but Arnau knew what had happened at that angle. The heavy axe blade would have shattered the Byzantine's spine right through the chain shirt.

It was over in moments. Only four Franks remained unharmed, two more sagging, badly wounded in their saddles, but they swept the icon up from the ground, whooping with victory, and began to ride off to the north, away from the main fight. Bochard watched them, and Arnau's lip curled in disgust. He couldn't identify the knights that had taken the icon – at this distance, their crests were a blur – but at least two were in red and white. He would have been willing to wager a good sum that the men even now riding back to the Frankish camp were Bochard's friends, de Charney and de la Roche.

He felt certain the icon would somehow find its way onto a Venetian ship bound for Acre by nightfall. What had the Franks taken in payment for securing Bochard's greatest prize, Arnau wondered bitterly? Perhaps it was simply adequate warning to ensure they won the first engagement in which the Byzantines had really stood a chance? Perhaps the chance to capture the leaders of the city?

That realisation suddenly broke through his misery, and Arnau turned, frantically scanning the fight.

The main battle was all but over already, though a group of men raced for safety, and Arnau could see the standards of both Laskaris brothers and the emperor himself among them.

Groups of men, both horse and foot, were fleeing now in ragtag bands, racing for the gate of the Blachernae, pursued by howling Franks. It was a disaster of almost epic proportions. Most would reach safety, for the Franks were far from foolish enough to pursue the routing forces within the range of the artillery on the wall top, but a force of men raced after the emperor's party, and Arnau noted with distress a pair of figures rising from the scrub nearby, bows in hand. *Another* ambush!

Suddenly Bochard was moving. Ramon grabbed Arnau's arm and pointed, and the younger knight turned to see. The preceptor rode hard down towards the imperial party, and Arnau stared. He simply could not believe that Bochard might intervene so directly.

The preceptor raced down the slope, yelling something, though it was impossible to hear over the general row. The Warings momentarily turned as if to face him, but realised just as Arnau did that the preceptor's weapon was still sheathed. He was not coming in for the attack, but rather seemed to be yelling urgently.

Arnau watched with a maelstrom of conflicting feelings as Bochard made a desperate lunge forward in his saddle, throwing out his shield. An arrow struck it with a thud, punching right through. A second thumped into the emperor's horse, and Arnau realised that Bochard had almost certainly just saved Doukas's life. The archers were running now, their ambush foiled, though they made it little more than a hundred paces before snarling Warings reached them, pulverising both with half a dozen killing blows apiece.

Free now of danger, the emperor's party hurtled on towards safety. The emperor's horse was wounded and fought against him until one of the Warings with incredible strength and deftness reached across and dragged Doukas from his saddle onto his own horse.

The party raced for the gate, now well ahead of pursuit, the emperor's wounded horse running off at a tangent on its own.

'Come on,' Ramon said. 'I don't think we want to risk getting left out here.'

They turned and raced their steeds back to the Blachernae's gate. They overtook several bands of fleeing men and were grateful as they reached the gate that their red crosses had not marked them as enemies for the fleeing Byzantines.

As they passed beneath the gate and rode into the heart of the world's best defended city, they reined in and slipped into a side passage once more.

'Bochard sold them out. All for the sake of an icon,' Arnau snarled.

'Yet he saved the emperor's life,' Ramon reminded him.

'Convenient, eh? He ruins the emperor's chance of success, rips the city's most sacred protective icon out of their hands, is responsible for the deaths of hundreds and hands success to the

Franks. And what will be his punishment? He saved the emperor. He will be a damned hero, Ramon. It makes me sick.'

Ramon nodded. 'Certainly there will be no stopping him now. And he managed to do it all without once drawing a blade against any of them. He remains, essentially, clear of guilt.'

'Maybe in *your* eyes,' Arnau spat, 'but in mine he just earned a spiked and flaming seat in the pit of Hell. And I suspect God above will consider him guilty enough to send him there.'

Ramon sighed. 'I fear that is the last sortie that will be made. Byzantium will now withdraw within the walls once more.'

Arnau nodded. A siege, then.

CHAPTER 19:
THE GREAT SIEGE

APRIL 9TH 1204

Bochard frowned and the two knights folded their arms.
'Do you intend to *"save"* each and every relic in the city?' Ramon asked, a touch of acid creeping into his tone.

'Do not needle me, de Juelle. This is the city of a *thousand* relics. It is our duty to preserve what we can. I have done an excellent job thus far, and regardless of your constant reminders, I am fully aware of the increasing danger. However, the defenders of the city know we are not their enemy, and as long as we do not place ourselves in peril with the ordinary citizens, we need fear no trouble from within. I have made certain arrangements to secure our safety among the Crusaders and their Venetian allies should they master the city. We will come to no harm there. We are effectively under the protection of both sides, and are officially not part of this conflict in any way. All that remains is to keep ourselves out of the line of danger, and we should come to no harm.'

'That sounds more reasonable than it is. The Venetian ships are readying to sail. You must have sent a hundred treasures to Acre already. Where will you draw the line? When will it be enough?'

Arnau snorted quietly. He knew just how many treasures still awaited shipment in the man's room, and until Balbi's ship could dock safely, they would likely remain there, too.

'I do not intend to save *every* relic, de Juelle. Even if the locals were willing to relinquish their treasures, which many still are not, we simply do not have the resources and time to do so. But I have made it my business to secure the most important and sacred items.'

'Of that we are well aware,' grunted Arnau, his face folding into disapproval and earning a sidelong look of warning from Ramon, who added, 'What artefacts could possibly be worth this danger?'

Bochard's face twisted as though struggling with himself over something. Finally he bit his lip and planted both fists on the table, fixing the pair with a level gaze.

'All right, since you seem unwilling to simply take the word of a man whose word is untarnished and under oath of truth. There are two treasures remaining that *must* be saved from the coming disaster, and it is for them that we must remain.' He sighed and looked about conspiratorially. 'At the Holy Apostles lies the shroud of Our Lord, and in the Mangana monastery the spear of Longinus.'

Arnau blinked, remembering that time in the first few days in the city at Holy Apostles when Bochard had asked about those very relics and been told where they were kept. He intended, then, to remove two of the most important relics in all the world from this city. Bochard's determination was clear. The young knight could still not place their acquisition above the expediency of departure, but the preceptor's reasons were a little more transparent.

'I see you understand now,' Bochard murmured. 'Naturally the keepers of these relics are loath to part with them, but every day of this worsening situation shakes their resolve a little. I shall secure both. Indeed, I am on the cusp of doing just that. I give you my word that when I have those treasures, we will depart with no further fuss.'

'That might be too late,' Ramon said, though his voice faltered now. Clearly, he had underestimated the value of the items the preceptor still sought. The shroud in which Christ had been buried, to shed when he rose upon the third day, and the head of the spear the Roman Longinus had thrust into the Saviour's side on the cross. What treasures they were, to rival anything kept in Rome.

'Leave me to my work,' Bochard said. 'And cause no trouble. You go to observe this siege, yes? Not to take part in it.'

'That is our intention,' Ramon said quietly.

'Good. Should I secure those remaining items, I shall attempt to send word to you. God go with you.'

'And with you,' the two knights replied in a rather formulaic manner, turning and leaving the room. As the door clicked shut behind them and they gathered up their shields which lay propped against the wall in the corridor outside, Arnau turned to Ramon, speaking quietly.

'That was not a promise, was it?'

'Far from it. It is my stated intention to not take part in the siege. Sadly, often plans can go awry. Especially when one's viewpoint is a little too close to the enemy. Come, Vallbona.'

The two men left the building and crossed to the walls. There was no sign of Sebastian, and had not been since the early morning. He had disappeared before dawn, likely to form part of the city's garrison. No one had the heart to deny him that. Once upon the city walls with Octa and two of his Warings, they travelled down the slope of the hill towards the water. Even as they neared the walls of the Golden Horn, they could see the shapes of the great Venetian vessels detaching from the far shore and beginning to pull out into the water.

The fleet had separated into sections and covered the inlet in a great line perhaps a mile long, war galleys with their artillery towing great rafts filled with soldiers interspersed with the transport craft also crammed with men and horses, but also with siege weaponry.

'This is going to get messy,' Arnau said, peering at the worryingly large fleet. 'The Franks are part of this force every bit as much as the Venetians. How can we hope to maintain our stance in not attacking the Crusaders?'

Ramon gestured onwards and broke into a light jog, Arnau running alongside. 'It is easy enough to tell the difference in most cases, and I believe we can position ourselves with little danger of facing Franks. Fight those of whom you are sure, and despite Bochard's certainty that the Franks will not touch us, that will not apply in this fracas. If a man makes to wound you, you wound him first. God will separate the just from the wicked in the end. You know who you are.'

And that was that.

They reached the sea walls and started to move along them. The enemy fleet looked set to hit this stretch of the defences – the same one with which they had achieved such success the previous season – all the way from the Blachernae to the foreign enclaves, past the burned-out sections of the city. This was, in some ways, an advantage for the defenders. There was little to worry about inside the walls now, and plenty of space in the destroyed regions for the mustering of men and equipment. Moreover, Doukas had established his command post at the top of that burned-out slope, near one of the few churches to have survived two conflagrations more or less intact. From there the emperor and his officers could see the entire stretch of the city under threat.

Arnau peered down over the parapet. The silting up that had all but rendered the Prosphorion harbour useless these days had affected the waterline along most of the southern shore. One long stretch had escaped it, the water lapping against the stones of the ancient defences in that specific place where the Venetian galleys had come against them the previous year. In many places, though, silting had moved the shoreline away from the walls, in some cases to more than a hundred paces distant.

Ramon kept them running past such areas towards that section where the walls met the sea directly. Arnau nodded to himself as he ran. Sensible. The Venetians would land the Frankish Crusaders on the shoreline where they could, but where there was no available shore, it would be the Venetians' ships in direct assault. Ramon had reasoned it through and put them in a position where they would invariably face the excommunicated Venetians, whom both men could resist with clear conscience.

They reached the nearest edge of that great stretch and came to a halt, breathing deeply. Thank the Lord the weather had warmed as spring came to the city. In the frosty winter it had been perilous running on the slippery white stones of the wall top. Now at least the temperature was comfortable and the skies were largely clear.

As they reached that section in direct contact with the water, they arrived at the recent works to heighten the walls and found themselves climbing rough-hewn timber stairs up onto the wooden hoardings that raised the effective fighting height by more than ten feet. It felt strange to be standing on timber rather than stone now, but the additional height made a great deal of difference.

Arnau readied himself, shield on arm and sword drawn, peering out over the wall top as a couple of Byzantine infantry shuffled along to make room, their faces betraying uncertainty about the loyalty and effectiveness of the red-crossed knights beside them. The young Templar's heart picked up pace as he spied the fleet coming towards them.

The enemy were no fools. In the centre of their fleet, the Venetian warships were more prevalent, the transports and rafts fewer.

'Hail Mary, graceful Mother,' Arnau said, eyes fixed on the nearest of the Venetian ships. 'The Lord be with thee; blessed art thou among women, and blessed the fruit of thy womb, Jesu. Holy Mary, Mother of God, pray for we sinners now and at the hour of our death. Amen.'

'Amen,' responded Ramon.

The Warings and the Byzantine soldiers nearby looked at them quizzically, unable to comprehend the Latin in which Arnau had prayed, but all present nodded their understanding as the two knights crossed themselves.

All too aware of the danger posed by fire to the timber additions, the men of the city's defence began to prepare. The outer face had been covered with stretched hides, giving additional protection from missiles, but also from flame, for now the Byzantines threw bucket after bucket of water down them, soaking the outer face of the new section, making it sodden and almost impossible to ignite.

In addition to the huge barrels of water brought up here from the nearest cisterns, there were braziers again. Atop the towers stood catapults and bolt throwers of ancient design, yet effective despite their antiquity. Arnau frowned as several soldiers moved an odd contraption into position ten paces away along the parapet. A barrel with a pump handle atop it, reminiscent of those used to spray water on fires, fed a long hose that ended in a metal tube some six feet in length. This the men kept below the battlements, hidden from sight.

'Greek fire,' Octa said quietly, noting Arnau's puzzlement.

The young Templar shuddered. He'd not seen the weapon in use, but its reputation was dreadful, and he'd some idea of the effect from its use on siege weapons and fireships.

'Just one could be spared on this stretch. The majority are being prepared along the walls where the enemy will land, rather than attacking directly from their ships. Sadly, much like the imperial navy, the firethrowers have largely gone from the city's forces, with no attention paid to their upkeep and replacement under the Angelids. Few men are trained as *siphōnarioi*, and few know how to prepare it.'

Arnau frowned. 'If you had this weapon, why was it not used last year?'

'Inadequate supplies,' Octa replied. 'Theodoros Laskaris has had crews building, manufacturing and teaching in secret for months to achieve what we have here. The equipment and knowledge both had all but vanished from the army.'

Arnau nodded. That sounded like Laskaris. While the city floundered under its joint fools on the Byzantine throne, the silent Laskaris, away from court, had devoted his time to preparing for when the city stood up for itself once more.

The ships closed in. Arnau paid attention to them now, almost able to see the faces of the men aboard. The vessels looked like arrows from this angle, arcing towards the walls, their grimacing occupants like demons, preparing to destroy and burn.

Demons...

For truth is not in their mouth; their heart is vain. Their throat is an open sepulchre, they speak guilefully with their tongues. God, judge Thou them. Fall they down from their thoughts; after the multitude of their wickednesses, or unpiousnesses, cast thou them down; for, Lord, they have stirred thee to wrath.

The words of the psalm thrilled through him, filling him with righteous fury. His knuckles whitened in their tight grip on his sword. He would make the Venetians pay today for their assault on a Christian city.

He glanced at Ramon and noted his companion's lips moving in silent prayer. He could see the same determination on his face.

The attack began first back along the wall, towards the Blachernae, where the silting had taken the shoreline furthest from the walls. There, fast Venetian transports disgorged their cargoes with the same speed and horrific efficiency as on that first day, when the knights had leaped ashore, already ahorse, to rout the Byzantine defences in Galata.

The transports thudded against the shore and huge ramps immediately dropped from their bows, men howling and bellowing, charging up and over, flooding onto the ground. No cavalry this time, for horses were no use against city walls. This time, huge swathes of men-at-arms in their drab greys and browns were spotted with the colourful surcoats of knights in their midst. Some were carrying scaling ladders, others spears and more bows and crossbows.

Arnau, safe in the knowledge that he had several minutes before his own wall section was threatened, leaned forward and peered west along the ramparts, watching intently. Those men on land were already running at the walls, their siege ladders arcing up and teetering, ready to slam down against the stonework. Behind them, horses were dragging wheeled siege weapons from more ships and trundling them down to the grassy shore, where men swiftly made them ready for war.

Other Crusaders were carrying huge timber-framed tunnels covered with hides, which they ran forth and butted up against the walls to cover engineers as they began work to undermine the ramparts.

It was all so quick that it stunned Arnau. Men were screaming and falling as arrows and rocks fell into the mass of invaders below, but it was a scattering of damage in a sea of Crusaders, and did little to prevent the covered tunnels and ladders and engines moving into place.

Then he saw something that made his soul curdle. Something he would never be able to unsee, and that would haunt his future dreams.

A long nozzle appeared through the battlements. There was a terrible, thunderous belching sound, as if from the throat of a dragon, and suddenly something poured from the tube. Golden and red, the Greek fire spurted forth not like water, but more like some glutinous soup, dragon's breath at its heart, all engulfed in clouds of acrid black smoke.

The terrible weapon had an instant and horrifying effect.

The sheds covered in hides already glistened where the shrewd Venetians had thoroughly wetted them against fire arrows. It made no difference against the Byzantine siphons. The liquid fire spattered against the sheds and instantly engulfed them in terrible, roiling flame. Men screamed and howled. Arnau watched in mounting horror as men emerged aflame and dropped to roll and put out the fire, but the act did nothing to lessen the conflagration. Rolling did not extinguish this fire, for it burned on and merely spread across the ground where the men rolled. Others threw themselves into the water in desperation and even in this found no solace, for the fire merely burned on the surface of the water itself. A hapless man who had already been badly torched and had dipped below the water, rose in relief from the deeps that had extinguished him only to find he had emerged into liquid flame that coated his face and hair.

Arnau uttered a short and devout prayer for the man's soul. Frank or Venetian, Christian or heathen, no man deserved to die like that.

Other pots of the stuff were being hurled to strike the siege engines, and catapults and bolt throwers were bursting into flame before they could be used effectively against the city. Arnau turned away from the dreadful sight only to remember that another such demonic device rested by the parapet mere paces from him. He shuddered with revulsion.

The first ship to reach the walls did so a little to Arnau's left and he stood, watching impotently as the Venetians launched the first stage of their naval assault. With its prow still facing the wall, the ship's crew threw out their anchor astern, keeping the vessel pointed at the ramparts. A bolt thrower in the bow began to thud and crack, launching great arrows up against the parapet, and a dozen archers on the deck loosed at will, peppering the wall with shafts as, behind them, one of those long sailcloth gantries was unfastened from the mast and swung out towards the wall.

Doukas's defensive measures had been good. Perhaps not quite good enough, but good. The extra height on the walls caused two difficulties for the Venetians. Firstly, their ingenious boarding ramps no longer had the height advantage they'd enjoyed the previous year, and secondly their archers and bolt thrower were too close with the walls' new height to effectively attack anyone atop them. Consequently, the arrows almost uniformly clacked off the stonework or thudded into timber, one or two thrumming high into the air, passing way over the heads of the defenders.

The Venetians were no fools, though. While they had watched Doukas's men heightening the walls, they had adjusted their gantries to suit. Though there was little they could do, for they could not heighten their masts, they had extended their gantries as far as practicality allowed. Arnau watched the walkway swing around and could see that with the extra length, it was almost unmanageable. It dipped this way and that several times before reaching the wall and when it did, it was still a little short, so that the men aboard it were forced to run up at the wall top rather than leap down to it. The result was that unlike the previous year, the attackers were at the mercy of the Byzantine soldiers as they tried to rush the walls. Arrows ripped into the men along the gantry, and two soldiers hefted long pikes and began to jab and poke at the end of it, lancing a foot of steel into the torso of anyone who got too close to the defences. The young Templar squinted, hoping to see green tunics. He had no love of any of these men, and would kill them one and all to save the city, but should he spot the men of Almerico Balbi, what was a duty would become a pleasure. Sadly, they were not Balbi's men on that ship.

A thud drew Arnau's attention and his head snapped back to the right. A second ship had struck the wall to that side, and the same tactics were being used. Arnau watched, feeling a little sick, as the siphoneers readied their dreadful weapon.

He shivered.

The Venetian arrows clacked, clattered and thudded into the wall below them, a rock from a catapult making the entire timber extension shake a little. Arnau felt a moment of panic as he watched the siphoneers desperately holding their barrel still as the timbers shook. The idea of that entire thing spilling or exploding on a timber wall top was unthinkable.

The ship's mast-ramp swung and dipped, the unwieldy extended weight making it hard to control, and almost broke as it swung down to near deck level. Arnau could see the grey-clad men on the ramp clinging on for dear life and shrieking as they were thrown about. One toppled, losing his grip and plunging to the deck below, where he landed with an audible crunch. Finally, the crew got the gantry under control and managed to swing it to the wall.

Arnau knew with a sickened feeling what was about to happen. The Byzantine artillerists heaved the siphon tube straight, while one of their number lit a long, pitch-soaked taper the length of a spear. He stood back, burning spear lifted. In perfect unison, three groups of siphoneers worked together. Those holding the tube thrust it out of the wall, directly into the mouth of the Venetians' canvas-and-timber gantry. The man with the burning spear pushed it out of the next embrasure along, flaming, pitch-wrapped tip at the tube's nozzle. And a third pair pushed down on the pump handle, hauling it up with grunts of effort and then pushing it down again, repeating the process over and over until it became a rhythm.

Arnau wanted to look away. After what he'd seen even from a distance in the other direction, he was not sure he could stomach a better view, yet there was an appalling fascination to be had in watching, and he found that no matter how much he might wish it, he simply couldn't turn away.

The liquid fire gushed forth from the pipe, directly into the gantry like an open mouth. The men inside did not stand a chance as the burning gobbets splashed across them and ignited their clothes, their flesh, their hair – even their iron armour burned.

But worse was to come for the Venetians. The liquid fire poured down the sloping gantry, murdering men all the way until it reached the far end, where it poured freely down the mast and onto the ship below. As it fell, it became a flaming rain that deluged the men on the ship, spots of liquid fire falling among them, burning faces, arms, backs, killing indiscriminately and refusing to be extinguished, no matter what the sailors did.

In moments, the entire galley was aflame. The attack had failed utterly, and the siphoneers stopped pumping, extinguishing both the nozzle and the spear by holding them under water until the remaining drops of fire burned themselves out. Then, efficiently and very, *very* carefully, they lifted that dreadful weapon, barrel and all, and took it further away along the wall, looking for where it was most needed.

Arnau prepared as the next ship faced him directly. He gripped his sword tight, trying to banish from his mind's eye the image of men tearing at the liquid fire eating their faces.

The same tactic was used once more. Arrows clacked and thudded in front of and beneath him, not quite able to crest the wall, the ones that did arcing so high that they were more likely to skewer a gull than a soldier.

He remained behind the parapet, not risking opening himself to a stray lucky shot, and listened carefully. He heard the noises below as men fought to control the heavy, swinging gantry and felt the bang as the timbers of the walkway thudded against the wooden wall top. They were coming.

Sure enough, the clacking of arrows stopped, lest the Venetians accidentally hit one of their own, and Arnau rose next to Ramon, the three Warings and half a dozen Byzantine infantry crowding to help.

The first man up the gantry in a cote of burgundy and mustard-yellow looked desperate. Perhaps he had seen what had happened to other attacks on the wall. Indeed, as Arnau rose before him he saw the man flinch, likely half expecting to see a dreadful steel tube pointed at him. It said much about the terror of the Greek fire that when it turned out to be a heavily armoured trained killer with a sword awaiting him, Arnau could read the relief on his face.

The Venetian reached the wall top and Arnau bit down on notions of brotherhood. These were men excommunicated by the Pope, who had engineered a war against an innocent city. They were wicked, and they deserved what was coming.

Appropriately steeled against the attack and murmuring words of praise and prayer even as he swung, Arnau delivered the first blow against the crew of the Venetian warship *La Simitecola*. His sword came down in an overhand chop with immense force.

The man screamed as he failed to raise his shield high enough in time, and the sword struck his upper arm a few inches below the shoulder. The chain shirt once again prevented a true cut, but the arm was shattered in several places and almost severed entire, the shield dropping, its weight stretching the arm where it was now held together only with muscle and flesh.

The screaming man was far from dead, but effectively blocked the gantry for his comrades, and Byzantine archers from a nearby tower were now raining arrows on them along the canvas length. In desperation, two of the beleaguered men on the gantry reached forward and unceremoniously pitched their screaming comrade with the broken arm over the side to fall to his death below. Ramon made the first of them regret that. Barely was the screaming man out of the way before Ramon's slice, coming with full force, took the man behind in the elbow. The damage was appalling, striking below the end of the short mailed sleeve, where only his bulky linen arming jacket protected him. The arm smashed and came free, sword, hand and forearm all crashing to the canvas and wood floor beneath him. The man howled in shock and agony and the Venetian behind him tried to push past until an arrow from the tower took him in the neck.

A cry from their left suggested trouble and, given moments of grace now, Arnau looked that way. A surge of men up the gantry had managed to secure a foothold where a lucky blow or two had removed the two spearmen keeping them at bay. There were Venetians on the wall top. Ramon was already running to help and Arnau considered joining him, but the same was now happening here. The bridge being fully in place, men were swarming up it, bent low against arrows and running to engage the men on the wall top.

Arnau parried a vicious blow and struck back, sword thudding against a raised shield. The man tried again and Arnau parried a second time. He drew back his blade to strike, but never got the chance as the next Venetian shoved the one in front, who staggered forward and fell against Arnau, the two of them falling to the timber walkway in a tangle.

Struggling to free himself, Arnau saw the Venetian draw his head back, unable to bring any other weapon to bear in the tangle, preparing to butt him. Sensing space open to his left, Arnau waited for just a fraction of a second and then threw himself as best he could in that direction. He was rewarded with a thud and a cry of pain as the man, already committed to the head-butt, smashed his helmet instead into the timber floor, knocking the sense from himself. Before he could recover, a Waring axe buried itself in his back, smashing through the chain shirt with disturbing ease.

The Templar struggled and managed to rise only with the aid of Octa. His sword had gone in the fall, and a tiny thrill of panic ran through him. Another Venetian on the wall top came at him, and Arnau did the only thing he could. He smashed out at the man with his shield, hard. The Venetian tottered back and wobbled for a moment, crying out.

Arnau lowered his shield in time to see the man he had punched with his shield fall backwards across the wall top. Miraculously, the man succeeded in arresting his deadly plunge, with one hand, gripping his mace, wedging in the timber and holding him up.

With a satisfied and very unnerving smile, Arnau reached down with his free hand. His fingers wrapped around the heavy iron flanges of the mace just as his boot pressed down on the man's own desperate grip.

'Mine,' he said with malice as the Venetian's fingers broke, one by one, until finally he lost his grip and fell with a scream. Arnau lifted the mace with relish. It had been years since he'd wielded his old mace, since the German knight had trained him in swordsmanship, eschewing the blunt weapon.

He rose to find himself surrounded by Warings. Granted a moment's reprieve from the fight, he looked this way and that. The sights he caught were more than a little encouraging. For the first time since this entire conflict had begun, the Byzantines were truly ascendant. The Venetians were unable to get more than the tiniest foothold on the walls, and when they did, swiftly had it ripped away from them once more. Over where there was a visible shoreline below the walls, the various covers and rams and machines the Franks had brought across were almost universally broken or swathed in sheets of flame. Whole areas of the ground burned, and in places the sea was even alight. Men down there still struggled on, but it was becoming increasingly apparent that they were not going to overthrow Alexios the Fifth today.

With renewed spirit and vigour, Arnau launched back into the fight, mace swinging with precision and strength, voice raised in Latin song that would almost certainly confuse the Italian warriors racing to take the walls.

He smashed and hammered, crushed and battered, Warings at his side, holding back a tide of Venetians and singing songs of battle.

It was, for the first time in months, a good day.

CHAPTER 20:
THE VENETIAN FURY

APRIL 13TH 1204

The city breathed. For days now, the city had breathed. The Venetians had swiftly abandoned their attack, taking the Frankish army with them, fleeing back across the Golden Horn to lick their wounds in Galata. Songs of thanksgiving had rung out in Greek from every church that afternoon and evening. For the first time in a year, Byzantium had struck a blow against the invaders and had done so with vim. Some said the Venetians and Franks would leave, that they would have had enough.

Arnau and Ramon, and those in command too, knew differently.

Many of the Crusaders *were* perhaps having second thoughts. Maybe some Venetians too. But Montferrat and the leaders of the Franks would be angry, pushing to avenge their losses. And the Venetians? Well, it was the considered opinion of anyone in the know that the Doge Dandolo would flay himself and throw his own peeled body into the ocean before he would give up Constantinople.

This was just a lull. A time for the enemy to rethink their tactics.

Still, given the unexpected moment of peace, Preceptor Bochard had redoubled his efforts to acquire those two last great treasures he felt needed removing from the city. Ramon and Arnau had argued over them in the privacy of their room. Arnau felt that, no matter the value of those relics, the time had come. They faced a stark decision.

Arnau knew in his heart that whatever the preceptor ordered, if they stayed and the enemy came again, then he and Ramon would not be able to stand back with swords sheathed. They would have to fight. And he could not drag his conscience around to fighting for the Crusaders. He felt certain that God would favour the Byzantines in this. He knew what was expedient and what was expected of him, and what his orders were, but they were all immaterial, because he also knew what was *right*. If he stayed, he would have to fight the Franks, and that would most certainly destroy any goodwill or guarantees they had with Bochard for the Templars' security. So Arnau knew he had to defy Bochard one way or another. He would have to leave against orders, or take the fight to the Franks. Certainly there was little chance now of Sebastian doing anything other than standing with his countrymen on the wall.

Thus it was that they had spent their days out of the apartments watching the enemy across the water, keeping clear of Bochard in an effort not to be restrained further. Thus it was, too, that they came this morning to be standing on the wall top above a minor gate that gave out onto a small narrow foreshore at the foot of the burned-out hill below the imperial camp and the church where it had been centred. Of all the gates in the stretch, it was one of the lesser ones, yet it stood at an angle where the wall bulged out slightly into the inlet and therefore gave an unparalleled view both across the Golden Horn and along the wall to either side.

The gate was under the command of a tourmarch, who seemed to Arnau a little young for his role, yet gave out his commands with admirable authority and confidence. Under his command three dozen men held the gate, including four archers atop the wall, two small artillery crews on the flanking towers – a bolt thrower left and a catapult right – and sundry infantry with spears, swords and axes. The only Warings in evidence here were the three who had come with them, including Octa.

'Are they moving?' Arnau breathed. 'I think they're moving.'

'Aye, Roman,' called a soldier from the tower to their right, just a few steps higher than the walls, 'they come.'

Arnau uttered a silent prayer beneath his breath, glancing to either side at his companions as he did so. Ramon was likewise engaged in prayer. Sebastian stood with his head bowed, clutching his battered and worn icon of the Holy Mother. Arnau frowned. He'd not realised the boy was shaking. In truth, and somewhat to his chagrin, he had been rather self-absorbed this morning, anticipating what was to come, and had paid little attention to the young squire. Regretting that, he reached out.

'There is no need to fear.'

When the squire looked up, Arnau almost recoiled at the mix of despair and fury in the lad's face, tears on his cheeks.

'Sebastian?'

'I die today, Brother Vallbona.'

'What?' Arnau frowned, and the squire thrust the icon out. His tears had soaked the painting, darkening the ancient wood.

'The Theotokos cries for me this day as she did for my parents.'

'Sebastian, those are your own tears.'

'No, no they aren't. But I'm not afraid. I shall die. But I shall sell my life dearly to those unholy bastards out there.'

Arnau continued to shake his head. 'Try not to put yourself in danger. They are just your own tears, Sebastian. We will see this day out, all of us.'

Sebastian simply gave him a sad, fatalistic smile and turned back to the enemy, icon gripped tight once more. Someone nearby shouted that the enemy were approaching.

Arnau felt his heart pick up pace as he watched the Venetian ships putting out to the water once more. Four days had passed since their failure and flight, but finally it appeared that they felt confident enough for a second try.

There was not a breath of wind this morning, nor had there been in the hours since the knights had risen from their beds, and the enemy were forced to rely upon oars rather than sails. Arnau watched as the ships slowly set forth. He had to grant once more that the Venetians, for all their faults, were clearly consummate seamen. Their ships moved in precise formation.

Their tactics had clearly changed, though. Instead of transports interspersed with war galleys, this time the galleys alone formed the front lines, transports towing rafts behind them. Apparently, the Venetians meant to secure a bridgehead now before landing the Franks. They had clearly learned their lessons after the burning of so many knights and their siege engines on the shoreline.

One thing became clear as they pulled out into open water. Venetian ingenuity had struck again. In several places, two war galleys had been tightly bound together, forming more or less a twin-hulled ship, one using their port oars, the other their starboard. Due to the doubled weight they pulled by oar, these vessels were necessarily slow and set the sluggish pace for the entire fleet. Yet they came.

'Why the twin ships?' Arnau murmured.

'The enemy are devious,' replied the tourmarch nearby. 'Who can read the minds of such devils?'

Arnau simply nodded, gripping his mace. He had managed to retrieve his sword in the aftermath of the fight, but had kept the mace, his long-favoured weapon. It felt comfortable in his grip.

He couldn't help but feel that the Venetians were making straight for him. With a sidelong glance at Sebastian and his icon, the notion occurred that perhaps it was the lad they were coming for, but he quickly dismissed it. If one looked along the fleet's line, the centre was more or less opposite. Of course, logic suggested that the reason for that was the imperial camp which lay atop this very stretch of hillside. Arnau wondered whether perhaps they had been unwise in choosing as their vantage point the more or less central position on a direct line between the enemy force and the emperor himself.

Ramon began to pray very quietly. Oddly, though he did so in Latin, the devout look of the man began to infect all those around him and, in moments, the Byzantines all around the gate and towers were also praying, Sebastian with them. Ramon looked up as their voices picked up volume, falling in together in one great song of praise, drowning out the Templar in their midst.

Arnau was rather surprised to find that his Greek, shaky upon arrival at the city, had so improved over the year that he was translating the words of the singers without effort. He listened as his eyes remained locked on the approaching ships.

'Blessed is the man who has not walked by the counsel of the ungodly, for the Lord knows the way of the righteous, and the way of the ungodly shall perish. Serve the Lord with fear, and rejoice in Him with trembling. Blessed are all who put their trust in Him. Arise, O Lord: save me, O my God. Glory to the Father, and to the Son, and to the Holy Spirit, now and ever, and to the ages of ages. Amen.'

Those atop the towers and wall punctuated the prayer with three shouted 'Alleluias'.

Arnau nodded his approval. Had he retained one iota of doubt about their course and the godly nature of these Easterners, it evaporated in the face of their piety. Whatever dogma kept them from the Church of Rome some might consider a great rift, but to Arnau their brotherhood was clear, while those vicious Franks out there with their eyes set solely on murder and pillage were no more godly than the pagan raiders of old.

The Templars were in the right place, doing what was right.

The prayer died away now and in the strange stillness the lack of breeze created, three sounds wove a tapestry of tension: the constant cawing of seabirds above, the sounds of armour and creaking of timber along the walls, and the distant splash and groan of the ships closing on them.

Arnau heaved in a breath. He felt the tiniest relief as the ships closed, that the one facing him directly was just a single warship, unlike the twin-hulled monstrosities to either side. He heard the tourmarch issuing his final orders and moments later the artillery began to loose, finding their range, ammunition plopping into the water only twenty paces ahead of the ships.

'One hundred and fifty paces,' a lookout called.

Artillery was adjusted.

'One hundred and twenty.'

A second barrage. More shots could be heard from the other tower tops now. All along the walls, the defenders were finding their range. The second release was better. The stone splashed into the water close enough to a hull to throw water up onto the side. The bolt smashed into the prow, sending flying splinters through the air, flensing any crew nearby.

'Ninety paces.'

'Prepare. Weapons ready,' called the tourmarch. Arnau needed no urging to brace his shield and test his grip on the mace.

A third barrage and this time the huge stone smashed into the deck of one of the twin hulls off to their right, causing alarm and chaos, though not enough to slow the vessel. The next bolt took a crewman directly, plucking him from the deck and carrying him overboard into the water to die in the deeps.

'Sixty paces.'

Arnau could see their faces now. And finally, at this close distance, he could see why the ships had been bound together. Those same wood and canvas gantries were hauled out from the masts, but there was none of the dangerous swinging and dipping they had seen a few days ago. The twin hulls had provided a much more stable base, and allowed for a greater length to be added to the walkways.

He watched in dismay as the first of these swung out forward, so long that there was no hope of it falling short before the walls. The Venetians had prepared once more in response to Byzantine success.

This wall top, he realised, was going to be under only a little pressure. The worst trouble was going to strike either side, and then perhaps on the foreshore below the gate. Readying himself, he waited. At another command, the archers dipped arrows into the braziers and loosed them at ships.

'No Greek fire to spare this time?' he said over his shoulder.

Octa rumbled. 'Very little fuel. Laskaris only had one season to gather the resin required, and even that in secret. We used much in the last assault.'

'This will have to be won the hard way, then,' Ramon said. He glanced over at Arnau. 'Sebastian is his own man today. Do not fret so much over him that you lower your own guard.'

'Thirty paces,' bellowed the lookout. The artillery was firing at will now, as were the archers. The single warship struck the ground on the foreshore directly in front of the gate and men were leaping from it already, racing for the walls. Behind, the transport and raft it towed were now coming alongside to disgorge their own cargo. There would be time before they were massed enough to present a threat, especially with archers loosing down at them and men dropping rocks and bricks gathered in small piles. The real danger lay to either side.

He looked right and could see that at least the Venetians were having difficulty there. The shoreline continued along the foot of the walls that way, and though it was narrow, little more than fifteen paces out, it was almost as long as the reach of the enemy's gantry. The one to the left was in no such difficulty, the water almost lapping the wall's base.

The ship to the right hit the land, and its ramp swung. It grazed the wall a couple of times, men shouting in alarm from both the wall top and the gantry itself.

To the left the enemy were going to be trouble. That long bridge had slammed against the parapet and before it could be moved or anchored by either side, the first figure was attacking. The enemy had learned. Early on they had sent their fast-moving, lightly armed men to man the gantries, keeping the weight down. Now, given the new stability of the twin hulls, they had taken the chance of putting their best men on the mobile bridges.

The knight who leaped from the bridge to the top of the next tower along with the grace of a cat wore a hauberk of chain, his head covered with a full helm, a surcoat emblazoned in blue, shield and heavy sword held ready.

He landed steadily and swung at a spearman, who literally fell back to the ground to avoid the cut. The man regretted his leap in an instant as two Warings appeared as if from nowhere, axes flying, and turned the man into sliced meat, but he was only the first, and before he had stopped screaming, two more men had leaped from the bridge. The two newcomers managed to cut down a pair of spearmen before they were submerged beneath Byzantine soldiery.

Arnau chewed his lip. They were pushing hard, but if it held like this, they stood a chance. He peered back to his right. The ship there was still in trouble. The sailors were doing their best to push forward despite the land lying in the way, their bridge swinging this way and that, unable to quite find purchase.

He glanced down. The forces that had landed were increasing in number all the time, fed from that transport that had now grounded, and they fought hard. A group were already bringing up a hefty, hand-held battering ram, and several siege ladders had been brought ashore. Arnau was about to be caught up in the action.

Somehow he felt it before it truly made itself known. Just a breath that brushed the wisps of hair poking out from his mail coif. Then a gust. He closed his eyes for a moment. *The Devil had lent his strength to the Venetians.*

A moment later the wind began to blow from the north, across the water, the first gust strong enough that men paused, surprised, in the middle of the action to be certain. The Venetian ships, their sails down in the hope of this very thing, suddenly burst into life. The great canvas sheets billowed and filled and the ships all along the walls suddenly lurched forward, even those already grounded. Men fell over in the bridge on the ship to Arnau's left. To his right that gantry that had failed to connect properly was suddenly slammed against the tower's timber top. With a roar of defiance, and before Arnau could yell at him to stop, Sebastian had turned and run that way, lending his blade to the defence of that stretch of wall. Torn for a moment, Arnau almost went after him, only restraining himself with recollection of Ramon's warning.

The gust went in a heartbeat, and the ships rocked, but then came another, pushing the ships against the walls. This time, the Venetians were ready for it. As the ships lurched, men threw out ropes and grapples, catching the timbers of the parapet, looping their ropes around stays and masts and whatever came handy to prevent them sliding free.

Pinned now to the walls, the gantries were solid and steady, and men rose all along them and rushed the towers to either side. Arnau felt his confidence slip as armoured knights threw themselves onto the tower tops and began to hack and cut and chop at the Byzantine defenders. Unless someone did something there was the distinct possibility that they would lose the towers, and if they did that...

'Here they come,' Ramon shouted, and Arnau ripped his attention from the endangered towers to either side, returning to his own peril.

Below, the ram was now swinging back and forth, held by a dozen men as it thudded repeatedly against the timbers of the gate. The young Templar knew how the gate itself had been strengthened with extra bars and blockages. He also knew it could still take only so much punishment and, perhaps due to lack of foresight, it had been given less attention than the more major gates, this being little more than a postern.

A ladder hit the wall top just in front of Arnau and he momentarily tucked his mace beneath the shoulder of his shield arm, lending his strength to the Byzantine spearman who was trying to push it back. With Arnau's help, he managed to push the ladder a couple of feet from the wall, where another infantryman managed to get a Y-shaped pole behind it and push, grunting with effort. The ladder arced away, teetered for a moment, and then fell back among the men who had raised it, cries of panic arising from those men who had already been climbing it and even now were tumbling back to the ground, breaking bones.

Arnau pulled his mace free again. Another ladder had come up nearby and the defenders were trying to heave it back. Ramon lent his own hand, but the Venetians and Franks were better prepared this time. Arrows and crossbow bolts came in a cloud in an attempt to clear the battlements before the ladder. Arnau watched several Byzantines fall backwards with cries of pain and alarm, shafts jutting from their bodies. The air filled with curses and sprays of blood. For just a moment, Arnau's heart lurched as Ramon fell back with a shout, but the older knight recovered a moment later, straightening and turning so that he could see how the bolt had punched into his shield. It was almost in the centre and had probably grazed Ramon's arm. The older knight discarded the shield, and Arnau noted that the bolt's passage had snapped one of the leather grips inside, making it unwieldy.

Men were at the battlements now, climbing up that ladder. Franks and Venetians both wrestled with the defenders, pushing to crest the parapet. Just as Arnau was contemplating rushing over to help, a thud announced a second ladder here. He leaped forward with two other Byzantines to shove the ladder away, and was met with another barrage of missiles. An arrow took the man to his right in the throat just below the jaw, throwing him backwards. The one to the left dropped like a stone, hiding behind the battlements as shafts flew past. Arnau pushed on alone, only realising his folly as an arrow struck him on the helmet above his right eye. The impact almost knocked him over, sending him staggering back, his hearing overcome with a ringing noise.

As he righted himself slowly, several paces back on the wall, shaking his head, he realised his helmet was pressing against his brow, dented by the blow. Other men ran for the ladder, and Arnau felt his heart skip as he watched Hell unfold in the blink of an eye. One moment the tourmarch and two infantry were running forward as the archers below reloaded, reaching out to push the ladder. The next, all three had gone. The Venetian galley before the walls had found its mark with the catapult mounted on the deck. The stone had hit the parapet, wrecking the top rungs of the ladder, but smashing through the timbers of the newly raised battlements. The stone itself had struck the tourmarch, obliterating him in a heartbeat as the ragged pieces that remained rained down over the burned-out city inside the walls. The men to either side of him were flensed by a cloud of splinters of shredded timber, some a foot long. Arnau stared in horror at the pair as they hit the wall walk, still alive and moaning as the blood pumped from a hundred wounds around the wooden points that covered them like some dreadful parody of a hedge-pig.

Arnau took time from the panic on the wall top to swap hands with his mace again, rip the misericorde from his belt and quickly dispatch the pair with as much care as possible to prevent the dreadful, lingering death they faced. Rather than put it away, he gripped the narrow dagger in his off hand now, the shield still on his arm, mace in his right.

There was an odd stillness for a moment in the aftermath of the horror, broken suddenly as a man appeared atop the ladder and threw himself over the shattered parapet onto the wall walk.

Arnau bellowed formless noises of rage and threw himself forward, mace raised. The man delivered a strong sword blow to the nearest Byzantine and looked around for his next target, eyes widening as they lit upon the red cross of the Templar before him, just before the mace came down and smashed into his kettle helmet, mangling the iron and driving it deep through cracking bone and into the Frank's brain. He shook, made an odd gurgling noise as red and grey matter leaked down his brow from his ruined cranium and he fell away to die, shuddering, on the wall.

But another man was behind him now, and another just climbing over. A third ladder hit nearby, and arrows slithered through the air once more. Greek defenders fell back, peppered with shafts.

Arnau glanced left and right, and his morale slipped once more. Both towers were in real trouble now. The one to his right was the scene of vicious fighting as men struggled to prevent a strong force of men widening their hold on the top. To the left, though, the news was worse. The Franks totally controlled the tower's top. Small groups of colourful knights were already beginning to push outwards along the wall top, some of them naturally closing the gap between that breach and where Arnau fought desperately to hold ground above the gate. Worse still, men were pouring along the gantry over there, and then splitting up to either support the push along the wall one way or the other, or piling through the doorway and heading down into the tower, fighting for control of the floors below. His momentarily wandering gaze caught brief sight of Sebastian off to his right, fighting like a madman, still alive and spattered with blood.

'The walls are falling,' he bellowed in the direction of Ramon, who was engaged in single combat with a man in a blue and white surcoat, head enclosed in a full helmet. Ramon either failed to hear in the press or ignored him, intent on his own troubles.

Suddenly, Octa was next to Arnau, nursing a wound on his left arm but hale as ever besides that. 'You should leave. We cannot guarantee your safety now.'

Arnau had to laugh at the absurdity that in this violent melting pot of Hell, the Waring still thought they were protecting the Templars. 'You need every hand.'

'We need the hand of *God*,' snarled the big northerner, then pushed past him, roaring and swinging his massive axe. An unwary Venetian, looking smug as a Byzantine victim fell away, continued to look smug even as his head left his shoulders with the mighty swing of the sharp axe. The body crumpled, folded and fell forward as the head tumbled out over the wall to fall back among his comrades.

Swallowing his dismay at the turn in the tide of the war, Arnau stepped back, allowing the Warings to take the lead here, then started to jog towards where Ramon was struggling to hold back a pair of men with swords and bright surcoats, and without a shield.

There was a terrible sudden noise and Arnau felt his sword arm flower in a dozen points of pain, like Greek fire splashing across the flesh. He staggered, turned and stared. Another shot from the catapult had struck the parapet. Men standing where Arnau had been only moments before were flailing on the floor, pinned with a hundred hard timber spears torn from the walls and sent forth in a cloud. Octa was gone, the only sign of his erstwhile existence his axe rocking slowly to a halt on the floor. Only one of the Warings was visible, and he was staggering this way and that, clutching his head.

Arnau, suddenly more than well aware of the pain in his arm, looked down.

His mail shirt had probably saved the arm, but it had not prevented damage. The sharpest of the splinters flying here at the periphery of the explosion had forced their way between the links and drawn blood, which was even now beginning to stain the steel. He flexed his arm. It hurt like Hell itself, but it moved and nothing seemed torn or broken. Gritting his teeth, he knew he could still swing the mace, as long as he tried to ignore the pain. At least his rib had long since healed.

'I shall acknowledge the Lord by his rightfulness; and I shall sing thanks and praise to the name of the highest Lord.'

And he meant it. Had he not been moved for some reason to turn from his duty there and go to the aid of his friend, he would even now have been with Octa at the gates of Paradise.

He lived.

God had saved him. He must not throw away that gift. Gritting his teeth, he ran on, mace rising, fiery pain rippling all along his weapon arm. The man on the right facing Ramon had no inkling of danger until Arnau's mace smashed into his shoulder, shattering bones and pulverising flesh. His shield fell away from useless fingers as he shrieked. He turned, but even had he had the strength in his agony to fight, he was not fast enough. Arnau's mace flew again, taking the man full in the face mid-swing, ripping his jaw away, mashing his nose and pulping his eye. The dying, ruined man fell away, keening in an odd, eerie way from his broken face.

Ramon, free of the trouble of having to hold off two men at once, swiftly and neatly dispatched the other with a swipe to the neck. As his victim fell away with a yelp, Arnau looked this way and that.

'This stretch of wall is falling.'

Ramon followed the direction of his gaze, nodding slowly. The next tower was now being used as an entry point for more and more men, and the other tower, which had been harder fought, was finally under Frankish control. Parties of enemy knights and men-at-arms were busy fighting their way along the wall top from both directions, heading towards this gate. Any time now they would meet, and anyone above this gate was doomed, utterly trapped, with men to both sides along the walls, and below outside, still climbing ladders. Indeed, even now more men were pouring up and over onto the gate top over the ruined parapet. The enemy had stopped loosing stones and arrows up here, for fear of hitting the Frankish knights who would now be able to secure the parapet without a great deal of difficulty.

Suddenly, out of the chaos and through the mess left by the last terrible blow, Arnau spotted Sebastian staggering towards them, mace in hand, drenched with blood and clutching a limp arm.

'Are you all right?' he yelled across.

Sebastian's eyes danced wildly for a moment before settling on Arnau. He nodded slowly. 'I think so. My arm. Broken, I think.'

Arnau turned to see another man clutching a shoulder and limping. He pointed at the unknown Byzantine and yanked his imperial scroll from his belt pouch. 'Get him back to the Blachernae and find a doctor for you both.'

The soldier gratefully took the document and gestured for Sebastian to accompany him. The squire looked uncertainly at Arnau for a moment, and the Templar grinned. 'Those were your own tears, Sebastian. Today's not your day.'

They descended the nearest staircase beside the gate, returning to the ground inside the city where Sebastian bade them farewell, staggering off with the limping infantryman, heading for the palace and relative safety. Men were running this way and that along the walls, shouting, others toppling from the parapet with alarming regularity. Small units of Warings were running in to lend fresh support, but the current focus seemed to be the sound of fraught combat from within the gatehouse.

The walls looked lost, but that had happened once before and the tide had yet been turned by the Warings. As long as the gate below held, there was still hope. Ramon had clearly come to the same conclusion, for when their eyes met again, the older knight gestured into the archway of the gate with his chin. Arnau nodded and the two men hurried inside, pushing their way in amid a tangle of Byzantine defenders, making to support those holding the gate. He reached the portal with some difficulty, Ramon at the far side, weapons out and heaving their bulk against the wood to help hold it against the battering of the enemy. Already the timbers shook under repeated blows. Arnau cringed as the great wooden portal thudded into his shoulder, dust scattering down from the archway above in a choking cloud. He could hear the shouts outside; no words were audible – just sounds of anger and violence.

With a heart-stopping crack, the shining steel curve of an axe blade appeared through the timbers mere inches from Arnau's face. Splinters of wood flew in a dozen directions, one drawing blood from the young Templar's nose as it passed. Even in the midst of this terrible fray, he found the time to say a quick prayer in thanks that only his nose had been blooded. Many a knight had lost an eye or more to the splinters of a lance, after all. A bloody nose was nothing.

The door shook again. He looked up instinctively. The white surcoat, emblazoned with the crimson cross of the order, was visible on the far side of the gatehouse. Ramon, a shining pure-white beacon amid the dun and grey of the local men-at-arms, shook his head with a grim expression. The gate was lost. It was only a matter of time.

An arrow thrummed through one of the many small holes that had already been smashed through the gate, taking a swarthy spearman in the throat and hurling him back to the cobbles to cough and gurgle out his last moments. Arnau paid him no more heed than any of the other poor victims of this terrible fight. He had boundless sympathy for these people, yet even that had been stretched with the chaos, death and disaster all around them.

'The gate is falling,' his fellow knight shouted across the rattle of local tongues, somewhat unnecessarily. Anyone could see now that the gate was done for – certainly the young Templar with the bloody nose.

Before they could do anything more there was a dreadful crack, and the huge, heavy beam that now constituted the last obstacle gave a little, the iron loops in which it sat coming away from the door with a metallic shriek. The entire gate scraped inwards by a foot, a gap opening in the middle. Arnau could see them outside now – hungry and afire with the desire to kill and maim. He had seen those looks in another such desperate defence, at Rourell half a decade ago. These men would not be satisfied with anything less than grand slaughter and total victory.

Arnau lurched back as the gate groaned inwards, and a pike thrust through the gap tore through the surcoat at his shoulder, taking wisps of material with it and grating across the chain shirt beneath. This second close call drew another prayer of thanks from the young Templar even as he brought his mace down and smashed the head from the pike in the press. Beside him, a man in a gleaming scale shirt suddenly jerked upright, arms thrust into the air and weapons forgotten as a spear slammed into the gap beneath his arms, impaling organs and robbing him of life.

Another thud.

The gate groaned inwards a few more inches. Now grasping arms and jabbing weapons were reaching through the gap, hungry for flesh. Mere moments remained.

Regretting he could do no more, and noting a similar look in his brother's eyes, Arnau de Vallbona withdrew from the defence of the gate, ducking an arrow and backing away.

It was not his fight, had never been his fight, yet leaving it felt like the worst of betrayals.

How in the name of God had it come to this?

Arnau ran.

CHAPTER 21:
THE WORLD'S END

APRIL 13TH 1204

B
arely had they turned and started back along the wall from the falling gate before they encountered a small party of men coming the other way, hailing them. Arnau had come to a stop with Ramon as a group of Warings halted and Redwald emerged from their number.

'Templars, how goes the wall?'

'Without the direct hand of God, the entire shoreline will be in Frankish hands by sundown,' Ramon had reported bleakly.

Redwald had nodded, his face betraying no emotion. 'Theodoros Laskaris is at the imperial pavilion on the hill. He has asked for you.'

Arnau had turned to Ramon, who simply nodded. 'We were bound for the palace and the preceptor, but we will see the commander first.'

The journey up the charred slope of the city was slow and laborious and the sun was beginning to slide from the sky as the two knights crested the burned-out slope and approached the imperial encampment. A small force of infantry was in evidence, along with half a dozen tents that housed the senior officers and nobles. At the centre stood a grand pavilion, guarded around its entire circuit by alert-looking Warings.

As they neared the centre of Byzantine command, they paused and turned, looking back down the slope towards the Golden Horn. It was easy to see why Doukas had chosen to command from here under a temporary roof rather than the comfort of a palace. Between the two fires that had burned large swathes of the city flat and the general slope of the hill, from here the officers could view the entire theatre of war, from the Blachernae off to the left at the edge of the city, to the tower below the acropolis hill where the chain had once been anchored.

And the view was disheartening. In the quarter of an hour in which they had trudged with difficulty up the detritus-clogged, burned-out streets of the city, things had gone from bad to worse down on the walls. Even at this distance it was clear that a stretch of walls containing three gates and perhaps a dozen towers was already under enemy control. For some reason, the Franks were still concentrating on keeping command of those walls and had not bothered sending forces further into the city, centring their attention on the breach they had created.

Even to Arnau's untrained eye it now looked hopeless. No matter how good the officers were or how brave the men, their chances of pushing the enemy back off the walls and securing them were next to nil. One glance at Ramon's face told him that the older knight had come to the same conclusion.

With a sigh, they turned and strode towards the great pavilion.

'We have been called for by Theodoros Laskaris,' Ramon told the Waring by the entrance. The guard nodded, clearly expecting them, and gestured to the door.

The two men entered the immense tent, the biggest Arnau had ever seen.

A great table stood in the centre, covered with a map of the city and a hundred wooden markers showing the position of units. It was notable that the black ones, which seemed from the positioning to represent the Franks, were predominant. Arnau immediately felt uncomfortable as there seemed to be an argument in progress and they had walked into the very midst of it.

'You advocate terms?' snapped the emperor, pointing an accusatory finger at a Waring with an impressive braided beard and ice-blue eyes. 'You are my guard, loyal to the death. What gives you the right to dictate imperial policy to me?'

The big man leaned on his axe with arms folded. 'I command the Warings, Majesty, and we remain loyal, but the day you made it clear that we were to function as part of the city's military in defence of Constantinopolis, you also put the city's care partially into my hands, and therefore my duty is to inform you that we have lost.'

'Never.'

The big Waring waved a hand towards the door, causing everyone momentarily to look in the direction of the two Templars, who flinched at the attention. 'The walls have fallen. We can throw every man at them to try and retake them, but we will lose. Once they breached, we lost. Everyone knows it. Now we can either fight on like some hopeless martyr's last stand or we can save what we are able. What *you* are able. We are in a weak position now, but it may yet be possible to bargain with the Frankish leaders. Not the doge, but the Franks. Give them what they want. Buy time for us to work. It might take months, maybe even years, but this need not be the end. But if you insist on fighting to annihilation, then it will be.'

Doukas roared at the man. 'Ceolwulf, you are my guard and you will obey my commands.'

'Of course, Majesty. But while we fight to the death to protect you, I will continue to advocate terms.'

'Where can we hold while we regroup?' Doukas snapped, glancing about him.

'The Blachernae?' a courtier mused.

'Too close to the fallen walls. And too accessible from them.'

'The Bukoleon,' Theodoros Laskaris said.

The emperor nodded slowly. 'Separated from the main walls, waterfront, self-contained. And on the far side of the city from the enemy. Yes, there we can gather and plan while we hold any advance. How many divisions can we recall while keeping the Franks bogged down at the walls?'

As several officers now involved themselves in the discussion, Theodoros Laskaris turned and hurried across the tent to the two knights. Gesturing for them to follow him, he pointed to an interior doorway that led to another section of tent. Inside it was rather gloomy, and it became more so as the commander let the flap fall closed behind them.

'You called for us?'

Laskaris nodded. 'You have served the city and the empire nobly through your time here, my friends. What we face now though is extinction, and you cannot be a part of that. Your preceptor can say what he likes, but you cannot stay, or you will likely perish with the rest of us.'

'What will you do?'

'Stand by the emperor until he either flees or falls, and then, when that happens, raise another and another until the last grocer in the city wears a crown to defy the Franks. We will do what we must. The council of nobles remains at the Haghia Sophia, arguing about their own perils. The emperor will rally what forces he can at the Bukoleon with a view to securing the more important sections of the city and gradually forcing the enemy back. It will be hard fought and there is more than a strong chance of failure, but we are men of Constantinopolis, the last of the Caesars, and we will fight until we die and bow our necks to no Frank.'

Ramon nodded. 'In a perfect world we would stay and help, but our order cannot afford to deal with the repercussions of knights of the Order falling into Frankish hands in the defence of what the grand master will consider a heretical city.'

'I have secured you passage,' Laskaris said quietly. 'Do not make it well known, for in the coming hours there will be many thousands seeking such a thing.'

'How?'

'There is a small harbour at a place called the Hebdomon, just two miles along the coast from the Golden Gate. The place is both an imperial summer residence and the location of the external cavalry and infantry barracks. It has remained empty since the siege began, but I have arranged for a small fishing boat to dock there in secrecy. It will carry you across the Marmara Sea and to safety.'

'Is it safe to travel?'

Laskaris shrugged. 'There should be none, or at least very few, of the enemy in that region, at the very far side of the peninsula from the fighting. In the coming hours the city's people will likely begin to see the end and flood from the walls. You would be best served leaving now before that happens, lest refugees come across your boat and seize it for themselves.'

Ramon smiled sadly. 'Thank you, Laskaris. It has been an honour to know both you and your brother. I pray that somehow this day can still be turned and your people saved.'

Laskaris shook his hand and then turned to Arnau and did the same. 'Good luck, my friends.' And with that he turned away and marched back into the tent to his emperor's side.

'I thought you were set on not leaving until Bochard did?'

'I was.'

'Bochard will not leave now,' Arnau breathed. 'The Franks will command the city within a day, and then he will feel vindicated and safe. He will not allow us to drag him away now.'

'Then we must be as persuasive as we have ever been. His few cronies among the Franks might have helped him thus far and offered him protection, but you and I have crippled his chances. With the red cross shown defiant on the walls, neither the Franks nor the Venetians are going to consider giving any quarter to us. If he does not leave with us this evening, he will almost certainly fall foul of them.'

Arnau nodded and the pair slipped from the side room, shuffling around the periphery of the great command tent and out of the main entrance. Once outside, Ramon broke into a jog, armour and weapons jingling, and Arnau picked up his pace and fell in alongside. They passed the smoke-blackened walls of the church and picked their way at speed through the burned bones of the city, making for the highest hill by the walls, where the top end of the Blachernae lay. As they ran, they kept their eyes on the walls down by the water. The sun was starting to slide towards the horizon, but there could be no doubt that the Franks were the masters of the shoreline now. No counter-attack was going to push them back off the walls, Arnau felt certain. Moreover, their struggle to take as much wall as possible had now brought them to the Blachernae Gate. Any time now, the great imperial palace at the western edge of the city might fall to the Crusaders.

Would they pause when night fell, or would they push on to take the city entire during the night?

They reached the Blachernae breathless from their run, a mile and a half of nervous tension, first through charred remains and then finally through the untouched region of the city. They spoke not a word on the journey. Everything they might have said, they had either already done so, or felt loath to do. The Blachernae reared up like an ornate mausoleum now to Arnau's eyes as they reached the gate and were admitted without question by the Warings on guard.

Arnau sucked in a deep breath as they crossed the courtyard and made for the apartments they had called home for a year. He knew this confrontation was going to be difficult. Indeed, he could see no way to succeed in persuading Bochard, but they had to try. One last time, they had to try.

As they reached the doorway that led in to their rooms, Arnau heard an alarm raised, disturbingly close. He paused, hand going to Ramon's shoulder. 'Listen.'

'They've reached the Blachernae,' the older knight confirmed. 'They will assume the emperor is here, or at least men of import. They will want to secure this place before nightfall if nothing else. Come on.'

Arnau followed Ramon through the door and up the stairs. The corridor that led to their rooms was short, but poorly lit by the sinking sun, and Arnau watched the shadows with nervous eyes, half expecting enemy assassins to leap from them. Bochard's door was shut, but there were noises within, and the thin line of golden light showing from beneath was repeatedly interrupted by moving shadows.

Arnau almost leaped out of his skin as their own door opened right next to his shoulder, and his hand went to the mace at his belt, ripping it free as he spun.

Sebastian stood in their doorway. His face was grimy and forlorn. His mail shirt was flecked with dirt and drying blood and his left arm was now strapped tightly to his chest, the most basic of ministrations, likely all the beleaguered medics would have time for on a day like this. In his right hand, the young man held a mace much like Arnau's, which had clearly seen much use.

'Is it over?' he asked in a ghost of a voice.

'For us,' Arnau said quietly. 'We must leave. The city is being overrun, and the Blachernae is next.'

'My people.'

'They will fight on, though the cause be lost. It would appear that the courage of ancient Rome still runs in your people's veins, Sebastian. But we must go before the city is lost. Will you come?'

Sebastian looked lost for a moment, and Arnau felt a wave of sympathy wash over him. The boy had fled west and found sanctuary with the Order only to be brought all the way back to the land of his birth and made to watch it destroyed. Would it be better for him to forget the Order entirely and stay with the Byzantines, or to turn his back on this for good and return to the Order with them? It had to be the boy's choice.

He said nothing, but stepped out of the room to join them. Arnau slid his own mace back into his belt as Ramon hammered on the preceptor's door.

'What is it?'

The older knight pushed the door open and stepped inside, followed by Arnau and Sebastian. Bochard was standing at a desk with a dozen small books laid open and bookmarked. His squire was busy wrapping up a bundle in the corner.

'De Juelle,' Bochard said with distaste. 'I see you continue to disobey me at every turn and throw in your lot with heretics. I should have known better.' His eyelid danced with a frantic speed that made his face hard to watch without one's eyes watering. 'You have been an impediment and an embarrassment since the day we arrived. Upon our return to Acre I will speak with the grand master and have you punished appropriately. You and Vallbona both. And this young man, too. He could have been a good Templar, true to the Order, until you two got your hooks into him.'

The three men moved further into the room, Ramon squaring up to the preceptor.

'Whatever you think is going to happen when the Franks come, Bochard, cast it aside. Unless your three friends happen to find you first, no one else is going to give you quarter. Already the Franks overrun the southern edge of the Blachernae. They will be in these rooms within the hour at the latest. We must go. For a year now, Vallbona and I have been telling you this, but the time has come. We can no longer tarry. Gather your things and prepare to leave.'

'No, de Juelle.'

'No relic can be worth this. Even your most holy lance. Staying will not mean you save it from harm. It just means that you and I will perish in this city alongside it. We have to go. Laskaris has secured us a boat. We have a means of escape, but we will not have it for long.'

'No, de Juelle. The spear remains in the Mangana. I will not leave without it.'

'Do not be a fool, Bochard. This is prideful behaviour, not piety. Not a display of Christian value but one of sin.'

'Sin?' Bochard snapped. 'You have the audacity to lecture me on sin?' He took two forceful steps forward towards the three of them. 'You who come here to my rooms bedecked for war? You who come fresh from fighting for the honour of heretics who deny Holy Mother Church? You who wear upon you the blood and gore of Christian knights in flagrant contravention of our order's most sacred rules? By God, de Juelle, I should not demand your punishment. I should demand your excommunication or even your death for what you have done. Have you any idea how this will be seen at the mother house? They are not as forgiving as I.'

He turned to Sebastian then. 'And this one! Did you truly corrupt an innocent young brother with your madness, or has he been a heathen hiding in plain sight all along? See how he brandishes in front of his preceptor a mace still covered in the brains of a knight of God. Appalling. Unacceptable!'

His hand darted out and snatched the wavering mace from the distraught boy's hand.

'A weapon of the Devil, used against Christians.' He stepped back. 'No, I am not done here, de Juelle. What you do is your own affair, since you have shown scant regard for my command throughout our time here. If you truly cling to that cross you wear, then you will hold this place against any troublemakers until those Franks who hold the Order dear can reach us and guarantee the safety of both our persons and all I have achieved. If you flee, like a coward, you forfeit both your honour, such as it is, and the last claim you can make to serving the Order.'

Arnau glanced at Ramon. The older brother was enduring the most dreadful inner struggle. Ramon felt the preceptor was wrong. He knew that leaving the city was the right thing to do, but to flatly refuse an order from Bochard would mean the end of his life as a Templar. Should Bochard survive, he would see them all stripped of their mantles and punished, perhaps terminally. Should he fall, they would be beholden to reveal all that had happened to the masters in Acre, for lying about it would only compound their sins. Ramon was caught in the most awful quandary.

'You have two relics left to find?'

Bochard shook his head. 'Already the shroud of our precious Lord lies with these treasures, ready to move. Only the spear remains.'

Ramon huffed. 'The Mangana is on the acropolis headland at the other end of the city. Already the Franks and Venetians will be swarming up there, for as the high point and the political and religious heart of the city it will be vital for their control. There is next to no chance of any of us reaching the

Mangana. It is a fool's errand, Bochard. Can you not be content with what you have?'

Bochard glared at him. 'We must not fear the soldiers of Christ, for is that not precisely what we are, de Juelle? No, we shall remain.' He spun to his left, his hand thrusting out, still holding Sebastian's mace, using it to gesture to the stacked boxes in the corner of the room, where his squire was carefully wrapping something in linen. Something wet flicked off the mace and spattered across the squire's shoulder and face. Hugues jumped in shock and revulsion and dropped his burden, recoiling.

Something carefully folded and ancient tumbled from the wrappings and Sebastian, eyes wide, ran over to his fellow squire to help with his good arm.

'See what we have. All this I have saved from ruin, Brother de Juelle. All of this will be kept sacred because of me.'

'Pride is a deadly sin, Bochard,' Ramon reminded him in flat tones.

'So is the murder of other Christians,' snapped Bochard. 'Yet you happily cut down men of God on the walls for your heretic friends. I have told you once, and now twice, de Juelle, do *not* lecture me. I shall not tell you again. And while you kill our brothers, I—'

Arnau saw it coming. He jumped, but there was nothing he could do. In a horrifying, slow-moving tableau, he watched Bochard turn once more, gesturing sharply with that gore-coated mace at the relics in the corner, thrusting out his arm with violent fury. He saw Sebastian, who had helped his fellow squire gather up the fallen relic and was now moving across to stand with Ramon once more.

He watched in sick horror as the steel flange of the mace smashed accidentally into Sebastian's forehead. He saw the bone crack and the terrible weapon push inside. Sebastian cried out, his forehead crumpling.

Ramon moved instantly and Bochard, still turning, stared in shock. As though he might undo what he had done, he pulled his arm back instinctively, though it did no good. He could not unmake the wound. The mace, covered now with fresh gore, lowered. Sebastian took a shaky step forward. His forehead was mangled and blood was sheeting down, pouring over his eyes. He looked like a thing of nightmare.

Bochard dropped the mace as though it had suddenly become white-hot, still staring at Sebastian as the boy took another step. He gurgled something unintelligible and dropped to his knees, beginning to shake. Arnau looked back and forth in horror between the preceptor and the dying squire, his mind's eye hurled back over the months to that dusty road in Armenian Cilicia, and Bochard crouched over the body of an armoured youth, his face white.

The preceptor's face had gone pale once more, one eyelid jumping and flickering. His mouth dropped open wordlessly. Arnau stared at him and knew suddenly that something in Bochard had broken. Something that had been building since their arrival, and probably long before. Something since the death of the boy on the road? Most likely something since the death of so many civilians in the streets of Cyprus. Something had snapped.

'What have you done?' snapped Ramon as Arnau hurried forward and reached out to the shaking boy. With a closer view he could see that the point of the flange had smashed through the skull. He turned. Ramon was looking at him. He shook his head and turned back to Ramon's squire.

'I am so sorry, Sebastian. I really am.'

Had he needed confirmation that the lad had lost the power of conscious thought, it came as he drew his misericorde from his belt and lifted it, ready to deliver the *coup de grâce* and Sebastian's blood-soaked eyes just followed the movements with no fear, moving on instinct alone. With a sense of infinite sadness, he reached to the waist of Sebastian's mail shirt, lifting the heavy links with his left hand. As it reached the level of his shoulders, Arnau carefully positioned his knife, adjusting it a couple of times due to the increased shaking of the boy and then, with as much force as he could muster, drove the narrow blade deep into the squire's heart. Pulling the blade back out with a gout of blood, he allowed the mail shirt to fall and cut off the crimson flow. The lad continued to shake for a few moments more, falling face first on the flagstones and shuddering in a growing pool of blood, but quickly shook to a halt and then lay still. Reaching down, it took only moments to find the icon the boy had carried his whole life with the order. It was dry. Had it truly cried that morning? Somehow Arnau was a lot less sceptical about it now than he'd been earlier.

He turned as he rose to his feet, icon gripped tight in his hand, about as angry as he'd ever been.

The fury he felt evaporated at the first sight of Bochard. He'd intended to cast the icon at Bochard with some snide comment about the value of relics, but his grip remained tight. The preceptor was staring at the body on the floor with a look of abject horror. Every snarling accusation Arnau had felt building up inside ready to launch at Bochard died on his tongue. Nothing Arnau could possible say to Bochard could be worse for the man than what he was clearly currently inflicting upon himself.

'I...' was all the preceptor could manage.

'We are leaving,' Ramon said in a dead, flat tone to the preceptor. Bochard simply nodded, wide-eyed, still staring at the bloodied heap on the floor.

He turned to Arnau. 'He is gone. At peace now.'

The younger knight nodded, silently, then reached down and gently rolled over the body so that the squire's blood-filled eyes peered up sightlessly at Heaven. He drew a cross lightly over the horrible wound on the forehead, cringing as he did so, then looked up.

'We commend to you, oh Lord, the soul of this your servant Sebastian, and beseech you, Christ, Redeemer of the World, that, as in your love for him you became man, so now you would grant to admit him into the number of the blessed. May all the saints and elect of God, who, on earth, suffered for the sake of Christ, intercede for him so that, when freed from the prison of his body, he may be admitted into the kingdom of Heaven: through the merits of Our Lord Jesus Christ, who lives and reigns with the Father and the Holy Spirit, world without end. May the blessing of God Almighty the Father, and the Son, and the Holy Ghost descend upon you and remain with you always. Amen.'

He rose slowly.

'Do you suppose someone will bury him? I hate to think of what will happen otherwise.'

Ramon nodded. 'I hope so, but we cannot focus on that now. It is time to leave.' He pointed at Bochard and then at the door. 'Go.'

Meekly, as though commanded by a superior, Bochard stepped over to the door, face still grey and eyes wide, body moving like an automaton. As Ramon guided the stunned preceptor, Arnau gestured to the man's squire, who was cowering in the corner near the relics, terrified.

'Come on. We are all leaving.'

Hugues nodded, still bordering on panic, and struggled to gather up armfuls of things.

'Don't be stupid man, leave them.'

With a hesitant nod, the squire dropped back most of what he was carrying, hugging to himself the one hastily wrapped package that Sebastian had helped him gather up so recently. Arnau hadn't the heart to tell him to leave it, given the way he was clinging so tightly to it.

Urging the terrified squire from the room, Arnau followed the others out into the corridor. At Ramon's gesture, he ducked into their room. They had brought little with them that they could not afford to lose, and Arnau gathered up the bare essentials and thrust them in a leather bag, throwing it over his shoulder and following the older knight back out into the corridor.

Bochard was standing at the window.

'They come. They come now,' he said, his voice strangely hollow. Arnau leaned in to peer past him. At the very limit of his vision, far off to the left, he could make out fighting on the palace's boundary wall. The Franks were in the Blachernae and closing on this area. If they did not leave now, they might never get to do so.

Ramon was already at the stairs, hurrying down them with a clatter and shush of mail, urgency in his every movement. It was perhaps another sign of how Bochard had been thrown by his action that he simply stood there, staring, until Arnau nudged his shoulder and pointed to the stairs. 'Go.'

The preceptor did so, still in his mechanical way, as though not truly with them, his limbs being moved by some phantom puppeteer. The squire, hugging his bundle, followed on. As they burst from the doorway below, Arnau's heart leaped into his throat. To their left a mob of Crusaders, the colourful surcoats of knights mixed in the steel and drab jackets of their men-at-arms, was surging across the grass. A force of eight Warings had emerged from another doorway and was running to intercept the much larger force. It would be a slaughter. The Warings would be swiftly overcome by Franks. Ramon gestured to the gate.

'The horses,' shouted Arnau, pointing towards the stable building, horribly aware that it would mean running in the direction of that violent conflict to retrieve the beasts.

'No time. Come on.'

Leading the others, Ramon ran across to the gateway. A glance up and left as they ran showed that more Franks were on the wall top coming this way, overcoming small parties of defenders as they went. Once they reached this gate, they could control all access to and from the palace. Anyone inside would be effectively trapped. How close they had come to being part of this great tragedy.

Arnau threw up silent thanks to the Lord as they reached the archway. In the last light of the day he could just make out the barred gate blocking their way and the four Byzantine spearmen, their weapons crossed, denying the Templars any exit.

'Stand aside,' bellowed Ramon in Greek, but the men remained still.

'Let us out,' he snarled.

One of the guards shook his head. 'By order of the Blachernae's commander all gates are to remain barred in the current crisis.'

Current crisis? What did the man think was happening?

'There is precious little point holding this gate, man,' Ramon spat, pointing back out into the courtyard. 'Hundreds of howling Franks are already inside, heading this way, and they're atop the wall, too. Now open the damned gate.'

The man had the grace to look concerned, and Arnau stepped forward to join his friend, hand going to his waist, pulling the mace from his belt. As he raised it there was a blood-curdling howl at his shoulder making him jump in shock, and suddenly Bochard was on him, gripping the mace and bellowing like a wounded animal. Arnau, shocked to the core, reeled back and put up no resistance as Bochard tore the mace from his hand and cast it away as though it stank of Hell itself. Panting, the preceptor, still wide-eyed, stared at him. Arnau started to feel distinctly uncomfortable under that glare, and perhaps the seeming mania of the preceptor had got to the Byzantines too, for they were now hurrying to lift the bar from the gate, more to get rid of the raving madman before them than for Ramon's benefit.

The sounds of combat rolled across the courtyard outside as the great timber gate was swung open. With just a nod to the guards, Ramon led the others outside, and Arnau felt a mix of panic and relief as they emerged into the open. The Blachernae had fallen. In a matter of minutes, the imperial apartments themselves would be ransacked by marauding Franks. They would be standing at the window in the Templars' room where they themselves had waited over the past year, watching the siege ebb and flow outside the walls.

They were out of the Blachernae now, but still in a city being swiftly consumed by a victorious enemy force. Indeed, the Franks and Venetians presented only one of three great dangers that Arnau became aware of in an instant. In addition, he could see a flood of humanity surging through the city, fleeing the fighting and the Franks within the walls. Such a desperate mob could do anything and might be almost as dangerous as the enemy. And finally, above and beyond all that, in the increasingly mauve sky of sunset, rising black clouds spoke of fresh disaster.

The city was on fire again.

CHAPTER 22:
BYZANTIUM'S FALL

APRIL 13TH 1204

A rnau shoved the man hard until he staggered, tripped on the kerbstone and fell back with a cry. Others were pushing and shoving now. He felt someone grabbing his mantle and, as he pulled away, felt the material tear. Freed from the grasping hands, he followed the others into the alleyway. Someone behind him bellowed and he turned and lashed out with a mailed fist without even looking. His punch connected with some bony part of a figure now largely hidden in the shadowy alley.

He ran.

Ahead, the squire was clutching his precious bundle and trying to guide Bochard who was still moving with a sort of detached mindlessness, as though not fully in control of his own faculties. Only Ramon was alert and ready, leading the small party.

The sun was down now, just at the level of the horizon, casting a last reach of golden fingers over the fallen city. Shadows lengthened and deepened in every corner, giving the streets a dangerous, eerie look. The last day of Byzantium was almost at an end. Arnau shook his head. He had to stop thinking in such poetic terms about one of the worst disasters of which he'd ever heard.

Constantinople *was* dying, though. Half occupied by bloodthirsty and victorious Franks and Venetians, flooding with desperate, terrified and angry citizens all hoping to get out beyond the walls to safety, sections burned out, others freshly aflame, the emperor and his Warings retreated to a waterside palace to make a last stand and the council of nobles as useless as ever.

Arnau had thought that escaping the Blachernae into the city before the invading Franks closed them in was paramount, and that relative safety would await them outside. How wrong he had been. They had emerged into the city just before the Franks stormed the gate house behind them, seizing control of the Blachernae palace complex, and had hurried along the wide thoroughfare towards the large sprawling monastery of Saint Saviour and the great Mese street, breathing heavy sighs of relief.

But as they approached the monastery, they began to meet crowds of refugees, and suddenly the red crosses on their chests marked them out as targets. Those more able and angry among the fleeing Byzantines bellowed their hate and anger at the Westerners among them and rained fists upon them as they passed, assaulting and accusing. They had escaped the first press of refugees with bruises and contusions and slipped away, racing through narrow alleys until they were alone.

Ramon and Arnau had to take control of this journey, as had been made clear in that first moment of trouble. Bochard was broken. When the Byzantines had attacked him, he had neither fought back nor made to defend himself. As Arnau had looked around in the press for him, he had seen Bochard standing defenceless with his hands raised, a look of blank acceptance on his face. Arnau had been forced to drag him away. The squire had been little help either. All he seemed to care about was the bundle he carried, which he hunched over and protected like a helpless child. So it was that the two knights had taken the roles of van- and rearguard, herding their companions along.

From the backstreets near the monastery, they had kept to the narrow alleys, avoiding the floods of people on the main roads, moving slowly and carefully. Clearly now, with the chaos and the panic, the crowds of Byzantines presented as much of a danger to the knights as the Franks ever had. Thus they kept to the shadows.

The Mese had presented difficulties. Their goal was the Golden Gate, since the other gates in the city walls had been filled with rubble and blocked with beams and iron bars to present a better defence against the Crusaders. The citizens might be flooding towards the nearest exit, but they would be disappointed. From their tours of the walls during the preparations, Arnau and Ramon knew well that the only gate that could realistically open to disgorge the population was the Golden Gate. Unlike most of the openings in the land walls, the Golden Gate consisted of a huge and powerful towered gate with a second, still-strong outer gate beyond it, connected to the ramparts with walls of its own, forming a small fortress. With the moat running around the outside, it was defensible enough that the emperor had left it without being completely sealed, against the possibility the Byzantine forces might need a ready portal from which to march.

Sooner or later every desperate man, woman and child in the city would find themselves at that gate, filtering through.

At the Mese, then, the small party of four men had been forced to cross the flood of humanity in the great wide street. They had spent a quarter-hour lurking in the shadows, waiting for a lull in the movement, but it had soon become clear that there would be no such lull.

Taking a deep breath, they had forged out into the flow like a man attempting to swim across a fast and strong river. It had taken every bit of strength they could muster to stay together, Ramon and Arnau keeping close, herding their companions through the crowd as angry Byzantines landed blow after blow on them, howling their hatred of the West.

Now Arnau pulled into the shadows again, breathing heavily. They had made it across the greatest of Constantinople's streets and into relative safety. Their chain shirts had absorbed much of the violence against them, since most of their assailants used only fists and elbows, and at the very worst a makeshift club. But still, when – *if* – they finally got to rest, the aches and pains would catch up and make life truly miserable. At least no one had broken a bone yet.

Bochard's squire rolled his shoulders, hissing at some wound he had taken in the mobile beating, checking his precious cargo. Bochard stood limp, like a discarded doll. His face was a mass of bruises from the beatings he had taken. Arnau and Ramon had agreed from the first moment of trouble not to draw a weapon. They would defend themselves as best they could, but these people were only attacking them out of terror and righteous anger, and neither man felt they could deliberately hurt the refugees.

'The time has come to hide our crosses,' Ramon said.

'How?'

The older knight reached up. A line of cord hung from one side of the alley to the other, drab washing pinned to it. He grasped a voluminous tunic and pulled until it came free. In moments he had removed his mantle, folding it and stuffing it into his belt, having to loosen it by several notches. Then he shrugged into the huge grey garment. He still looked like a Westerner, but at least he did not stand out as a Crusader now.

Arnau looked around, up side streets until he spotted what looked like a long brown cloak. Grabbing it, he did the same. It smelled of smoke and damp wool, which made his stomach churn, but it would help him move through the city unmolested and was therefore, right now, more valuable than gold. A few more minutes and they managed to find garments to cover the other two. The squire slipped into his without argument. Bochard numbly accepted what they did as they removed his mantle and covered him with a green woollen tunic. Arnau did notice a flinch as the cross came off and another as the wool settled on his shoulders. Was it automatic? Had Bochard been a brother of the Order for so long that even when his mind had apparently disconnected from his body, he still felt the wrench of his cross being removed, or did it perhaps indicate that Bochard was still there somewhere, and might be coaxed out once more?

Suitably disguised, they moved on. A few minutes later, they crossed the Lykos River – a narrow stream that passed through the city down to the sea – via a narrow stone bridge. Here they passed a small party of monks fleeing in their rich gowns, clutching to their chests all they had of value as they fled their church, knowing what was coming.

The two groups passed one another without a word, and the Templars moved on through alleys and narrow streets until the buildings finally petered out into an orchard. Taking a breath, Arnau and Ramon got their bearings, eyes falling upon the distant line of tower tops that marked the city wall off to their right. A small collection of close towers marked a major gate in the walls and, given the position of the Lykos, Arnau knew it for the Gate of Saint Romanus through which Alexios the Third had taken his army against the Franks only to flee with the job unfinished. The Romanus Gate meant they had come little more than a third of the way across the city in all that time. Even now the sun had finally disappeared, lending a growing inkiness to the world.

'We've not come far,' he said, disheartened.

'Further than I'd thought,' Ramon replied. 'Remember we've passed through the most built-up area and the biggest street in the city. From here there's a lot of open land until we're nearly at the Golden Gate.'

Arnau nodded. It *would* be a relief to cross arable land. They spent the next half hour moving, which was a blessing after their five-minute scurries punctuated by fifteen minutes of hiding from locals. Fields and animal pens, orchards and barns went by with the city walls always on their right, keeping them moving in the correct direction. The only buildings they saw were farms and occasional chapels or monasteries.

Early on they moved through another suburban cluster and two more major roads, as they passed groups of subdued, desperate locals all pouring towards the Rhegium Gate, where Arnau knew well they would be turned away, the gate blocked.

Finally, they began the descent of the last hill, the glittering waves of the Marmara Sea off in the distance. They passed through a final orchard and entered a narrow street between high houses. The built-up southern region of the city awaited now. There was no sign of activity in the narrow streets and it was only as they emerged out onto the southern branch of the wide Mese that they encountered another flood of humanity, though these were not making for the Circus Gate at the end of the road, since that gate had been sealed for more than a decade by imperial decree for some arcane reason Arnau could not recall. Instead they were now all flooding south, making for the Golden Gate.

There were, in fact, so many of them that Arnau wondered whether the entire population of Constantinople was trying to squeeze through the one exit. Would the Franks find the whole place deserted when they moved further in the morning?

They found none of the trouble here that they had encountered earlier. Their disguises helped them blend in with the crowd, but more crucially, the press of humanity was so tight that it was almost impossible to raise one's arms to shoulder level, and nobody could possibly make room for a scuffle. After another ten minutes amid a dark press of miserable humanity, they found themselves on the Via Egnatia, herded slowly and uncomfortably with all the rest towards the distant sight of the Golden Gate, the huge, square white stone towers almost glowing in torchlight.

They were almost there. Once through that double gate, they would have left the city and it was then just a matter of a two-mile walk along the coast to the hidden boat in the Hebdomon harbour. The human tide carried them closer and closer. Just inside the Golden Gate there lay a small square, surrounded by houses and shops and radiating streets. They had seen it from above a couple of times over the past year, and it had always looked spacious and pleasant. Now it resembled nothing more than a cattle market, filled with milling, lowing refugees all moving at the pace set by the narrowing chicane of the gate itself.

'Trouble,' hissed Ramon, just ahead, turning to look at Arnau and pointing over to their right. The younger Templar peered that way and his heart sank. A cart stood to the side of the square with several figures stood atop it. Amid the men-at-arms they could see a man in red and white. Franks. How in the world had they come here? He realised with irritation that while the four of them had moved slowly by necessity, the Franks could easily have come along the walls from the Blachernae at pace, for the garrisons on the wall tops had all either fled or been recalled to the seafront palace where the emperor rallied his remaining forces. It would have been very easy for the Franks to beat them here. And if for just a moment he wondered *why* they were here, it was quite simply the best place to be if you were looking for someone. It was the only feasible exit through the walls. Anyone they sought would have to pass through here.

It was clear, when he considered it, who they sought. Red and white meant it was probably one of Bochard's friends. They were not here for violence or looting, for they had taken a raised vantage point and were peering at the crowd. They had to be looking for Bochard.

'Keep calm and keep your face away from them until we're through the gate,' Ramon hissed.

Arnau nodded and they moved steadily forward with their herd, ever closer to the safety of the gate.

'For why though I shall go in the midst of the shadow of death, I shall not dread evils,' a voice suddenly shouted.

Arnau turned wide-eyed disbelief upon the preceptor, who had thrown his arms in the air.

'For thou art with me,' Bochard bellowed. 'Thy rod and thy staff; those have comforted me.'

Arnau tried to reach him past the squire in the press, to pull his arms down. He'd picked a damn fine time to break his silence and find his faith again.

Ramon was struggling with him now, but it was too late. One glance at that cart and Arnau could see men pointing. Suddenly, the press of humanity seemed not to be as close as it had been only moments before. As the Franks began to shout and brandish weapons, heaving their way with casual brutality through the crowd, the citizens pushed to be further and further away from these men, and the four Templars swiftly found themselves in a widening circle, facing the approaching Franks.

Bochard was still shouting his psalm, arms raised, eyes darting this way and that.

'And that I dwell in the house of the Lord, into the length of days.'

'I'm not ready to dwell in the house of the Lord quite yet,' barked Ramon, hand going to his belt and ripping free his sword. Arnau yanked out his mace, desperately hoping that Bochard wouldn't try to take it this time, but the preceptor was off on another psalm now, preaching to the crowd.

The Franks closed slowly in a line. Arnau was hardly surprised to see three nobles among them, men he now knew: Otho de la Roche, Geoffroi de Charney... and Almerico Balbi. Two Franks and a Venetian, then. And Balbi's inclusion spoke of ill intent for sure. His eyes strayed across the men-at-arms with them, and he realised with a frown that only two of them bore the colours of the Frankish knights. The others wore the dark green of Balbi's Venetians.

'Hand over the relics and the preceptor,' de Charney said in surprisingly reasonable tones.

'What?'

'Preceptor Bochard will remain under our protection, and the relics he has amassed will be kept safe, but none are to be removed from the city at this time by the command of Doge Enrico Dandolo and the lord of Montferrat. Hand over your relics.'

Arnau snorted. 'You might want to have a word with your Venetian friend, then. He's been creaming off the best of Bochard's shipments for his personal coffers for months.'

The Italian's face, usually bearing a pleasant smile, slipped into a mask of hatred for just a moment before the smile returned and turned upon his companions. 'He lies, of course.'

Arnau smiled now. The faces of the two Franks suggested that they were perhaps more inclined to accept Arnau's word than their pet Venetian's. He looked at Ramon, who shrugged.

Bochard stopped his recitation and frowned at the men.

'Preceptor?' de Charney said, concerned.

'He is not himself,' Ramon replied. 'An accident.' He turned to the squire. 'Give him the shroud.'

The squire, wide-eyed, looked at Bochard, who seemed completely oblivious.

'Give him the shroud,' repeated Ramon.

Arnau grimaced. 'You know they have no intention of giving the shroud up to the authorities,' he replied quietly, gesturing to the squire to stay back. 'Such a treasure is worth a king's ransom. De Charney and de la Roche might have more noble intentions, I suppose, but you know how the Venetians work. It will become Balbi's price for his ships. The shroud will end up in a vault in Venice. I wonder how long anyone who knows its fate will last once the authorities begin to look for it.'

Balbi's eyes flashed dangerously, and now the other two Crusaders were glancing uncertainly back at their companion. It was a gamble, turning them against one another, but they had to do something, and if it was true that the two Franks had connections to the Order, then perhaps they could be brought into the light of truth.

'Give them the shroud,' Ramon said again.

'Balbi will steal it for himself just as the Doge Dandolo has stolen a whole empire.'

'I do not care right now,' Ramon grunted. 'Give it to de la Roche or de Charney alone, then. Whichever of them has it and for whatever purpose, the shroud will be safe, for everyone covets it. Give them the shroud,' Ramon said a fourth time, and then to the three enemies, 'Bochard stays with us, though. He needs help. The Order can look after him.'

Hesitantly, unhappily, Hugues walked forward, holding forth the tightly wrapped bundle he had been clutching to his chest. De la Roche stepped out and took it, a look of reverence on his face. The squire flinched as he let go, and for just a moment Arnau thought he might just try to grab it back, but in the end, deflated, he stepped back to the other Templars.

'And any other relics you took from Bochard's room,' snapped Balbi in a thick Venetian accent.

'There are no other relics. We are not thieves.'

'I do not believe you,' Balbi snarled. 'Separate and drop your weapons so that my men can search you.'

'I give you my word,' Ramon said, 'which is my bond, and unchallenged as a knight of the Temple, that there are no other relics among us.' Arnau winced, thinking of Sebastian's icon in his belt pouch.

The two Frankish knights shared a glance and nodded. 'I am satisfied with his word, Almerico,' de la Roche said, then turned to Bochard. 'Will you come with us? You will be protected.'

Bochard simply stared at them.

'He stays with us,' Ramon said firmly.

'Search them,' snapped Balbi angrily, waving at his men.

Arnau hefted the mace. He had no desire to fight the Franks, especially now these two were seemingly being reasonable, but the Venetians were a different proposition entirely. Especially Balbi and his thugs.

'No brother should keep company with an excommunicated man,' Arnau said quietly. 'Inviolable rule of the Order. So if you insist on pressing me,' he snarled, 'then I will show you the quality of my steel.'

De la Roche stepped out between them all, turning to the Venetian nobleman. 'That's enough, Balbi. Let them be. A Templar's word is good.'

The Venetian snorted. 'Did you hear him? He knows we have the shroud and he knows it's not going to the doge or his friends. Did we not agree that there should be no witnesses? The shroud is too valuable.'

Arnau took a step forward, and noted that Ramon had done the same. The other Frank, de Charney, now stepped out in the middle beside de la Roche.

'Don't push things, Balbi,' the Frank said. 'We agreed to remove certain things of value before the rank and file begin burning and looting monasteries. We never intended to keep it for ourselves, but to remove it from the city for safety. I have no quarrel with the Temple, and they are as relieved to see such treasures saved from the sack as anyone, are you not?' he finished, turning a meaningful look on the knights. Ramon nodded.

'Do not think you will secrete away such a treasure without my share being weighed,' Balbi snapped. 'Or perhaps I ought to take the whole thing myself. After all, without my ships and my men, you would all still be floundering about on the shore below the walls, burning with Greek fire.'

'You overstep your bounds,' de Charney snapped as Arnau's prediction about the Venetian seemed to be coming true already.

'Oh come now,' Balbi laughed. 'Did you ever think I would let you take one of the richest prizes in the world for yourselves and leave me with just a few coins for my troubles? "No witnesses" need not be limited to Templars, de Charney. We are already under papal excommunication. What harm might I come to in killing a few more renegade knights?' He gestured at the Templars. 'I should have let my men pull their triggers that night. How foolish. I shall not be so sentimental and short-sighted again.'

Arnau felt an odd mix of emotions as de la Roche and de Charney suddenly backed towards them, drawing their swords and falling in alongside the Templars. Two men-at-arms came to join them as Bochard's squire drew his sword. Ramon shook his head at the young man. 'Just keep the preceptor safe.'

Arnau chewed his cheek as he pondered. With the two knights and their men, they had effectively six swords. Balbi had more than a dozen with him. Undoubtedly at least he and Ramon would be better warriors, but they were also tired and bruised and outnumbered.

He sighed. He'd thought it was over, yet here they were, only two dozen paces from freedom and still fighting Venetians.

'To the Devil with you,' he spat, and leaped. His mace caught the shield of a panicked-looking Venetian man-at-arms, crumpling the upper right quadrant. The Venetian made to counter with his drawn blade, but Arnau was already pivoting on the right foot he'd led with, spinning around the man's shield side and moving on to another target. On the periphery of his vision, he could see the others leaping into the fray, but he had his eyes set on Balbi.

A grey-clad fighter swung a sword at him and he had to lurch to the side to avoid it, throwing his mace up to block. Employing one of the more impressive moves Lütolf had taught him all those years ago, he rolled his wrist and turned, his arm following the fluid roll, his mace moving in a clean instant from a block into a strike. It was easier done with a sword, but he managed regardless and the Venetian reeled as his own blade was knocked to the side while the Templar's mace hurtled up into his chest.

There were a dozen or more cracking, breaking noises as the weapon struck the man's breastbone and ribs, caving in his chest. Arnau moved on, leaving the dying man to collapse on his own.

Beside him, Ramon sang his own song of battle, blade biting deep into a Venetian neck even as another of the enemy threw himself forward. They were neither natural swordsmen, nor well-trained, these men, but desperation and numbers still made them a fearsome force.

'Mine eye is troubled of strong vengeance,' Arnau bellowed suddenly, slamming aside a man-at-arms with a bruised shoulder, whereupon one of the Frankish knights dispatched him with a heavy blade. 'I wax old among all mine enemies.' His gaze locked on Balbi, who was watching him with a troubled yet spiteful smile, as he pulled another of his men in between them for protection. 'All ye that work wickedness depart from me, for the Lord hath heard the voice of my weeping.'

The Venetian swung a blade and Arnau dived forward, coming close inside the swing and smashing the butt-end of the mace into the man's face at very close quarters. The man-at-arms' teeth shattered under the blow and Arnau threw him roughly aside where he staggered and made a feeble attempt to cut at his attacker before Arnau's mace smashed him to a pulp.

'The Lord hath heard my beseeching; the Lord hath received my prayer,' he snarled the words of the psalm. Balbi was running out of men, but at the last, as he backed up against a stone trough, he pulled his last man in the way, a big bruiser with a mail coat over his green shirt and carrying a heavy sword.

Arnau was beyond caring who he faced now, flooded with the unquenchable desire to send Balbi to his divine judgement. His mace swung hard. The big man deflected the blow with his sword and, while he recovered the weapon for another attack, swung a mailed fist. The blow caught Arnau on the jaw even as he tried to dodge out of the way and he felt the pain flow through his face. Refusing to be distracted, he threw himself at the man. The Venetian tried to back away, but Balbi was behind him, pushing him forward, and he took a shoulder barge from the Templar hard, spinning to the side. He lashed out in the press with the hilt of his sword, and Arnau yelped as the heavy iron thudded into his left shoulder, numbing the arm.

He spun. The Venetian recovered in moments as Arnau pulled back, trying to right his sword for a more effective strike, but Arnau was fast. As he spun, his mace flicked out. It struck the recovering man-at-arms on the side of the head and filled the air with blood as readily as with screams.

The big man fell away, gurgling in agony and Arnau tested his jaw and shoulder, reassuring himself that despite the aches neither was broken, before finding himself face to face with Almerico Balbi.

In that sneering face, Arnau found everything he had learned to hate this past year. The Franks were misguided children, doing wrong because they were led to, for all they should have known better. In time they might regret what they had done and suffer for it, but they were at least redeemable. It was the Venetians who lay at the root of all the evils that had fallen Byzantium. Venetians who perverted the Crusade in the first place. Venetians who had led them to sack the city of Zadra. Venetians who had sunk the fishing boats on the first day they reached the city of Constantinople. Venetians who had twice engineered ways to take the walls. Venetians who had demanded sums that no emperor could readily meet in order to further the cause of invasion. Venetians who had cheated and miscounted the loot in order to continue their campaign. Venetians. All Venetians. And now it was Venetians who threatened Christian knights and brothers of the Temple all for the sake of avarice.

Standing before Arnau now, Almerico Balbi was all of them. He was every pox-ridden degenerate of the doge's fleet. Every man Arnau had seen kill soldiers on the walls. Every last one of them.

With an incoherent bellow of rage, Arnau swung his mace. Balbi lifted a rich, ornate sword into its path and stared in horror as the heavy iron mace head simply snapped the blade and continued its swing unabated, smashing into the bicep of his sword arm, mashing muscle and breaking bone.

Balbi was done for with the first wound.

He fell back, screaming, broken sword falling away. Arnau refused to relent. Still snarling his hatred in the form of accusation and blame for everything the Venetians had done, interspersed with Bible verses of wrath and vengeance, he struck the fallen, beleaguered Venetian again and again.

It was only when strong arms gripped him and pulled him upright that he realised Balbi had been dead for some time as the young Templar repeatedly pulped his remains with the gore-coated nightmare of a mace.

He rose, shaking. A flash of memory struck him. *A gore-coated mace. Sebastian with a caved-in forehead.* He looked down at the weapon in his hand in horror, and then at the mashed mess that had been Balbi on the ground. With a grunt he cast away the mace, suddenly certain that his days of wielding such a weapon were most definitely at an end.

Still shaking, he turned.

De la Roche and de Charney had been the men who had pulled him off his victim. Both were lightly wounded. Ramon cradled what looked like a broken arm. Bochard stood at the back, eyes wide and staring, his squire keeping him still. The Venetians were all gone, either dead or fled into the radiating streets the moment their master had been turned into a pulp of nightmare.

'It is over, Templar,' de la Roche said, sword in one hand, shroud of the Saviour tightly wrapped in the other. 'Be assured that this will be preserved for the good of all Christendom.'

Arnau could not bring himself to answer. He was shaking uncontrollably. The wrath was gone, though, replaced with a hollow ache. He turned to Ramon.

'A boat awaits us, Vallbona,' the older brother said, wearily. 'And I think Constantinople is lost to us. Time to go.' He nodded at the two knights. 'Go safe and God watch over you.'

De Charney and de la Roche bowed in return, and Ramon gestured for Arnau to follow, turning back to the gate. The other two joined them. Arnau, shivering, coated in blood but with empty hands, staggered forward, exhausted eyes roving ahead of them.

For just a moment, he thought he saw the face of Redwald the Waring amid the flow of humanity, a cloaked man beside him, and then the figure was gone, lost in the press.

Without a further word, the fugitive populace leaving space around the wounded and gore-coated men, the four Templars passed beneath the Golden Gate, leaving the city for the first time in a year and walking wearily out to freedom.

EPILOGUE

Constantinople lay on the horizon, a lump jutting from the glittering, moon-swept waters of the Sea of Marmara. Lights twinkled and blazed, though the pall of black hanging above the city and blotting out the indigo sky made it clear that not all of those burning points of light were intentional.

The city was dying.

The Byzantine fisherman and his son who had agreed, for a good sum from Laskaris, to ferry them to somewhere safe, murmured to one another as they changed tack and started to run for the southern shore. They had seen no Venetian ships patrolling. The invaders had won, and knew that the city had no vessels left, so had recalled their ships.

Bochard lay quietly in the boat, his head on a rolled-up mantle, his squire by his side, face full of concern.

'What now?' Arnau sighed, watching the city slip into the distance.

'We make for Cyprus,' Ramon yawned. 'Wherever this fellow takes us, we secure a ship for the four of us. I still have a sizeable purse of money, and while Byzantium may have fallen, I'm sure its gold will still be good.'

'And at Cyprus?'

'We see that Bochard is taken care of and send word to Acre that he is there.'

'But we don't go to Acre?' He tried to keep hope and relief from his tone as he spoke. He had been driven and excited about coming east to fight the enemies of all true Christendom, but had, instead, been forced to choose between Mother Church and what his soul said was right. Ramon had too, but in his usual pragmatic way he seemed to have dealt with the issue and coped. Arnau was not sure he had. What had happened in Constantinople had changed him in ways he had yet to truly measure, and had altered his perceptions entirely. He was beginning to understand how those men who lived with clear monochrome views like Bochard were too brittle, and snapped with a troubling wind, while men like Balthesar who had always allowed understanding and an open mind to drive him were perhaps the best men to represent the true faith.

He would never be a Lütolf, no matter how pious the man had been, and he could never be so accepting of their role as Ramon. Perhaps, somewhere inside, he was turning into the old knight who had spent his early life as a Moorish mercenary before finding redemption.

'I see little point,' Ramon said, stretching. 'The Crusade will clearly never leave for Egypt now. The Crusade is, in fact, over. The Franks and their dogs now have a new empire to settle instead. And it appears that we were of peripheral enough value in the first place that the grand master assigned us to escorting Bochard, keeping him out of the way. No, I think Rourell is where we are bound once more. Home, Vallbona. Home and peace and contemplation for a time.'

Arnau nodded, peering off across the water. Peace. The word had a pleasant ring to it.

It was about time they found some peace, although somehow he knew that God had something in store for him. Peace was unlikely to enshroud him for long.

He turned his back on the fallen city and gazed west. Somewhere far out there lay home. He'd been excited to leave and head east into unknown lands and Saracen-filled deserts. Now, though, he'd had his fill of the East. No, Iberia was where he belonged.

Home.

He sighed, clutching Sebastian's icon tight, and behind him an empire breathed its last.

HISTORICAL NOTE

The Crusaders' sacking of Constantinople heralds one of the most critical turning points in history. Its importance is hard to overestimate. Firstly, there is the religious aspect. Until this point, while there had been schismatic differences between the Catholic and the Orthodox Church, it might be said that they were not insurmountable. While they might have considered one another heretical, there was this sort of 'wayward child' or 'difficult uncle' aspect which meant that both sides felt that reconciliation was always a possibility. What happened in 1203–1204 and the consequent Latin occupation of the empire killed that off for all time. Thanks to those years, the Catholic and Orthodox Churches have remained apart to this day.

Furthermore, the history of crusading changed. After three great ventures to free the Holy Land from the grip of the Muslim peoples, the detour and dreadful acts of the Fourth Crusade meant that there would never again be a Crusade of the old sort. That is not to say that the Christians and their enemies would not be at odds. The 'Northern' Crusades pitted the Knights Teuton against the pagan and heretical lands around the Baltic. The Reconquista in Spain would only end with the capture of Granada in 1492. But after this there would never again be a great multinational, papal-led expedition to free Jerusalem from the hands of the Saracen. This was the end of the 'great' Crusades.

Moreover, the damage the Crusaders inflicted over those years and during the succeeding regime essentially ruined Byzantium. While the ousted Byzantine empire, living in exile in Anatolia, would regain control of Constantinople a number of decades later, the damage had been done. Byzantium had still been the Roman empire. It had been the bulwark and bastion at the edge of Christendom, holding back the enemies of the West. The weakening of Byzantium by the Franks and Venetians left it in no real position to defy the Turks, who then steadily encroached upon the empire until the day the conqueror Mehmet finally overwhelmed the city for good in 1453 and ended the Roman empire after a pretty good run.

One interesting aspect of this siege and sack was the looting. Records show just how bad it was, but physical evidence even more so. Just a cursory glance at Saint Mark's cathedral in Venice will reveal the bronze horses stolen from the hippodrome in Constantinople, as well as a statue of the Roman tetrarchy moved to Venice. Marble, columns and mosaics in the basilica came from the sacking of Constantinople, and a visit to the basilica's treasury will reveal many treasures stolen in 1204. Gold, gems, treasure, coin, artworks and anything of value was taken from the fallen city. Among these things, we know that relics were removed. The ones I have mentioned in this text are all noted in one source or another as being kept in Constantinople, and some of them disappear from the historical record during the sacking.

Although the known history of the 'Turin shroud' only begins much later, there are tantalising hints of its earlier existence. It is noted in more than one source as being kept in Byzantine Constantinople, and the knight Robert de Clari, whose brother was one of those two knights who finally broke through the gate on that fateful day in April incidentally, wrote in his long chronicle of the Crusade that 'there was the shroud in which Our Lord had been wrapped [...] And none knows – neither Greek nor Frank – what became of that shroud when the city was taken.' Better still, a letter from Theodoros Angelos to the Pope in the following year says: 'The Venetians partitioned the treasures of gold, silver, and ivory while the French did the same with the relics of the saints and the most sacred of all, the linen in which Our Lord Jesus Christ was wrapped after his death and before the resurrection. We know that the sacred objects are preserved by their predators in Venice, in France, and in other places, the sacred linen in Athens.' One Otto de la Roche becomes Duke of Athens in the following months! Only twenty-five years later another de la Roche is recorded as a Templar master. The connections were just too good not to build into my story. Moreover, history puts the shroud in the hands of a de Charney in France in the following centuries. Although any Templar connection to the Venetian Almerico Balbi is my own invention, the Balbi were an important Venetian landowning family, and though Templar links in Venice are not well advertised, a certain area of the city was once given over to the Order. To create a small conspiracy involving these three was a fun fiction of mine built upon legend and odd known facts.

The spear of Longinus and the crown of thorns were both recorded as being in the Mangana monastery. The great icon of the Virgin was kept in the Blachernae church and paraded around the city. It disappeared from the city more or less as I told it, though not with Bochard's involvement. Truly, Constantinople was the city of a thousand relics, far richer in them than mere Rome. And the Templars have long held a reputation as collectors of relics. How much of this is truth and how much part of the endless mill of Templar rumour and legend will likely remain unknown, but remember that all of Christendom was obsessed with relics and their value, and the presence of a more important relic more or less guaranteed the expansion and prosperity of a city.

This leads me to Bochard. I may be doing the man a disservice, I suppose, for Reynald Bochard is also a real historical figure. His time as Master of Cyprus is based upon the truth, ending in trapped Templars and huge bloodshed, following which even the Templars decided they couldn't really hold the place they had inherited from Richard I, moving it on to the brother of the King of Jerusalem. I have exaggerated nothing there. Indeed, I may have played down how badly that ended. Bochard more or less disappears from history after Cyprus, but turning this otherwise unknown yet pivotal figure into a disaffected failure seeking redemption made sense. In truth, initially the part of relic hunting in this tale was just meant to be a side plot that made Bochard want to stay through the siege. It was only on unpicking the threads mentioned above that I knew it had to become more than just a minor part of the story. And you may have spotted perhaps some signs of PTSD in

Bochard in the closing chapters after he shocks himself rigid. Recent academia has produced interesting works on the evidence of PTSD as an affliction as far back as Roman times. Bochard, then, I think we can label ill rather than mad or dangerous.

So now you know about some of the characters: Bochard, de la Roche and de Charney. Let me tell you something of the future for the rest. We'll start with what happens to the city. I've intimated that it never truly recovers. That perhaps makes it sound worse than it was. Though it had been permanently weakened, there were brief flowerings in which the city flourished. From 1204 the city remained in Latin hands, subject to the Church of Rome until 1261. The Byzantine emperors ruled in absentia from Nicaea, only retaking Constantinople half a century after their ousting.

But what of the characters you've come to know? Well, in truth, little of it is good. Alexios Doukas did indeed flee the city on the night of the sacking through the Golden Gate, and his fate was not to die in the city. Moreover, Constantine Laskaris attended the meeting of nobles in the Haghia Sophia that night where, in the absence of Doukas, he was made emperor. He fought on for only hours before the Warings deserted him and he too was forced to flee the city. He would rule in exile, continuing to stand against the Latins, for almost a year. Theodoros also made it out that night, reaching Nicaea unharmed.

Having fled, Alexios III Angelos went into exile where he, unbelievably, eventually ended up with Alexios V Doukas, marrying his daughter to the man. Angelos's failures had not ended in Constantinople, though, for in the end, he blinded his son-in-law, Doukas, and fled approaching Crusaders once more. Hurrying hither and thither, Angelos eventually ended up being captured in battle by none other than Theodoros Laskaris, after which he was imprisoned in a monastery where he died. The blinded Alexios V Doukas (Mourzouphlos – 'the monobrow') was captured by the Latins eventually and taken back to Constantinople. There he remained the defiant hero he could have been, refusing to accept charges of treason and instead labelling the young pretender Alexios IV a traitor. He was thrown to his death from the column of Theodosius, a martyr to the end.

It would be Michael Palaeologos who would recapture the city and become the next emperor to rule from Constantinople. Interestingly, he was the great grandson of Alexios III Angelos, but for those intervening years of exile in Nicaea building back to power, you might be interested to know that the dynasty of emperors were the Laskaris. Indeed, it was our very own Theodoros Laskaris who ruled in Nicaea from 1205 until 1222. His brother Constantine had ruled from the last days of the siege until 1205 when he died in battle against the Latins.

I've done my best with locations. I am fairly familiar with most of them, though the more troublesome parts are the Golden Horn walls and the Blachernae. Little remains of the Golden Horn walls and the fragments left only give us tantalising glimpses of what they might have been like. As such, I have built my story from primary sources, secondary sources, maps and photos I have of the place, as well as the amazing 'Byzantium 1200' online project. I urge you to look the latter up, by the way. The Blachernae is even more troublesome, most of it having disappeared beneath shanty housing for centuries, and more recently even those shanty houses are disappearing to be replaced by modern buildings. I have walked much of the Blachernae, but its original form is very hard to discern now, barring fragments currently being reconstructed and odd pieces of terrace wall in gardens and car parks here and there. There may or may not have been a wall between it and the city. It might have been just a low boundary wall, combined with terracing. Or it may have been more. I have chosen to make it a solid defence, partially based on the fact that the emperors would hardly shut themselves up in the Blachernae with the Warings if it was not defensible. I have based it also partly on views from the 1493 Hartman Schedel map. The 1922 Pervititch plan shows a lesser wall enclosing the palace area, along the terrace line, which similarly fits. Sadly, the gate where the city's fate was decided is now covered with a padlocked door as part of a garage and not preserved as the significant monument it should be.

Placing the Crusader camp was troublesome, since neither records nor archaeology traditionally identify its location, and so also was the bridge mentioned in the early stages of the siege. Moreover, the battle between the Crusaders and the Byzantine army near the Frankish camp that ended with the emperor leading his fleeing men back to the city is recorded as ending with the two sides facing each other over a wide watercourse, or 'canal', that fed the city. Such a channel no longer exists, and it seems extremely unlikely that it ever did. Although there are records of aqueducts running along the hillside near the Golden Horn, any watercourse feeding drinking water to the city outside the walls would be underground due to terrain and hygiene. Still, I did a certain amount of research into this, even consulting the amazingly clever archaeologist Kerim Altug in Istanbul, who sent me some incredibly useful texts that informed this book. Locating the Crusader camp was even more troublesome, but I pinned it down to Balci street near the Horn, north-west of the walls, courtesy of a recent find and associated article provided by the most excellent Twitter user and website 'The Byzantine Legacy'. Other locations can still be visited, including the Bukoleon, the land walls and the Golden Gate. The church of Holy Apostles was destroyed following the Turkish conquest and the Fatih mosque built on the site. Similarly, while there is a Galata tower which is a tourist attraction, it is a later Genoese structure and not the one from this text. The base of the tower that held the chain is now the Yeralti mosque in Beyoglu.

Interestingly, there is no mention of the use of Greek fire in the siege. Given how much of Byzantine military history revolved around this dreadful and still largely misunderstood weapon, I decided I needed to add it – for colour if nothing more. Given the state of the ruined Byzantine fleet, I figured that perhaps something similar had happened to Greek fire. My descriptions of its use come from Anna Komnena's almost contemporary description: 'This fire is made by the following arts. From the pine and certain such evergreen trees inflammable resin is collected. This is rubbed with sulphur and put into tubes of reed, and is blown by men using it with violent and continuous breath. Then in this manner it meets the fire on the tip and catches light and falls like a fiery whirlwind on the faces of the enemies.'

Some readers might have been thrown by the name 'Waring Guard'. Yes, this is another spelling of the famous Varangian Guard. They were once drawn from the Scandinavian and Rus peoples exclusively. By this time, though, they were almost entirely populated by men from England, Anglo-Saxons who were disenfranchised by Norman oppression from the mid-eleventh century onwards. Many Saxon English who wanted to live free fled to Constantinople to join the Guard. Names like Octa and Redwald are English. The Guard were fanatically loyal to the emperor, and converted to Orthodoxy when they joined.

I'm going to leave you alone to mull this over in a moment, but I want to explore something else before I go. Part of what drove me to write this book was my abiding desire to make this series different and explore new and intriguing aspects with each volume, other than merely Templars on Crusade or Templars with weird occult leanings. Realising that just a few years after the date of the second book, the city of Constantinople suffered this fate, meant I really wanted to explore it. Although I would be limited to writing the specific timeline of the war, I felt it was worth attacking. Because – and bear with me here – though the Templars are not noted as being in the city at the time, it is certainly possible that they were. Imagine if you will the moral quandaries faced by a Templar in the midst of this war. Would it be much different from my approach? Who knows?

In terms of bibliography, I would point you in the direction of two fictional Templar series: Michael Jecks's Puttock and Baldwin novels, and the Brethren trilogy by Robyn Young. Branching out from that, I would recommend Gordon Doherty's Strategos series, which is set in the Byzantine world around a century earlier, and Prue Batten's Gisborne books, which cover much of this territory over similar times. As well as a slew of Osprey military history books and numerous texts on Constantinople I already owned, I would particularly recommend Ernle Bradford's *The Great Betrayal* for the Fourth Crusade. For my favourite Spanish Templars, perhaps look to Judi Upton-Ward's *The Catalan Rule of the Templars* and for slightly less academic angles on this particular plot, Barbara Frale's *The Templars and the Shroud of Christ*.

Most of all, I would recommend a visit to Istanbul. Nothing will bring this tale to life like walking around the sites.

Thank you for reading and I hope you enjoyed the book. If you did, please leave a review as they really do keep authors afloat. And keep an eye out for book four, which is already in process. *The Winter Knight* will see Arnau de Vallbona in Germany, dealing with the legacy of his old friend Lütolf of Ehingen.

Simon Turney, February 2019

Printed by Amazon Italia Logistica S.r.l.
Torrazza Piemonte (TO), Italy

10976092R00210